DIAMOND
THE BLACK DRAGON

Dara J. Carr

DIAMOND

THE BLACK DRAGON

Dara J. Carr

Harrison House Publishing

Harrison House Publishing
www.theharrisonhousepublishing.com
info@theharrisonhousepublising.com
ISBN: 978-0-9996147-4-7
Library of Congress Control Number: 2019932205
Harrison House Publishing and the "HH" logo are trademarks belonging to Harrison House Publishing.

PRINTED IN THE UNITED STATES OF AMERICA

FORWARD

When you read through the story you may find several places where the laws of the land do not jive with what is being said. When I look at other stories, be it in movie, a book or television, I have found that some authors will use "Poetic License" to change things to fit their plot. If you watch the movie, "Liar, Liar," there is a glaring discrepancy where the law does not fit the outcome of the court case. If the proper legal decision were used in the movie it would ruin the plot (plus it might give a lot of minors an idea of how to try to get away with something). In "Star Trek" and "Quantum Leap" they constantly misused the laws of physics. A Certain US Senator said that he was being fired upon by the Khmer Rouge, while he was in Viet-Nam, even though that political group did not appear on any political scene until after the USA was out of Viet-Nam. If other authors of fiction and science fiction can use it - so can I. If a United States Senator can boldly get up and be some kind of historical revisionist then who are you or anyone else to say that I cannot. If you try to say that I cannot improvise, revise or use poetic license, then all I have for you is a very loud, sloppy raspberry.

This story is fictional. No actual person or event is depicted. Any similarity with any person, living or dead, or any event, is entirely coincidental and unintentional.

TXu 2-100-909

OTHER BOOKS BY

DARA J. CARR

The Semi-Dragon Tale

Revenge Cometh Forth

Here Are My Shorts (a collection of short stories)

Volunteer...Spy?

The Original Owlam

What New Things We Can Learn?

The Lies We Tell to Survive

Countless Enemies and Discoveries

Enemies From Beyond

More Troubles, More Enemies

Reflections and Beginnings

What New Occurrences Do We Face?

She is Back!

They Are Back!

DIAMOND THE BLACK DRAGON

1

It was his last chance. Each candidate was given 10 attempts at successfully hatching an egg, and raising one of the great flying reptiles. Each man was given one egg at a time and then had to go from there. If any man failed to come up with a living dragon after ten tries, he was tossed out and placed in some menial labor job, somewhere as far from the dragon forts as was geographically possible.

Kovarin knew his chances were slim. There had been seventy-eight men who had gone to the tenth egg...only thirteen had succeeded at that point.

Supreme Commander Dozzbin was the one who passed out the eggs to the Candidates. He had received his exalted rank, because he had the largest and meanest dragon...currently. Rank was determined by the man who had the largest dragon. Leadership capability was ignored. Might makes right, and Dozzbin had the mightiest dragon...currently. He had the final say as to who got which egg. His rank gave him more prestige than the entire Supreme Tribunal of Elders. Therefore he had the Tribunal in his pocket (and by their throats)…and Dozzbin hated Kovarin's guts.

Dozzbin had been the one who had assigned the other nine eggs to Kovarin. Each one had been the smallest of the batch. The smaller the egg, the less chance of survival for the hatchling…in many cases. None of Kovarin's assignments had hatched.

He was reading through the instructional scroll for hatching. He had practically memorized the thing after several hundred readings. He had also read, several hundred times, the guide on caring for the young dragon.

He snickered to himself. 'Dragons…hah!' They were nothing more than giant flying lizards. Their intelligence was better than most reptiles. They were nothing, compared to those legendary talking dragons from the northern wastelands of Tuvalow, however, they could be trained. Start when they are newborn hatchlings and you could control them for life.

The females did not have strong wings like the males. They were usually seen with the ground defense forces and primarily used for breeding. The only time that a female would fly was when she was in heat and trying to get away from, one or more, hormone crazed males.

The males were separated by size. The extra-small ones (who usually were smaller than a canine) were neutered and the master of that dragon served…whatever purpose could be found for them. The small ones (usually the size of a small equine) were neutered as well, because the Tribunal and the High Command wanted larger and larger dragons, just to scare off invaders. The small ones served a higher purpose than the extra-small - but not much higher.

The medium ones were sized by how long they could stay airborne (with a rider). If they could get off the ground, carrying a rider, they were allowed to be in the defense forces. Those who could fly, only if they did not have the weight of a rider, were neutered as well. The mediums, of course, had more prestige than any of the smalls.

The large and extra-large were the battle force. Their bodies were measured, from nose to tail, in order to see which category they fit into. The large ones achieved a low officer rank for their rider. The owners of the extra-large were the high ranking officers. The large and extra-large were used in the main battle wings for fighting, reconnaissance and breeding.

Right now, he would be happy with anything. What came out of the egg did not matter as long as it lived. Ever since he had been given a ride on one of the big battle dragons, by his uncle when he was a boy, he had dreamed of the day that he would be the master of one of them. A dream that would be totally destroyed… if this one failed to hatch as well.

He went to look at himself in his mirror. His face showed the worry and concern of the frustration of losing nine hatchlings. He wished that he could change his face. He wished that he could change his overall appearance. He was shorter than most of the other candidates and other riders as well. He was not the shortest, however, he came close. He had always been heckled about his appearance since he was a boy. His head was almost shaped like a triangle. He had a large forehead and a tiny little jaw. When he had been going through hand-to-hand combat training, even then, the (so called) grownups had heckled him about the shape of his head: "Aim for the top of his head, cause you might cut yourself on that tiny jaw!" "Aim for the top, cause you might miss that tiny little jaw." They also heckled him when he ate. He had to cut the meat and vegetables into smaller portions, because he could not get large chunks into his small mouth.

His brown hair was thinner than most of the other people his age and as a result, he looked older than he really was. When he had successfully finished all of the mandatory training to receive a dragon egg, he had been one of the youngest in his class.

He washed his face and went back to the instructional scroll. He put the scroll down and started the ritualistic preparations of the hatching sand pit. There was plenty of time. The eggs would not be ready for distribution for three more days.

Sift the sand thoroughly in order to remove any foreign debris. Boil it in clean water for cleansing purposes, sift through it again for debris then pour the hot sand into the pit. Make sure the temperature in the pit stayed as constant as possible, before and after the egg had been introduced into the pit. Any radical change in temperature could endanger the unborn.

He checked the temperature rod as he did his work. It should register somewhere between 38A and 48A. His rod was in place and was showing 44A. Perfect! He continued with the process. He could probably have done it in half the time, as many times as he had done it, however, he did not want to make any mistakes on this one...his very last chance. The boring process took one and a half days.

After finishing the long process, he slowly walked around the dragon hatching chamber. Exactly thirty-one paces across. He knew every step by heart. As many times as he had walked around in the chamber, he still always pondered on the past. Who had used this particular chamber before him? How many had been successful? What rank had they achieved? How big and what gender had their dragons been?

His thoughts were interrupted by a knock on the door. He stood there, rather bewildered, for a moment. The distribution would not be taking place until tomorrow evening. Who was it? Could it be Dozzbin, coming here to give him more childish ridicule? The knocking came again, louder and more persistent. He was in no mood for any of Dozzbin's trash talk at this time. He slowed his pace, hoping that whoever it was, they would go away.

Out of the large hatching chamber, through the archway, into his barrack room. He was at the door. The knocking kept on rattling the door. The inevitable was coming, might as well face what was coming. He clenched his teeth and opened the door.

He let out a sigh of relief. It was Namanti, the primary secretary in the hatching area. She stood there with her usual smile and that friendly look in her eyes. Her long, thick curly red hair hung down like a mane, all the way to her waist. She was the tallest of all the women in the secretarial force, however, she was still short compared to all of the dragon candidates. She was dressed in her usual garishly colorful attire.

She addressed him in her usual perky manner. "Were you asleep?"

He swallowed hard. No matter what mood he was in, or what he was thinking about, whenever he saw her, his mind was changed. It might be those flashing blue eyes or the soft pouting lips. It could be the fact that she was the only woman in all of the hatchery who treated him with any form of dignity.

She moved her arms up over his shoulders and started caressing his neck. "Are you too busy…or have you finished the preparations for your egg?" She let her words trail off.

"Just waiting for the egg," he said quietly. "I'm hoping for the best…as usual.

She giggled. "I'm sure that it'll come out alive this time."

He gave her his best half-hearted smile.

She walked in the room and frowned. "Hey, why's it so hot in here?"

He looked around rather puzzled - and then thought of the hatching pit. "The pit! You know that it has to be kept in a specific temperature range."

He led her into the hatching chamber. He reached for the temperature rod, pulled it up and looked at it. It was showing 45A. That was still in the proper range. He checked the glowing coals that surrounded the pit, on three sides.

He held it up for her. "See, everything is normal."

She had a puzzled look on her face as she squinted to read the rod.

"It's supposed to be between 38 and 48…so the egg will

hatch," he said.

She frowned as she looked at the gage. "Uh-huh, hatch, but not cook."

"Huh? What do you mean - cook?"

"Is it supposed to be this hot?"

"Look at the rod."

"I am." She pursed her lips and looked even more perplexed.

"So…what's the problem?"

She looked up at him, shrugged and gave a wan smile. She took the rod and perused it again. She suddenly had a bit of anger in her eyes. She dropped the rod, turned and headed back through his bedroom to the door. "I'll be back later, Candidate. I won't be able to come by, once the egg has hatched, but I will be by again, before it does." She gave him a provocative smile, winked and then headed out the door.

He could do nothing but give her a weak and confused smile. He was still a little tired from the workout of cleaning the pit. He sat back down on his bed, picked up the guide scroll and re-re-re-re-re-re-read another passage on the care of the egg and the hatchling.

He was startled awake again. He had fallen asleep while reading one of many passages that he had memorized…a long time ago. Someone was pounding on the door again. He stumbled getting out of bed, grabbed his robe and fumbled around putting it on as he staggered to the door. He took a deep breath, got his balance and bearings…and opened the door.

"I told you, I'd be back," said Namanti cheerfully.

"What? But…they'll be here soon…either today or early tomorrow…with an egg!"

Her smile got bigger. "I brought you something." She dug down into her pants and pulled out three temperature rods. "I think that maybe these'll help you."

"What are you doing with those?" he whispered loudly. He felt like shouting at her, however, he did not want to bring any unnecessary attention to himself right now. "No one is supposed to have those…except…the Candidates. They're too expensive to be thrown around in someone's…uh pockets."

"I'm only trying to help," she cried. "It's just…that… you've had so much trouble…in the past. I thought that you could use them…and I…" Her eyes started to tear up. She tossed them on his bed. "Here! They're yours to worry about now." She turned and stormed out of the room.

He picked up the rods. All three of them were registering normal body temperature of 38A. Well, why not? She had been carrying them inside her clothing. Well, they were working.

His anger changed to curiosity. He looked closely at the three rods. They seemed different. No, they *absolutely* were different compared to the one he had been using for the nine previous eggs. These were identical to each other, however, very different in appearance to what he was used to. He went to the pit and pulled his rod out for comparison. His old one looked almost the same except the numbers were in a different pattern... and rather sloppily painted on the tube. He dropped one of the new rods in the pit by accident as he was comparing. He let it lay for a few moments as he was again comparing the ones in his hands. He stood there contemplating for a few moments and then picked up the fallen rod. He nearly lost his lunch. The one that had been in the sand was now registering 61A. In just those few short moments, it had shot up from 38A to 61A. Could that be possible? Had he been cooking the eggs? In the instructions, you were absolutely *never* supposed to allow the temperature to go above 55A. He placed all four of the rods in the sand. He watched as the three new ones all rose quickly to 61A. They then started slowly crawling up, even higher. He did not know whether to spit, curse, shout, cry or fill his pants. When they all finally stopped moving up, all four were at the same level. The three new ones were showing 81A. The level on his old one was at exactly the same level, however, the number at that level was 39A.

He started kicking the coals away from the pit, partially to cool it down and partially to take out his frustrations. After removing most of the hot coals, he ran back to his living area and started shuttling as much cool water back to the pit as quickly as he possibly could. He had a water pump that fed into a big bathtub, and he was pumping away furiously on it in order to get enough water. He plugged the drain hole so that he would not lose any water while attempting to cool the sand pit.

Dozzbin had given him that temperature rod. He had used that same one on all nine of the other eggs. Dozzbin had said that

Kovarin would never have a dragon, and had done what he could to assure that his prediction came true.

He checked the new rods between each trip with water. They finally started registering that he was cooling the sand down to a tolerable level.

He walked back into his bedroom, with the old rod and one new rod. He stuffed both of them into his left armpit and waited. After counting to 100...twice, he pulled them out and checked. The new one was registering normal body temperature of 38A. The old one was showing -1A, 39 degrees lower than what it should be showing. 81A would be high enough to cook the embryonic dragon, in the egg, but not enough to make the water in the sand boil.

He spent the next few hours checking and rechecking the temperature in the sand. He could not help but think of what the repercussions of the discovery would be. Dozzbin had full control of the Tribunal and he was the Supreme Military Commander. Whom could he trust?

When he finally got the temperature in the sand at a constant, in the safe zone, he took the bad rod and hid it carefully in the large hatching chamber, along with two of the new rods. The walls looked like a cave so there was no problem with any odd shaped areas of the wall.

The fourth law: Willful and malicious destruction of a dragon is punishable by either banishment, dismemberment or death, as shall be decreed by the Tribunal.

The fifth law: Repeat offenses of the fourth law receive a mandatory death penalty.

This was a violation of the fourth law and 8 violations of the fifth law. It was his responsibility to report the crimes to the Tribunal. However, he had to prove that it was Dozzbin and not himself who willfully committed the act. He was stuck. He waited the rest of the day, contemplating the predicament.

2

He heard the bell start tolling. He counted seventeen. Seventeen eggs were being distributed to the candidates. There were currently twenty-six candidates ready to accept an egg. He was number fourteen on that list. He did not have a hard time guessing which one was going to be his...the last and the smallest.

All who were to receive an egg were to open the big door between the hall and the hatching chamber and wait. He felt even more frustrated as the wait went on and on. He saw two eggs being taken by on large carts that were big enough for a man to crawl inside. It took four men to help those particular Candidates with their eggs.

He kept waiting. Each egg that passed by was getting smaller and smaller. His feet started going numb and his back started hurting.

The Senior Tribune, Tremyath finally faced Kovarin. Tremyath was dressed in the ceremonial brown robe. He had three different robes, one for each of the colors of the dragons - bluish gray, brown and gray. The one that he would wear, on the occasion of distributing the eggs, was the color of the Supreme Commander's dragon. He wore a large gold medallion with a dragon's claw on it that hung around his neck from a silver chain. He had a head full of snow white hair and bloodshot brown eyes. He normally spoke in a low monotone voice that could calm anyone…when he was just talking to you. When he was chastising someone, that same voice could be raised to a level that hurt your ears and seemed to make the rafters vibrate.

Dozzbin stood to Tremyath's left, in full battle dress. Fur lined black leather boots that came up to the knee. Thick brown wool pants that were topped off with a wide black belt. A shiny steel breastplate that was rounded and had ten built in sheaths, for the deadly throwing knives that were carried by all of the Dragonmen. On his head was a highly polished steel helmet that looked more like a crown, with the symbol of rank on the front of it - a gold sunburst with carved alabaster dragon wings on each side. On his side hung a sword, that was nothing more than ceremonial, seeing as how no Dragonman had ever been involved in hand to hand combat. His lips were hidden by a big black mustache. He had an eternal look of contempt in his small gray eyes, at least he always looked at Kovarin contemptuously.

Tremyath started the ritual. He seemed to be looking straight through Kovarin as he spoke: "Has this man passed all of the qualification tests for Candidacy?"

Dozzbin sneered and said: "Barely!"

Tremyath closed his eyes and sighed. "That is a yes or no question, not a critique, Dozzbin. Please respond correctly."

Dozzbin clenched his gauntleted fists, and spat a "yes" through his teeth.

Tremyath closed his eyes and sighed again. He opened his eyes and looked at Dozzbin, with disgust in his eyes. He regained his composure, looked directly into Kovarin's eyes. "Do you have any problems, at this time, concerning the acceptance of a dragon egg, my son?"

"Just one," said Kovarin softly.

Tremyath's eyebrows went up. "And what is that?"

"Just before the bell sounded, I broke the temperature rod...for the hatching pit."

Dozzbin growled in anger. "You clumsy fool! What makes you...?"

Whatever he was going to say was drowned out by the klaxon like voice of Tremyath: "Hardly a crime and hardly a reason for reprimand!" His voice went back down to a less painful volume. "As I recall, Dozzbin, you were responsible for the destruction of no less than four rods...and that was only with five eggs. This man is on his tenth egg and this is his first damaged rod."

Dozzbin stood shaking and huffing for a few moments. "Right you are, Senior Tribune." He turned his attention to Kovarin: "Candidate! What was the reading on your rod, just before it was broken...or did you think of looking?"

"It was 44A, Supreme Commander," Kovarin said calmly. He noticed a glimmer of laughter in Dozzbin's eyes.

"Very well," growled Dozzbin. He reached into a place inside his belt. "Here's a new one. As it is written in the regulations,

I must tell you that the price of the one you broke, must come out of your pay. Any objections?"

Tremyath seemed a little disturbed at how quickly, and from where, Dozzbin had produced a rod. He frowned, shook his head, and turned back to Kovarin. "Are you, now, ready to accept the responsibility of the egg, Candidate?"

Kovarin looked at Dozzbin and smiled. He then turned to Tremyath with a more sober expression. "Yes, Senior Tribune, I am *more* than ready."

Another one of the High Tribunal appeared carrying the egg. It was exactly as expected. It was extremely small. This one could be easily carried in one hand, however, the Tribune member was very carefully holding it with both hands. It was not the smallest one that Kovarin had seen - it was also not the largest.

Kovarin took the egg carefully and reverently. As usual it was much heavier than it looked. It was warm to the touch and very hard. It was an elongated oval that was dark brown with what appeared to be blue veins running throughout. He did not recall ever seeing the lines so pronounced or so dark.

Tremyath put his right hand on the egg and his left hand on Kovarin's forehead. "May the blessing of the god of Dragonkind be with you."

Before going back into the chamber, Kovarin once again gave Dozzbin a big grin. The commander did not show any confusion in his face, however the way he kept clenching his fists did give away the fact that he was troubled.

Kovarin closed the door, still smiling. He knew that there were several questions going through the commander's mind.

No point in dwelling on that. Time to take care of the egg. He went to the pit and placed it in the warm sand. He huffed. "Warm" not hot. He pulled one of the new rods out of the sand where it had been buried. The measurement was between 45A and 46A. He stuck it back in the sand along with the new rod that Dozzbin had just given him. Before placing it there, he noticed that this one had a reading of -1A. He shook his head sadly. Dozzbin had already been prepared with another faulty rod.

He went back to his room and sat down on the bed. For, approximately, the next 32 days, he would have to take care of the little egg. 32 days of checking temperatures and turning the egg.

He would have 32 days. He thought about the two massive eggs that had been wheeled by. They could take a little longer developing in the egg. They could also come out meaner than anything that could be handled.

The hatchlings came out ravenous. If they find their own food, you cannot control them. If you feed them all of their meals, during their first 30 days, they lose most of their desire to hunt and become somewhat dependent on their handler.

He had heard that the larger hatchlings had, in a few cases, caused fatal damage to their handler. Many had lost fingers - and hands - when trying to feed the larger ones. You had to get the meat to them and get your appendages back before they snap that sharp beak. The longer their neck…the further their reach. The larger the hatchling…the greater their hunger.

Another one of his contemplations, at this time, was whether or not he was going to press charges against Dozzbin. That man had some kind of control over the Tribunal, which seemed odd, however, Tremyath had seemed to be the one in charge during the presentation of the egg. That was a good sign.

So how to go about it. Tremyath had seen Dozzbin give Kovarin a new rod. His reaction had been surprise. Could he confide in Tremyath and have him believe that Dozzbin had been conspiring all this time? What would happen when he showed off that he had five rods - two faulty and three good? Would they believe that it was Dozzbin who had supplied the two faulty ones? Would they take Namanti's word that she had supplied three good ones? 'This is what creates ulcers,' he thought.

He lit one of his time candles. When it burned down to each one of the time lines marked on it, he had to go check the temperature of the sand. It also had lines on it for turning the egg. Four times a day, the egg had to be given a one quarter turn.

He sighed, picked up the instructional scroll and started reading again.

A knock on the door woke him up. At first he was surprised that he had fallen asleep. Then he considered all that had happened. He quickly looked at the time candle. He had been asleep for a very short time. He got up, went to the door and opened it to see Namanti with a hopeful look on her face.

She looked up at him shyly. "Are you still mad at me?"

He cleared his throat and made several unintelligible noises. It was rather difficult for him to look her in the eyes.

She folded her arms and tried to suppress a smile. "You aren't mad anymore, are you?"

He finally stumbled over a very meek: "No."

She lowered her chin and looked up at him from under her eyebrows, with a pouting look on her lips. "Don't I at least get some kind of apology?"

"That's one thing...that has never been very easy...for me."

"Well, why don't you invite me in?"

He glanced back at the time candle. Why not have someone in here to keep him company? "Well, if you have the time..."

She giggled and entered.

"It's almost time to turn the egg, and I have to check the rod," he said.

She looked at the time candle. "No, it's not," she snickered. "You think that I don't know how those time candles work?"

He cleared his throat. "I still want to check the rod."

"Which rod?"

"Is that an accusation or an inquisition?"

"Either...both...or curiosity," she said grinning.

"All right, it's one of the rods that...you gave me."

"No need to get huffy. Let's go check it."

"You have to be quiet in there. The hatchling should only hear…"

She grabbed his nose and squeezed. "I know the rules," she said with laughter in her eyes. "I've been around, long enough, to know that the hatchling should hear, only, your voice. I'll whisper."

He made a few gyrations with his face to clear his nose, from the pinch. They went into the chamber.

He pulled both rods out, to check the difference. The good one had a reading of 46A. The bad one showed 7A.

Namanti pulled on his arm and whispered in his ear: "Why do you still have that goofy one in there…you know that it's bad?"

"I've had *this* goofy one, for less time than the three that you gave me. I received this one from Dozzbin, at the time I was given the egg."

"But, he…how? I mean, how he could have come up with another bad one…unless…?"

He gave her an innocent inquisitive look. "Unless…?"

She put her hands over her face shocked. "Oh, my! He's the Supreme Commander…and…he gave you a bad one…on… purpose?"

"*Two* bad rods."

"What? You mean that Dozzbin…gave you the other bad one…as well?"

"He said that I would never be a Dragonman. He's done everything he can, to make true, his prediction."

There was a tear trickling down her cheek. "You must report this…to the Tribunal. It's terrible. It must be done."

He sighed and shook his head. "Report it to whom? Dozzbin has all fifteen of them, wrapped around his little finger. They always vote, unanimously, the way he desires. To which one of his toys should I give the report?"

A loud hissing noise came from his bedroom. The time candle had burned down to the mark. He reached over and tenderly gave the egg a quarter turn. He stabbed both of the rods back into the sand, one on each side of the egg.

The two of them quietly left the hatching chamber.

He was awakened, abruptly and rudely, by a hard slap on his chest. He looked up at Namanti who was shaking her right hand, and had a pained look on her face.

"Huh! Whuzzat for?"

"Your stomach!" she said angrily. "When was the last time you ate something? All those gurgling noises. You fell asleep right in the middle of a conversation and your stomach started… roaring."

The hunger was rather intense. He had to think for a moment. He had been so worried and mad enough at Dozzbin that he had completely forgotten about eating. He looked toward the hatching chamber.

"I checked them again for you," she said with a smile. "The good one shows 45A and the stupid one shows 6A."

She then shoved a bag, with some fruits in it, in his chest. "Eat!"

He was not sure where she had come up with the fruit, however he gratefully accepted them.

"It won't do much good, for the egg to hatch, if you end up dying from starvation."

"Okay, okay, I'll be more careful."

"I'll see you again after you're more rested and can talk business. I have some other things to take care of."

After she departed, he was really worried. She knew what had happened. She had been around long enough to know the proper procedures, temperatures, rules and laws. Is she going to tell the Tribunal what happened? If she does tell them, who will she put the blame on? Would she tell them about the rods she had supplied? Is she going to use this information to blackmail me, or Dozzbin, or both of us? The possibilities made his head hurt.

He had to report this mess - but to whom? Dozzbin was the Supreme Commander of the War Forces. His orders were absolute. His crime was obvious…to Kovarin and Namanti…but so was his control of the Tribunal.

The only thing that Kovarin could think of at this time was to hatch the egg and surprise Dozzbin. Once the egg hatched and, by the gods, it lived, then hopefully Dozzbin would give himself away…not likely.

3

The days dragged by. Anxious anticipation kept him awake…most of the time. The only thing that allowed him to get any pleasure was when he was visited by Namanti.

When he was alone, he spent many long boring hours, waiting, wondering and praying. When Namanti was there, he was able to get a little sleep, because she would watch the time candles and help keep track of the turnings.

By the twentieth day he was a nervous wreck. With twelve long days still to go. He was laying on his stomach while Namanti massaged his sore back. Under normal situations the massage would have been very relaxing. Not today…not now.

"I'm worried about you," she said. "I have an iron skillet that's softer than the muscles in your neck."

"I can't help it. I need this egg. I need it to hatch…alive. It's my last chance and I still haven't figured out what to do… about Dozzbin and those two rotten rods."

"There has to be something that you can do. I mean Dozzbin killed those other eggs…not you…"

"But, I'm the one who is responsible for making sure that

everything is exact and perfect…in the pit."

"Oh quit thinking so negative. I know that you'll think of something. It's not as if it were totally hopeless."

He mumbled something unintelligible.

"You need to get out of the room for a while. You're so pale. The lines under your eyes look more like bruises."

"I can't afford to leave," he snapped! "If I do, Dozzbin or some cohort of his, could sneak in here and foul things up. Besides that, you know the rules: As long as I have an egg, in the pit, I can demand that all my meals are brought here. If I leave and something happens - I'm responsible."

"Big deal. You're not eating most of the food. You're killing yourself, through starvation, worrying and very little sleep."

"I'll live. I've been through worse situations."

He propped himself up on his elbows. She slapped his shoulders. "Lay down! Quit checking that candle. It's been less than two turns, since the last turning…and the temperature is fine."

He buried his head in the hides. She could tell by the way his body was shaking that he was crying.

"It's all right," she said softly. "Get it out of your system."

Day 28.

Kovarin could not remember the last time that he had slept.

He could not remember the last time he had eaten. His stomach was making numerous loud noises. He ran his hands through his hair. His hands felt as if they were covered with some kind of slime. He could not remember the last time he had bathed.

He walked over to his mirror and was horrified at the zombie staring back at him. The last seven days of gestation, he was to be completely alone with the egg. It could hatch earlier or later than expected. Whatever...he had to be completely alone with the infant reptile.

Namanti had been there to remind him to bathe, eat and sleep. Now that she was not allowed in. She had not been here for the last six days. He had not been taking very good care of himself...except for natural body functions.

He glanced at the candle for the ten thousandth time. It had not burned down any noticeable amount since the last time he looked.

He went in the chamber and stared at the egg. He noticed a big difference between this egg and his failures. The blue lines on the others had faded. This one, the lines had darkened, they were almost black. He wondered if that was because the hatchling was still alive or that this one had not been cooked.

His stomach gurgled again. He went to his food tray. He was starving, however, nothing on the tray looked fit to eat. He went ahead and shoved...something...in his mouth in order to stop his rumbling stomach.

Day 29.

The egg sat there motionless in the sand. He noticed that the blue lines were even darker now and seemed even more pronounced as if they were growing as well. Hopefully the darkening of the lines was significant. The others had been cooked. This one had been kept at the proper temperature.

Day 30.

He heard someone ringing a bell in the hallway. An egg had hatched. Whoever the lucky candidate was, was ringing for the Meat Cutters.

The little monsters were born hungry. Since no one knew when any particular egg would hatch, bovine were slaughtered right in the hallway by the Meat Cutters and meat passed through a large chute, to the Candidate.

A second bell rang out for another successful hatching.

He went back to his pit. The egg sat idle. Each time before, he had been given the smallest egg. It should have hatched…first. Two had hatched already and his was still sitting like a lifeless lump.

He heard a knock on his door.

'What is this,' he thought. 'Not even Dozzbin is stupid enough to commit this horrid breach of etiquette…well, maybe he is. He's dumb enough to kill nine hatchlings.'

He shouted angrily: "Who's there? No one is supposed to

disturb me, at this time."

The knock was persistent.

He walked closer to the door. "Who's there?"

The man shouted back: "Open your meat chute… Grounder!"

Grounder?! The name given to those who failed all ten times. The deadline for the egg was not for another two days and someone was already predicting the worst.

"Open up," came the angry voice again.

Kovarin could not recognize the voice through the door. He decided to find out what this mocker wanted. He hit the latch and the door on the meat chute fell open. A scroll tube…?

The mocking voice called out again. "My dragon has matured. I don't need the hatchling instruction manual anymore. Maybe it'll give you some luck."

Kovarin heard a loud laughing, retreating down the hall. He had no idea why that man had done this and did not really care. He shut the door and threw the scroll as far as he could fling it in the hatching chamber.

Less than an hour later, someone was pounding on his door again. Whoever it was, was shouting something, however, his words were a little distorted by the thick door. He ignored it and stared at the egg.

"Move…you little…"

Whoever was pounding was now screaming.

Kovarin sighed, got up and headed to the door at a slow calm pace. He stopped at the door and stood listening to the pounding and screaming. 'Surely someone else has heard this idiotic uproar by now,' he thought. He put a doorstop near the door. If someone tried to force it open, it would jam on the doorstop and no one could enter. He opened the door slightly. The perpetrator tried to force it open and the doorstop did its job. The man could get nothing inside except his hands and a portion of one foot.

"Open up, you idiot!"

"The law states that no one is to enter, at this time. Read the rules and laws…idiot!"

"All right, so you win that argument. Now, give me back the scroll. I have to turn it back in, to supply."

Kovarin looked through the opening. The man who had been yelling at him was Kevrong - one of Dozzbin's favorite friends. Kovarin looked as innocent as possible. "Scroll?"

"Yes, you soon-to-be Ex-Candidate Grounder. The scroll that I gave you about a turn ago. I need it."

"I don't know what you're talking about. You said that you gave it to me? I haven't opened this door in over two days. How could you have given it to me?"

"I put the thing in your meat chute," said Kevrong desperately.

"Really? I'll go check." He forced the door shut. He walked casually into the chamber. He hit the latch on the meat chute and the door fell open and Kovarin looked at the chute as if he had never seen one in his life. He looked through the chute and saw Kevrong looking back at him. "I don't see anything in there," he said with wide-eyed innocence.

"I know it's not there, I just looked, Grounder."

"Wait a minute, you said that you put it in a chute...are you sure that is was my chute?"

"Yes," he screamed. "I'm sure it was yours."

"Well...anyone can open the chute...from the outside. How long ago did you...?"

"About a turn."

"Anybody could have come by...in that amount of time. If someone saw you put it in there, they might have wanted it for themselves."

Kevrong stood there sputtering.

Kovarin shrugged and closed the chute. 'Maybe I should have told him that I burned the scroll,' he thought. 'No, that would mean that I do know about it.'

Day 31.

He had vomited four times. The last two times it had been nothing but bile. After the conversation with Kevrong, Kovarin had decided to check that new scroll. He had found an official set of instructions, for the proper care of an egg and the hatchling. The scroll that Kevrong had so maliciously thrown in that meat chute, was a work of art. Each portion had been carefully done in some fancy calligraphy. Kovarin's old one, comparatively speaking, was a scrawled mess, done in haste. Each line on the new one was arrow straight. There was not one straight line anywhere on the old one. The new one was of top quality paper. His old one was thin, ratty and torn in several places, as well as a few odd stains. The instructions were different. The new one had illustrations. The old one did not. He was shaking with rage and terror as he read.

Day 32.

The egg had been cared for "properly", only for the last 30 hours, since reading and comparing the scrolls.

His stomach was churning and growling from emptiness but refused to hold anything.

Dozzbin had given him the altered temperature rods and instructional scrolls. He only had his word that Dozzbin had given him bad rods and instructions. Dozzbin had the Tribunal.

He contemplated the evidence with a few thoughts. Is this providence, finding this information at this time, or was it possible that Dozzbin had planned for all the information to come in at this time? Is Dozzbin bold (and arrogant) enough to let it leak, as a show of power? Is it a cruel and horrible coincidence? How would the Tribunal react to this information? Is Namanti going to start an insidious blackmail operation? How do you answer all these irritating questions?

Day 33.

Past due. Seventeen eggs had been distributed. He had heard the bells for eleven so far. 'Me and five others,' he thought. 'I have nine days before a size two egg is declared dead.'

Day 34.

Two more hatched last night.

He sat on his bed chewing on some cheese and bread.

Something popped in the pit. His heart skipped a beat. He nearly gagged on a piece of cheese and his bladder emptied. He had had a large bed fur wrapped around him and was having a terrible time trying to get out of it as he staggered, stumbled and fell (several times) trying to get to the pit.

When he finally got there, he nearly screamed for joy. The egg had spun, on its own, from the last position he had left it. There was a small triangular hole in the shell with a tiny black claw sticking out. The claw was *moving*. He grabbed the rope for his hatching bell and pulled on it violently. He was so overjoyed that he forgot every single instruction for taking care of the hatchling.

He ran back to his bedroom and grabbed the "good" instructions. He had it set at the point of hatching. Quickly skimming over the passages, he realized that he had forgotten his gauntlets. He ran back to the bedroom, grabbed them and was putting them on as he headed back to the pit.

According to the bad instructions, he was supposed to leave the egg alone and let the hatchling break its way out of the shell. The good one stated that he was supposed to help. The gauntlets were necessary because, even as a hatchling, it still had very sharp claws and beak. The gauntlets made his hands very clumsy, however, it could not be helped. He did what he could to break pieces away on the hard shell. He had to find the head quickly, before the little beast suffocated.

'What in the name of the punishments, did that mean?' All this time, it had been locked in an airtight birthing egg. Now that that wall was breached, it needed air.

He had to find the head. He wanted to smash the shell with his fist. He held back that temptation because of the damage it could do to his infantile dragon.

The bad scroll had said a little about talking. The new one said that you were supposed to talk, as much as possible, so that the hatchling would get used to recognizing your voice. He had practiced all kinds of things to say as he was cracking the shell away. Now, all he could do was spout a bunch of gibberish. He hoped that it was just his voice and not just words…at this time.

The right foreleg and right wing were free now, through the pieces that he had broken off. He found the base of the neck. The curve of it showed that the head was somewhere under the belly. He concentrated his efforts in that area. A large chunk snapped off and the head was finally free. Now, he had to get the rest of the neck free from its bondage. The dragon needed to straighten out the neck, in order to get that first breath of air.

The hatchling was clawing and snapping for all it was worth in a feeble attempt to break itself out. 'Maybe that was what started the relationship,' he thought. 'The man helps the vicious little snapper out of the shell and a bondage of friendship is the result.'

Two big pieces snapped off that freed everything from the base of the ribcage up. It craned its neck into a straight line, opened its mouth, inhaled and then snorted some yellow mucus out of the tiny nostrils.

The next move it made was to turn its head and sink its beak into the ring finger on Kovarin's right gauntlet.

"Oh, blather! I gotta feed you." He tried shaking the jaw lock off the gauntlet. The snarling little lizard was adamant. Kovarin sighed in frustration and pulled his hand out of the glove.

He reached out and grabbed the cord to the bell. That bell that had remained silent through nine other eggs was now singing the wonderful news of a live hatching - a new life…and it is hungry. He was supposed to keep ringing it until the meat bearers arrived and gave him something to feed the hatchling.

He opened the door on his side of the meat chute. "Come on, you lazy bums, where are you?"

It seemed to take forever. Finally a voice came screaming through the chute: "All right, all right, I'm here! Enough with the bell!"

Kovarin stopped ringing and looked through the chute. "Yeah, okay, now, give me some!"

"How much do you need?"

"I was given a size two egg. A big fistful should be enough

to start with."

The bearded man looked shocked for a moment. He turned away and Kovarin heard a muffled conversation going on just outside the chute.

A different man peered through the chute. "Candidate Kovarin! Did you really have a live hatching?"

"Yes, why?"

The man turned to someone to his left. "Hah! I told you, you deadskin! You owe me 50!"

'Those rats were making bets?' He was ready to break the man's jaw. The only thing that stopped him was the realization that *this* man had bet in favor of a live hatchling.

The first man reappeared with a bloody cleaver in one hand and a fist sized chunk of meat in the other. "Is this enough, for the moment, Candidate?"

"If it's not, I'll let you know." He grabbed the meat, shut the chute and headed for his treasured little charge.

The tiny beast was still in the same place, with the rear end still firmly stuck inside the eggshell. It was snarling in frustration at the gauntlet. It had not been able to get anything edible or small enough to swallow off of the glove.

He pulled out his knife and cut several small pieces off of the chunk of meat. He then took one piece and used it to entice the hatchling away from the gauntlet. He almost jammed the giblet through the nose before it finally released the glove. It snapped at the meat, twice before it held its mouth open. He dropped the meat in the hungry mouth. It bit at the piece in its mouth several times before it finally swallowed. It craned its neck and Kovarin could see the lump in the neck as the meat traveled down.

While it was swallowing, he pulled the gauntlet away and inspected it for damage. When the lizard snarled at him, he chuckled, and then fed it another piece of meat.

While it chewed on the second piece of meat, he picked up the "good" scroll and looked for the instructions on feeding. He remembered everything from the bad scroll, but was trying to ignore that information. Before he could find the proper place, he had to put two more pieces of meat in the lizard's mouth.

He found it. "Let's see, it says that the first meal should be approximately one seventh of the dragon's body weight… (?)." He nearly panicked. "How do you figure that…without scales?" He continued reading: This will usually have to be done by visual estimation. The easiest way to tell that the hatchling has had enough, is when it starts to regurgitate some of the meat back up. He looked up. "Okay, feed it till it pukes…that's easy enough."

Another thing from the bad scroll was that he was just supposed to feed it. The good scroll stated that he was supposed to tell the hatchling what was going on as it was being fed. As he popped each piece of meat in the hungry hatchlings mouth, he repeated over and over: "Eat, eat, eat, eat." The instructions had stated that you could use a different word if you wanted. If you did, then you had better remember that specific word for that specific action. He decided not to get spectacular, strange, unique or weird - if you are eating…say it.

It ate almost half of the fist-sized chunk before it slowed down. After one big belch and a few pieces of meat came back up, it looked as if it had the hiccups for a few moments. It did not snarl at him again, it just sat there looking around...contentedly.

Now that his hatchling was calm, he started removing the rest of the shell. It sat there and watched with, what seemed to be, somewhat of an indifferent attitude. With a full stomach, it was much more passive.

After removing all of the shell, he remembered that the old scroll had given instructions on bathing the newborn with an alkaline soap. He checked the new one. According to this one, he was just supposed to wipe away any embryonic fluids with a clean, warm, soft wet rag.

After the cleaning, he placed it in a small cage that had been provided, in regards to the size of the egg. He then place the cage back in the sand, to keep the little beastie warm.

Now was the time for some hard, serious reading of the new scroll. The differences, so far, had been anywhere between minor and monumental.

He rang the other bell for some food for himself. Now that he had a live hatchling, his stomach had abruptly stopped churning and was now growling. He felt much better. His feeling was closer to elation and celebration rather than relief.

He had barely turned around, after ringing the bell and there was a knock on the door. Were they waiting outside the door with it? He opened the door, not knowing what to expect. He saw the Senior Administrator, a short white haired man, wearing a long gray robe.

"Good afternoon, Dragonman. Congratulations on your hatchling."

Kovarin nearly choked on his words. "Dragonman" - he was now officially a Dragonman, now that he had a live one. "Thank...you...good Administrator. How may I help you?"

The elderly man looked somewhat perplexed. He smiled again and said: "Aren't you the one, who is on his tenth attempt?"

"Uh...yes...I am."

He closed his eyes and smiled. He nodded. "Yes, I suppose that you have forgotten some of the procedures, for a live one... after so many unfortunate failures."

"I'm going to go over them...again...right now."

"Very good. I have been looking for your paperwork, on requisitions of supplies. I can't seem to find any."

"I don't remember...requisitioning anything."

With a light laugh, the old man said: "You had to. You have to have a temperature rod and an instructional scroll."

'Dozzbin gave those to me,' he thought. "It has been quite a while. Maybe the paperwork just got...misplaced."

Another smile. "Maybe. I'm sure I'll find it somewhere."

"What did you want...right now?"

"Oh...yes. It is entirely possible that you forgot some of the procedures. You must not forget any of the procedures concerning your hatchling. I checked with the meat bearers. Judging from how much meat you requested, I suppose you won't need very much oil."

Kovarin felt a cold chill run down his spine. 'Oil?' "Uh…no, I suppose…I won't need…very much."

The old man held up a mug full of milky yellow liquid. "Do you think that this will be enough…for now?"

Kovarin was bewildered. His hands felt clammy and he swallowed hard. "I hope so. If it isn't, you know…that I'll contact you. I'm sure that you have a lot more ready…if I need it."

"Oh, yes, most assuredly," he said with a huge smile.

He gratefully took the mug of oil and thanked the old man. He started to close the door.

"Tut, tut, my boy…procedures."

"Huh?"

"The birth record…for the hatchling. I have it here." He handed Kovarin a small leather scroll tube. "Please get it back to me, as soon as you can."

Kovarin took the tube. "Uh…right…as soon as possible."

"Good day and again congratulations…Dragonman."

Kovarin felt twice as tall as he had been a few moments ago. "Good day and thank you, Administrator." He closed the door and leaned against it, looking at the newly acquired items with tears of joy running down his cheeks. The birth record sounded easy enough…the oil (?)…what was it for?

Start with the birth record. That should be easy. The first line was the time and date of the birth. This line had already been filled in. 'Apparently the old man did it when I rang the bell.' Second line: Name of the newborn. (?) 'I'll decide later.' Third Line: Gender? He had not bothered checking. Fourth line: Length? Oops, he had not measured. Fifth line: Wingspan? Double oops! Sixth line: Color? Black! He was going to make sure...later. It had been somewhat dark in the hatching chamber. Seventh line: Handler and Owner? Hey, one that he could answer easily. He grabbed his quill and wrote his name in. Looking over the form in disgust, he reminded himself to take the measurements and pushed it aside.

He picked up the instructional scroll. What is with this confounded oil? He read through the part about helping the hatchling and cleaning with the rags. Next were instructions on how to take the measurements required on the certification of birth. Next was the part on determining gender.

Next was the oil - hallelujah! Once the hatchling has been completely fed, you must coat the entire body in oil. When it was inside the shell, it was kept in an environment full of moisture. Now it is free and the skin will dry out very quickly and the hatchling will be very uncomfortable. It could scratch itself to the point of causing serious or even fatal injuries. It must be oiled at least once a day for the first 25 days of life. After that, it is to be determined by the Administrator or a Ringmaster, if any more oiling is needed and how often.

He grabbed the mug of oil and headed for the chamber.

The little beastie was now laying on the left side.

Considering the length of his little charge, if it stretched out both the neck and tail in a straight line, the cage would be too small. It lay there with the end of its tail sticking out between the bars.

He quietly opened the cage. He started smearing oil on the underside and exposed right side. As he rubbed the oil on it, the dragon jerked the legs every now and then. Each time it jerked, he froze and waited to make sure that it was still asleep. He was very careful as he oiled the wings. They seemed so fragile. After getting the tail, the neck and the head, he now had to turn the little beast. He stretched out the wings as he oiled them. It was rather slippery work, however, it was accomplished without waking the dragon. He finished oiling the rest of the left side.

Closing the cage with slick hands was a bit of a trial. He finally got that done and sat back, feeling rather proud of himself.

He spent the next few minutes rubbing his hand in loose dirt on the ground, trying to get all of the oil off of his hands. He had tried to wash it off and had watched the water just flow over the oil. He wondered if there were instructions on how to get all of that slick stuff off of his hands.

He went back and started reading the instructions again. He found out that some of the dragons would lick the oil off. It stated in the instructions that this was not a problem because the oil was not toxic. He would have to watch and see if the dragon licked too much off and then started scratching the licked area.

He looked back at the birth record. Name? What should he name the little beastie? He went back in the hatching chamber. He lit four torches and placed them around the raised sand pit.

The dragon was now laying on its stomach and in the firelight, with the oil all over it, it seemed to glitter and shimmer in the firelight. The black scales were still very visible even through the oil…but the glittering… "Like a diamond," he said. He looked up and smiled. "Yes…a diamond. That's your name, little one… Diamond. I don't know what your sex is yet…Diamond is a name that could go either way." He smiled and went back to the birth record. He could now fill in the blanks on color and name.

He checked the instructions on how to measure and sex… Diamond. He had the necessary equipment for measuring already in the bedroom. It was not any kind of expensive equipment, so he was not surprised that whoever had been here before had left it in the chambers. He took the necessary measuring devices, for a tiny dragon, back with him into the chamber. Once again he opened the cage and started carefully handling his new little friend. Diamond was still content to sleep.

He measured the length in steps. First, he measured the tail from the tip to the back legs. Then, the back legs to the front legs. Then, the front leg to the tip of the nose…or beak. He only had to measure one wing and multiply by two in order to get wingspan. He drew the numbers in the sand with his fingers. Any attempt at holding a quill after handling the oily dragon would have been impossible. He went back and used the loose dirt on the floor in order to clean most of the oil off of his hands before handling the quill pen.

The only blank that had not been filled in: Gender! He decided that that particular blank could wait…until after a good nap.

4

He woke up hearing a strange noise. It was coming from the hatching chamber. He got up and walked slowly to the noise. He was sure that the little dragon could not possibly be making that noise. It was a staccato buzzing sound. He got closer to the pit and found that it was Diamond who was making the sound. His neck was craned out and he was taking rapid in and out breaths. Each exhalation made the strange buzzing sound.

He heard a knocking on the meat chute. He went to it and opened it.

A man on the other side looked through at him. "Hey, Dragonman. It's about time that your charge should be bellyaching for the next feeding."

Kovarin chuckled helplessly. "Yeah, it's a weird sound coming out of its throat, isn't it?"

"Same amount as before?"

"Yeah…I haven't seen any growth spurt yet."

A chunk of bloody meat slid down the chute. He caught it and then went for his knife. He cut three pieces off before he reached the pit. As soon as he popped the first piece into

Diamond's mouth, the little beast shut up, swallowed and held the mouth open for the next piece. Kovarin cut and tossed as quickly as he could, all the time calmly repeating: "Eat, eat, eat." Seeing as how Diamond was not chewing, just swallowing, it was difficult to keep ahead of the hungry beast. Kovarin started cutting larger pieces. This at last gave him a little time between pieces. It took longer to swallow the larger chunks. Diamond still was not chewing, however, it had to do a few gyrations, with his neck and head, in order to get the larger chunks all the way down. After almost half of the big chunk of meat was gone, it started slowing down. It belched a couple of times but still held the mouth open for more. After a third belch, Kovarin decided that Diamond had had enough. Diamond looked up in anticipation and saw that there was no more coming. It laid back down in the cage.

Kovarin decided that this was a good time to really catch up on reading the good scroll. There was so much information in his memory from the bad one…he just could not trust anything that he had read. He rolled the scroll down to the last part he had read and started in again.

There was more information in regards to sizing. He felt like skipping it…until something caught his eye. The size of the egg did not always truly determine the size of the hatchling. This egg had been registered as a size two. According to the measurements that Kovarin had done…Diamond was a little past size three. According to another passage, in the scroll, the cages were only for sizes one and two dragons. The reason that you wanted to keep the tiniest dragons in a cage was because if they started flying, the tinier ones were very fragile and could end up having a tragic if not fatal accident. Once they reached size three, they were a little sturdier and did not have a strong possibility of any kind of bad accident while flying.

Kovarin did a quick check on the temperature of the pit, to assure that Diamond would be comfortable. He then reached for the door of the cage. Diamond watched him with some interest as his body jerked two or three times as if it had the hiccups.

Kovarin opened the cage, reached in, gently picked Diamond up and pulled it out. He laid Diamond down in the sand. Diamond hiccupped again while looking around at the domicile. It slowly got up and started waddling around exploring the sand pit.

Kovarin re-read the part on measuring the hatchling. He decided that he would do another measurement on Diamond.

That would have to wait. By now, Diamond had wandered almost to the exact center of the pit. Since all of the hatching pits were the same size and any one of them could handle one of the giant eggs, Kovarin would have to have crawled in after Diamond. He decided to wait until the next feeding, when Diamond would come to him. After the little beast was stuffed, complacent and hiccupping, then a measurement could be made with greater ease.

Diamond curled up and went to sleep. That was another part of the reason for keeping a size one or two in the cage: A dragon that small could have easily curled up in the wet sand and ended up with its nose under the sand and died from drowning or suffocation. Size three and up were not narrow enough to be prone to sinking and drowning.

Another thing that Kovarin checked on was the feeding

schedule. A new hatchling should be fed three times a day at regular intervals. So that is what the other type of time candle is for. The bad scroll had no annotation at all about the other type of time candle. Kovarin growled in disgust as he went back to his bedroom, pulled out the candle, placed it and lit it.

Again - time for some more studying. He read the part of determining gender and decided, again, that that could wait. He read the part about the necessary supplies and ordered a keg of oil, in order to make sure that he did not run out.

He was ready, ahead of time, for the next feeding. He obtained a fist sized chunk of meat in preparation. He went to the pit where Diamond was still curled up in the middle. He sat there cutting the pieces up and lining them up on the side of the pit…a little out of Diamond's sight. He waited.

Diamond finally stirred. The dragon straightened its neck and tail and stretched them. It then spread all four legs out and stretched them while wiggling all of the toes…or claws. It unfolded the wings, and flapped them rapidly for a few moments. Since it had its back to Kovarin, it did not see that there was anyone or anything else in the chamber. It then sat back on its haunches and started the "hungry" cry. It looked straight up and cut loose with that staccato buzzing sound.

Kovarin tapped the butt of the knife on the edge of the pit several times. Diamond stopped, looked around mostly forward, saw nothing and started buzzing again.

Kovarin chuckled to himself. He leaned forward. "Dinner is back here," he said merrily.

Diamond stopped crying and turned to look. It turned its entire body around, sat back on the haunches and started crying again.

Kovarin was a little surprised and amused by this move. 'Oh really,' he thought. 'You want me to come to you?' He held up a piece of meat. "You are going to have to come to me, little one," he said calmly.

Diamond stopped for a moment and then started back up, sounding a little more frantic this time.

"Over here," said Kovarin as he waved the meat around.

Diamond stopped crying. It looked at Kovarin and snorted. It got up on all fours and started waddling towards Kovarin. It started the hungry cry again. When it got close enough, Kovarin gave the meat. As Diamond got each mouthful, it slowly crept a little more forward until it was right on the edge. Now it was getting the pieces a lot faster and seemed much more contented.

Kovarin was watching the neck as it swallowed and it seemed that at times there was more than one piece in the neck at the same time. As fast as he could toss the pieces into Diamond's maw, they were being swallowed and the mouth was open ready for more.

"Do you taste it? Do you breathe…in between bites? Do you have some other way of breathing in between…?" He just shook his head and kept throwing pieces of meat into that seemingly insatiable hole.

He ran out of meat. In the other two feedings, Diamond

ran out of desire before the meat ran out. This time the meat ran out first. He had been starting to slow down as far as swallowing and then reopening his mouth. It sat there with his mouth open waiting for another. When it did not come, it closed its mouth and started looking around as if confused. It laid down in the sand and belched. It laid its head down and went to sleep again.

"Very interesting first part of your life, little one. Eat and sleep, eat and sleep." Kovarin shook his head. He pulled out the measuring devices. He reached down and gently straightened the tail and the neck. He then measured the length. He checked with his original figures and was a little astonished. 'Could I have been…that wrong?' he thought. 'Is it possible that Diamond has grown that much…that quickly?' He looked around the pit for any droppings. In the three feedings, Diamond had consumed something close to equal to his weight - at the very least and had not rid itself of anything.

He stretched the right wing out to the full length and measured. The wing was longer as well. He made annotations of the new information on a different piece of paper.

He noticed a place on Diamond's back that looked like a scale had been knocked loose. He lightly touched it with his finger and found that it was rather dry. He grunted to himself. He went back to where he had left the keg of oil and opened it. Diamond got another oil bath.

After cleaning the oil off of his hands, Kovarin heard another knock on the bedroom door. He went to the door wondering what was going on. Nothing was supposed to disturb the bonding between the Dragonman and his charge. He opened the door. The old man was back.

"Have you finished the hatchling's paperwork yet, my boy?"

"Uh…everything except…gender, Administrator."

"Please, my boy. I need to get my paperwork in order."

"Yes, Administrator Vock, I know, but…I just haven't felt like being that personal with…my little friend."

Vock smiled. "You may end up getting even more personal than you think…at times. It's best to get the preliminaries out of the way…as soon as possible."

Kovarin hung his head. "You're right. I'll get that done." He heaved a sigh. "I'll…go try it…now."

Vock's smile got bigger. "Good man." He bowed slightly and walked away.

Kovarin sighed. The scroll listed two different ways to determine sex. One was to find a certain skin flap, on the bottom in the rear and pull it open to inspect the genitals. It seemed too invasive, indignant and possibly injurious to the little beast - not to mention "disgusting". The other was to massage the bladder in order to stimulate urination, and then observe which way the stream was going: Forward, it was a male. Backward, it was a female. He walked up to the pit. The only movement was the rise and fall of the chest.

He sighed again and gently put his hand under Diamond. He lifted the right side of the body a little and started going by the illustration as to where he should start rubbing. Diamond started making a soft keening noise that sounded like a moan of gratification.

"Oh great! You're enjoying this...you little..." He kept rubbing.

Diamond stretched out the right rear leg and flexed the clawed toes a little. Then a spray of urine.

Kovarin flinched a little. "Okay, you *are* a male," he said flatly. "Now I can finish your silly birth certificate."

He remembered that the good scroll had given instruction that the hatchling should not be left to lay in its own urine. He picked Diamond up and moved him to a different place. He then scooped the *soiled* sand out of the pit.

He again had to clean the oil off of his hands before picking up the quill. He finished cleaning, unrolled the birth scroll and made the final annotation. He went to his door to call out for the Administrator. He opened the door and Vock was standing right there...with that same smile on his face.

Vock clasped his hands over his chest. "You probably chose the massage, didn't you?"

Kovarin cleared his throat as his face turned red. "Yes, Administrator, I did." He handed the scroll tube to Vock.

Vock took it. "Before you close the door, let me look at it."

"My dragon?"

"No, dear boy," said Vock stifling a chuckle. "The document. Let me see if I have any questions."

"Oh." Kovarin looked around a little sheepishly and stood there with his hands clasped in front of him.

Vock was reading the document with his eyebrows raised and that ever pleasant smile on his face. Suddenly his expression changed to a confused frown. He looked up at Kovarin. "Black?"

"Yes, black," said Kovarin nonchalantly.

Vock studied Kovarin's face looking for any kind of trickery. "Are you…sure that it isn't…dark gray?"

"No…black!"

Vock looked back at the document. "That…that's rarely happened before. I have seen several that were a *very* dark gray… but…black?"

"I'm quite sure," said Kovarin with a smile.

Vock stood there looking at the scroll while nodding. "I can hardly wait to see this one in…" he looked at the scroll carefully. "…*his* coming out. If he is definitely black and not dark gray, then he really will be something…unique."

"I was a little confused myself, when I first saw that little claw pop out of the shell. I thought, myself, that it was probably just a dark gray, but he most definitely…is black."

Vock stood there still nodding as he looked at the document again. He looked up at Kovarin. "Diamond?"

Kovarin smiled. "Once the skin was oiled, he seemed to sparkle in the torchlight…like a gem. I decided that it should be Diamond."

"Sounds very appropriate." Vock rolled the scroll up and placed it back in the tube. He looked back up with that big smile. "I shall endeavor to find your other paperwork. I will do everything I can to make sure that *this* does not get lost like *that* did."

They gave each other a courteous bow and Kovarin closed the door.

He leaned against the door wondering about what the next thing to do in regards to his new little friend. Better keep reading the good scroll. He was learning all kinds of new things. Kevrong (and Dozzbin) would be so irritated…if they knew.

Suddenly there was a lot of loud shouting in the hallway. Kovarin listened at the door to try to find out what was going on. He heard several people bellowing at each other. He could not understand what was going on because there were so many people shouting at the same time. The shouting sounded as if it were getting closer to his own door. He pressed his ear to the door in an attempt at hearing something…intelligible.

His right ear nearly got knocked through to the left side of his head. As he was trying to listen, someone started hammering their fist on his door.

The voice directly outside of Kovarin's door belonged to Dozzbin. "Open this door, you nefarious dastard!"

Next he heard Vock, screaming at Dozzbin. "What do you think you're doing? You can't interrupt the bonding!"

"There is no bonding, you simpleton! That scoundrel is

fabricating the whole thing. He does *not* have a live hatchling and I'm going to prove it…RIGHT NOW!" Dozzbin started hammering on the door again. "Open up, you mendacious curmudgeon!"

There were a few more shouts and grunts as Kovarin could hear several people wrestling in the hallway. One man was shouting: "Hold him!" Dozzbin was shouting back: "Get your hands off of me!"

Finally Vock broke in: "Commander, you're upsetting all of the hatchlings! Now, stop it."

Kovarin thought of his charge. If Diamond was being upset by all of that shouting, he needed to be there to comfort the little dragon. He ran into the chamber. Diamond was still sleeping peacefully, even with the din going on just on the other side of the wall. Kovarin opened the meat chute to listen in.

"All right! You are right," said Dozzbin still in a bit of an angry way. "I shouldn't upset the ones who *do* have live hatchlings. That one, however, is a liar. There is no way that he could possibly have a live hatchling. He's too incompetent. He's failed nine times before and now, you expect me to believe that someone that ineffectual has, all of a sudden, become proficient? NO! Not at all."

"If he is telling a tall tale…," said Vock, "…when the Ringmaster goes in, we will know. Until then, you have no authority to enter. No one may enter and upset the bonding."

"*I* have no authority? Do you know, who you are talking to? I am the Supreme Commander of the War Forces. Don't tell me that I don't have any authority!'"

"Here…you don't! I am Senior Administrator of the Hatching Hall. Here, I have the absolute authority…even over *you*."

"You mean that you are going to allow that charlatan to keep up his phony story…until it's time for…"

"We are not hurting for space right now. The next set of Candidates are already preparing their pits and we have at least five rooms that are totally vacant. You know the rules! If that man is fabricating then I will turn him over to you, once a lie is proven, and you can do anything that you want with him. If the Ringmaster proves a live hatchling…then you owe everyone in this hallway, Dragonmen, Candidates, Meat Cutters, Suppliers and Administrators - a huge apology."

Dozzbin scoffed. "You're actually going to wait that long? You're going to wait for the Ringmaster? All right! Fine! When the Ringmaster goes in and proves *no living hatchling*…then, you and everyone you named will owe *me* a huge apology."

Kovarin breathed a sigh of relief as Dozzbin stormed away. He closed the meat chute with a big smile on his face. Then his expression changed to complete horror…Ringmaster? Back to the scroll…to find out when the Ringmaster was supposed to visit. He had seen and heard several things about the Ringmaster, however he was not quite sure as to what the overall responsibilities were to and by the Ringmaster.

5

The Ringmaster was supposed to visit, at a time between the hatchling's nineteenth and thirtieth day of life. He would "install" rings in the lower jaw of the young. Since it was not practical and rather unhealthy for any dragon to have a bit in its mouth like a horse, you had to have something in the mouth to attach the reins to, in order to control the dragon when it was older.

The handler would be notified as to when the Ringmaster was coming and would be given a dose of an opiate (dose depended on the size of the hatchling). The dose was to be placed in the first few pieces of meat given to the dragon. The handler was to observe, as the dragon ate. When it went to sleep (not in the normal fashion, but under the influence of the drug), the Ringmaster was to be informed and he would then enter and perform the installation, as well as an examination. The installation had to be performed, very early in the life of the dragon, so it would not yet feel much (if any) pain. The doping was also necessary in order for the dragon to not know that someone else had been in the chamber.

The young dragon should not feel that much pain, but would be a little confused in regards to these new attachments. The confusion usually only lasted three to four days.

Once the rings are installed, the handler should measure his dragon daily because some of the dragons grew fast enough where larger rings were needed to replace the smaller ones. There is no concern as far as replacing the rings with larger ones because as soon as the holes are in the back of the mandible, they are there permanently. The holes grow with the dragon and this makes it easier to replace them with larger rings.

Kovarin looked up and just spoke to himself: "How many more surprises are there going to be…in this good scroll?"

The next four days were very much the same. Feed Diamond, wait till he drops off to sleep, set a new time candle for the next feeding and then measure him again.

Diamond was eating an enormous amount compared to what he was getting rid of. Kovarin cleaned very few droppings out of the pit and there was also very little of the white sand that had been "stained" yellow.

He called for Administrator Vock. When Vock showed up, Kovarin told him about the measurements that had been taken. When Diamond was born, he had just barely been a size three. Now, he was past size five and getting very close to size six.

Vock contemplated the information. "Is he eating more… at each feeding?"

"Yes, considerably more. His first feeding, he didn't finish a fist-sized chunk. Now, he can consume three times that much and still want more."

"Yes, he should. Tell the Meat Cutters, on the next feeding, to double your last order. Some of them do grow very rapidly…at first. Usually it's the very small ones that do grow like this - but not that rapidly. Keep me informed as to when the rapid growth starts slowing or stops altogether. This one is turning out to be *very* interesting."

"Thank you, Administrator. I appreciate any help that you can give."

"That's what I am here for, my boy." Vock smiled, bowed and then turned away.

Kovarin closed his door and sighed. He looked at the time candle. It should be hissing at any time now. He headed out of his bedroom to check on Diamond. He was stirring a little, however, he had not awakened yet.

Kovarin rang the bell on the meat chute.

One of the bearers responded. "How much this time, Dragonman?"

"Double the last order."

"Double? Are you serious?"

"On the advice of Administrator Vock, I am doubling it."

"All right, as you wish, Dragonman."

Several large pieces of meat came sliding down the chute. He picked them up and took them to the edge of the pit. He started cutting them into small pieces. He looked at Diamond, once again almost in the exact center of the sand pit.

Diamond stirred. He stretched out his front legs and neck and yawned. Then he stretched out his back legs and tail. He stood up on all fours and started flapping his wings. He moved them slowly at first. The flapping got faster and faster. Kovarin was watching him wide-eyed as Diamond's front legs rose out of the sand. He stopped flapping and yawned again. He looked around and saw Kovarin and waddled towards his feeder.

Kovarin was wondering when he would try his wings again…and get all four legs off of the ground. His mind went off to a dazzling ride through the clouds on a much larger dragon. He had no idea if Diamond would ever get that large…hope springs eternal.

His mind was brought back to the present situation as Diamond got impatient and started his hungry cry. Kovarin chuckled and started popping pieces of meat into the hungry maw.

Diamond ate a good portion of the meat that was there. He could not possibly finish all of it, because there was a greater mass of meat than Diamond's body weight. This time, instead of going back to sleep, after he got his fill, he wandered around the edge of the sand pit, exploring what there was of his (currently) small world.

As he was taking his tour he squatted and emptied his bowels. Again Kovarin noticed that he was taking in a huge amount and getting rid of only a small amount. That was the only reason that Kovarin could see as to why he was growing rather fast. Just how big was he going to get though?

Diamond was at the edge near Kovarin and started rubbing

his right side against the rocks that made up the perimeter of the pit. Oops! Oil time! He was getting some dry patches on his skin.

Kovarin quickly grabbed the oil mug and dipped it into the keg. He headed for Diamond while getting some of the oil on his hand. He started to rub the oil on the left side of Diamond's body when he noticed that there was a considerable amount of loose dead skin hanging off that had been unnoticed before. He remembered, from the good scroll, that the first shedding of skin could take place anywhere from four to ten days after hatching. He peeled the dead skin off with his right hand and applied oil with his left. Diamond stopped rubbing against the rocks and sat there giving off his contented keening while he was stripped of the dead skin and oiled. Most of it came off very easily. There were several small spots where Kovarin had to pay quite a bit of attention, in order to get a small piece off.

He piled the dead skin off to the side. He had an idea as to what he could do with Diamond's first shedding - throw this refuse into the face of Dozzbin. Maybe that would convince that villain that there was a live dragon in here.

Diamond rolled onto his left side, exposing his belly. Kovarin saw that this was the only place where there was any of the shedding left of Diamond's body. He quickly pulled it off and then finished oiling the little beast down, from nose to tail.

After getting his oil rubdown, Diamond went back to his favorite sleeping spot and curled up to sleep until he got hungry again.

Kovarin snorted. "Have a nice nap, you little spoiled brat."

He gathered up all of the dead skin and went to the door of his bedroom. He opened it and looked out into the hallway. One of the lower Administrators saw him and came immediately.

"Is there something I can help you with, Dragonman?"

"Yes, I was wondering if Supreme Commander Dozzbin is still causing a ruckus around here."

"Yes, Dragonman, he is still causing havoc, telling us that he cannot believe *you*."

Kovarin held out the dead skin. "Give this to him. That should tell the Supreme Commander something."

The man took it with a smile. "I don't know if it will satisfy that man or not. I shall certainly give it to him though."

Kovarin gave him a cordial bow and closed the door. He chuckled. He then realized that he had not started a new time candle yet. "What a bother," he said as he took a knife and shaved a small portion off for the time lost. He then lit it and ate some of his own dinner, before taking a badly needed rest.

He woke up and took a quick look at the time candle. He still had a little while before the next feeding. He could get the meat ahead of time and have it cut up before Diamond woke up.

He was preparing the meat, next to the pit when he saw Diamond wake up. Once again he went through the ritual of stretching the front then the rear.

He started flapping his wings again. This time he was

flapping them faster, with what seemed, a little more purpose. His front legs came off of the ground and then his rear legs went airborne. He suddenly let out a small "yeep" of surprise, stopped flapping and took a spread-eagle belly splat back down into the sand. His head was darting around, looking in every direction, as if he were trying to figure out what had happened. He had clenched his claws into the sand as if trying to clutch onto something. He looked up at Kovarin for a moment and then continued looking around in confusion. He stood up on all fours and took a look under his belly, still trying to figure out what that new sensation was that he had just experienced. In his cogitation, he finally decided that he was more hungry than he was curious (or scared) about leaving the ground. He waddled over to Kovarin for his repast.

Kovarin tried desperately not to laugh at the spectacle that had just taken place in front of him. He knew that certain animals took it badly if you laughed at them and he was not sure how this or any dragon would take being laughed at. Diamond had had a somewhat abrupt (and embarrassing) landing in the sand, he did not appear to be hurt, so just go on with the feeding.

After he had his fill, he once again did not immediately go to sleep. He again wandered around the perimeter of the pit, while hiccupping. This time, however, he stood up several times, on his back legs, and got a better view of what was around him and over the edge of the pit. After a few minutes of this exploration he went back to the center of the pit, curled up and went to sleep.

Kovarin sat there wondering how these creatures could have possibly survived, in the wild, before they became somewhat domesticated.

Since Diamond kept on going to the center of the pit, Kovarin now had to climb in and crawl over to him in order to take measurements and give the oil treatment. He noticed that the sand did seem to be warmer in the middle. He decided to try an experiment and place the coals, more on one side than the other, in order to get Diamond closer to the side for his naps. If he could get Diamond closer to the side, the measuring could be done much easier.

The next feeding started the same. Diamond woke up and stretched. He started flapping his wings rapidly again. He left the ground, "yeeped" again and belly flopped into the sand again. This time as he was looking around the room, trying to figure out what happened. He looked back at his wings and gave them a few apprehensive flaps. He studied his wings for several minutes and then decided that he, again, was more hungry than curious.

Diamond was now pushing size seven. He was growing rapidly and steadily. The measurements showed him as being just a little longer, and wider wingspan, with each feeding. Kovarin wondered just how big he might get at his current rate of growth.

The next feeding was about to take place. This time when Diamond flapped his wings, he hovered in place for a few moments. He looked back at his flapping wings, forgot what he was doing, stopped flapping and belly flopped again. Kovarin was finding it more difficult to keep from laughing out loud at the educational antics going on in front of him.

Diamond looked back at his wings and started flapping them again, with less apprehension than before. He started flapping harder and harder until he started going airborne again.

Kovarin was *really* glad that the sand was wet. If it had been dry, the wing flapping would have sent a sandstorm throughout the chamber.

Diamond slowed his flapping and went back down gently this time. He sat there in the sand panting heavily. The panting subsided quickly. He looked around the room again as if he were trying to figure out what he had just observed.

Kovarin leaned over the pit and started praising Diamond for his feat of flying. Again he was not sure if the dragons could feel emotion the same way as dogs, however, it would not hurt to treat him as if he did.

Diamond waddled over to Kovarin, minus the panting, while looking up at his face instead of at the meat. He sat down close to the edge and looked back at his wings. The breathing was normal. He looked back at Kovarin and opened his mouth, ready for food.

At the end of this feeding, Diamond started walking around again. He headed back to the middle and looked around as if confused. He started exploring again. He came to the area that Kovarin had placed most of the burning coal. He settled down in this warm sand, curled up and went to sleep.

"So that *is* what you *were* looking for...the warmest spot.

Hmph! Somehow, with all of the coals around most of the pit, the heat was being concentrated in the middle." He looked down at the contented, glutted, sleeping dragon. He smiled. "I'm learning more about you every day and you are learning more about you as well, my little friend."

6

Kovarin prepared for Diamond's next meal. He ordered an even greater amount of meat, after the last measurements had been taken. Diamond was now a full-fledged size seven and was well on his way to size eight.

After preparing the meat, he went back to his bedroom and waited for the time candle to burn down to where it started hissing. As soon as it did, he lit a new candle in preparation for the following feeding.

He went back into Diamond's bed chamber. Diamond was already going through his stretching routine. He started flapping his wings again. He rose into the air. He started flailing his legs and tail around and started flying forward…with very little control as to where he was going. He started yeeping and squawking as he flew…in no form of a set direction. He gained and lost altitude, he changed direction, several times, with no control over what he was doing.

The last part of his uncontrolled flight came when he very unceremoniously slammed into the wall. He landed on his back and started a new sound that Kovarin had never heard before. Diamond was doing the same thing as if he were making his hungry cry, with the rapid inhaling and exhaling. This time, however, the noise he was making was not a low buzz, but a very high-pitched, ear-piercing yeep. His legs, wings, tail and head were thrashing around as he did not seem to be able to right himself.

Kovarin ran to him and carefully did what he could to pick Diamond up. With all of the thrashing, and oily skin, Diamond slid down Kovarin's left leg. He immediately wrapped his legs and tail around Kovarin's leg and clamped on for dear life. His wings were still flapping a little and he stuck his head inside Kovarin's shirt, still keeping up with that horrid noise. Kovarin felt something wet and warm flowing down his left leg.

After several moments of trying to console Diamond, with soothing words and a calm voice, the noise started to subside. Diamond pulled his head out of the shirt and looked up at Kovarin's face. His beeps of panic started coming with less frequency and rhythm. He looked around, confused and slowed his yeeps even more. He looked down at Kovarin's predicament, having a four legged creature hanging on to one leg of a biped and stopped yeeping. He looked up at Kovarin's face and let out a few more yeeps of fear. Then he seemed to have stopped altogether.

Kovarin made the awkward walk to the pit, with Diamond still holding firm to his leg. Diamond let out a few more feeble yeeps. Kovarin raised his left leg up over the pit and continued saying soothing words to Diamond. The little dragon finally saw that he was in no danger and was back in the safety, security and familiarity of the pit. He eased his grip on Kovarin's leg and slid down to the warm sand.

He yeeped a few more times as if trying to remind himself

that he was afraid...of something. He could not remember what he was supposed to be afraid of and decided, again, that it was not as important as getting something to eat. He sat on his haunches and opened his mouth.

Kovarin started popping meat into Diamond's mouth. The episode did not seem to have curbed the little dragon's appetite. He still took each piece, swallowed immediately and had his mouth open, ready for the next chunk of meat.

Kovarin heard a commotion at the meat chute. Someone broke protocol and hollered through the chute. "What's going on in there?"

Kovarin was not sure what to do. Instead of answering he just kept feeding Diamond.

Again the voice called out: "We heard the dragon's cries of panic - what did you do to frighten him?"

Kovarin groaned. "He scared himself!"

"What? How does a hatchling scare himself?"

"He flew out of the sand pit and because it was his first flight, he had very little control and slammed into the wall and that's when he started yipping."

"He can't fly...he's too young...too small...what really happened?"

Kovarin was getting impatient. "I'm telling you the truth. Now, you are breaching etiquette. Leave me alone, while I'm feeding my dragon!"

The voice outside did not get any lower. "One of you two…go get the Senior Administrator…now!" The chute door closed. The rest of the conversation at the meat chute door was muffled and unintelligible.

Kovarin was relieved that they had stopped with the bothersome questions. He watched Diamond to see if any of that had upset the little beast. Diamond still, seemed to be, only interested in the next mouthful. Each piece was swallowed with the same speed as the previous one. Diamond kept eating as Kovarin saw that the supply of meat was getting very low. He did not know what to do if he ran out and Diamond still wanted more, now. There were only three pieces of meat left when Diamond finally swallowed a piece slowly. He lowered his head, looked around and then belched and started hiccupping.

Kovarin sat there somewhat nervous in the anticipation of what would happen next. He put the next piece of meat back down on his platter and reached for the oil. He dipped the mug into the keg and then placed the mug on the edge of the pit. Diamond saw the mug and sniffed. He came closer to Kovarin and just stood there. Kovarin got some of the oil on his left hand and started applying it to Diamond's right side. Diamond turned his head and watched as the oil was being smeared on his body. He lowered his head and started keening contentedly. He stood there like that while Kovarin oiled his entire body. Once the oil bath was finished, he curled up and went to sleep.

Kovarin cleaned the oil off of his hands and took measurements again. Diamond had grown…again…not much, however, he was still getting larger. He sat there watching

Diamond sleep for a while.

He decided that it was time to report…whoever that man was, for the breach in protocol. He went back to his room, washed his face put on a clean shirt and went to his door. He opened the door and was not sure who was more surprised. Senior Administrator Vock and three other top echelon Administrators were standing there waiting at Kovarin's door.

He looked from face to face. All four of them looked very somber. Vock did not have the usual friendly smile on his face.

"We understand that there was a situation, between you and your charge," said Vock inquisitively. "It is reported that you frightened your hatchling…is this true?"

Kovarin closed his eyes and let out a low growl. He took in a deep breath and opened his eyes. "*I* did not scare him. *He* scared himself. He's been trying his wings, the last few times before his feedings. This last time he took off and…had absolutely no control as to how to turn or navigate in any way…properly. He slammed into the wall and then started that panic cry. I soothed him and petted him until he stopped…that horrible noise. Then I put him back in the pit and fed him."

"That's impossible," said one of the other Administrators. "According to the hatching date, he is much too young and too small to fly."

Vock held up his hand to the other Administrator. "Nathak, please, let me…" He looked up at Kovarin with a bit of a stern look. "What my colleague says is true: Your dragon is much too young to fly. No dragon, this young, has ever flown…before."

"Nevertheless," said Kovarin flatly, "...he did! He has grown rapidly and he has tested his wings...more than once."

Vock clasped his hands in front of him. He took two steps closer to Kovarin. "You do understand...the punishment... for giving false evidence to myself...and any of the other Administrators...don't you?"

Kovarin leaned closer and got right in Vock's face and spoke in a slow intimidating manner: "I am not fabricating. I am telling you the absolute truth." He did not move.

Vock looked deep into Kovarin's eyes. He looked for any kind of flinch or blink or anything that would indicate deception. After several moments of staring each other down, Vock finally broke the silence.

"All right, Dragonman. If what you say is true...then your charge is growing...faster than normal." He leaned back and cocked his head. "Since that is the case, we must summon a Ringmaster...now. If he is growing and progressing this rapidly, we must get the rings in him, as soon as possible."

Another one of the Administrators protested: "Senior Administrator, you heard the words of Dozzbin? He says that this man is..."

"Yes, Acong, I remember Dozzbin's tirade. He said that this man was incompetent and that there was no possibility of a live hatchling. Remember, though, he did supply us with the skin from the first shedding. You cannot fabricate *that*...with words. Plus, now, we have the word of several Meat Cutters and aides, to the noise that came out of the chamber. Only one that is alive could make that noise. I will let the Ringmaster give us an eyewitness account of the dragon."

Acong held his arms out and shook his head in disbelief. "When!?"

"Now," said Vock impatiently. "Go get a Ringmaster!"

Acong cleared his throat. "Which one?"

Vock leaned his head back with his eyes closed. "I don't care," he snapped. He looked back at Acong. "Any…two of them…or all three, I don't care…just do it!"

Acong spun on his heels and headed off.

Vock looked back at Kovarin and smiled. "I hope…I *pray*…that you are telling the truth. I don't like any deception. I would dearly love to see that loudmouth, Dozzbin, getting slapped down…with the *truth*." He sniffed and cleared his throat. "When the Ringmaster comes, he is going to want to see *all* of your measurements. From that, he will determine which size rings to install. We will let you know when he shows up."

"I will have the measurements in my hand ready for him," said Kovarin cordially.

Vock bowed his head.

Kovarin returned the bow and slowly closed his door. He leaned back against the closed door. "Bring on the Ringmaster… all three of them if you want," he said with a huge grin on his face.

There was a knock on the door. Kovarin woke up and

looked around somewhat confused. Then he remembered that the Administrators had called for the Ringmasters. He took a quick look at the time candle - only half way down. Good, maybe the Ringmaster wanted to have a conversation before doing the deed.

He got up and went to the door. The knocking was not loud - it was persistent. He opened it and saw three men standing there with Administrator Vock.

Kovarin smiled. "Can I help you gentlemen?"

Vock smiled as he introduced the three men. "These are the Ringmasters. They are the three primary caretakers of the dragons. I introduce, to you, Ringmasters Tulluck, Felshon and Challoo."

Each man bowed his head as he was introduced. They did seem the type that Kovarin was expecting. All three of them had nothing of their original color to their hair. All three were different shades of gray.

Tulluck was a tall gangly man. He had a look in his blue eyes that spoke of years of experience and the wisdom that went with it.

Felshon had a medium build and had a patch over his left eye. The good right eye had a look of suspicion in it.

Challoo looked as if he had never missed a meal in his life. He also had a huge bushy beard that hung half way down to his waist.

Tulluck spoke first: "The first thing, Dragonman, that we want to see, is all of your measurements."

Kovarin smiled. He had the paperwork on a small table, right next to the door. He picked it up and handed it to Tulluck. Tulluck held it up so that all three men could peruse the information.

He seems to be growing at a very rapid rate," said Felshon.

"Look at the body to wingspan ratio," said Challoo. "That *would* make him *very* capable of flight."

"It's not entirely impossible...we've heard from others, that their dragons started testing their wings at this early age," said Tulluck.

Challoo looked at Kovarin with an inquisitive look. "You say...he's black. Are you sure that it is not...a very dark gray?"

Kovarin shrugged. "If he is dark gray...it is the *darkest* gray that I've ever seen in my life. His color hasn't faded. He still looks...very black."

"Interesting," said Felshon. "I know that I'd like to see this little one. I've never seen a black before."

"No one *really* has," said Tulluck as he shook his head.

Felshon looked at his colleagues. "So? What do we do? Do we go in just one at a time...or do we go observe together?"

Tulluck shook his head again. "I don't like the idea of too many people in there at once. However, if he's sedated, he won't know it...and we might just have to go ahead and 'ring' him... now."

Felshon grunted and pulled a pouch out of a large pocket on his robe. "How much do you think we need?"

"He's definitely almost a size eight…" Challoo looked at Kovarin. "…does he seem fat or…normal body dimension?"

Kovarin shrugged slightly and looked thoughtful. "His body has not fattened. He has just…grown…since the hatching."

Felshon raised his eyebrows. "Two full measures?"

"Just slightly less than that, I think," said Tulluck.

"I agree," said Challoo.

"Yes," said Felshon. "Slightly less…just to be safe."

All three men nodded approval. Felshon pulled a very tiny spoon and a small bowl out of another pocket. One of the Meat Cutters brought a small table up to him. He placed the bowl on the table. Challoo pulled a small clay bottle of water out of one of his pockets and poured a small amount of water into the bowl. Felshon opened the pouch and stuck the spoon in. He brought it out filled with a light brown powder. He held the spoon directly over the opening in the pouch. He then took a knife and leveled the powder off, in the spoon, with the knife, dumping the excess powder back into the pouch. He poured the powder into the bowl. He produced another spoonful of powder. He leveled it off again. This time, he shook the spoon slightly so that a little of the powder fell out after the leveling. He then added this to the mixture in the bowl. The pouch and the spoon were put away.

Tulluck pulled a small spoon of his own out and started rapidly stirring the powder and the water.

Challoo signaled to one of the meat cutters, who produced a fist-sized piece of raw meat and placed it on the table.

Kovarin was looking, with an inquisitive frown, as the measuring and mixing was going on.

Felshon tapped Kovarin on the shoulder. "Dragonman, do you let him bite pieces of meat off, or do you cut it to mouthfuls, yourself?"

"I cut them in small pieces…uh…mouthfuls and feed them to him…one at a time, Ringmaster."

"Very good. Would you please cut three *mouthfuls* off of this piece of meat?"

"I'll get my knife."

"That's all right, I have one," said Felshon. He pulled a knife out and gave it to Kovarin.

Kovarin took the knife and cut the meat. He made a mental note to himself, to sharpen his own knife, as this one sliced through the meat with almost no effort at all.

"Now," said Felshon, "cut a small hole in the middle of each piece."

Kovarin made the holes.

Felshon looked over at Tulluck. "Ready yet?"

Tulluck looked closely at the paste he had just made. "Yes, quite."

Felshon pulled out a different spoon. "Now, Dragonman, take this spoon and fill each hole with some of the mixture. Make sure that you use all of it."

Kovarin spooned the stuff into the holes in the meat.

"Very good," said Felshon. "On your dragon's next feeding, these will be the first three pieces that go into his mouth." Felshon turned to the Meat Cutters. "Go ahead and prepare the dragon's normal portion…at this time. This way, that meat will be of the same freshness as that meat."

Kovarin watched the Meat Cutter go to the outside of the meat chute. The man checked some annotation on a piece of paper hanging over the chute. He then cut a few pieces of meat, weighed them and placed them in the chute.

Felshon smiled at Kovarin. "Take these three pieces with you. Make sure that you keep them separate from the others. You can go ahead and prepare…" He looked at a small plaque, hanging just outside of the door. "…Diamond's next meal."

Tulluck spoke up. "How soon will the next feeding be?"

Kovarin opened his door wider. "You can see the time candle…right there." Everyone looked in at the candle.

"Well," said Challoo, "it seems that we have some time to sit here and puzzle over this fascinating dragon, before his next feeding."

"Remember, keep those three pieces separate," said Felshon. Also, make sure that you let us know, when the little one is asleep…from the drug."

Kovarin picked up the three "treated" pieces, gave a nod to each of the Ringmasters and went back into his room.

He took them to the edge of the pit and put them in a

special place. He then got the next feeding from the chute, and started making giblets out of the big chunks. After all of that was finished, he left the untreated meat on a platter off to the side and went back to his bedroom to rest and wait.

The time candle surprised him when it hissed that message of "time is up". Kovarin quickly went to his door to let someone know. The three Ringmasters were sitting on a bench, outside the door having a conversation, while sharing a bottle of some liquid. When the door came open, they all looked at Kovarin in anticipation.

"Ringmasters...the time candle just went off. I'm going to go feed him now."

"Right," said Tulluck. "That's as it should be. Let us know when he's been knocked out by the drug."

"Uh...right." Kovarin felt a little stupid. No time to worry about that. 'Those men are professionals,' he thought. 'They're ready and warned that it will happen soon. They probably also know that I am a little nervous about this whole situation.' He lit a new time candle.

Diamond was stretching his rear section out by the time Kovarin got back into the chamber. He looked up, saw Kovarin, turned toward him, opened his mouth and waited. He got a little impatient as Kovarin was getting situated and started his 'hungry cry'. This was silenced, as soon as the first piece of drugged meat, hit his mouth. He swallowed quickly and was ready again before Kovarin could get the next piece ready. Number two and then number three were down the gullet of the unsuspecting victim.

Now, Kovarin was pulling untreated pieces off of the platter and watched Diamond carefully as each piece was swallowed. He was waiting for any sign of slowing or drowsiness. Diamond swallowed over a third of the meat and showed no signs of slowing at all...yet.

Diamond finally slowed...a little. He suddenly tilted a little to his right. He stopped and jerked to an upright position. He looked around, confused. He opened his mouth. Kovarin threw another piece of meat in. Diamond was now showing signs of fading. He did not swallow as quickly. The meat was slower moving down his esophagus. He was looking around, between bites instead of immediately opening up for the next piece. Kovarin was wondering if he should stop the feeding altogether.

Diamond wavered again. He lowered his front legs to where he was now laying on his belly. He again started looking around in confusion. He looked up at Kovarin and opened his mouth. Before a piece of meat could be put in his mouth, his head started drooping down, slowly. He still had his neck held up, however, he could not hold his head up. His head slowly sank into the sand, nose first - with his mouth still open. His neck started relaxing and Kovarin did not like the angle that it was going in, so he reached down and pulled Diamond's nose out of the sand and straightened the neck. Diamond was slightly roused by the movement and tried to hold his head up, mouth open. His head sank back down, again, this time resting on his chin. The mouth slowly closed.

Kovarin watched for several moments for any sign of movement. All he could see was that Diamond was breathing normally - for when he was asleep. Kovarin sighed. It was done. Now, for the Ringmasters and what they have in mind.

He went to his bedroom door and opened it. The three men looked up expectantly. "He's asleep," Kovarin said flatly.

The three men filed into the bedroom.

Before Kovarin could shut the door, a fourth man came in pulling a cart that was too hot to stand near. There was a bit of smoke coming out of the top of the covered cart. The new man was huge. He towered over everyone in the room. He was heavily muscled and had a shaved head. He was wearing a thick leather apron and had many burn scars on his arms, like any blacksmith would normally have. He stopped with his cart in the bedroom and just stood there a little bit away from the hot cart. He did not say a thing.

Kovarin shrugged and followed the three Ringmasters into the hatching chamber.

The three men were all standing there gawking at Diamond.

"I just couldn't believe it…from hearing it," said Felshon. "A black! Who would have ever dreamed…?"

"Yes," said Tulluck. "His skin is so black…I can't tell if his eyes are shut or not." He got down as close as he could to Diamond's head. "Black skin over black eyes…it is…difficult."

Challoo gently straightened the tail and the neck. He then measured Diamond. "He is definitely a size eight." He chuckled. "A size eight that just a few days ago…hatched from a size two egg. Hard to believe."

"Supreme Tribunal Tremyath saw the egg being presented," said Kovarin. "He along with another member of the Tribunal and Supreme Commander Dozzbin."

All three men stood back and gazed at the little wonder again.

"A size eight, hatching from a size two egg…not uncommon," said Challoo. "But…it usually takes fourteen to twenty days before the dragon grows *that* much. For a hatchling… to grow *this* fast…remarkable!"

Tulluck took the measuring device. He stretched Diamond's right wing out and measured. All three men got close and again started shaking their heads in awe.

"He has enough wingspan," said Tulluck. "The wing to body ratio…is enough…for him to become…airborne." He looked at the other two with a strange amused look in his eyes. "Only a few days old…and he has the wings to do it." He looked at Kovarin and smiled. "Dragonman, I believe you! This hatchling…has the wing size to do it." He looked back at Diamond and smiled. "He just doesn't know how to control his flight path yet." He got his face down closer to Diamond. "You don't, do you, little one. You can fly…but not control it…yet."

"We *must* ring him," said Felshon flatly. He looked at his colleagues. "Who should do it?"

Tulluck snickered. "Challoo, that's your assistant out there. Might as well be you who rings the little one."

"Thank you for the honor," said Challoo. "My only

problem, right now, is trying to figure out…what size we should start him at."

The other two nodded in agreement.

Challoo stroked his beard. "As fast as he's growing, I would think that he could start…with size twelve…or thirteen even. The problem there is…a twelve…just might be a tad too heavy for him."

Felshon shook his head. "If he's growing this fast…I feel that…in two or three days, the size twelve won't be that cumbersome."

"Size twelve would be good," said Tulluck. "At least that way, if his growth continues, at the rate he's going, we wouldn't need to replace them until…he's grown to size fourteen."

The three men looked at each other and all nodded in agreement. Challoo went to the archway. "Bodor, bring in the cart."

The big man pulled the hot cart into the chamber. Kovarin felt the temperature go up several degrees as the cart came in.

"Bodor, we need size twelve rings,"

Bodor pulled an odd looking belt from around his waist. He laid the belt down on the floor and stretched it out. It was lined with shiny rings of many sizes. The small ones started at the left and they got progressively bigger, the further to the right that you moved. Bodor moved his finger up the line till he found what he was looking for and unhooked two rings from the belt. He handed the rings to Challoo and put the belt back around his ample waist.

Challoo looked at Kovarin. "Dragonman, I need your oil."

Kovarin pointed at the keg. "It's in there...take what you need."

Kovarin had placed a ladle on the edge of the keg. Challoo took the ladle, filled it with oil and then placed the two rings in the oil.

Tulluck and Felshon carefully moved Diamond closer to the edge of the pit. They rested his chin on the stone edge of the pit and then both backed away.

Challoo rested the ladle in the sand making sure that the oil did not spill. He pulled out a large gauntlet and put his right hand in it. He looked up and smiled. "Bodor, we are ready for the rods."

Bodor brought the cart a little closer to the pit. He pulled a metal cover off of the top of the cart. A larger amount of smoke came up out of the opening. He waved the smoke away. Using tongs, he reached into the hole and pulled out a long black tube that had a silver looking rod in the middle of it. Challoo pulled the silver rod out, picked up Diamond's head and carefully used the rod to poke a hole in the back of Diamond's lower jaw. The smell was atrocious as it burned through skin and bone.

Kovarin gasped. He watched for any movement by Diamond. None! The little dragon was so doped up, he felt nothing at all...or at least there was no indication that he felt pain.

Challoo dropped the rod into the sand pit and it sizzled a little. He threw the gauntlet off with a quick flick of the wrist.

He pulled one of the rings out of the oil, unclasped it and fitted it through the new hole.

Tulluck and Felshon came up and both nodded approval.

Challoo did some kind of thing with the ring that Kovarin could not quite understand. It seemed to be some additional pin that was added to the ring, to keep it in place and closed.

Challoo put the gauntlet back on and the procedure was repeated on the other side of Diamond's jaw. Again, Diamond showed no sign of noticing what had just happened.

Tulluck placed his hand on Kovarin's shoulder. "These rings, as we said, are size twelve. If he does grow to be a size fourteen, one of us will have to replace them with something larger. Since we don't know how big he is going to grow…we'll need you to keep the Administrators aware of his growth." He chuckled. "I never thought that I'd see the day that one of us installed, size twelve rings, in a hatchling that came out of a size two egg…only a few days ago." He shook his head and smiled. "Amazing!"

"Yes, quite amazing," said Felshon.

"Now…the other question," said Challoo. "Should we sterilize him?"

"I think that we need to hold off on that," said Tulluck. "We have absolutely no idea how large…he may grow."

"Yes," said Felshon. "It'd be a shame, to sterilize him, and all of a sudden, he's large enough to breed. That would just…not be…in any way, shape or form…acceptable."

Challoo nodded with a big smile. "Then…we are all in agreement. Keep an eye on his progress. If he grows large enough, he is a breeder. If not…then he gets…snipped."

Tulluck looked at the leftover meat. "Would he have eaten all of that meat…on a normal basis?"

Kovarin looked at the platter. "Oh, yes. If it wasn't for… drugging him, he would've easily downed the vast majority of that."

Tulluck nodded. "Next time he awakens, he's going to be *really* ravenous. We'll tell the Meat Cutters to add that amount… to your normal order."

"He'll be ready to eat all of that…and possibly more," said Felshon.

Tulluck added: "Right now, a time candle will be useless. The doping always throws their feeding schedule off. You'll just have to wait until he awakens and then set up a new time candle."

"Also…" said Challoo, "…he'll be a little confused by these rings that'll be slapping against his jaw. It'll take…maybe three or four days for him to get used to them. Once he does, he won't pay that much attention to them again." He chuckled. "I do hope that he does grow large enough to be ridden. It will be a magnificent sight…seeing a *black* flying with the other dragons."

Felshon came up and looked Kovarin in the eye. "You do know, don't you, that historically, the darker the dragon, the more fierce and dominant they've been?"

Kovarin cleared his throat. "Ringmaster, I wasn't sure…if

that was a rumor or not. You're saying that it is a truth?"

"Yes, it is, Dragonman." said Felshon. "He could turn out to be one of the strongest, and most nasty tempered beasts that we have in all of the Flying Battle Divisions."

After picking up all of their equipment, the four men left the chamber. Kovarin heard them close the bedroom door as they departed. He went back to Diamond and placed his head back down on the soft sand. He started oiling Diamond's body. He watched as Diamond's breathing did not change. He was sleeping peacefully - in spite of the invasive procedure that he had unknowingly gone through. A few more coals were placed near the pit…keep it nice and warm.

He sat there for quite a while just looking at Diamond. He was not sure what to do, until he remembered that he had not given Diamond his complete oil bath. He went to the keg, dipped out a mug full of oil, went back to the pit and slowly made sure that all of Diamond's body was completely oiled.

He felt a little better after giving the oil bath…a little better…but not much.

7

Kovarin could not help but think that he had helped in playing a very dirty trick on Diamond. Still a hatchling, he trusted the man who fed him in every way possible. He trusted the man for food. He trusted the man for oiling his skin. He trusted the man for a warm, safe place to sleep. Now that trust had earned him a session of being drugged and having two holes punched in the back of his lower jaw.

The rings glistened silvery, in sharp contrast to the jet black scales of the little reptile.

Kovarin sighed. "Will I ever get a chance to ride through the air on your back? Will you get large enough…to carry me? Will I ever be hooking reins up to your jaw rings…in order to fly with you? After doping you like that…will you still trust me?"

Kovarin sat there next to the pit with a large amount of fresh meat for the one who trusted him the most. He stretched. He had been sitting there for at least three turns, waiting for Diamond to awaken. They had stated that the drugging would throw the feeding schedule off…a little. What is a little? Is it a little for the dragon? Is it a little for the handler?

Diamond snorted. He raised his head up a little. He craned

his neck and front legs out and stretched them. The tail and rear legs were stretched next. He sat up on his haunches and spread his wings out to their full extent and flapped them a few times. He raised his head a little higher, and for the first time that Kovarin could remember, he saw Diamond yawn.

Diamond looked over at Kovarin and opened his mouth. No hesitation, no suspicion, just hungry, just "feed me". A piece of meat went in and he swallowed. His mouth was ready for the next piece before the lump of meat had traveled the full distance of the neck.

So far, the jaw rings had gone unnoticed. Diamond was only concerned with getting his stomach filled with a big load of fresh meat. He was not moving his head very much, except to open his mouth and receive another lump of meat.

The pile of meat on the platter was getting smaller and Diamond was not slowing down. So far he had eaten more in this one sitting than he had ever downed before. They said that he would be ravenous. He did not look like he was eating any differently…except for the amount. Kovarin figured that as long as he was getting something in his mouth, on each opening, he would not have time to start his hungry cry, so no matter how ravenous he was, that situation was being taken care of…rapidly.

Diamond caught a piece in his mouth and did not swallow immediately.

'Finally,' thought Kovarin. 'He's just about full.'

Diamond sat there for a few moments before he did swallow, and then opened his mouth waiting for another piece.

There were only four more pieces left on the platter. The little glutton had hogged almost all of it down and was wanting more. Another piece was popped into his mouth. Diamond took three breaths before swallowing this piece. He opened his mouth again. Kovarin gave him another piece…only two left. Diamond swallowed and flopped down in the sand.

Kovarin decided that a good back scratching might get some trust back. He moved to where he could get his hands on both sides of Diamond's back and he started scratching. Diamond started keening as he welcomed the feeling. The keening was interrupted a few times as Diamond belched or hiccupped. The keening tapered off and stopped. Kovarin realized that Diamond had gone to sleep.

He gave Diamond a slow rub down along with his regular oil bath. He shook his head. Diamond was totally unaware of the trick that had been played on him. He still trusted his handler… with his safety…and feeding…and life.

He pulled out the measuring devices and checked Diamond's progress. He had not grown so much as the width of a hair, since his last feeding. At first Kovarin worried about it. Then he remembered that Diamond had not had a full feeding last time. His sedation had prevented the full measure of what the gluttonous little reptile would have normally eaten. He sighed and decided to not worry until the next feeding and measuring. If that showed zero growth…that would be the time to worry about…no flying…and sterilization.

He went back to his bed chamber and made the annotation in regards to zero growth and his notion as to why there was no growth. He set a new time candle, fed himself and flopped down on the furs on his bed to get some sleep.

Kovarin woke up. He was somewhat shocked at first. Something was in his bed…with him…and it was moving. He lifted one of the furs up…and saw Diamond…in the same bed.

Kovarin quickly checked himself for any injury. Those claws could tear you apart, without the dragon realizing that it had inflicted serious, possibly fatal, injuries. He breathed a sigh of relief as he saw no tears in his skin. He saw a few gaping holes in a few of the furs. Holes that had not been there…before Diamond got hold of them.

He sat up in dismay. Why was Diamond not in the pit? Why was he here…in bed? Then he remembered a passage…from the good scroll: *If your dragon ever crawls in bed with you, you have forgotten to keep the sand pit warm enough for the dragon.*

Kovarin growled at himself. In all of his worry over the possible negative attitude that Diamond might have because of the drugging and ringing, he had forgotten to completely check the coals by the pit. He slowly crawled out of the bed, covering Diamond with, what was currently, the warmest parts of the furs. He headed into the hatching chamber, with a torch, in order to get a good fire started with some new coals.

He looked down as he went through the archway. He saw Diamond's clawed footprints in the dirt…from the archway to the bed. He looked carefully at the ground between the archway and the pit…no dragon footprints. There were some droppings, scattered in a line, between the pit and the archway. He wondered if Diamond had flown from the pit to the archway. It was possible. Had he learned some control…over aerial navigation? He decided to make an annotation in his scroll for keeping track of the measurements, about this phenomenon.

He got to the pit. Most of the coals, near where he had controlled the sleeping location of Diamond, were just ash. He uncovered some that were still hot and glowing. He got his shovel and poured some more fresh coals on the hot ones. He stuck the torch in the middle in order to aid in getting the coals started faster.

They were not catching fast enough for his approval. He went back to his bedchamber and got some of the oil from his lamp. He took it back and poured some of the oil onto the cold coals. This started a better fire and some of the coals were catching. He breathed a sigh of relief and pulled the torch out.

He went back to the bedchamber and checked the time candle. He grunted in exasperation. It would be just a little while before the time candle would go off and he would have to start another feeding.

He went back to the meat chute. The Meat Cutters were already there, gossiping. He gave his order. He quickly cut up the first chunk of meat and then went back to check on Diamond. No movement…other than breathing. Back to the chute and start cutting more meat.

While cutting this meat, he heard the time candle hiss. He kept cutting. Moments later, he heard Diamond start his hungry cry. He cut the rest of the meat as rapidly as he could. He then gathered a large handful and headed for the bedchamber.

Diamond was sitting on the furs, voicing his disapproval about the tardy feeding. Kovarin shoved a piece of meat into Diamond's mouth and backed off a little. Diamond swallowed and opened up for the next piece. When he did not receive it, he looked around confused. Kovarin was backing off, trying to entice Diamond back into the hatching chamber.

At first Diamond did not move, other than to start his hungry cry again. Kovarin held the piece of meat out and did not move. Diamond finally got the message and headed for Kovarin. He got his piece of meat and Kovarin backed off again. Diamond started crying between each piece of meat. He thoroughly disapproved of the mobile feeding, however, he wanted the food, more than the distaste for the procedure, and if he had to move to get it - so be it.

Kovarin remembered that there were droppings in the path. He did not want to get any of that on his feet nor did he want Diamond tracking it around. He glanced back as he was moving and steered himself and Diamond around the "line of debris".

Kovarin selected a rather large chunk of meat and popped it into that hungry maw. Diamond had to do a little movement of the mouth, in order to get the large piece to the back of the throat. Kovarin picked that time to reach down, grab Diamond and get him back into the pit. Diamond looked around, a little perplexed at this adjustment. He did a few more gyrations with his head and then swallowed - mouth open, ready for the next piece.

The feeding continued normally, until Diamond was satisfied. He laid down on his belly in the sand. Kovarin was surprised to see that there were several more pieces of meat left on the platter…and Diamond was not begging for more.

Diamond suddenly started looking back and forth. He was moving his head rapidly as he made the movements. He stood up on all fours and his wings spread out to their full length, but did not flap. He kept looking back and forth. Kovarin finally realized that Diamond had finally noticed the jaw rings.

Before, when he was feeding, he did not pay attention to the fact that something might be touching his lower jaw. Now, there was no meat going into his mouth, and, something was touching his jaw. He could not see what it was. This made him a little nervous, as he could not figure out, or see, what kept touching him…on both sides…on the lower part of his jaw. He never once made any motion with his claws to investigate the area being touched. He simply kept looking for the mysterious thing that kept touching him that he could not see.

After several minutes of the frustratingly pointless search, he dropped down on his stomach. He laid his head in the sand and folded his wings against his body. He belched, let out a frustrated snort and promptly went to sleep.

Kovarin sighed in relief. It had looked a little comical, however, he could not laugh. He still felt a little guilty about the drugging and ringing.

Time to take another measurement. He checked the new measures with the last ones. Diamond *was* still growing and it definitely had something to do with the amount of food he ingested. He was now a large eight and well on his way to size nine.

"You still have a long way to go, my friend," said Kovarin.

The harnesses and saddles that were made were for a dragon of, minimum, size twenty-five. Only a few dragons smaller than that had ever been able to carry a rider on their back and get airborne. Anything smaller than a size forty was sterilized. This way the dragons would continue to get bigger and bigger. Only the largest were able to breed. Only the largest and most ominous looking ones would get to fly in the battle units.

Kovarin snorted in disgust himself. Battle! The dragon units had never fought in any battle. They were just used to scare any, wannabe, invaders off. Most of the rumors of how these beasts acted in battle had been started by the people of High Country. The north, east and west borders of High Country - all ocean. There were very few places that a ship could dock because the entire perimeter was high cliffs. South of High Country were the kingdoms of Peegruch and Joktel. Again the border was one very long series of high cliffs. No one could invade without a tremendous amount of ropes and ladders. The only country that had any kind of regular airborne military was High Country…and they had never been in a battle in the entire history of the country. They still spent a great deal of money on that particular defense because it was one of the very few countries, in the world, that had never been invaded - because of the rumors and tall tales invented and perpetuated by the propagandists of High Country.

There were other countries that had attempted an alliance with High Country, however, when they were told that the Dragon Squadrons were for home defense only and not to help someone else in their war, the treaties seemed to quickly dissolve into nothing.

The dragons were bred and trained in the capitol city: Dragon City. After being trained and ready for "combat" the trained lizards were all distributed along the shores and the southern border. They would fly and make a big show. That was what kept High Country from being invaded - fear of a rumor.

Kovarin did not care about the rumor. What he cared about was the fact that now he had a dragon that he was responsible for and it was growing. If Diamond grew large enough…IF… he would be able to do these patrols. Kovarin would have the prestige. He would be honored. He would be part of the biggest hoax that had ever been perpetrated on the world, however, he would enjoy, immensely, riding on Diamond's back up in the air… just because he could.

Kovarin smiled as he looked down on his peacefully sleeping charge. This little one was the ticket to all of the honors that were bestowed on a Dragonman. He decided that he needed more information from the scrolls. So much had been left out of the bad scroll and he was finding out, by accident, some of the things that should have been there.

He checked the coals at the base of the pit. He threw a few more on, just to make sure. He headed back to his bedchamber and checked the time candle. He pulled out the scroll and continued reading.

He had been wondering why the Ringmasters were content, in regards to allowing for bigger rings to be installed, later. Why? What was the indication that Diamond had not stopped growing?

It had to be here somewhere…hopefully.

After some more reading he finally found it…or them. The two signs that a dragon was getting close to the final growth size… all from the neck up. While a youngling was growing, their skull was mostly rounded. As they started to reach maturity and their final growth stage, they would start developing ridges on the top sides of their skull that would eventually sprout two large horns. This was for both male and female.

The male had another development at the base of the skull. He would start growing his "neck flare". It was almost like another wing, however, it was used only when the males were fighting for supremacy. They would make their flares stand straight out, giving the appearance that their head was four to six times the size it actually was. As long as their flares were standing out, they were either challenging or facing a challenger in combat. When they were at peace, the flares folded back against the neck and were hardly noticeable. If two males were locked in combat for supremacy, and one of them had had enough and was surrendering, he would fold his flares back against his neck and slink away. The victor would usually keep his flares out, at their full glory, and roar at the loser.

Kovarin put the scroll down, placed a weight on it to mark his place and went to the pit. He checked Diamond's head and neck. There was no sign of the horn ridges or the neck flares at all. Kovarin laughed in joy to himself. Diamond still had some growing to do. How much was unknown. The main point was that he was *not* finished growing…yet.

He went back to the bedchamber to read the next section.

This was on the "combat for supremacy". Kovarin was wondering, because of those nasty claws and sharp beak, how did they keep their dragons from tearing each other apart? He was amazed to find out that the combat was mainly roaring at each other while showing off their flares, some aerial acrobatics, body bumps and head butting. No clawing, scratching or biting was mentioned at all.

Once again he remembered that the bigger your dragon - the higher your rank. If your dragon was a smaller one who was mean enough to defeat a larger one - then and only then would the man with a smaller dragon get into the ranks of the upper echelon.

He looked up at the chart that showed the rankings. The five largest dragons were: Thunder, size fifty-one - rider: Dozzbin. Glutton, size forty-eight - rider: Brashtok. Bloodletter, size forty-eight - rider: Gonterro. Monster, size forty-seven - rider: Heth. Eating Machine, size forty-six - rider: Invelton.

Because of the size of Thunder, Dozzbin was the Supreme Commander War Forces. Prior to Thunder, there had never even been a size fifty dragon. Around a century ago, there had been one size forty-nine. Thunder had rewritten the book on size.

Glutton and Bloodletter were currently the only size forty-eight dragons. Between Brashtok and Gonterro, neither one would admit which one was slightly larger than the other. Since Glutton was listed before Bloodletter, it was assumed that Glutton was larger (by the smallest of margins). Brashtok flew Glutton as the Battle Division 6 Commander. Gonterro flew Bloodletter as the Battle Division 4 Commander.

Monster was currently the only size forty-seven dragon. Battle Division 1 Commander Heth was his rider.

There were two size forty-six dragons: Eating Machine and Purge. Eating Machine was listed as the fifth of the top five, so he was at least, the width of a fingernail, larger than Purge. Eating Machine was ridden by Invelton, the Battle Division 5 Commander. Purge was ridden by Nossiturm, the Battle Division 2 Commander.

The smallest of the Battle Division Commander's dragons was Protector. He was a size forty-five and was ridden by Ayponch, Battle Division 3.

There were a few listings for the other dragons who had obtained a length of size forty or higher. There were thirty-seven of them and they were all Battle Division Sub Commanders or Battle Group Commanders.

Kovarin, right now, would be happy if Diamond could eventually grow to size twenty-five. Then he would get above the rank of Dragonman and go to the rank of Unit Force Level Three, Dragonrider. Diamond was creeping, quickly, to size nine and did not have his horn ridges yet. Anything was possible.

The time candle hissed. Kovarin sighed happily. Time to go throw some more meat down into that bottomless pit…and hope that he grows some more…quickly.

8

Twelve more days had gone by and many more feedings of the hungry (and growing) Diamond. The once tiny dragon was now a size twelve and pushing size thirteen. There had been another shedding and Kovarin had been more than happy to request that the vacated skin be rubbed in the face of Dozzbin...again.

Kovarin was oiling his sleeping dragon. A feeding had just been finished. Even though Diamond was sleeping he was contentedly making a keening noise as he was getting a full body rubdown with the oil. Kovarin liked hearing that noise. It made him feel relaxed and happy as well. When Diamond had first hatched, one mug of the oil had been sufficient to last for three applications. Now, it took four mugs for just one oil down.

He finished the full oiling. He cleaned the oil off of his hands and took the regular measurements. He sat there in shock for a moment. With a big grin on his face he carefully and slowly moved Diamond so that the neck and tail were stretched out straight. He measured again. He sat there giggling silently in complete elation. Diamond *was* now a thirteen...and a very short distance from size fourteen. His last growth spurt had been rather significant

He quickly checked for any skull ridges or neck flares. Nothing! He once again cleaned the oil off and went to make the annotations of growth. He wrote the new measurements on his scroll. He sat there feeling very smug. He kept looking at the figures, getting a bigger smile each time he read them again.

A knock on the door. It startled Kovarin a little. Distress changed to curiosity and he went to the door. He opened it and saw the three smiling faces of Tulluck, Felshon and Challoo.

Kovarin smiled back. "A wonderful welcome to you, good Ringmasters. What can I do for you on this fine day?"

"We would like to see the latest measurements, Dragonman," said Felshon. "There's no telling, how fast your unique one, is growing."

In his joy, Kovarin forgot that he had the paperwork in his hand. He went back to his desk to find it and was momentarily confused and concerned because he could not find it on the desk. He started looking around, slightly panicked, until he noticed it…in his left hand. He then flushed a little from anger and embarrassment. He went back to the three men and held it up for them to read.

At first all three looked at it with curiosity. All three faces changed, in an instant, to an open-mouth, shocked frown.

Felshon looked at Kovarin. "This…is…true?"

Kovarin gave them a cordial smile. "What would happen if I lied?"

Felshon closed his one eye and chuckled. "That would be

bad…very bad indeed."

"Especially since we're all so very interested in monitoring a very distinctive dragon," said Challoo. "You wouldn't…couldn't get away with any form of deception."

"I think that his rings should be changed…soon," said Tulluck. We had stated earlier, that we should wait to see if he grew to be a size fifteen, before the changing. Now…as fast as he's growing…it should be now."

Challoo cleared his throat. "When is the next…feeding?"

Kovarin opened his door wider and pointed at the time candle.

"Oh," said Challoo. "I have plenty of time to get ready." He walked over to Kovarin's time candle, pulled one out of a pouch on his side and made a comparison. He pulled out a knife and cut his candle shorter than the one Kovarin had. He then lit the candle. "We'll be back, to set up the opiates, for his next feeding." He looked at his two colleagues. "And we will then, again, examine this little wonder."

The three nodded in agreement, with huge grins on their faces and all three departed.

Kovarin was about to close the door when Administrator Vock showed up. 'Another visitor?' thought Kovarin. "Administrator…can…I help you?"

Vock stood there for a moment shaking his head with a very pleasant smile on his face. "Dragonman, I can hardly wait to see what you have, in this chamber. There have been times in the past when I have seen, one or two of the Ringmasters…interested in one specific dragon. But…all three! That has never happened before. You have something…marvelous…in this chamber. I'm itching from head to toe with anticipation to see this wonderful specimen."

Kovarin smiled. "At the proper time, Senior Administrator. You will not be displeased."

Vock smiled and bowed his head cordially.

A very short time before the time candle was supposed to go off, there was a knock on the door. Kovarin answered and saw the three Ringmasters, with that small table, mixing the opiate concoction for Diamond. One of the Meat Cutters was waiting with a large slab of meat. Again, once the drug was ready, Kovarin had to cut holes in the meat and place the drug in the first three pieces of the meal. He took the three doped pieces into the chamber.

A Meat Cutter was already dumping large pieces of meat into the chute. Kovarin retrieved them, set them on the platter and started cutting the slabs into bite-size pieces.

He set the three special pieces up first and waited. He got closer to examine Diamond's eyes. The Ringmasters had been correct. Because of the fact that Diamond's eyes and eyelids were the same color and nearly the same texture, it was very difficult to tell if his eyes were open or not. It was difficult until Kovarin saw a slight movement. For the first time, he actually saw Diamond open an eye. He leaned back somewhat startled. The movement had been so slight and hardly noticeable. It would have been totally unseen if Kovarin had been further away.

Diamond raised his head up. It appeared to Kovarin that he saw several blinks as his friend was waking up. Diamond opened his mouth wide in a yawn. He did his ritualistic stretching.

Kovarin picked up the first piece of drugged meat and readied himself. He still felt a little guilty over the first drugging… now he was doing it again…it was not any easier on his conscience.

He looked at the piece of meat in his hand and chuckled. This single hunk of meat was larger than the entire first meal that Diamond had eaten. Diamond had grown that much in…Kovarin could not remember, off the top of his head, just how many days old Diamond was.

Diamond sat up on his haunches and opened his mouth. In went the first drugged chunk - swallow. Then the second - swallow. Then the third - swallow. Now, untreated meat.

Diamond's neck was now large enough that Kovarin could not see the full progression of each chunk as it slid down the esophagus. He could only see that Diamond's ever growing mouth was opened and ready for the next chunk.

He kept an eye on Diamond for any wavering, compared to what had happened with the last drugging. It took some time (and most of the meat), however, Diamond stopped for a moment and shook his head. He weaved a little, shook his head again and opened wide. Kovarin threw another piece of meat in his mouth.

Diamond's left foreleg buckled. He righted himself…

momentarily. He then laid down on his belly and swallowed the piece in his mouth. He opened up for the next hunk.

Kovarin threw in another one and watched carefully.

Diamond swallowed quickly and took the next three pieces in rapid succession. The next piece sat in his mouth for a few moments. He looked around, somewhat confused, before he finally swallowed. He tried to open his mouth again, however, his head started sagging down and he was not able to open up completely. His nose hit the sand.

Kovarin was ready this time. He carefully pulled Diamond's head up and straightened the neck out. He laid the head down as if it were the most fragile thing he had ever touched in his life.

Diamond snorted twice and tried to open his mouth again. His lower jaw was on the sand, so he raised the upper…a little. The upper started slowly going down and Kovarin watched his dragon's eyes. He saw an eyelid slowly close. Again it was difficult to see because the eyes and eyelids were so close.

Diamond snorted one last time before he started breathing slowly and regularly. Kovarin watched him for several minutes to make sure that everything was…normal (?).

He got up, cleaned the blood from the meat off of his hands and went to his bedroom door. He sighed and then opened it. All three Ringmasters were still there looking at him in anticipation.

"He's asleep," said Kovarin flatly.

"Excellent," said Challoo jovially.

All three men came in…and went to Kovarin's bed. They started rubbing their hands all over the furs that he slept on.

Kovarin looked at the spectacle, somewhat mystified, somewhat horrified. "What…are you…doing?"

Tulluck looked up. "We are getting *your* smell on our hands. This way, there's less confusion for the youngling. There'll be some odd smells…that he's not familiar with, but as long as it's mixed with your smell, he'll accept it."

Kovarin shook his head. "But…you didn't do that before."

"He was much younger…then," said Felshon. "He's developed a lot more since that first meeting. We want to keep the confusion down as much as possible."

At first that statement did not make sense. Then, as Kovarin contemplated the logic…it did make sense. These are the Ringmasters. They are the ones who are experts in the growth, care and treatment of any and all dragon ailments, ills and blessings. He shrugged and headed into Diamond's chamber as the Ringmasters continued pawing the furs.

Felshon came in first. He stopped and smiled as he looked out of his one eye at Diamond. Kovarin thought he saw a tear go down the man's cheek as he slowly walked towards the pit.

Tulluck came in next. Like Felshon he stopped and stared at Diamond with a smile on his face. He then came forward, tilting his head from side to side as he approached, looking at Diamond from the nose to the tip of his tail.

Challoo finally came in. He, like his colleagues, stopped

in the entryway. He stood there momentarily…and wiped tears of joy from his eyes. He wiped his nose on his sleeve and started approaching…almost in a reverent manner. He cleared his throat twice before he could speak. "History…is being made…right here…right now. For me to live at this time and…see…actual history in the making…I thank the Great Maker."

The other two Ringmasters nodded in agreement.

The three of them just stood there for several moments just staring at Diamond in admiration.

Tulluck finally broke the silence by loudly clearing his throat. "Yes, this is history in the making - and if we just stand here, looking stupid, it'll just pass us by." He looked at each of his cohorts. "To work, gentlemen!"

Felshon wiped a tear away. "Yes, to work!"

Challoo turned away from Diamond and hollered through the entryway. "Bodor! Size nineteen!"

Tulluck started measuring Diamond from nose to tail. Felshon started measuring the wings.

Challoo got very close and started scrutinizing Diamond's head. He looked closely at every part of it. "Not a sign of it…yet. Neither has started growing."

Kovarin felt a little left out. "Not a sign…of what?"

Challoo looked up at Kovarin. "His horns…his flares. There's no sign, yet of the horn ridges or the budding of his neck flares."

Kovarin felt like jumping for joy. He, instead gave Challoo a very sober gaze. "So…he's still got a lot of growing…to do?"

Tulluck chuckled. "He's less than the thickness of a fingernail away from size fourteen."

"His wingspan…is incredible…for one so young," said Felshon.

"His growth," said Challoo. "Never before, has one… come from a size two egg…and grown this large…this fast."

"I am curious," said Kovarin. "Which part of history is being made or rewritten?"

Tulluck chuckled. "One, he's black! There are three instances, in the history scrolls, where someone thought they had a black. In each one, after each shedding, they all three started fading to dark gray. Your charge has gone through three sheddings…and hasn't faded at all…that I can see."

"A size two egg," said Felshon. "The largest dragon, that any size two egg produced, in the past, was a dragon that grew to be size fifteen…and that took a lot longer than what we're seeing here. Since there are no horn ridges on his skull and no budding of the neck flares…he should grow…way beyond…seventeen or eighteen." He looked at Kovarin. "There's a good chance…that you *will* be a rider!"

Kovarin's heart started pounding in his chest. In spite of what Dozzbin had done, he could be on Diamond's shoulders, soaring through the clouds with a Battle Division.

"Right now," said Tulluck, "we're going to have to move

him."

Kovarin was yanked out of his dream. "Move? What? Where?"

"Move," said Tulluck. "You…and him. Since he is growing so rapidly and he hasn't started the budding of his horns or flares…we feel it's the best thing, if we move him from this hatching chamber, to a much larger one. You've said that he has proven himself capable of flying…already. While we haven't witnessed this ourselves, the wing to body ratio proves that he is more than capable. If he grows much larger and is not moved, he could very easily hurt himself…badly…in this chamber. Therefore, while we've been in here checking…there are others who are preparing for the move."

"You won't have to do a thing," said Felshon with a smile. "The need to move him, while asleep, is crucial. We have an army of men, standing by, waiting for the order, and they will move you and your dragon to a much larger chamber."

Kovarin swallowed hard.   He had hidden the bad temperature rods in the wall of this chamber. He was wondering how he could get them out of here without arousing any suspicion. He looked over at the wall where they were buried. He swallowed hard again.

Felshon left the chamber and went into Kovarin's bedroom. He heard the door open and a muffled order given. He could see that there was a flurry of activity in his bedroom, as numerous men started picking things up and moving out with them.

Bodor had entered the chamber with the new rings…and

a fur from the bed (?). While Challoo was changing the rings in Diamond's jaw, Tulluck went to a wall in the chamber and hit it several times with a metal rod. A large portion of the wall started moving.

Kovarin's heart started beating rapidly again. The chamber door to the inner sanctuary was being opened. Only the Dragonmen, or their family members, were allowed to enter that hallowed ground. He had finally made it. He was going to enter and see the great inner sanctum of the dragons. He watched, trying to maintain control of his bodily functions, as the lower part of the wall started rising outward and upward. He could now see where eight men straining as they were turning a large wheel that pulled the wall up. He could see, at first, a lot of feet. Then a lot of legs and more of bodies as the wall kept slowly moving up. There were dozens of people out there, waiting to see this spectacle - Diamond, the black dragon.

Apparently the news had spread all over High Country about this mysterious little dragon. They had come to see for themselves, the dragon that was black and growing faster than any other dragon had ever done before.

While everyone else was watching the wall move up, Kovarin quickly went to his hidey-hole, scraped the dirt away and pulled the hidden temperature rods and bad scroll out. He put his hands behind his back and shoved all of them into the back of his pants. He then side-stepped all the way back to his bedchamber, trying to be as unnoticeable as possible among the mass of activity, found his longest cloak, threw it over his shoulders and prayed that it would hide the unusual bulge in the back of his pants.

He headed back to Diamond's chamber. The doorway to the inner sanctum was more than half way up. Kovarin could now see some of the breastplates of the men outside. They had worn their best dress uniforms for the occasion of just looking at Diamond.

Kovarin thought to himself. 'How many of the Battle Division Commanders are here?'

He started seeing the ranks. The Battle Group Commanders had a five pointed star on their breast plate. The Battle Division Sub Commander had a five pointed star overlaid clawed wings. The Battle Division Commander had a seven pointed star with overlaid clawed wings.

He scanned the crowd and was shocked when he saw, off to the left, all six Battle Division Commanders. He counted the points on the stars and he counted the men, just to make sure, three times. They were all wearing their full dress uniform. The battle uniform had the knife sheaths built into them. The dress uniform breastplate proudly displayed their rank. They all had the black leather boots that came up to the knee. Each one had wool pants and a cape that matched the color of their specific dragon. Kovarin was not sure how to distinguish which one was in charge of which Division until he noticed that each one had a number, on the right shoulder of the breastplate that was made of gold. They each had their Division number embossed on the side of their helmets as well.

Kovarin gawked a little as he tried to distinguish each one. There was a list, of each of the Commanders, displayed in the room of each Candidate. He ran the list through his head that had been read 10,000 times. Heth, Battle Division 1 Commander. He had a brown cape. Battle Division 2 Commander Nossiturm and Battle Division 4 Commander Gontero were wearing bluish-gray capes. The other three were wearing gray capes. Each cape was slightly different because they would get a cape that was as close to the shade of gray, brown or bluish-gray as their specific dragon.

He scanned the rest of the men. He saw numerous five pointed stars, with and without the overlaid clawed wings. He also saw Dozzbin, off to the left of the Battle Division Commanders.

'So...' he thought. 'All of the top four ranks are well represented at this...spectacle. All of the Battle Divisions are currently being led by the Wing Commanders so that all of the top echelon could be here to actually see a *real* black dragon.'

Now it finally hit Kovarin as to just how unique Diamond really is. A black who had shed, several times, and stayed black. He hoped that the main feeling among these men was awe and not some idiotic hope of seeing some one-of-a-kind freak.

Three men brought a, very long, four-wheeled cart into the chamber.

Challoo tapped Kovarin on the shoulder. "We'll be taking Diamond out of here on that cart. We need your help in picking him up and placing him on it."

Kovarin tried to say something and only gargled. He loudly and embarrassingly cleared his throat several times. "All right...so where do you want me?"

The look on Challoo's face gave a non-verbal answer of:

"A very stupid question!" Challoo closed his eyes and sighed. "You will handle Diamond's head. This way, the main thing that he smells…is you! We try to keep all the different smells to a minimum, therefore, with you, blocking all other scents, he should notice, only yours…if he awakens."

Kovarin shook his head. "More and more, I'm learning… just how wise and experienced, you and your two colleagues are in your devotion to caring for the hatchlings. The care that you take and show towards these dragons…I am so *very* impressed."

Challoo smiled, closed his eyes and gave a polite nod of the head. "I thank you for your kind words. We do not seem to get enough…positive comments…from many of the Dragonmen."

"You gentlemen have nothing but respect from me," said Kovarin, trying to sound as sincere as possible.

Again, another polite nod of the head from Challoo.

Several men were staring silently at Challoo and Kovarin as they had exchanged pleasantries. They watched as the two men walked up to Diamond. Kovarin dutifully took his place, as close to Diamond's nose, as he could get.

Three of the men shoveled some of the sand, from Diamond's birthplace, onto the cart.

The cart was put in place and they all carefully picked Diamond up. As they moved him to the cart, they paid very careful attention to make sure that none of his legs got caught under him and his wings were kept folded, in their normal position, against his back.

Tulluck pulled the temperature rod out of the sand and gave it to Kovarin.

The cart was tall enough that Kovarin could stay close enough to Diamond to keep his head cradled against his stomach. Diamond would not be able to smell anything strange…hopefully.

Challoo placed his hand on Kovarin's shoulder again. "You, Dragonman, will set the pace. We will not go any faster than you."

Kovarin chuckled nervously. "Uh…where are we going?"

"When we get outside, just look for *your* pennant. Each door has a pennant that matches the color of youngling that dwells within." Challoo chuckled. "There *is* only *one*…black pennant. That, is our destination."

Tulluck went to the opening. He held his hands out at the congregation waiting outside the door. "Gentlemen…if you would, please."

Several of them licked a finger and then held it up. After getting the wind direction, everyone moved to where they would be downwind from the group as Diamond was paraded by.

Everyone now looked at Kovarin in anticipation. He in turn looked at Challoo, questioningly.

"It's your call…as to when we move," said Challoo with a smile.

Kovarin flushed. They were all waiting for his direction, in the task. "Oh…well…let's…go!" He smiled.

Challoo leaned towards Kovarin. "Do you wish to lead or follow?"

"Huh…oh…I'll follow. You gentlemen probably know… better than I do, where we're going."

Four more men came into the chamber with wheelbarrows and started shoveling some of the sand, from Diamond's "former" pit. Once they had filled them, they passed the procession, heading for a place on the other side, where a man was slowly waving a black pennant over his head.

Kovarin sighed with relief. Now he knew where he was going. He started rubbing Diamond's head. He heard a low dull growl of contentment coming from Diamond. 'Keep him as calm as possible,' thought Kovarin. He kept rubbing. Usually Diamond would be making some kind of keening noise, however, he was drugged and that was probably messing up more than one of Diamond's normal sounds.

They left the chamber. Kovarin was now, finally able to look around at the precious home of the Dragonmen. It was an enormous box canyon that stretched for some distance off to his right before it curved to the left. To his left was a wall that curved around to where their destination was. However long the canyon was, the hatching chambers were at the very end. He figured that it was a good strategy in keeping the hatchlings safe and protected at this end of the canyon.

High up on the walls, Kovarin could see several, very large, dragons peering down at what was going on beneath them. On what appeared to be the highest perch, up there, he saw a mammoth dark brown dragon. That one had to be Dozzbin's Thunder. Thunder was the size fifty-one...biggest toughest and meanest dragon of them all...currently.

Kovarin scanned right. On two lower perches, he saw two big bluish-gray dragons. Those had to be Glutton and Bloodletter - the two size forty-eights. Further to the right was another brown. That had to be Monster, currently the one and only size forty-seven. A little further on was a gray...Eating Machine. Going further down, he saw another blue-gray and a gray. Those were the dragons of the other two Battle Division Commanders who were not in the top five - Purge and Protector. He was a little awed at the sight of all of these dragons, along with their important riders. They were here to gaze upon, and hopefully show respect, to a true black...not a dark gray, but a black.

He looked back a little at the cliff face from where he had just emerged. It was not as high as the side where the seven biggies were currently sunning themselves. On this side there were several very large dragons, all bellowing and flaring at each other, trying to determine pecking order, between them.

Two of the bellowing dragons, a gray and a brown, took flight from the cliff, now behind Kovarin. All of the men in the procession and the audience cautiously turned their attention to the two flying dragons. The dragons snarled, bellowed and flared at each other as they flew, hovered and attempted to get a better tactical position over each other.

Kovarin heard Challoo quietly saying a desperate prayer.

"Please stay away from us, please go off to the side, and

please end it quickly." Challoo repeated each statement several times as he (and everyone else) watched the two flying combatants.

The brown suddenly rushed at the gray. The gray did a strange flap of his wings and a twist of his tail and the brown missed. The gray then lashed his tail at the brown, smacking the left wing and throwing the brown's flight off kilter. The gray turned and flew after the floundering brown. The gray slammed his entire body into the top of the brown. The brown hit the side of the canyon and started falling, completely out of control, causing somewhat of a landslide of rocks and dirt as he clawed at the face of the cliff. The man who had been waving the black pennant, retreated into the chamber he was standing next to, just a heartbeat before the brown hit the ground, very close to where the pennant bearer had been standing.

The gray hovered overhead bellowing at the brown. The brown turned himself over and wavered a little. He looked up at the gray. His neck flares folded back against his neck, his head drooped down and he started walking away, awkwardly. Several of the non-combatant dragons that had been watching started flaring and bellowing at the loser. The noise was deafening.

One of the Battle Group Commanders held his fists up in victory, with a huge smile on his face. Another Battle Group Commander kicked the dirt under his feet, turned away and muttered a few obscenities under his breath. Several other men congratulated the smiling man, while the angry one walked off by himself, grunting and growling in anger and consternation.

"We're lucky that that was a quick one," said Challoo. "Come on, gentlemen, let's get going...before there's another challenge."

The procession continued. The man with the black pennant came back out of the chamber. He looked up very cautiously before he came completely out into the open and held the pennant up high.

As they were walking along, most of the Dragonmen just stood and watched. They walked away as soon as Diamond passed by. Some smiling, some gawking, some staring in awe or disbelief. There were three others who were walking along, scrutinizing Diamond very carefully.

Kovarin looked over at Challoo. "Who are those three men?"

Challoo smiled. "They are the Tailors. They're the ones who make the special uniforms for the Dragon riders. They have to do everything they can, in order to get your uniform as close to your dragon's color as they can. If Diamond does grow, to where he can fly and carry you, they *will* have to get a properly colored uniform ready."

"But…why are they looking at him so closely? Black is black…what could possibly be the problem?"

"I've talked to them several times…and according to them…there are at least twelve shades of black."

"I'd have to say that there are probably eleven shades of dark gray and one shade of black. I cannot agree…"

"They are the professional Tailors, Dragonman. Let them do their job. It *is* what they do best."

Kovarin shrugged and kept walking along with the procession. Because of the hidden "items" digging into his backside, he was very glad that it was a slow march.

He looked back up at the dragons sunning themselves above. He wondered if Diamond would ever be able to go up there and sun himself. He wondered if any of the smaller dragons were allowed up there.

Off to the left, he noticed numerous other dragons sunning themselves. They seemed rather disinterested in the fight that had just taken place and each other.

Kovarin pointed up at them. "What's wrong with them? Why didn't they scold that loser…like the other ones did?"

Challoo chuckled. "Those are the females. They don't have a pecking order problem with the males. They have their own way to establish dominance…between them. With the males…it's usually the biggest that is the most dominant. With the females, it is whichever one can last the longest in a fight."

"So…they can be violent…as well?"

"Very violent, very noisy and very lengthy battles."

"Any fatalities?"

"As long as the Dragonman can control his beast…no! If he loses control of his dragon…who knows?"

"How could the Dragonman possibly control a size forty or larger?"

"That's why you spend so much time, talking to your

charge as its growing. No matter how much noise is going on, Diamond will hear and recognize your voice. Once he's been trained, he'll also respond, favorably to those commands."

"So, how and when do they mate? I mean, if Thunder is the largest and meanest, doesn't he get to do all of the mating?"

"No, he doesn't. He'd have to spend all of his time here, with all of the large females. The largest thirty-eight males take turns here at the sanctuary. This way, we still have only the largest breeding, while we don't have to worry about any male challenges when a female goes into heat."

"If only the largest females are allowed to breed...how do they come up with so many...small eggs?"

"It all depends on how many eggs that particular female lays in that specific mating. If she only comes up with one egg - very large. If she comes up with...oh, say nineteen or twenty - most of them are rather small."

"What's the most that any female came up with?"

"That record was set, over two hundred years ago. A dragon, named Blue Tart, came up with forty-one eggs in one mating."

"That must have put a strain on the Meat Cutters...trying to keep all of those hungry mouths fed."

"No, only five hatched. In most cases, the smaller eggs don't hatch. We do have a standard that measures something smaller than a size one. Of the 'waste' eggs, maybe one out of a fifty will hatch. Of the successful 'waste' eggs hatchings, maybe one out of a twenty will live…more than fifty days."

"Do you let them hatch…if you get any…waste eggs?"

"We allow them to hatch. Then we observe them. So far it has been the same…in most cases. We have had one of the waste egg hatchlings live as long as two years…once."

Kovarin rubbed Diamond's head as they walked along. He did it to comfort Diamond, if there was any discomfort, and he was checking to see if there was any sign of the horn ridges starting to form.

He contemplated what Challoo had been saying and he marveled at the size of the canyon. Of course it would have to be big because of all of the larger dragons that they were trying to breed.

They kept on heading to the new home for Diamond. He had not thought that it would take this long, however, it was a little further than he had anticipated and they were going at a very slow pace.

He looked back at the one they had departed from and did a quick comparison. "Why is the opening so wide…on this new one?"

Challoo chuckled. "Because of the possibility of Diamond emerging, with his wings partially extended. In this new one, he'll have the luxury of being able to spread out a little before he comes out…when he finally gets his horns and neck flares and is mature and large enough and has received a little training."

"Why can't you start training him now?"

"We don't yet know how big he's going to be. If he gets to be a size twenty-three, and does not yet have his horn ridges... then we will start training him for controlled flight. If he gets his horns and flares...before he is a twenty-one...then he'll probably not be a ridden flyer and will have to be trained for something else."

They finally reached the new chamber. The new home for the dragon that was causing so much gossip. Kovarin was stunned at the difference in size. This cavern floor was easily four times the size of the one he had departed. The pit for Diamond was about three times the size as the last one. The roof above was almost two and one half times as high as the last one.

He looked for where his bedchamber was. At first he could not see an opening. The last one had a hand carved archway, between the dragon chamber and the bedchamber. This one had a natural tunnel that separated the two.

The men with the wheelbarrows were shoveling Diamond's old sand into this new pit. There was one man who was carefully checking the temperature with a "good" rod.

Kovarin looked at Challoo somewhat concerned. "Is this going to be his permanent home?"

"Oh, my no, Dragonman. Once they've matured, they do not really like to live inside...anything anymore. They prefer to be outside...where they can bellow and fight with each other... and sun themselves."

Once again they had the task of picking Diamond up and moving him. He was carefully placed in the warm sand.

Challoo pulled the rod out of the sand and looked at it closely. "I believe that you have one rod too many at this time, Dragonman."

Kovarin pulled the rod that Tulluck had given him out. "Which one would you prefer, Ringmaster?"

Challoo smiled. "This one is already doing the necessary job...so, I'll take the one that you're holding back to supply."

"Senior Administrator Vock will be happy about that," said Kovarin with a smile as he handed the rod to Challoo.

Out of the corner of his eye, Kovarin saw Dozzbin, standing just outside the chamber, with a look of horror on his face. The horror changed to confusion as Challoo took the rod, gave it a quick look and then placed it in his waistcoat.

Kovarin looked at Dozzbin, smiled and gave him a courteous bow of his head. Dozzbin responded with clenched teeth and stomped away.

The outer door to this new chamber was slowly closed. All of the men who had helped move Kovarin and Diamond headed out, one way or another and now Kovarin was once again alone with the unsuspecting Diamond sleeping peacefully.

Kovarin left Diamond's chamber and went to check on his own. He grunted in frustration as he looked at the bed frame. All of the furs had been just thrown on the bed. Now, he was going to have to go back to arranging them to where they were comfortable and even again.

The work desk was identical to the one from the other

chamber.

He checked the two armoires in the room. The one had all of his clothing hanging in it and the other had all of his other necessaries. He hung up the cloak and went back into Diamond's chamber to try to find a nice little hidey-hole for the bad rods and scroll.

9

Kovarin had been able to get a little sleep. He awoke and went to check on Diamond. Once again, the drugs had thrown Diamond's feeding schedule off. He should have awakened and started bellyaching for food at least a half turn ago. Instead he was just lying there grunting. Kovarin went ahead and ordered enough meat to feed Diamond, once he did wake up. He would still be hungry.

After almost a full turn of grunting and just slight movements of his head, Diamond finally awakened. He did his stretching and yawning. He stopped and looked around. The quick movements of his head told Kovarin that Diamond had realized that something was not right, however, he was having a problem figuring out what it was. He pushed up with his front legs and then sat up on his rear legs. He was giving the chamber a complete once over. He started giving off his hunger chant.

Kovarin held up a piece of meat and waved it around. "Hey, Diamond, food! Do you want to eat or just complain?"

Diamond looked down at Kovarin. He was still giving off the hungry sounds. Now, he came back down to all fours and opened his mouth. In went the first piece of meat and the chant finally stopped.

After eating less than half of what was expected, he sat up on his hind legs and looked around the room again. He seemed to realize that something was different, however, his reptilian brain could not perceive what it was.

Kovarin kept talking to him in a soothing manner.

He went back down on all fours and opened his mouth. He swallowed six more pieces and then started looking around again. He stepped out of the sand pit, went to the wall and started running around the wall of the chamber. After taking three laps around the perimeter, he stopped and stuck his head through the opening into Kovarin's bedchamber. He snorted twice and headed back to the sand pit. He flopped down on his belly and snorted again. He looked at Kovarin, opened his mouth and started the hunger chant again. Kovarin threw more meat in as fast as Diamond would take it. The pile of meat was down to only two pieces before Diamond belched and decided that was enough.

Kovarin cleaned the blood off of his hands while still talking to his bewildered beast in a soothing manner.

Diamond stood up on all fours and started flapping his wings. He raised up off of the ground and hovered in one place for a few moments. He then started moving around a little. Slight movements of his tail helped him adjust his direction. Slight changes in the angle that he was flapping his wings changed his altitude, direction and speed.

Kovarin tried to sound as encouraging as possible. He was thrilled, seeing his dragon was flying. He could hardly wait until Diamond could go outside and not be limited by walls and a ceiling.

The first chamber had been big enough for Diamond as he was. He was still growing and this new chamber definitely gave him more room to do what he needed to exercise his wings and anything else he needed to do.

Diamond came back down slowly. He landed in the sand pit and was panting heavily for a few moments. The panting stopped quickly and he laid down in the sand. He snorted several times, yawned and went to sleep.

Kovarin now used this time to check the temperature in the sand. It was fine.

He grabbed the measuring devices. He carefully measured the right wing. Then he checked the full length. He was astounded. Very little growth. Then he remembered - the last time that Diamond had been drugged, he had grown very little. Maybe there was something about the drug that stunted growth of any type…as long as the drug was in his system. Kovarin checked again for horn ridges (as if he needed to)…nothing. Neck flares… nothing. Good! He has not stopped growing…yet.

He lit another time candle, and went back to the task of oiling Diamond down from nose to tail. The oiling was now becoming a major task, considering how much Diamond had grown, especially trying to turn him on his side to oil the underside.

With that job finished, Kovarin cleaned up, went to his bedchamber, ate some food for himself and snuggled into his bed furs for a good long nap.

Kovarin was awakened by the loud hiss of the time candle. He was beginning to hate that thing. He sat up and scratched himself in random places. He relieved himself in the chamber pot. He set up a new time candle and realized that it was the last one he had.

He went to his work desk, wrote out an order for some more time candles as well as more oil for Diamond. He placed the order and the full chamber pot outside the hall door of his bed chamber.

He walked into his dragon's sleeping chamber. While he was checking the coals along the side of the pit, Diamond let out a few growls and snorts and clawed the sand a few times with his left foreleg.

"So…you're capable of dreaming, my friend." Kovarin sighed contentedly and went to check on what the Meat Cutters were dumping down the chute.

He took the meat, prepared it and waited for Diamond to wake up.

After feeding, flying and patrolling, Diamond was back in the pit asleep. Kovarin measured him and was pleased with what he saw. Diamond was now a full-fledged size fifteen, well on his way to sixteen and had no sign of horns or flares.

He had wondered why Diamond slept so much. He had asked Challoo that question. It was because of all of the growth spurts. All of his energy was being used for growing. He had very little left for anything else - grow and shed. Now that he was a few days older, he was able to do a few other things between his long naps, however, it was not very much. He still would use most of the nutrition to grow, rather than run around.

This was another reason as to why they wanted to wait for any training. Wait until his growth slowed down, then he would spend more time awake and could then be trained…depending on just how big he finally would be.

Over the next few days, Diamond continued to eat enormous amounts of meat and sleep most of the time. He grew… size sixteen, size seventeen, size eighteen, size nineteen…

Once again, he had to be drugged and fitted with new, larger rings. This time Challoo put in size twenty-seven rings. It was a bit of a tight fit, however, they did not want to keep on drugging him over and over in order to give him new, larger rings.

Size twenty…size twenty-one…! Kovarin checked for horn ridges or flares. Nothing! Diamond was a twenty-one and still growing. He remembered that if Diamond were to grow two more sizes, without the horns developing, then they would start training him for flight. He would be fitted with a saddle and harness and would receive training from a specialist at training the flyers.

Size twenty-two…size twenty-three…! Kovarin called for the Ringmasters in order to confirm the size and get the training started.

This time they did not drug him. This time, they came in after he had finished feeding and had fallen asleep on his own. They confirmed the size and ordered the Master Flying Trainer to be notified as soon as possible.

Kovarin could hardly hold back his elation. He was going to be a Dragonrider, not just a Dragonman. He wondered how Dozzbin was taking that particular piece of information.

There was a knock on the door. Kovarin answered. Standing there was a very tall and burly man. He had thick black hair that covered his ears and a beard that showed gray on his chin. He was wearing a sleeveless leather shirt that showed huge muscles in his arms. He had on the boots and pants that would normally be worn, when flying.

"Good afternoon, Dragonman, I am Master Flying Trainer Shondark. I'm here to evaluate your dragon for a proper fitting of a saddle and determination for training." He had a deep booming bass voice.

"I welcome you, Master Trainer. I've been looking forward to this day for…I can't remember how long. I've watched my dragon take his first flight…when he had no control at all and slammed into the wall. Now, he is able to control where he goes when he wants."

"Good, we need to use that and discipline him to the saddle and reins. May I come in and see him, Dragonrider?"

"Oh, yes, Master Trainer…please…come in. He's sleeping

right now. He just finished feeding and is taking his usual long nap…for growing."

Shondark walked in and headed directly to the dragon chamber. He stopped and stared for a moment when he saw Diamond.

"By the Great Maker, he is black. I would've never believed it. I've seen some very dark grays…but…" He shook his head and chuckled. "This one is…*absolutely* black."

He took several laps around the sand pit, stopping and scrutinizing Diamond as he went along. He finally stopped his walking and scans and stared at the front shoulder area where the saddle would be fitted.

"Can't do much right now," he sighed. "Until he starts growing his horns, we can't really be sure how big a saddle will be required. I hate to start on one…only to find out that it won't be big enough…at the end of his growing stage."

Kovarin was a little perplexed. "So…nothing's going to be done…now?"

"Oh, no, I'm going to go get a trainer saddle for him. We'll put it on him and get him used to the feel of the saddle. Once the trainer is on him, you need to comfort him as much as possible. He probably won't like the feel of it, but he needs to get used to it and not be afraid of it. Any kind words that you can say to him will be very helpful"

"You don't have the trainer with you?"

"No, I came to see what size to start with. Those things

are heavy and bulky and I don't like dragging several of them with me, trying to guess which one to use in advance. I'll be back after his next feeding and we'll put it on him. It'll be a little loose, but that's okay, because we don't want him shocked by something that's too tight."

"I trust your opinion," said Kovarin with a polite bow of his head.

Shondark returned the bow and headed out. He looked at the current time candle before he left.

Kovarin sat down at his work desk and giggled with glee. His goal was finally within reach. He would have to hold back and listen to all of the Ringmasters and Master Trainers in order to keep from fouling things up. 'Now is not the time to get impatient,' he thought. 'Let things happen in their own time and soon enough, I'll be on his shoulders and up in the air.'

Shondark showed up with the trainer and four other men. It was not a saddle at all, it was just the inner portion that would be touching the dragon's body. The portion for Kovarin would come later after Diamond was used to this strange new contraption and had stopped growing.

Kovarin saw why Shondark had brought several men with him. It took all of the men in the room to shift Diamond up to where they could get the straps under him, both behind and in front of his forelegs. He marveled at how when Diamond was first born, he could be lifted with one hand. Now it took six men to move his front legs and body, in order to get the trainer saddle in place.

After the saddle was in place, Shondark took his own measurements. He determined from that just how fast Diamond was growing and when they would need to get a larger trainer on him. Two of the assistants left and came back shortly with two larger training saddles that they planned on keeping in Kovarin's bedchamber...until needed.

Then they departed.

Then as Kovarin was preparing the next dinner for Diamond, the dragon awakened. He woke up and did his stretching. He did not notice it at first. When he did, he turned his head back with that long prehensile neck and looked at the new addition. He sniffed at it, growled and snorted several times.

Kovarin tried to be as comforting as possible, saying: "It's all right, Diamond. It won't hurt you. It's there for a reason. You're all right. You're safe." Over and over he repeated all of this as soothingly as possible, while Diamond carefully looked it over.

Diamond started biting at the saddle. If it had been made of any weaker material, he would have bitten through it the first time with his large, sharp and powerful beak. He walked out of the pit and headed for the wall. He started scraping the strange thing along the wall in an attempt at dislodging it from his shoulders.

Kovarin followed and grabbed his head, trying to comfort Diamond and distract his attention away from the saddle. Diamond raised his head up and Kovarin was lifted completely off of his feet. He looked around a little as if trying to figure some other method of dislodging the parasitic thing. Kovarin held onto the big neck and tried rubbing Diamond's head. It did little to comfort the dragon, at this moment.

Diamond bellowed and shook his head. Kovarin was temporarily deafened by the noise and accidentally grabbed one of the jaw rings as he was being shaken. Diamond froze. He slowly lowered his head. When Kovarin's feet were on the ground, he let go of the ring. Diamond immediately started scraping against the wall again. Kovarin grabbed a ring and Diamond froze again.

The rings were in a very sensitive area and Kovarin realized that this was the way you control your dragon…with pain…if you have to. It hurt him inside to cause this pain, however, he knew that it was necessary. He tried to talk as calmly and soothingly as possible. Each time he let go of the ring, Diamond would continue to try scraping the saddle off.

Kovarin finally decided that he had to take command. He grabbed one of the rings and started leading Diamond away from the wall. Diamond made several grunts and growls of protest, however, he had to give in to the painful pulls at the back of his jaws. Kovarin led him into the sand pit. He let go of the ring and started rubbing Diamond's head. It took several moments before he started his comfort keening. That lasted for a few minutes… until he started his hungry cry. Kovarin sighed, stepped out of the pit and started throwing large pieces of meat into that big hungry maw.

After feeding, Diamond tried his wings again. He looked back at the saddle again and snorted at it again in a somewhat disgusted manner.

It was four more feedings before Diamond got used to the saddle. He finally figured out that it was not going to hurt him. He finally figured out that he could not get it off. He surrendered to leaving the thing alone.

Another knock on the door woke Kovarin up. He stumbled to the door rubbing the sleep out of his eyes. Shondark was standing there.

"It may be time to change the saddle to a larger one," said Shondark.

"If you think so," Kovarin yawned. "Do you have your crew with you?"

"Yes, I was just wondering when the next feeding was."

Kovarin looked at the time candle. "We've got plenty of time to change the saddle."

"Good!" Shondark signaled to his men and all of them came in and headed to the sleeping dragon.

They once again had to go through the arduous task of moving the sleeping beast in order to get the straps undone and out. When they pulled the trainer off of Diamond, Shondark growled and backhanded one of his helpers, knocking the unfortunate man down flat on his back.

"Fool! You forgot to oil the inside of the saddle! You're never going to be a decent trainer if you keep making stupid mistakes like that!" Shondark growled as he looked over Diamond's shoulder area. He turned to Kovarin. "Dragonman, do you have sufficient oil on hand?"

"Uh…yes," said Kovarin a little shocked and fearful.

"Good, where is it?"

Kovarin pointed.

Shondark looked down at the fallen man who was rubbing the swollen side of his head. "Well…what are you waiting for? Go get the oil!"

One of the other assistants leaned towards Shondark and whispered. "When are you going to give up on him?"

"As soon as I can find someone else…who has at least half a brain…that can be used for…something…positive."

The man that had been slapped came back grunting under the weight of the small barrel. He placed it next to the sand pit and pulled the top off. Shondark dipped his hands into the oil and started rubbing oil liberally over the area that had been covered by the saddle. "Doesn't look like it did too much damage." He grunted. "Of course, their hide is awfully thick and tough. It would take quite a bit to do any *real* damage."

Another one of the assistants brought the next larger trainer into the chamber.

Shondark looked at the saddle and then started looking closely at Diamond. "Where are your last growth measurements?"

"I…uh…took one measurement…after you saddled him," stammered Kovarin. "I haven't taken any measurements…since."

"I think that we need to do it…now."

"Okay," said Kovarin, feeling a little guilty over his negligence.

The man with the swollen face sat off to the side as everyone else took part in taking the measurements.

Shondark shook his head. "When I put that saddle on him, he was a twenty-three. Now, he's just a fraction away from being a twenty-five."

Shondark and Kovarin both started feeling Diamond's skull for ridges.

"Still smooth," observed Shondark.

"Yes," agreed Kovarin. "There's no way of telling...how much bigger he's going to get...yet...is there?"

"No, not yet."

A different assistant oiled the interior of the new saddle. Kovarin smeared even more oil on Diamond's shoulder area. Then they went through the arduous task of getting the larger saddle on Diamond.

After they finished the job Shondark looked at the one with the swollen face. "One more foul up...you're gone. I don't care who your father is, I can't tolerate any more of your mistakes. Now go! You can start the clean-up back at the work shed."

One of the assistants looked up after the swollen face departed. "One more foul up? Just one? Are you seriously, *finally,* going to get rid of him...or is this just another threat to try to...?"

Shondark scowled at the assistant. "I've had it with him!

I purposefully sent him back there, because he always forgets something. I usually don't have to look very hard to find what he forgot. At least in there, he can't do anything that'll possibly hurt one of the dragons."

The three assistants all looked at each other, snickered and nodded.

Kovarin was a little curious. "Is he really that bad?"

Shondark huffed. "I'm surprised that he can get food into his own mouth without injuring himself…severely."

The three assistants all chuckled.

"Anyway," said Shondark, "keep an eye on Diamond, make sure that he doesn't injure himself and we'll start his training as soon as we can keep him awake…and not sleeping while growing."

Again Kovarin was curious: "How is it that you know so much about the dragons? I mean…what kind of experience do you have that…?"

"*We* are Dragonmen," said Shondark. The difference between our dragons and yours…ours are too small to be ridden. My dragon is a female that I named Gray Bonnet. She's a size fourteen."

Each one of the assistants introduced themselves.

"My name is Chul. I have a male named Bigmouth. He's a size eleven."

"My name is Vollost. My dragon is a size nine named

Runner."

"I'm Yoll. Mine is a female named Flapper. She's a ten."

Kovarin felt a little sick. "And…the one who just left…he actually has a…dragon…that he's responsible for?"

Shondark cleared his throat in disgust. "Kullto…has a male…a size six that he named…" He rolled his eyes. "…Blue Terror. The silly little thing is afraid of his own shadow and has been knocked around by size four and three dragons."

Kovarin's eyebrows went up. "Last in the pecking order?"

Chul scoffed. "Dead last!"

"Anyway," Shondark rubbed his hands together. "We'll be keeping track of Diamond's growth and try to get some training in…if we can ever get in here when he's awake. So, we'll be leaving you alone for now. I'll let Challoo know about the size. He'll make the determination for the next changing of the jaw rings."

The four men departed, leaving Kovarin to contemplate. He had heard that those with smaller dragons were not allowed near the flyers. Now he had just been informed that they were not hidden, but given the chance to excel in assisting with the care of the flyers. He started wondering if the Ringmasters each had a dragon of their own…or the Meat Cutters…or the Administrators. He chuckled to himself wondering. How many of the other people involved with all of this, had their own miniature dragon?

After three more feedings, Diamond was now a size

twenty-six. Shondark was eager to make attempts at training him and Challoo was eager to try to get some larger jaw rings on him. With Challoo, that could happen at any time…that Diamond was asleep…which happened to be most of the time. Shondark, on the other hand, had to get him before he was totally sated with meat and nodding off.

Challoo did replace the twenty-seven rings with thirty-one rings. Easy enough to do when Diamond was soundly unconscious. He also checked for any sign of horn ridges.

Kovarin took over rubbing Diamond's head as soon as Challoo had finished the examination. "How many of the other dragons are still growing?"

Challoo looked a little confused. "What do you mean?"

"There were sixteen other men who got eggs when I did… how many of them are still growing?"

Challoo giggled. "You're the only one that still has a growing dragon. There's a great deal of attention…drawn to this one. One: Because he is *still* black and has not faded to dark gray. Two: He hatched from a size two egg and now…size twenty-six with no sign of horn ridges."

"How is it that mine is the only one that's still growing?"

"Let me think. There were two size nineteen eggs in that last distribution. One of them produced a female. The other one…a male that hatched with his horn ridges ready to break skin. He grew from a size nineteen to a twenty-one and his horns are in full blossom. He is *not* a flyer. The funny thing there is, that he was one of Dozzbin's favorites. That's why Dozzbin gave him a larger egg." He chuckled. "We have no idea how much any one of the hatchlings are going to grow. There was a fourteen egg that has produced a size forty-four female. Then there were all of the smaller eggs. Two didn't hatch. All of the others have reached full growth and that one female is the only one from that last distribution that'll be able to mate…unless Diamond keeps growing. In that case he'll be able to be a flyer and a breeder. We can't predict anything about him yet…except the fact that he is not finished growing."

"Has anyone ever taken this long…to grow to full potential?"

"No." Challoo snickered. "I think that Diamond heard some of the things that Dozzbin was saying and is growing so big out of spite."

"From what I hear, there are a lot of people who don't like Dozzbin."

"We've been hoping, for some time now, that a new dragon will come along and unseat Thunder. That'll help demote Dozzbin and get him out, away from a lot of things in our personal lives."

"Not to sound as if I'm not interested in that, I just wanted to know what you think about Shondark coming in here and training. Is Diamond ready to see a new face…and accept it?"

"Oh, yes, he is. I'll be in here as well. We want to see how he accepts the new people. We want to see how he'll react to them. Plus, we do need to start his flight training as soon as possible."

Kovarin was a little surprised at the last statement. "He already knows how to fly!"

"Yes, he can fly. The problem is that you don't know how to control him in his flight. That is part of the training: Not just him - you!"

"Sooo…when does it start?"

"At his next feeding. Shondark and I will both be in here and we will see what his reactions are and start the training."

10

So, the training was to start. He was well on his way to being a size twenty-seven and many were eager to see him trained properly. They also needed to see how he would react to other people.

When it came time for him to awaken and start his next feeding, Tulluck, Felshon, Challoo, Shondark and two of his assistants - Chul and Yoll - were all in the room. Yoll had also brought his little brown, size ten female, Flapper, into the room as well. She had leashes attached to her jaw rings, for control and protection…if needed.

As Kovarin was preparing the meat, he leaned over to Challoo. "I thought that there was only going to be two of you in the room."

"I got outvoted," said Challoo sarcastically. "I still think it's a mistake having this many people in the room, but…we're all professionals."

Kovarin looked back to his bedchamber. The only one who had not entered the room was Challoo's assistant Bodor. He was quietly standing there waiting for any instruction from Challoo.

The prepared pile of meat for Diamond was sitting next

to the sand pit. Kovarin looked back at Flapper several times to see if she was going to try for the meat…she seemed to be totally disinterested in the meat. 'Either she's already been well fed, or it's true that they don't eat that often…once they're mature,' thought Kovarin.

Flapper snorted and slowly wandered towards Kovarin.

'Oh great,' thought Kovarin. 'She is going to go for the meat.'

She stopped by Kovarin's left side. She sniffed at him several times. She then started licking his left arm.

"She likes you," said Yoll chuckling.

Kovarin looked back at the little female. "Are you sure?"

"Yes," said Shondark. "That's the way these dragons show their like and approval of other people…or dragons. They lick them. The more she licks you, the more she likes you."

Kovarin cleared his throat and chuckled. "Apparently… she likes me…a lot."

"She is *very* friendly," said Yoll with a chuckle.

Flapper stopped licking when Diamond snorted loudly. She backed off as he snorted again.

"My charge awakens," announced Kovarin in a mockingly dramatic fashion.

All six of the men stood side by side, behind Kovarin. They let their arms simply hang at their sides. Yoll pulled Flapper closer.

Diamond opened his mouth in a gaping yawn and started stretching his neck and front legs. He stretched out his wings to their full extent and brought them back to his body. He then started stretching his back legs. He stopped suddenly and started looking around at all of the strangers. He stood up on all fours. He individually stretched each one of his back legs again and started slowly walking forward, looking at the line of men.

His attention went down to Flapper. She had her neck craned up, looking back at him. The two dragons slowly moved closer to each other and they bumped noses. Her tongue came out and gave his beak a few licks. He snorted once and then started licking her as well. Yoll breathed a slow sigh of relief. Diamond crept a little closer and started licking Flapper's neck and then her body. She crouched down on her belly and continued licking Diamond's neck.

Challoo looked at what was going on and quietly spoke: "Not sure whether she's acquiescing to him because he's a male or because he's almost three times her size…but, the two of them are getting along…very well."

Diamond now switched his attention to Yoll. The man stood there as calm and quiet as he could be. Diamond gave Yoll a quick lick and then switched his attention to the next man in line.

Shondark stood there being scrutinized by Diamond with his eyebrows raised. Diamond sniffed several times and went on to the next man.

Shondark grunted and chuckled. "No accounting for taste, is there?"

Chul was the next one to be sniffed. Diamond snorted at him a few times and went on to Challoo. He gave Challoo several sniffs and then turned to Felshon.

"I wonder if I should be hurt," said Challoo glibly.

"He likes who he likes," said Felshon with no emotion.

Felshon received a few sniffs and a grunt. Diamond turned to Tulluck. He sniffed Tulluck from top to bottom. He licked Tulluck's chest.

"I approve of you too," said Tulluck with a big grin.

"He's never licked me," said Kovarin inquisitively.

"He doesn't need to," said Tulluck. "You feed him. He accepts the food from you…that's approval enough from him… for you."

"Hold up some food for him," said Shondark quietly.

Kovarin picked up a piece of meat and held it in front of Diamond's nose. He sniffed at it and opened his mouth. Kovarin placed the meat in Diamond's mouth and quickly pulled his hand back. Diamond slowly closed his beak and swallowed. He backed up into the pit and looked down at Kovarin who held up another piece of meat. The mouth opened and in went the meat.

While the feeding was going on, Felshon and Challoo departed. Since Diamond had approved of Tulluck, they felt that they would leave him to deal with anything that might happen.

The pile of meat was getting smaller. Kovarin was wondering if the Trainers were going to do anything. They were talking about beginning his training and now all they were doing was watching him eat. He looked back at Shondark and the two assistants. They were doing practically nothing - just watching. Kovarin shrugged and kept tossing meat into Diamond's open, hungry maw.

When the pile got down to eight chunks of meat left, Shondark put his hand on Kovarin's shoulder. "That's enough for the moment."

Diamond was sitting there waiting for the next piece of meat. It did not come and he started his hunger cry. Kovarin could not understand how he could possibly be feeling hunger. The amount of meat that he had eaten clearly outweighed the little female dragon that was still sitting back there.

Shondark looked back towards Kovarin's bedchamber. "Vollost…are you in there?"

Vollost came into Diamond's chamber. "Yes, Master Shondark, I'm here and I have it."

"Good, bring it in."

'Bring what in?' thought Kovarin.

Vollost came up with a small keg. There was a sickeningly sweet citrus smell coming from the keg. Vollost pulled the top off of the keg and the smell got even stronger.

Kovarin felt like he was going to gag from the smell. "Is that stuff necessary?"

"Absolutely," said Shondark emphatically. "Get some of it on your fingers."

Kovarin looked at Shondark in horror. "Why?"

"You need to start training your dragon…just do it."

Kovarin fought off a wave of nausea. He stuck two fingers into the gelatinous muck and pulled some of the sticky stuff out.

Shondark got close to Kovarin's ear and whispered. "Now, start giving him the command 'down'."

Kovarin shrugged. He sat there and repeated "Down" several times. Diamond kept up the hungry cry.

Shondark whispered again. "Get hold of one of his jaw rings. Don't jerk it, just get hold of it."

Kovarin reached up. Diamond saw an empty hand and pulled away a little. Kovarin almost had to jump to get hold of a ring. As soon as he caught hold of it Diamond froze and stopped crying.

"Now," whispered Shondark, "slowly and easily pull him down and repeat the command - *down*."

Kovarin did as he was told. He heard a bit of a high pitched protest come from Diamond. He pulled slowly and carefully down and repeated the command. As soon as he got Diamond's head down, Shondark hooked a leash onto the ring.

Shondark again whispered. "Now that you have him down, rub that goo on his tongue and let go."

Kovarin shrugged. He rubbed the stuff on Diamond's tongue, quickly withdrew his hand and let go of the ring.

Diamond pulled back made a few smacking noises of some

kind with his tongue as if he were carefully tasting the muck. He leaned forward a little and sniffed at Kovarin.

"Get some more on your fingers," whispered Shondark.

Kovarin complied. "What is this stuff?"

"It's a mixture of some fermented fruits and ovine blood."

Kovarin was not sure whether he wanted to puke or pass out. "What good does it do?"

"The dragons love it," said Shondark.

Kovarin noticed that Flapper was sniffing at the keg and Yoll was having a bit of a difficult time pulling her back. He steeled himself. "Okay, now what?"

"Take the leash."

He took it and just held it.

"Don't pull on the leash, just give him the command."

"What command?"

Shondark gave a little growl of frustration. "The one we're working on!" he whispered angrily.

Kovarin felt a little stupid. He started repeating the command again. Diamond did not move.

"Use the leash," said Shondark.

Kovarin pulled on it.

"Don't jerk it! Just give him a hint," said Shondark.

Kovarin pulled on it easily. Diamond started leaning down, growling. As soon as his head was down close to Kovarin, Shondark again told him to give Diamond the goo. He rubbed the stuff on Diamond's tongue and eased up on the leash.

Diamond again smacked his tongue. This time, he got very interested in the keg. He started moving towards the keg. Vollost picked the keg up and backed away, while Shondark grabbed hold of the leash and just held Diamond in one place.

"Okay," said Shondark. "He likes it. He has to learn that the only time he gets it is when he obeys a command."

They went through the ritual several times before Diamond finally got the message. If he was told "Down" and he bent his head down, he got some of the tasty (?) goo. If he did not dip his head down, he got nothing but a painful pull on the jaw ring… until he complied.

After almost one turn of one command, Shondark told Kovarin to give Diamond the rest of the meat. Kovarin had some of the goo on his hand and it got on the meat. Each piece of the last eight that went into Diamond's mouth spent a few more moments than normal in the mouth before being swallowed.

After the last pieces of meat, Diamond laid down in the sand and went to sleep. Tulluck, Shondark, Chul and Vollost helped Kovarin in oiling Diamond's body.

Yoll was having a difficult time controlling Flapper. "Hey, do you mind if I give her some of the *treat*? She's about to go crazy!"

Shondark and Tulluck both laughed.

"Go ahead," said Shondark. "It'd be cruel to not let her have some of it right now."

Yoll got a handful of the muck and held it up. Flapper sat there begging like a canine. He rubbed the stuff on her tongue and pulled his hand back. She sat there for several moments moving her tongue around, thoroughly enjoying the gooey *treat*.

"Go ahead and take her out of here before she goes completely mad," said Shondark.

Yoll pulled her out.

"So," said Kovarin. "Did we accomplish anything positive?"

"Oh, yes," said Shondark. "He's getting the message. Do what you're told and you get a reward. Soon enough, we'll be able to teach him two or three commands in one setting. He seems to be much smarter than some of the dragons that I've trained in the past."

"Should I order some more of that…what did you call it… *treat*?"

"No, we'll bring it with us," said Shondark. "You don't want to keep it around here. Diamond will break into it and… well…remember that it is fermented. That dragon…Glutton…he somehow got into the storehouse and got hold of fourteen kegs of the stuff one time. He crunched the kegs in his beak, swallowed all of the *treat* and got very, *very* drunk. That's quite a sight, watching one of the big ones trying to move around…or fly…

while he's hammered."

After all of the men had departed, Kovarin went back and checked on Diamond. He sighed. "Yes my friend, there are going to be a few things happening to you…in the next few days…that you won't like. I'm afraid that it is necessary." He walked back to his bedchamber and collapsed onto his bed furs. He fell asleep rather quickly.

Kovarin was awakened by someone hammering on his door. He got up and staggered to the door and opened it.

Shondark was standing there with a smile on his face. "Are you ready for the next round of training?"

Kovarin grunted in disgust. He looked back at his time candle. Unfortunately it was almost the time that Diamond would be waking up - hungry. "I've…gotta talk…to the…Meat Cutters."

"We already have," said Tulluck as he walked in the room.

Chul, Yoll and Vollost came in the room as well. Vollost was carrying one of those smelly little kegs of *treat*.

Shondark had been the one at the door, however, he was the last to enter. He was pulling on the leash of a gray dragon (that was trying to get at the keg of *treat*). "This one is my dragon," he said. "She's a size fourteen and her name is Gray Bonnet."

Her name made sense to Kovarin. The dragon was a medium gray, all except for the top of her head and her horns, which were dark gray. He nodded as he thought that the name was rather appropriate.

As the men stood around waiting, Shondark went up to get a close look at the time candle. "Vollost will set the new time candle for you, while we're in the big chamber taking care of Diamond."

Kovarin, who was still trying to get totally awake, just grunted approval.

Gray Bonnet squawked her disapproval as Shondark pulled her away from the keg of *treat*.

"You know that you're going to have to give her some of that," snickered Yoll.

"Yes, but not now," said Shondark as he pulled back on the leash harder again.

Kovarin stumbled into the big chamber towards the meat chute. It took quite a bit of meat to satiate Diamond now. Several very large slabs of meat. He had obtained a small cart for moving the meat. He piled eight of the slabs onto the cart and moved them to the pit. He went back to the chute and picked up eight more and considered the thought of obtaining a wheelbarrow for moving the meat. It now took four trips with the cart to move one of Diamond's meals. He went back to the pit and started cutting the meat for Diamond's bite sized chunks.

As Shondark dragged Gray Bonnet into the chamber she finally stopped her protesting squawks when she saw Diamond. She started bobbing her head up and down and from side to side, all the time keeping a close eye on him.

Diamond finally stirred. He did his normal ritual of yawning and stretching. He was not as surprised to see strangers as he had been the last time. He did not really notice anything different until he saw (or smelled) that there was a different female in the room. He took a few steps closer to her and sniffed. She pulled back from Diamond, squawking the whole time. Shondark would not let her retreat very far. He kept pulling her back. Diamond got his nose up against her body and sniffed. She flattened herself on the ground and dug the claws of all four feet into the dirt. He licked her several times. He pulled back, went back to the pit and started his hungry cry. Kovarin shut him up with a large chunk of meat in his mouth.

After he had been fed most of the meat, another training session started. This time he was more willing to accept commands and obey them as he kept on getting a finger scoop of the *treat* on his tongue…when the action was consistent with the order.

Gray Bonnet was becoming almost uncontrollable as she saw Diamond getting *treat*, but she was getting none. Finally Shondark stuck his hand down in the *treat* and then smeared it all over the upper part of her carapace beak. She sat down and contentedly utilized her long tongue to lick the stuff off.

They put Diamond through a long session. He got used to *Up* and *Down*. He had a little problem with the concept of *Left* and *Right*. His eyes started to look a little glazed over.

"Master Shondark," said Chul. "I think that he's had a little too much of the *treat*. He appears…or his eyes don't look normal."

Shondark took a close look. "Uh, boy. He's still immature.

It'll be a while before he can really hold his...*treat* without getting drunk." He took a deep breath in and out. "We'll end the session now. Give him the rest of the meat and we'll let him sleep it off."

Gray Bonnet had smelled the *treat* on the last pieces of meat. She headed over to them to get some more goodies for herself. Diamond noticed her trying to get at his meat. He leaned his head forward and bellowed at her. She scrambled behind Shondark making a few of the panicked yeeping sounds. A moment later, Gray Bonnet's head popped up just behind Shondark's left shoulder. Her gaze went down to the meat and back up at Diamond...several times.

Kovarin fed Diamond the last few pieces of meat. There was, again, a little of the *treat* left on his hands, so Diamond was more than willing to accept it with great relish. He wavered a little and flopped down.

Shondark looked at his assistants. "Vollost, take the *treat* out. Chul, get the oil. We'll help measure and oil our big baby." He turned to Kovarin. "Where are the measurements from the last session?"

Kovarin felt a cold chill run down his spine. "I...uh...we didn't...or I forgot...to take any measurements...last time." He swallowed hard looking rather guilty.

Shondark scowled at Kovarin. "Indeed! Let's make sure that we don't forget...this time." He shook his head. "Where?"

Kovarin looked a little confused. "Where...what?"

"The measuring devices!"

Kovarin closed his eyes and flushed. He chuckled nervously. "Yes…I…I'll go get them." He went back to a shelf in the tunnel between the two chambers and retrieved them. "Here…I…" He felt like an idiot. "I won't forget again."

Shondark sniffed. He looked back at Diamond. "Let's get him measured before we oil him."

Chul and Yoll carefully stretched a wing out and they measured. Shondark looked a little surprised at the results.

"Okay, now the other," said Shondark still frowning.

They did the measurement. All of them looked at the results with a little (or a lot) of surprise.

Shondark looked down his nose at Kovarin. "The last time you measured…wasn't he just a hair away from…being a twenty-seven?"

"Yes…just a little bit," said Kovarin nervously.

Shondark shook his head and chuckled. "He's past twenty-seven. He is now full into twenty-eight. There's a good possibility that at this rate…he'll be a twenty-nine…in no time."

Shondark and Kovarin both checked his skull and neck. Still no sign of the ridges or flares.

Kovarin could hardly hold back his elation. "Shall we oil him now and…let him grow…some more?"

With five men doing the oiling, it took quite a bit less time to accomplish. After the others departed, leaving the warning that he was almost out of oil, Kovarin sat there looking over Diamond thoroughly, while giggling helplessly. Each time he saw the results of the growth spurts, it brought on new heights of euphoria.

Over the next nine days, Diamond continued to grow and get more training. He was now a size thirty-three...with no ridges on his skull. Challoo replaced his jaw rings with size forty rings.

They had just finished another session and Kovarin stood there looking at the big rings. "Size forty," he whispered. "If you do get that big...not only will you be a flyer...but you'll be part of the...*elite*. You'll be a breeder! There's only thirty-seven of those...males...and all of *them* came out of a size eighteen egg... or larger."

He pondered what it must do to one of the big females to lay an egg that large. He shuddered.

He, for the thousandth time, felt Diamond's skull for the bone ridges. Nothing! His skull was still smooth and round. 'Thirty-three...and still growing,' he thought. He leaned down and kissed Diamond on his head. He then went back to his bedchamber, wiping oil off of his lips and spitting the bitter stuff out of his mouth.

Kovarin woke up. He heard a soft knocking on his door. He was at a bit of a loss to figure out who it was. Shondark, Tulluck and Challoo all pounded on the door. Vock also knocked a little harder. He checked the time candle, sniffed and got up. He scratched himself in random places as he went to the door. He opened it.

"Long time, no see," said Namanti happily.

He looked her up and down. She was wearing one of her normal garish outfits. He cleared his throat...several times. "Yes, it has...been a while...since we last...talked."

"Would you like to...rekindle...," She leaned forward a little with a very friendly manner. "...some *good* memories?"

"I...I'm not sure...I can let you in...right now. Diamond is still training and...I don't know...whether or not..."

"Oh come on," she said pouting. "Me and Dozzbin seem to be the only ones who haven't been in there with you lately."

He shook his head. "It's only been the Ringmasters and the Flying Trainer."

"...along with all of their assistants," she snapped back.

"I...still don't know if I can..."

She folded her arms. "Yes, you can!" She grunted in disgust. "Do you think that this is the first time I've talked to a Dragonman with a sleeping dragon in the next chamber?"

He was not ready to hazard a guess at that question. He opened the door wider. "Come on in."

She gave him a big smile as she walked in.

He closed the door and looked at the time candle again. It seemed that there was enough time for a little conversation.

He woke up when the time candle gave off that loud hiss. He remembered that he had been talking to Namanti and did not understand how he had fallen asleep. He heard some panicky squawking coming from Diamond's chamber. He looked around for Namanti. She was not in the bedchamber. He headed into Diamond's chamber…and had to stifle a loud laugh.

Namanti was standing- in a recess in the uneven cave wall. She was holding up her hands in a feeble attempt at trying to hold Diamond off, from licking her. Each time he licked her, he went from the knees to the neck. Each time he licked her, she gave off another terrified squawk.

She saw Kovarin. "Help…me! He's…going to…eat me!"

Another lick and squawk.

Kovarin could not help himself. He started laughing openly. "Don't worry…he's not…trying to…hurt you. He's… trying to show you…that he likes you."

"Why…why… (squawk)…is he licking me…if he's not… trying…to eat…me?"

"Affection," said Kovarin as he headed for the meat chute. He opened it and found the fresh meat sitting there. He placed several slabs on the cart and moved them to the pit. As usual, it took four trips with the cart to get all of the slabs of meat to the "dining area". He cut the meat into the, now normal, large pieces for Diamond and set them off to the side.

Namanti was still in fear of her life. "Give…him something…to eat…before he eats me!"

"He won't eat you! He only eats what I feed him. I haven't cut you up to bite size pieces, so he won't eat you." He finished cutting the meat and looked back at Namanti's predicament...with a grin. "Diamond! Eat!"

Diamond turned away from Namanti. He saw the meat piled up. He looked back at Namanti and then sauntered over to the pit. He climbed into the pit and took his normal seat, waiting for the food.

Kovarin started tossing the pieces into Diamond's mouth. Namanti came up behind Kovarin and watched, still with fear in her eyes, as Diamond swallowed the big chunks of meat so easily. She sniffed a couple of times. "You said...that he was...licking me...for *affection*? Did he want me to...do something with him?"

"No, he was showing that he likes you."

"What happens...if he doesn't like me?"

"He either ignores you or growls at you."

"Oh...uh...so...he was...being *nice*?"

"Yup! He likes you...a lot. The more that he licks you, the more he likes you."

She grunted in disgust. "I'm covered in...dragon spit... because he *likes* me?"

"Yup!"

She let out a long sigh of relief. "I need to use your chamber pot."

"Haven't you ever been this close to one of the dragons...

before?"

Her shoulders sagged. "No," she said helplessly. "No one has ever let me get...close enough...to touch one of them before. I'm not part of your...precious inner circle."

He snickered a little as he kept on heaving chunks of meat at Diamond's open mouth. "Now, you've met one...up close and personal. He approves of you...so you can be happy knowing that he doesn't hate you."

She grunted. She headed back to his bedchamber. She was in there for just a moment when she let out a cry of surprise.

Kovarin heard Shondark shouting. "What are you doing in here?"

Namanti just stammered for a few moments.

Kovarin turned to see Shondark dragging the squawking, Namanti back into Diamond's chamber, by her arm.

Shondark glared at Kovarin. "What's the meaning of this?"

Kovarin tossed another piece of meat into Diamond's mouth. He turned. "Is there a problem?"

Shondark rolled his eyes. "Uh...yeah! She shouldn't be in here!"

Namanti looked up at Shondark indignantly. "And you should?"

Shondark glared at her. "I'm the Master Flying Trainer... who are you?"

"I'm the master of information," she spat back sarcastically.

"We can't have her getting in the way of your dragon's training. He has to be trained…without any kind of outside…" he looked around trying to think. "…distraction!"

"If it helps," chuckled Kovarin, "he approves of her. He gave her more licks than he did to that little female dragon, Flapper...or Gray Bonnet."

"That was a controlled situation. Part of his training, seeing how he would react to another dragon," said Shondark impatiently.

"We now know that he approves of a female human as well," said Kovarin with a bit of a giggle.

"And what happens, when you decide to get married?" Shondark was now scolding. "Are you going to tell the woman, who is going to wear your *crest*, that your dragon has a greater approval of this woman than her?"

Kovarin scoffed as he tossed another piece of meat. "I haven't come across too many women that I approve of. Whoever wears my *crest*…it has to be someone that I approve of as well."

Namanti was getting tired of being pushed around. She tried to pull away from Shondark's grip. "Legoame!"

He looked back at her angrily. "What for?"

"So I can leave!"

Shondark shook his head, growled and rolled his eyes.

She struggled some more against his grip. "Are you gonna

let go of me?"

"I haven't decided what to do with you yet," he said menacingly.

She leaned her head towards his hand and tried to bite his hand.

He shoved her back towards Kovarin's bedchamber. "Get out!"

She muttered several obscenities under her breath as she stomped out.

As she left, Chul, Vollost and Yoll walked in, looking back at her rather confused. Chul and Vollost were carrying a larger training saddle. Yoll was pulling Flapper in by her leash.

Shondark sat down next to Kovarin as he kept tossing meat. "You don't realize…what damage she could do…with your future relationships."

Kovarin looked at Shondark confused. "*Which* kind of future relationships?"

"What woman is going to wear your *crest*, with any pride, when or if your dragon approves of that woman much more than he approves of…the woman that you marry? What's the high command going to say about a dragon that approves of that worker…more than…any of them? The number one woman that your dragon should…be affectionate to is…whoever your wife is…no other woman should be…approved of." He sat there with his elbows on his knees and his head resting in his hands.

"It's not like he never got a whiff of her scent before," said

Kovarin a little defensively.

"Shondark looked up. "What…when did…what?"

"I've had her in here several times…taking care of paperwork. She sat on my bed furs…among other places in the other room."

Shondark glared at him. "Did you ever bother reading the instructional scrolls? If you do something like that, you were supposed to bathe and get new furs. It's in the instructions!"

Kovarin swallowed and looked at Shondark confused. "I don't…uh, remember reading…that particular passage." He stared at the disgusted trainer for a few moments trying to think of something else to say. His contemplations were interrupted when Diamond started complaining about having to wait for the next piece of meat. He tossed the meat into Diamond's mouth. "Besides…he got more of her scent than that."

Shondark looked at Kovarin with even more disgust on his face. "What?"

"There was one time…when I forgot to check…the coals. Diamond was, I think, only a size eight at the time. He left the pit and crawled under the…bed furs…with me."

"…and got a snoot-full of her scent," muttered Shondark. He growled a little. "No wonder he approved of her so…*readily*. He finally got to see…what went with the scent that's been… all over this place…since he first hatched. It was too familiar to ignore…or disapprove of. *You* are the one…who is going to have to explain this…to some poor unsuspecting young woman…some day."

Kovarin cleared his throat. "So…what kind of…training… are we going to try to accomplish…today?"

Shondark sighed a few times as he was thinking. He sniffed. "Today…you're going to sit on his shoulders and give him instructions from that position. He needs to get those instructions from there, because most of them will be given while he is flying anyway."

"Okay," said Kovarin sheepishly.

It took several attempts before Diamond would allow the new weight of Kovarin on his shoulders. Once he accepted it and was rewarded with *treat*, he stopped growling. With longer reins hooked to the jaw rings, Kovarin was able to lead Diamond around the chamber for quite a while. Diamond still seemed to have a few problems with it, however, a glob of the *treat* smeared on his snout seemed to give him the necessary urge to fully accept this new phenomenon.

They also wanted to get him used to flying, so after he tested his wings and hovered a few moments, inside the chamber, he was again rewarded with more *treat*.

After the training and finishing the feeding, Diamond fell asleep again. The five men all worked on oiling and measuring.

Shondark looked at the new measurements. "Congratulations…you now have a size thirty-four…with no sign of horn ridges." He looked Kovarin directly in the eyes. "If… he makes it to size thirty-seven…and still has no ridges…there is a strong probability…that you also have a breeder, as well as a flyer." He turned back to stare at Diamond. He stood there scrutinizing from nose to tail with his arms folded. "All this… from a size two egg." He shook his head with a smile. "No wonder the Ringmasters can't shut up about him."

Kovarin cleared his throat nervously. "Should I…uh…go ahead and change…my bed furs?"

Shondark's arms dropped to his side and his chin was against his chest. He sighed. "No! There's absolutely no reason… now." He looked at Kovarin somewhat disgusted. "Your charge has been getting *that* scent from day one. If you take it away now…*that* will cause confusion."

"Okay," said Kovarin uneasily. "Got it!"

11

Nine days later, Challoo changed the jaw rings to a larger size. This time Diamond received size forty-six rings. Diamond was now a size forty…with no sign of the horn ridges or flares. He had entered the great inner circle. He was a flyer, who would supply his handler with upper echelon rank and he was now the thirty-eighth male who would be allowed to breed…once he matured. No dragon had ever taken this long to go from hatching to maturity. Of course no dragon had ever reached size forty, after hatching from a size two egg.

Namanti had come back, several times, for more paperwork and supply discussions with Kovarin. She still did not like the idea of being licked, from stem to stern, by that huge raspy tongue. The only way to keep him from licking her was for her to rub the top of his head - hard. Kovarin had rubbed Diamond's head with his knuckles. Namanti's skin was a little too soft for that procedure, so she would use a small brush instead. Diamond did not mind, as long as he was getting a good head rub.

Shondark was getting even more upset over Namanti's familiarity with Diamond…and vice versa. He kept warning that this could cause irreparable damage with whoever Kovarin chose as his spouse.

When Dozzbin was informed that Diamond was now a full-fledged size forty - flyer/breeder, after unscrewing himself from the ceiling, he decided that he was going to get a good look at Diamond himself. Kovarin informed the Administrators that Dozzbin would not be allowed in the chamber, without several escorts…Vock himself being one of them. The Administrators did not question Kovarin's demands in any way at all. Dozzbin was allowed to stand in the archway that separated the two chambers. He stood there with his arms crossed tightly over his chest and just glared. He did not get close to Diamond at all.

After one of the training sessions was over and Diamond was asleep, the Tailors came in and compared several pieces of fabric to see which was closest to the color of the dragon. After seeing Diamond up close, there were two pieces that they did not even bother bringing into Diamond's chamber. They narrowed it down to two specific ones and seemed to not be able to agree on which one was closer. Kovarin and Shondark both got a little miffed at the way they were quibbling and ordered them to take the argument outside - somewhere away from Diamond.

Kovarin was informed that there had been another session of egg distribution while Diamond was still in growing and waiting for maturity. A group of fourteen eggs had been distributed. Eleven had hatched and nine of those had already matured.

Kovarin decided to start looking a little closer at the instructional scroll again. He had a burning question running through his mind: Since Diamond is now as large as many of the dragons that had been perched on the south cliffs, why was he not able to go out and establish his position among the males? It took four days of privately scanning through the scroll before he finally got his answer.

The males do a lot of wing slaps, tail slaps, body slamming and head butting in order to establish dominance. Any male, who does not have his horns yet - the skull was too soft. If an immature male were to go out there and start head-butting with mature males, he would get his skull crushed. No immature male, no matter how large he was, has ever survived any of the dominance battles with a mature male. After reading that passage, Kovarin spent several hours a day, rubbing and closely scrutinizing Diamond's head. It was not just a case of what rank would be worn when Diamond finally matured...it was survival. The flares (no matter what size) were just for show...the growing of the horns and the thickness of the skull were the difference between life and death.

Kovarin was taking one of his naps in between the feeding/ training sessions. He was awakened by a knock on his door. He looked up at the time candle. It was too early...for Shondark or anyone else that he could think of. The only possibility was... Namanti? He got up and threw a robe on. He went to the door ready to admonish Namanti because he *needed* some sleep. He opened the door and was even more surprised at what he saw. Standing there, with a smile on his face, was one of the Assistant Hatching Administrators.

Kovarin tried to get past the sleepiness he felt. "Uh...can I...help you...Administrator?"

"Yes, Dragonrider, I am Assistant Administrator Bruthik.

I've been asked to come here and inform you that, a gathering…
or party has been put together…in your honor, for you to meet
some of the eligible young ladies of our Capital City. They're
all hopefuls as far as being the wife of a Dragonrider. Since your
Diamond has caused quite a stir, there are those who are very
eager to see just whom…you would choose…of these nice young
ladies…to wear your *crest*." He stood there with a rather stupid
looking smile on his face.

Kovarin stood there speechless for several moments.
"You…want me to go…to this *thing* and display myself…like a
piece of meat in a market? You want me to sit there while all of
these girls are giggling and whispering and gossiping about me,
and trying to bid the highest price for me?"

"Oh, no, Dragonrider! It's nothing like that. They'll be
there and it'll be…your choice entirely. They decide nothing."

"Have I ever met any of these…eligible young ladies?"

"I…I have no idea. They *are* from some of the *finest*
families…of High Country. They will be there for *you* to…
choose."

He scoffed. "So *they* are the meat that's on display…for
me!"

"Well…yes."

"Who's going to watch over Diamond while I'm…
shopping?"

"It should be someone…that *you* trust."

He looked down and shook his head. "When?"

"In three days…in the evening."

"I don't have anything…proper to wear…for some gala banquet."

He smiled real big. "Oh, not to worry, Dragonrider. The Tailors will have something for you by then. They're working very diligently to make your uniforms."

"Really, what will my rank be?"

"Until you…possibly replace one of the Battle Group Commanders, or higher, it is recommended that you wear the rank of Wing Commander."

"I don't have the proper emblems…in my hands."

"Again, not to worry, the Tailors are taking care of that… as well."

"Uh…what time…in three days?"

"That will be determined by…the latest feeding time of your charge…Diamond. Once he's been fed and bedded…you'll then be taken, by coach, to the ballroom…where the banquet is taking place. You don't have to worry, it's just a short ride from here. The young ladies will have to come in to the city…they have much further to go…and no responsibility…to a dragon."

'Probably no responsibility to anything…if they're a bunch of snobby, aristocratic little stuck-up wenches, who have nothing better to do other than sit there in front of a mirror and check their makeup, or go out and drink tea with each other,' thought Kovarin. He cleared his throat. "So three days from now…after which feeding?"

"If you could give me some…estimated time…as to when his feedings are normally taking place…I could give you, and them, a better estimate of…when." Again the stupid smile.

"The only thing that I can give you is an estimate. It seems that the training that he's currently going through, is throwing his sleeping schedule off. Usually he'd go back to sleep after eating and unloading his bowels. Now, Shondark comes in and keeps him awake long enough to do some training…"

"So, just add that to the intervals…that should give us some closer estimate that I can give to the others."

Kovarin was about to give him an estimate when he saw a tiny little brown dragon crawl up, from behind, onto Bruthik's left shoulder and started flapping its wings. He stopped and stared, confused, for a moment. Bruthik looked down where Kovarin was staring.

"Oh," said Bruthik happily. "Meet my charge. This is my dragon. I call her Shoulder…because when she's awake, that's where she prefers to be perched. When she's asleep, she's usually curled up in this, gourd on my side." He pointed to a dark ball like gourd, hanging in a net off of his belt.

"Interesting," said Kovarin in a curious manner. He leaned closer to get a better look.

Shoulder arched her head back and started retreating down Bruthik's back. She started doing some kind of chittering that sounded like a scolding of some sort.

Bruthik looked down at her. "Now, now, now, little one.

That's not polite." He stuck his right index finger into a small pouch on his right side. He put his fingertip up near Shoulder. She sniffed at his finger and then started licking the *treat* off of his finger, ignoring the stranger that was staring at her.

"I'm sorry, Administrator," said Kovarin. "I...I've never seen...any dragon...that small...that was alive."

"Yes, she is one of the smallest size ones that has ever survived. She's just the length of a fingertip of being a size one. If she were much shorter, she would have been a waste and would probably not have survived. She's almost three years old now."

Kovarin could not help it. He continued staring at the tiny little brown as she moved her gaze around, scanning the scenery of Kovarin's bedchamber.

Bruthik waved his hand in front of Kovarin's face. "Uh, Dragonrider...the estimated time...please."

Kovarin snapped out of his hypnotic state. "Oh...yes." He went over and sat down at the work desk. He made a few calculations and then wrote down a time. He went back to Bruthik. "This is the closest that I can come up with, Administrator. Diamond should be fed, trained and asleep...by this time...I hope. If not, it shouldn't be too far off."

"Very good, Dragonrider," said Bruthik as he took the paper. "Until then, have a very pleasant time." He turned without waiting for a response. As he walked away, Shoulder turned and looked back at Kovarin with her head up high as if she were ready to attack (or run in fear) at the slightest movement by the man.

Kovarin chuckled as he closed the door. 'So, that's a size one,' he thought. He held up his right hand and looked closely. Each size of the dragons was measured by the size of a man's hand - from the wrist to the tip of the middle finger. If the dragon was shorter, from nose to tail-tip, then they were considered a waste, because they rarely lived. Once their length was longer than that, they had a high probability of survival. Each size length was determined by that same hand measurement. Diamond exceeded the length of forty hands stretched out together. Thunder was just over fifty-one hand lengths. Many times Kovarin had wondered just whose hand had been the original one that had established the standard that everyone was going by now.

He went to look at the list of the upper echelon commanders. Since Diamond was now a forty, someone on that list would eventually be demoted. There were five size forty dragons on the bottom of the list. Battle Group Commander Aj was at the very bottom. Since he was listed last, his bluish-gray dragon Dastardly would be the one dropped down to Wing Commander. Aj was the Battle Division 2 Group 3 Commander, who would not be the happy one. That did not matter to Kovarin. They all had to go by the same rules. Kovarin knew it, Aj knew it…and Dozzbin knew it.

He looked up the list. There was still the possibility that Diamond could grow to be a size forty-four. Those were the Battle Division Sub Commanders. Twelve of them and the shortest one on the list was a bluish-gray name Soar, ridden by Zadusk. He was one of the two Battle Division 4 Sub Commanders. If Diamond kept growing, he would oust that one.

He continued up the list. Protector - a gray that was the shortest of the six Battle Division Commander. Ayponch was his rider - Battle Division 3 Commander...for now.

Then...there was the top five dragons. Number five on the list was a gray, size forty-six named Eating Machine. Invelton was his rider. Battle Division 5 Commander.

Monster was fourth on the list. Bloodletter was third. Glutton was second. Then there was Thunder. Thunder was the one and only dragon to reach size fifty...and he had continued to fifty-one.

Kovarin stood there looking at the list dreaming. He knew that he and Diamond were now on that list...just exactly where... only time and those maturity showing horns and flares would finally tell.

He looked, with a huge grin, at the emblems of each rank. The Battle Group Commander, which he was absolutely guaranteed at this time, was a gold five pointed star. The Battle Division Sub Commander, which might be within reach, was a gold five pointed star overlaid with a set of clawed wings. The Battle Division Commander was a gold seven pointed star with clawed wings. The Supreme Commander was a sunburst with wings. He prayed that the horn ridges would not show up...until Diamond could compete with Thunder. He was getting very envious of that position.

Namanti stood there, with her fists on her hips, glaring up at Kovarin. "You want me...to sit here...and...watch over him...

while…you're out…ogling…your possibilities of a wife?"

"He trusts you," pleaded Kovarin. "He likes you."

"He takes a layer of my skin off, each time he licks me," she said through clenched teeth.

"It'll be after a training session. He will have been fed and he'll be tired from the training session and he should spend the entire time asleep. You won't have to worry about a thing. Just be ready to ring the bell, if anyone, like Dozzbin, tries to do anything funny."

"You're sure? He'll be asleep…the entire time…until you get back?"

"I'm not going to spend six or seven turns at any party. I'll be introduced to them, I'll have a polite little discussion with each one and then I'll tell them I have to leave to think it over…no way that's taking over…uh…two maybe…three turns…at the most." He smiled at her with his arms outstretched…pleading.

"You're gonna pay me for my time!"

"If you insist, yes."

Her shoulders and head sagged. She stood there shaking her head. She looked up at him, frowning, and let out a long sigh. She looked through the tunnel at Diamond as he lay there in the sand pit asleep. She pointed at Diamond and looked up at Kovarin. "That's all that I'm gonna be looking at the whole time, right?"

"Unless you go in there and purposely wake him up, that's all you're gonna see."

She let out a long sigh. "Okay."

12

The night before the party, the Tailors came in. He tried on the uniform and was feeling rather smug. The emblem of the Wing Commander was on the chest of this dress uniform. He stared at the silver clawed wings that spread across his chest, while the Tailors looked at virtually every stitch of the black uniform that he was wearing. He sighed and snickered. His favorite color was red. Now, he was going to have to get used to the shade of black that matched Diamond…the one and only black dragon.

The Tailors were fretting and fussing over the stitching and tightness or sagging in certain areas. They were making all kinds of annotations on paper as they were using "tailor" vocabulary that Kovarin could not even begin to understand.

He looked over at his work desk. The three Tailors had brought their dragons with them. There was a brown size three and two gray size twos that were running around exploring the top of the desk. None of them seemed to have the courage to jump down off the desk. When one of the tailors would go to the desk to make annotations, one of the dragons would either jump onto them or go up to them and nuzzle them for attention. They would smile, cuddle their dragon and then push them back to make their notes.

Kovarin had initially heard that if you did not get a flyer, you were given some insignificant job somewhere else. He was now seeing that that was a totally false rumor. Tailors, Ringmasters, Administrators, Meat Cutters, Flying Trainers, and even a member of the Supreme Tribunal. Each and every one of them had a non-flying dragon. They still had a dragon and they took that responsibility seriously. This entire country depended on the dragons for their defense…even though it was a gigantic fraud. As long as the fraud continued…High Country was safe.

The men who had dragons were looked upon with respect. The ones who had flyers were looked upon with awe. Of all the dragons in High Country, of which there were tens of thousands, there were less than six hundred males that were flyers. Including Diamond, there were now thirty-eight males and twenty-two females that were breeders.

The night of the banquet, Shondark had insisted that Namanti was incapable of doing the job alone. Kovarin finally gave in to allowing Chul and Vollost keep a watch outside in the hallway. They could sit there with their two little males, Bigmouth and Runner. Assistant Hatching Administrator Acong came to help keep watch, with his little dragon, a size three, bluish-gray male named Trouble. Namanti felt a little safer with this arrangement as well. Dozzbin may have been foolish enough to try something against a secretary - highly unlikely that he would be crazy enough to take on three men who could sound an alarm.

Kovarin headed out to the coach, proudly wearing his new uniform. The boots felt a little odd and would take some getting used to. He thought about the breastplate and the other parts of the battle uniform that would feel different as well. He *was* going to get used to it. He was now a full-fledged Dragonrider. He would have to wear that responsibility as well as the uniforms.

The black coach looked enormous. There was enough room in the back to seat six people comfortably. There were lanterns on each corner of the coach that had already been lit. It took four equines to pull the monstrosity. He was wondering why they had used this to pick him up. It was something that was more fitting for royalty. Then he remembered - he was now a member of the top elite. He was a Dragonrider…with a dragon that was big enough to be a breeder.

He got up into the back of the open coach. He looked out to the west and saw the sun just disappearing over the horizon as the coach started forward. He snickered to himself. The sun was setting on his life as a nothing (according to Dozzbin). He was now an important man, who was having a banquet thrown in his honor. While the rest of Capitol - Dragon City, was throwing a ball for Kovarin, Dozzbin was probably throwing a massive fit because of Diamond…and the fact that Kovarin was the rider.

As he sat in the rocking coach he made a mental note to talk to the Tailors. The shirt was rubbing and digging in a little in the left armpit. He tried to adjust it a little during the ride. It would not cooperate. He tried sitting differently. He tried lowering his shoulder. He tried holding his left arm forward. Nothing helped. 'Wonderful,' he thought sarcastically. 'Perfectly rotten start to what is supposed to be a nice evening.'

The coach arrived at the banquet hall. He had to stifle himself from laughing out loud. They were honoring him, by decorating the hall…with the color of his dragon. It looked more like a funeral for a major dignitary was about to take place.

Waiting at the place where he was to get out of the coach were two men. One man, whom he did not recognize, was wearing a bluish-gray uniform…with a large black, silk sash. The other man…was one of the Master Tailors.

"Good evening, Dragonrider," said the Tailor with a smile. "I am here to see if there are any…last moment adjustments…that need to be made before your grand entrance."

'Oh, thank the Great Maker,' thought Kovarin. "Absolutely," he said. "I am getting badly chafed…in the back of the left armpit."

"Oh dear," said the Tailor. He quickly jumped up into the coach. "It'll be better in here. That lantern will give me enough light to see what needs to be done."

Kovarin turned to give the man all the room he needed to work. He felt a little snap and heard a pop and the pain was instantly relieved. "I don't know what you did, but it helped already."

"I just cut a few stitches…to see…Oh, my! It appears that it has already chafed you to what would definitely be painful. There is a raw patch of skin back here. I'll make a few adjustments and you'll be able to make the evening…without too much more discomfort."

Kovarin sat there patiently while the Tailor did his patch job. He looked down at the other man standing there. The man was wearing the emblem of a five pointed gold star on his breastplate - the emblem of a Battle Group Commander. He was very tall and lean. There was light brown hair sticking out from under his dress helmet. He stood there, stoically waiting for the Tailor to finish his work. Kovarin wondered if this was the man whose dragon was going to be ousted from the top command because of Diamond. Surely they would not be doing that now. They would have to wait until Diamond has his "coming out".

"There," said the Tailor. "That'll hold for now. If you have any other problems, I'll be at the party…somewhere around there."

"Thank you, Tailor," said Kovarin gratefully. "I don't know what you did, Master Tailor, but it feels much better."

The Tailor smiled and motioned for Kovarin to depart the coach first. Kovarin smiled back and stepped down. He looked up and realized that this other man was *very* tall. He could rest his chin on Kovarin's head while standing flat on his feet. Kovarin saluted the tall man. "Good Evening to you, Battle Group Commander."

The man grunted. "Battle Group Commander…for the moment. As soon as your Diamond has his 'coming out', I'll become a Wing Commander."

"I take it that you are…Battle Group Commander Aj?"

He closed his eyes and gave a polite nod. "Yes. Battle Group Commander, Battle Division 2 Group 3...for the moment."

"I hope that you're…not too bitter…over…"

He raised a hand and smiled. "Oh no. There is no room

for any bitterness. I knew that it'd happen…sooner or later. I was just hoping for…later."

"It is the rules that we all have to live by."

Aj sighed deeply. "Yes. It is what originally gave me my rank…and now it is why I'm…sinking…a little." He looked at Kovarin with a bit of a strained smile. "Please understand and forgive me…if my congratulations to you seems a bit… melancholy."

"I understand, Commander. I can only imagine how you feel. As you said, though, you knew it was coming…seeing as how you have the shortest size forty."

"Actually, I don't. Of the five size forty dragons, my Dastardly is in the middle. The problem was in the dominance battles. Both Rash and Stonehead are shorter, however…they both…clobbered Dastardly in their respective battles. Not much… that I could do about that."

Kovarin nodded. "Is that why you are the one greeting me…here? Is there something in the protocol that…?"

"Oh, no," said Aj with a smile. "I asked to be the one to greet you, because I did want to have a moment of privacy and let you know that I'm not really upset at all. I knew when I first put on the uniform what could happen and I'm glad that I'm only being dropped down one rank."

"It could be disastrous…to be dropped further."

"Yes…anyway…we've had our little chat. I now have the honor of introducing you to some special people who are coming towards us…uh do you know any of them?"

Kovarin looked up the stairs and saw three men coming towards him. He smiled as he recognized his uncle. The other two were complete strangers. "Yes, I recognize my Uncle Onjono. That huge cheesy mustache and those great grinning teeth, under that duster…he's the one who introduced me to the joy of dragon riding."

"Oh really?"

"Yes, He gave me a ride with him…several years ago on Bird Eater…and I found out, quite by surprise, how that mischievous dragon got his name."

Aj looked a little surprised. "You mean…he does…do that? I thought that it was just a…"

"No, I saw him do it. He snuck up behind a very large bird…and snap! No bird! There were, however, two wingtips that fell from the sky."

Aj clicked his tongue. "So…it's *not* a rumor." He shook his head. "Uh…let's go and meet the other two."

One of the men was wearing a gray uniform with the emblem of a Battle Division Commander. The other was wearing a gray suit. Those two along with Onjono were all wearing a black silk sash. Aj and Kovarin saluted the two officers as they got closer.

Aj started the introductions. "Since you are related to Battle Group Commander Onjono, I'll dispense with that. I would like to introduce you to Battle Division 5 Commander Invelton and

Dragonholder Kredemon." He looked at the others. "Gentlemen, Wing Commander Kovarin."

Invelton was a tall, stern looking man who had a salt and pepper mustache. Kredemon was not quite as tall as anyone else in the group. He had short brown hair, a lean build and a very friendly smile.

They all shook hands cordially.

Kovarin was a little confused as to all of this 'outside' stuff that was going on. "To what do I owe this special meeting…if you don't mind my asking?"

Invelton laughed. "It is customary, at an occasion such as this, for you to meet the parents."

Kovarin was even more confused now.

"I, Battle Division Commander Invelton, am the man who is the Dragonrider of Eating Machine…Diamond's father."

The other man's smile got even bigger. "I, Kredemon, am the Dragonhandler who is responsible for Queen Gray, Diamond's mother."

Kovarin was a little stunned for a moment. "Oh…I… never…even thought of parentage before. I was just…so happy to have a live hatching. It completely slipped my mind."

"That's quite all right," said Kredemon. "The main thing to worry about for you, in the future, is that any time Queen Gray goes into heat…you must keep Diamond…away…until she has mated."

"Yes…yes…yes…uh…any…siblings that I might have to…avoid?"

"Yes," said Invelton. "Just one other breeder. A female named…" He looked up and groaned. "…Whine!"

Kovarin was taken aback. "Whine?"

"Yes, Whine…the Dragonhandler - Tadyotho…wanted a male. He's not very happy with a female."

"I think that we know who the real whiner is," said Kovarin in a chiding manner.

They all got a chuckle out of that.

Invelton added: "There are two other breeder siblings…of Diamond's. These, however, are males - Sky Chaser and Crunch."

Kovarin was not really interested, he just decided to add to the conversation. "Are they represented here, tonight?"

"Oh, yes," said Invelton happily. "Sky Chaser is a size forty-four. His rider is Frand - Battle Division 1 Sub Commander. Crunch is ridden by Azzitok who is a Battle Group Commander in Division 1 Group 2."

Kovarin leaned back and cleared his throat. "Our family is very well represented here…and in the upper echelon altogether."

Kredemon, Onjono and Invelton all nodded happily in agreement. Aj just gave them a somewhat strained smile.

Kovarin looked at Onjono. "So, Uncle, is Bird Eater still up to his dirty little tricks?"

Onjono shrugged. "It's…difficult to stop him. He enjoys it so. He so loves it when we're patrolling the northeastern cliffs. There's a lot of…very large birds in that area…less now, of course…but they are there."

Kovarin turned to Invelton. "Division Commander, you are the ranking man, so I guess that you're going to lead the way."

Invelton smiled. "Yes, I'm the ranking man…however, this gala affair is in your honor." He gestured politely with his hand. "You may lead the way."

The Tailor had joined them during their friendly chat and now all six men headed up the stairs to the elaborate main entrance. At the doors there were two more Dragonriders, one Dragonhandler along with Teeha - Onjono's wife.

Teeha came up to Kovarin and hugged him. "Ah, Kovarin, my favorite nephew," she said with a huge smile. She backed away a little. There was a tear in her right eye. "It's a terrible shame that your parents couldn't be here…for this. That fire that…" her words trailed off and she sniffed. She touched his cheek. "I know that they would be so proud."

He lowered his head slightly. He remembered that day, not long ago, hearing about the fire that had killed his parents. He cleared his throat. "Yes, it would be nice if they could've been here. That's just another reminder…of how fragile…life can be." They hugged again. He stood back. "Let's try to think happier thoughts now."

"Yes," she agreed.

"Uh…Aunt Teeha, where's my cousin Erashan?"

Her smile got bigger and her eyes shone with pride. "He's just about to finish his Candidate qualification. We're hearing that he's doing very well. He should be finishing very soon and maybe getting an egg…hopefully soon."

Kovarin looked at his uncle. "This family is going to be very well represented, what few of us there are, among Dragonmen."

Onjono nodded with a smile, every tooth shining brightly under that huge, carefully groomed mustache.

"There are three others that you need to meet," said Aj.

Kovarin looked at the two.

A big man with a huge jaw and mouth held out his hand. "I'm Battle Division 1 Sub Commander Frand. I ride Sky Chaser - one of Diamond's brothers."

Kovarin shook his hand. The man had a strong grip. "Commander, it's good to meet you." He chuckled. "Especially under these circumstances."

Frand smiled and nodded.

The other Dragonman held out his hand. "I'm Battle Group Commander Azzitok. I ride Crunch…another brother."

Kovarin shook his hand…not quite as hard a grip. "Commander, good to make your acquaintance." He turned to the third man.

This one had a rather insincere looking smile. He was a rather small man who looked rather undernourished because of his skinny body. "I'm Tadyotho…I'm the Dragonhandler for Diamond's sister - Whine."

Kovarin blurted it out before thinking: "Why, by the first dragon's claw, did you name her that?" He felt like an idiot for asking, however, the damage was done and he tried to cover it up by showing no emotion at all.

Tadyotho smiled. "I named her that because of a strange sound that she makes, when she's asleep. Most people don't believe that, but if you want, I'll take you to her when she's sleeping and you can hear her."

Kovarin chuckled. "I just might take you up on that. I've heard a few strange sounds out of Diamond…awake and asleep."

Tadyotho nodded.

Kovarin looked around at the people surrounding him. "There seems to be a rather large group of flyers here. Is there anyone out on patrol?"

"Oh, yes," said Invelton with a laugh. "The only ones who are here, are the ones who're related to Diamond…or you. We've come to welcome you to the elite group of flyers and breeders. You have the newest size forty and…we felt it would be polite to greet you…especially on this occasion."

Kovarin looked a little startled. "Uh…you haven't heard… the latest update?" He looked up. "Of course, it's very new…and I guess that it just hasn't been broadcast about yet."

Invelton looked a little concerned. "What, what, what, what, what?"

"His…latest measurement…" said Kovarin with a bit of a guilty smile. "He just…broke the line…to forty-one. According to Ringmaster Tulluck, he's officially a forty-one…*now*."

Azzitok put his hands to his chest. "Oof! You've just entered my territory. My Crunch is a forty-one." He leaned a little closer with his brow furrowed inquisitively. "Any sign of his horn ridges yet?"

Kovarin smiled smugly. "No sign of ridges *or* flares yet."

"I think that he may be competing with me soon," said Frand. "My Sky Chaser is a forty-four. If Diamond doesn't have ridges or flares yet, then…he could easily be growing to a forty-five…or larger."

Invelton cleared his throat. "Commander Aj…get in there and inform the Herald. He needs to announce a Dragonrider for a new forty-one instead of a forty."

Aj saluted and quickly headed to the person in question.

Invelton looked around. "Let's hesitate a moment while the announcement is being *corrected*." He looked at Kovarin. "No ridges or flares and he did break the line to forty-one…when?"

"Just the last measurement, before I headed over here," said Kovarin proudly.

"This is going to get a few noses out of joint," chuckled Azzitok. "The Herald knows, possibly before the members of the Supreme Tribunal know that Diamond is a forty-one."

Everyone got a snicker or chuckle out of that observation.

"They *need* to get an occasional slap down," said Invelton with an air of evil pleasure.

Aj came back. He raised a hand and smiled. "Ready!"

Invelton gestured to Kovarin to lead on. "You're prospects and public await you…Dragonrider."

Kovarin swelled with pride. That word had never sounded like such an honor before. He had just been called a Dragonrider by the man who had the fifth largest dragon in existence. He strode forward feeling taller with each step. As he headed for the entrance he wondered if Dozzbin was going to be here…and what the man would be eating.

The Herald was watching him approach. At a certain point the little gray-haired man snapped to attention and banged a rather large gavel on a small table, three times. The banging echoed throughout the banquet hall and all talking ceased.

The Herald took a deep breath and started his introduction. Kovarin was rather surprised at how loud the little man's voice was as it echoed through the room. "Ladies and Gentlemen, announcing the arrival of our guest of honor. Dragonrider, Wing Commander Kovarin. Dragonrider of the newest size forty-one dragon, the famed black dragon - Diamond."

There were four members of the Supreme Tribunal present. All four of them had surprised looks on their faces. One of them turned to one of the others and Kovarin could see him mouth the words: "Forty-*one*?" He heard Invelton chuckling behind him. The Herald and the other Dragonriders had known before the Tribunal…about Diamond's status.

He was greeted with a round of polite applause. A man in a very stiff looking outfit came up to him with a tray of crystal goblets that contained a red liquid. Before he could take one of the drinks, Invelton grabbed his arm.

"I think, Wing Commander, that you should refrain from drinking any wine," said Invelton. "You have several young ladies to talk to and it would not be polite if you were…drunk…before you got to the last two or three of the hopefuls. Remember, you *must* be polite."

"Yes," said Kovarin. "The fruit juices."

Invelton, and the rest of the people who came in with Kovarin all took goblets of wine. Kovarin was steered to a large punch bowl, where a man in another stiff looking outfit, ladled a cup full of juice from the bowl. Kovarin took the cup with a smile. Before he could take a sip of the juice, there was a rather short, petite, young woman standing next to him, receiving a glass for herself. She had very long brown hair and big brown eyes. She was dressed in a black evening gown and wore black gloves. He felt that before the night was over, he just might, *really*, be a little tired of that color.

"Hello," said the young woman. She held out her hand for him to kiss. "My name is Vaya. I hope you don't think that I'm being too forward, but, I just had to be the first one to meet you."

He smiled as he kissed her gloved hand. "I was told that I was going to be meeting several prospects for wiving…so, no I don't think that you're being too forward. I had to meet somebody tonight and someone had to be first."

She blushed and put her hand over her mouth in a coy manner. "Yes. I don't have anyone in my immediate family who is either a Dragonrider or Dragonhandler and it would be a great honor for our family if I could get married to one. You would find me a good catch, because my father and four of my uncles are in the Senate. You're status would improve greatly if...*when* you choose me."

He was not sure what to say so he took a sip of the juice. It was some kind of mixture and it had a tart but pleasant taste. 'Diamond has assured my status,' he thought. "It sounds as if your family has been more interested in politics than defense of the homeland." He looked up as if thinking. "Five relatives in the Senate...my, my, my...that does lend itself to some rather high status."

She pointed. "Why don't we go out on the balcony, where we can have a...somewhat private conversation?"

"Isn't that a little too private? I mean if we are out there..."

She giggled. "It's customary, for the prospectives to go out there where they can have a more intimate chat. All of the people can still see us with the big doors open, so we are still... chaperoned."

'Customary?' he thought. 'Uncle Onjono, why didn't you inform me of some of these...customs?' He gave a polite chuckle. "If it is customary - then who am I to break tradition?"

She took his arm and they went out to a small white marble table near the edge of the massive balcony. He looked around and figured that they could have had the entire party out here...

if they had really wanted to. He looked over the edge and saw a huge round fountain below. Even in the dim light of the eight torches, that surrounded the fountain, he could see some large fish swimming around in the shallow water.

Before he could continue any polite banter, she, with her back to everyone in the ballroom, got down to business. The smile left her face and she talked in a complete business-like manner. "I *am* the best prospect. None of the other girls have as many as five relatives in the Senate, the Tribunal, the Judges or the Dragon Command combined. Now, *after* you give me your *crest*, I will allow there to be two children. One just seems to simply be too little and three, or more, is out of the question. After I've gone through the trouble of giving you two children, I don't expect to be bothered by you anymore. So, you can go chase whatever you choose and keep your hands off of me. We shall be seen, in public, at *all* of the functions and we will make the appearance of being happy at all times. I don't ever want to hear about any obligations that a wife has to her husband. Are there any questions...so far?"

'By all that's holy,' he thought, 'how do I get out of this conversation...without choking this little menace to death?' He cleared his throat and blinked a couple of times trying to think. "I really don't have...any questions...at this time."

"Good." She continued on with her scroll of demands and commands and would not let him get a word in edgewise. When she finally ran out of commands (and air in her lungs), she took in a deep breath. "Then can we call it a match and...?"

"Uh...moment, young Vaya...remember that I must be polite. I need to give each one of the others some of my time.

Plus, no matter whom I choose, it wouldn't be fitting to announce my decision…tonight."

She stuck out her lower lip and frowned. "Oh…foo! That's right. No matter what the situation, we must always be polite. That can be so *very* bothersome." She sighed. "All right, I'll give you some time with the others and await your decision… to choose me." She smiled and walked away.

He did everything he could to hide his repulsion as she departed. Judging by how many people were scrutinizing him, there could be disastrous results if he…stuck his tongue out at her…or made some lewd gesture…or looked as if he were going to lose his lunch. He tried to cover some of the emotions by downing his drink.

As Vaya departed, another young woman was approaching. She, like just about everyone else was dressed in tonight's color of black. She was a little taller, and did not have as small an overall build. Her hair was a little shorter and a lighter shade of brown and she had big almond shaped blue eyes. She was carrying two cups of juice with her.

"Good Evening, Dragonrider," she said in a husky voice. "I brought you a fresh glass. Vaya has a way of souring the juice with her presence….and her ego."

'Oh wonderful, they're well acquainted with each other,' he thought. "I don't know about any souring," he said with a chuckle. 'More like turning the drink and the entire evening into a turpentine bath,' he thought. He cleared his throat. "…and you are?"

She held out her hand for a kiss. "I am Natiski. I'll bet that she told you of all of her uncles and her father in the Senate…even though there are five of them, they're really not that good. They haven't brought any new, good legislation into play."

He thought: 'And you know this…how?'

"My father, who is on the Supreme Tribunal, doesn't think very much of them…or her for that matter. One thing that you should know is that you never go with the first one…that you meet. Just let her stew and fret, while I help you forget about her."

'Oh help,' he thought.

She started in on her own list of demands, commands and absolute rulings. The difference between the attitudes of these two young ladies (?) was negligible at best. She would wear his *crest* and get all of the honors and prestige while he was to stand off to the side…permanently.

After nauseating him with a little more of her rhetoric, she became equally upset over the fact that he "had to be polite" to the other girls.

As she departed, he noticed that she did not look back. She was giving him a full show of the swinging of her hips as she walked away. As soon as Natiski was completely off of the balcony, the next one came out. She apparently did not want to watch him ogling the last girl. She wanted to be the total center of attention as she made her entrance…no distractions at all. She had two cups of juice in her hands as well.

She seemed a little taller than number two. She had waist

length, dark raven hair, which he wondered if it had been colored for this occasion. As she got closer he was able to see, what looked like, laughter in her eyes. The black formal dress that she was wearing did little to hide the fact that her hips seemed a little large…for a girl her age…whatever that is.

He downed the contents of his second glass and put it down on the ledge. As she approached he tried to look as cordial as possible for her…hoping that she was not as snooty as the first two…snobs.

She handed him the fresh cup and held out her hand for a kiss. He took the cup and kissed another gloved hand.

"Good evening, Dragonrider." Her voice was higher than the last girl, however, her manner of speaking was immaculate. "I am Imathaka. I help complete the circle. Vaya's father is in the Senate, Natiski's father is on the Supreme Tribunal and my father is one of the Judges in the High Court."

'Legislative, Executive and now a Judicial,' he thought. 'I wonder if any of these girls represent the military.' "Really?" He tried to avoid sounding pompous. He was hoping for an improvement and did not wish to spoil it by showing her any kind of attitude.

She read off of her scroll, spoiling any belief that she was a better person than the other two girls. This one was "generous" enough to allow for four children…if it should happen, by some unforeseen accident, to occur.

Once again he had to fight back the urge to try to choke some sense into this girl as well. Again, after she had read off of her scroll of demands, he had to remind this one as well, that he had to be polite to all of the girls.

This one departed, swinging those large hips. He did not like the idea of walking too close to her…that sway could be injurious…if you did not take any necessary precautions. The next one did not appear until this one was out of sight as well.

After Imathaka was off of the balcony he again threw the last bit of juice down his throat.

The next one made her entrance. This one appeared to be about the same height as the last one. She had long brown hair, blue eyes and instead of having huge hips…this one was top heavy. She was not ashamed of showing a large amount of cleavage. She seemed to want to put on a better show than other women.

She held out the fresh cup of juice with the appearance that she was being overly kind. He took the cup and gave her the obligatory kiss on the hand. She also seemed to be making special effort to hold her chest up so that her endowment appeared even larger.

When she talked, she seemed as if she were somewhat breathless. "Good evening, Wing Commander. My name is Teevasha. I know that the others have tried to impress you with their connections to politics. I don't have any such nonsense to worry about. My family has owned the Palsiton Winery for over 300 years. We don't need to dabble in politics…just competition with other wineries." She chuckled. "As if the other wineries were able to compete with us."

"Palsiton? I've heard that that is the best in the country."

"Oh, yes. We have a wonderful history. We have wines, only for the most discriminating..." She got an evil grin on her face. "...and only the richest of all the families of High Country."

He smiled (hoping that it did not look too strained). "Do you export any of your wines?"

She put her free hand up, closed her eyes and sucked in her breath. "Oh, absolutely! The Queen of Jebeltau *bathes* in one of our finest."

'My, what a lush,' he thought. "That sounds expensive."

She giggled, taking special care to make sure that her chest jiggled. "She can afford it. She's a Queen!"

"Yes," he admitted, trying to keep from gagging over her obvious show of the...obvious.

She now read from, her imaginary scroll. There was not very much difference between her and the others - she gets all of the assets and he gets all of the liabilities. He listened to her drivel on for a while before reminding her (as well) that he had to be polite.

Teevasha made her exit and the next one came in. This one was a little shorter than Teevasha and was a little on the heavy side. She had long blonde hair and shiny brown eyes. She seemed to have an overabundance of jewelry...around her neck, her wrists, her fingers, hanging off of her ears and a couple of rings that were visible on her toes.

She brought him another cup of juice and received the obligatory kiss on the hand.

"My name is Cha-Ashi," she said in a somewhat tenor voice. "I'm not like some of those others, who are trying to impress you with their political affiliations. My father is the one who supplies over half of the herding beasts that feed the big dragons." She smiled. "Without my father, your dragons would starve."

'No they wouldn't,' he thought. 'We'd get the food beasties from some other rancher.' "How nice," he said with a now practiced false smile. "I know that my Diamond really appreciates everything that goes into his mouth."

"Diamond," she said with a big smile. She looked at the ornamentation on her hands and wrists. "Yes, I like that name."

She did exactly like the others. She read off of her scroll of demands and commands and was not interested in anything he had to say.

When Cha-Ashi left, Kovarin was a little surprised to see Onjono come out on the balcony. He came up to Kovarin looking a little bored.

"Well, nephew, what do you think so far?"

Kovarin turned away from the people inside that were gawking at the two men. "I don't think that you really want to know what I think."

"Yes, these…situations can be a bit of a strain…on your patience."

"Did you know that those…Prissy Little *Its*…were going to be like that…every one, so far?"

Onjono looked thoughtful for a moment. "Prissy Little Its…that's one of the most…polite things that I've ever heard those…young ladies called. Most of the time it's something… much worse."

"So I'm being polite. I probably still have a few more to go."

"Yes, you're only half way through. There are five more to go…from what I understand."

"Five   more?"   He   groaned.   "So why   are   you   now,   interrupting   the   *niceties*?"

"I thought that you could use a break. Go somewhere and use a chamber pot. Either empty your bladder…or your stomach, depending on how you feel right now."

"This isn't your first one of these…debacles…is it?"

"How could you tell?"

"You know what's going on…what they're saying…what they're demanding…and commanding. Why didn't you warn me?"

Onjono sighed. "If I had told you in advance what the… Prissy Little Its are like, would you have believed me?"

Kovarin stared at his uncle for several moments. "Probably not. I still don't believe their audacity."

"You have five more to go through. Again, do you wish to…relieve yourself?"

Kovarin shrugged. "Why not?" He looked around. "I just

don't know where the closest outhouse…or chamber pot is."

"Follow me," said Onjono flatly.

They walked to one end of the large balcony. There was a rather dull looking door, compared to all of the others, that Onjono led him too. As soon as the door was opened, Kovarin knew what the room was for…by the smell.

"How quaint," said Kovarin in a sarcastically. "An indoor outhouse."

"We are on the second floor…of a very large building. Can you imagine trying to run down the stairs…if you had to go really badly?"

"It'd be…a comically horrible waddle…if you're thinking of what I'm thinking."

Both men chuckled as they each picked a "hole" and relieved themselves of the earlier drinks. After finishing, they went back out onto the balcony and faced into the wind and inhaled deeply…to get some of the smell out of their noses.

Kovarin sighed. "Back to the…one sided fracas…I suppose."

Onjono laughed. "When we get back into their sights… don't say anything funny."

"Why not?"

"Those girls have some massive egos, but those same large egos are also very fragile. If they see us laughing, then each one will decide that we're making fun of her."

Kovarin thought of something clever to say. He checked himself when he saw that they were getting close to the table (where the used cups had been cleared away in their absence). Some people were already looking out and scrutinizing the two men. 'Shut up and save the jokes for later,' he thought.

The next contestant was already on her way to the table before he got there. Onjono had taken a quick left turn back into the main ballroom, leaving Kovarin alone...ripe for the picking. This girl looked somewhat young and about average height for...a teenaged girl. She did seem a little skinny. Her brown hair hung down and almost covered one eye. She had a rather provocative look in her big hazel eyes. "My name's Soondi," she said in a somewhat nasal voice.

Again, take the cup and kiss her hand. Try to start some kind of small talk before she starts on her demands...oops...too late.

Soondi's father was a baron of one of the northwestern provinces. One uncle was the High Sheriff in the same province. Another uncle was the Chief Jailer of the same province.

'Keep it in the family,' he thought. He had to think it...he could not get a word in at all, once she started on her speech. Once she finished, he had to remind her, as well, about being polite to the others.

She departed after giving him another alluring look. She wandered back into the ballroom.

The next one that came out, Kovarin had to fight to keep from staring. He had rarely ever seen a woman this tall. She was by far the tallest one of the entire lot. Her build almost made her look masculine - her walk did not sway from that idea as well. He swallowed hard and hoped that she did not notice. He was thinking that he did not want to get into a physical wrestling match with her…she could very possibly win.

She handed him a fresh cup and held out her hand for the kiss. "Good evening, Dragonrider," she said.

Again he was rather surprised. She had a baritone voice. He could not remember the last time he had heard a woman (or girl) whose voice was that low. He kissed her hand. "Good evening…young lady."

"My name's Teebatay. My father is not like any of the others. He's not a politician or a rancher. His job is to collect all of the excess grains, fruits and vegetables and make sure that there is enough for everyone to have enough of the different breads and such."

"Sounds like he does have an important position."

"A lot of other people don't think so."

He smiled. "Where would we be without the grains, fruits and vegetables? We'd be competing with the dragons for the meat."

She smiled. "So you do understand…somewhat…his position."

"I can easily respect him."

Now she went off into her sermon on his responsibilities to her and her attitude about the situation.

'More self-serving drivel,' he thought.

When she left he decided to check and see if she had the walk from the back that he was used to seeing on sexy young women…nope! Not this one. This was definitely one where you might just have to pull the pants down, in order to properly determine gender…if you did not know her.

The next girl was one of the shorter ones…and one of the heaviest. He had heard the term "full-figured". She was a blue-eyed blonde with a somewhat heavy build. She was not fat… just a little plump. Her name was Leeltow and she did not have a list of demands that differed from the others…very much. Even though she was heavier, she did seem to be a little nicer than the others and she was still good looking.

The next one came out. Kovarin could not hide his surprise as his jaw dropped when he saw her. She sashayed her way up to him, with some very over-exaggerated movements of her hips. The movements were so overdone that she spilled some of the contents of the cups on her wiggle-walk up to him.

"Good evening, Dragonrider," she said in a very cheerful manner. "My name is Jeendala."

He blurted it out before he could stop himself: "How *old* are you?"

She was momentarily taken aback by his question. Her expression was one of surprise, then a slight frown, then a somewhat mocking smile. "I'm seventeen," she said with a grin.

'Bull what?' he thought.

She was absolutely the shortest of the bunch. She had long brown hair, flashing green eyes…and the skinny frame of a (very young) girl-child who had not yet reached puberty.

She giggled. "There's lots of people who have trouble believing that I'm as old as I am."

'With good reason,' he thought.

"I'm used to it," she said with a mischievous grin. "The other girls are all jealous of me…for my appearance."

He still could not hide his shock. He did, however, finally find the gumption to accept the cup of juice and kiss her tiny hand.

'If I take this one…they'll all think I'm a child molester,' he thought.

She started in on her lecture. One of the big differences (that again made him wonder about her true age) was that she wanted to wait, at least five years, before bearing any children.

He had to take a deep breath and think carefully about not saying what he was thinking. 'Is that so you have enough time to grow some boobs and some body hair?'

When this one departed back to the ballroom, she again put on her bogus show of a sexy walk.

Finally the last one made her appearance. She was not as attractive as some of the others and she was rather slender. She was about the same height as most of the others. She let her long brown hair hang loosely behind her. Her steel blue eyes seemed to have a challenging look as she slowly sashayed up to him. She gave him a friendly smile as she held out a fresh cup of juice for him.

"My name is Towetha."

He once again was given a list of demands and commands. It was very similar to the ones that he had heard before. He wondered if they got together and dreamed these ideas up as a group...or was it taught in some "prissy little it" school.

After Towetha departed, Kovarin stood there looking down at the fountain below. He heard footfalls behind him and wondered who it was that was coming up now. He turned and saw that Onjono was once again coming out for another...rescue (?), conversation (?).

Kovarin sighed and met his uncle. "What now?"

"They await your decision."

"Got any advice...before I put my neck on the chopping block?"

"Yes, turn around and we'll both face away as we have our chat."

Kovarin turned back and stared back down at the fountain.

"First of all, nephew, what are you thinking?"

He scoffed. "I'm thinking...of all ten of those...*girls*... floating, face down in that fountain."

Onjono snickered and made every effort that he could to look as if he had some coughing spasm. He cleared his throat. "I told you - don't try to be clever. Those girls, and their parents, have some very fragile egos. If either one of us laughs, they'll *all* think that we're laughing at them."

"Okay, I can live with that. Any other advice?"

Onjono took a sip from his goblet. "Yes! It's one that I hope you'll heed."

"What?"

"Don't make any decision tonight!"

"That's the best thing I've heard...at any time tonight. I will definitely heed that one."

"Good. I want you to think of what you heard from each one. This is a decision that you'll have to live with...for the rest of your life."

Kovarin growled.

"I'm serious...no matter what you do, most of them will be disappointed. Uh...are there any of them...that you're thinking about?"

"There's one that I'm *absolutely* saying no to."

"Really? Which one would that be?"

"That little scamp - Jeendala."

"Any particular reason why?"

"Don't tell me that she's seventeen years old. I doubt very seriously that she's a day over...twelve...maybe even as young as ten."

Onjono frowned and shook his head. "I've...wondered

about her myself. They're all supposed to be between the ages of fifteen and nineteen. Anyway, you asked for advice. Okay, here it is: Choose the woman that appeals to you the most as far as her attitude and personality. Don't let any political or money aspects come into play...unless they all seem the same and the only thing after that is money or status. The wrong decision will just make both of you miserable. Think of whom will be there...for you, as well as someone that *you* want to be there, for her. I would say: Choose the one who has helped you the most in the past, but, you have no history with any of them. You may have to take each one of them into Diamond's current home and see how he reacts to them. His reaction can be very important. That may help. The decision is not easy...I know. As soon as I heard that this was going to be one of these...parades of the...Prissy Little Its, I was worried for you." He turned and faced Kovarin. He sighed. "Do what *you* think is best...but *don't* make any decision tonight."

"So, how do I get out of here?"

"You beat a retreat to the outhouse...after you do what is necessary...exit out the other door, and I'll go make the necessary apologies for you...informing them that you have decided to think on it...for a while."

Kovarin turned and faced Onjono. "Thank you...Battle Group Commander." He saluted. "I will try to...make the best decision...I can."

Onjono returned the salute. He turned and headed for the ballroom to tell all of the young ladies that they would have to wait. Kovarin headed for the outhouse...and then home to Diamond.

13

Kovarin wandered back to his room. He was followed by the Tailor, who once more scrutinized each hem and line, took the uniform and departed to make the corrections. Kovarin sat down on his bed furs, contemplating what had happened over the last few hours. He suddenly realized that Namanti was not in the room. He was slightly panicked over this and quickly headed into Diamond's chamber to check on him.

He stopped and was a little perplexed at what he saw. Namanti was sitting on the edge of the sand pit, rubbing Diamond's head with her brush. Diamond's head was resting in the sand, right next to her leg.

She looked up when she heard Kovarin enter and scowled at him.

Again he was a little surprised. "What's the matter?"

She glared at him. She wrinkled her nose and started chewing him out in a whiny whisper. "I'll only be gone for two, maybe three turns…it's been over five! He'll sleep the whole time! That's all you'll see of him, is asleep! I thought I heard something, I came in here and he woke up! The only way I can keep him from licking me is to rub his head. If I stop, he'll wake up and start licking me again. My whole left side is covered in dragon spit…including my hair!"

Kovarin chuckled. "The Trainers and the Meat Cutters will be here soon…and they'll occupy his time with feeding and training. He'll let you go then."

"Are you sure that all of this licking is just…affection?"

"Would the Ringmasters and the Trainers intentionally fabricate a story about that?"

"Would you please…do something to distract him? I want to get in your tub…and wash. I smell like his breath. It's nasty! My robe is…" She held up her left arm and let out a grunt of disgust.

He walked over and started rubbing Diamond's head. Namanti got up, quickly tiptoed away and headed to the bedchamber. He heard the water pump going at a rather fast rate as she tried to fill the tub as quickly as possible.

He went back to looking closely at Diamond's head. It was still rounded. He smiled. 'You still have some growing and maturing to do, my big, young friend.'

He got up slowly. He heard Diamond let out a snort. He waited for a moment to see if this was a move at waking up. When there was no more movement other than a slow regular breathing, Kovarin smiled and headed back to his bedchamber.

Namanti was vigorously trying to get the smell out of her dress. She was sitting in the full tub rinsing the garment off and occasionally smelling it for any residual saliva. After she was convinced that she had cleaned it sufficiently, she started on her left arm and shoulder. "You owe me, Dragonrider," she spat at him. "First you said that you wouldn't be gone that long…hah! Second, you said that he would sleep the whole time - wrong again! All this time…I could've been taking care of paperwork." She gave him an angry stare. "I have to wait here until my clothes dry out," she snarled.

"Nothing can dry…while it's in the water."

She started wringing the water out of each garment. As she wrung out a portion of something she would hang it over the side of the tub and continue on down. He held on to the part that was out of the tub. When she finally got to the end, he shook each one out and hung it on a rack to dry.

He picked up his robe and headed back to the tub. "You're going to need something to wear…until that dries." He pulled out his coin purse. "How much for babysitting Diamond?"

She scowled back as she was now cleaning her hair.

"I'm eternally grateful for what you did."

"Give me the towel…when I'm finished. I still smell like…his breath. I don't want to leave here smelling like this."

Kovarin was awakened by someone kicking his feet. He looked up and saw Shondark standing there looking a little repulsed. He chuckled in a bit of a guilty manner. "He should already be awake," said Shondark, trying to avoid any conversation about Namanti. "Is there anything that might have possibly interrupted his sleeping time?"

"Uh…last night…I had to go…to that ball…in my honor. They had a bunch of those…young aristocratic females for me to look at…as a possible wife. While I was gone, Namanti was here…to make sure that no one pulled anything…" He let his voice trail off a little looking at the bored face of Shondark. "She…uh… said that she thought…she heard something. She went in there, he woke up…he gave her another one of his big, long, affectionate lickings and the only way she could get him…to go back to sleep was to rub his head. I don't know…how long he was awake."

Shondark turned without saying a word. He headed to Diamond's sleeping quarters. Kovarin followed attempting to look somewhat decent, in nothing more than his robe.

Challoo was in there already with his assistant Bodor. Chul, Vollost and Yoll were also there, with Yoll's little brown female, Flapper. Flapper came scurrying up to Kovarin with her wings extended and slightly moving. He stopped as he looked down at the little dragon. She gave him a quick lick on his chest, turned and went back to Yoll.

Chul pointed at the meat chute. "The Meat Cutters have already filled the order."

Challoo was looking at some figures that he had written on a piece of paper. "If he wasn't a forty-one before, he most definitely is now." He looked back at Diamond and chuckled. "He also, *still* has no sign of horn ridges." He looked at Kovarin smirking. "I'd say that you will, in all probability, have, at the very least, a forty-five…by the time he's finished growing."

'That's the area of Battle Division Commander,' thought Kovarin. 'Is it possible that I could be competing with…Dozzbin for…Supreme Commander?' Kovarin chuckled. "Who would've thought? This from a size two egg!"

They went through another long feeding/training exercise. When they finished, they were all a little tired. A new time candle had been set and Kovarin closed the door behind the last of them as they departed. He thought of getting himself a good nap. Namanti was still sitting there with a towel wrapped around her.

He cleared his throat. "Uh…you're…still here?"

She giggled. "I don't know if my robe is dry…or not."

"Did you check?"

"I haven't bothered checking. I didn't want to get up… with all those men in the area. I didn't feel like getting ogled by all of them…either in here or in the hallways."

He looked at the mixture of dirt, blood, oil and *treat* on his hands. He went to the tub and pumped it hard, several times to get a good lot of water. He cleaned his hands and face. He went and checked her clothes. "They're all dry now."

She looked at him disdainfully. "Would you mind going into Diamond's chamber while I get dressed?"

He snickered and headed back to the sand pit. He stood there smiling while staring at his *now* big dragon. He stood there until he heard the door in the other room being shut…hard. He headed back to his furs for a good nap.

After twelve more days of feeding and training, Diamond was still growing. His growth spurts seemed to be slowing. Challoo was confident that this meant that he was getting close to maturity. He still did not have any sign of his horn ridges though.

"Let's keep this a secret," said Kovarin. He looked at all of the men in Diamond's chamber. "Just tell people that his growth has slowed and his ridges are not showing yet. The rest…keep it a secret."

"That's not really fair…to others," said Challoo. "I don't understand why you want to surprise everyone in such a great manner."

"We wouldn't be doing anything in a fair manner, if we kept it a secret," said Shondark. "Someone needs to know."

"If we tell anyone about this…the information will get to Dozzbin," said Kovarin. "I don't want him to know. It's him that I want this information kept from…all the way up until the revelation is made…to all."

Chul got his thoughts in: "What about Senior Administrator Vock? Will you trust him?"

Kovarin placed his hand on Chul's shoulder. He tapped the shoulder several times with pursed lips. He nodded. "All right. Vock! You go get the Senior Administrator. We'll talk to him…privately."

Chul looked to Shondark. "When should I…?"

"Now, boy!" Shondark looked at him angrily. "This is the one thing that Dragonrider Kovarin has agreed to. Go now…get

Vock!"

Chul departed. He was not running, however, he was not moving slowly.

Shondark gave Kovarin a nasty look. "Can we continue the training session…until Vock gets here?"

Kovarin sighed. "Yes…by all means. We don't want to interrupt the training." He cleared his throat. "Shondark, would it be possible for one of your apprentices to…go get Tulluck and Felshon…as well? I mean…we may need a few witnesses…to the actual information."

Shondark looked over at Vollost. "You heard the request, boy. Go! Find them and tell them that this meeting is just a little urgent."

Vollost departed as well.

Tulluck and Felshon both arrived together. They both seemed a little tipsy.

"They had a little too much wine at their last meal," said Vollost.

"I think they'll sober up…when we tell them," said Shondark.

A few moments later Vock showed up. He seemed a little upset at not being told why, just being told that it was urgent. His frown turned to shock as he entered Diamond's lair and got a good look at the dragon. He then put his hands over his mouth and started laughing with joy as he looked up and down the big immature dragon. Tears started coming out of his eyes. "Oh, my…he's still black…and so big." He stopped and tried to regain some composure. "Uh…why am I here?"

At that moment, Diamond moved his head closer to Vock and got a good sniff. He gave Vock a lick that went from Vock's chest all the way up to his forehead.

Vock started laughing again. He addressed Diamond: "I thank you, big fellow, I like you too."

"Senior Administrator Vock," said Shondark with a guilty smile. "The reason that you are here…is to help us keep a secret."

"A…secret? What do you want me to…?"

"It's a surprise for all," said Kovarin with a smile. "It's a surprise that we don't want Dozzbin knowing about…until Diamond has his *coming out*. Then…we lower the boom…and let Dozzbin blow a blood vessel."

Vock grunted. "Over what?!"

Shondark handed a piece of paper to Vock. He looked at it with a little impatience. The look on his face went to surprise and then shock. He looked around the room at all of those present and got affirmative nods from all of them.

Vock was now a little flustered. "Does…he have…any sign of the ridges…or flaps?"

"None at all," said Challoo with a shrug. "He's still growing and we have no idea…how large."

Vock looked to Shondark for more affirmation.

"No ridges…no flaps," said Shondark. "No way to tell…

when he'll stop…growing."

Vock shook his head. "It seems…such a dirty trick. I can't lie to them…I have to…"

"It's not a lie. You're just…not telling them the whole story," said Challoo. "There's very few people who…like Dozzbin. I don't know…of really any…who do like him. When Diamond has his *coming out*, the show that Dozzbin puts on will be priceless…especially if he doesn't know."

Vock closed his eyes and shook his head. "It makes me feel…*dirty*! However, I'll keep the secret. If for no other reason…just to watch Dozzbin hit the roof. I just hope that the Supreme Tribunal doesn't get too upset with us…keeping a secret from them."

Two days later, Diamond's skull was changing. His horn ridges were finally growing in. The flaps at the base of the skull started coming in as well. Diamond seemed to be in several different kinds of misery as all of his new growth was centralized to his head area. Challoo, Shondark and Kovarin all had to pay special attention to oiling the flaps and horn ridges and scratching the miserable itches that Diamond was feeling.

Challoo chuckled. "It shouldn't be too much more time now. I'd say two days at the most."

"I agree," said Shondark looking a little smug. "Two days from now, we'll see Diamond leave this chamber. He'll go out there and make his first challenges. I wonder who he'll challenge first."

The next day, they made the cut for the horns to sprout completely. His horns came in very nicely. The ridges were on the upper sides of the skull. The cuts were made in the back of the skull for the horns to penetrate without any further pain. As they rapidly grew, they grew straight back out of the back of his skull and when they were at their full length, the tips pointed slightly up. The horns were the only part of Diamond that was not black. The horns were an odd shade of yellow.

To Kovarin, the flaps seemed to grow at an incredible rate as well. After one feeding, the flaps were just a piece of wrinkled looking skin that surrounded the base of the skull. At the next feeding, the flaps were longer than his hand. After another feeding, they had tripled in size.

Kovarin looked to the Ringmaster. "Is that normal?"

Challoo looked puzzled. "What?"

"The flaps," said Kovarin. "Do they suddenly sprout and then…grow at that…unbelievable rate?"

"Oh, yes," said Challoo with great confidence. "Everything is going as it should be." He chuckled. "He's going to look magnificent when he spreads those flaps. I can hardly wait to see it."

The day arrived. It was obvious to the Ringmasters and the Trainers. Diamond did not eat very much. His horns were at their full extension. His neck flaps formed a very large circlet around his head. He also did not go to sleep after an incredibly small meal. He was walking around the perimeter of the chamber, looking impatient. He was looking…for what he did not know. The only thing that was going on now was that his primal instincts were kicking in. He was no longer a hatchling infant. He was not an adolescent. He was a fully mature dragon, ready to face the rest of the world - and he seemed to know that this area was not it. He was tiring of the isolation and the cramped quarters. It was time for him to get out…and fly.

Challoo and Shondark left with the paperwork. They informed all those necessary that a mature male, who was a flyer as well as a breeder, was ready to come out and challenge the world.

Kovarin had been informed that it would take a few turns before the *coming out* could take place. The reason for the delay was because of the notoriety of this unique black dragon and the news of how this monster had hatched from a size two egg.

Diamond continued taking laps around the perimeter. Occasionally he would come away from the wall and test his wings. He would flap them to the point where his front legs would come off of the ground and every loose piece of dirt was flying through the air. After each time, testing his wings, he would growl a little and then go back to the wall patrol.

A few times, Kovarin tried to appease him with a little *treat* on his carapace beak. He would accept it and lick it off as he continued his impatient march around the wall.

Kovarin had also been told that as soon as the outer door

was opened and Diamond had departed the chamber, he would never return. Once a dragon experienced the "open", they became very claustrophobic. As a result, Kovarin would now have to vacate the bedchamber that he was currently occupying. He would get new quarters, befitting his rank…whatever that was going to be. He was very sure what that rank was going to be, and there was one certain person who was in for a very nasty surprise. There was going to be a group of men who would come in and move his belongings to his new quarters. They were not going to come in and move Kovarin's possessions until after Diamond had departed the big chamber. They were afraid of what might happen if there was some unusual noises while Diamond was going through his pacing.

Kovarin had also retrieved the bad scroll and the bad temperature rods from their hiding place. He was not sure what he was going to do with them, or when, however, he knew he had to keep control of them.

He had been issued a new, and supposedly permanent, saddle. Since the horns and neck flaps were fully grown, they were very sure that his growing pains were over. He was as big as he was going to get. The new saddle was waiting off to the side. Right now, Diamond did not need the distraction of the saddle. Once the door was opened, he would be rather busy…challenging and/or being challenged.

Chul finally came back to the chamber. He carefully walked up to Kovarin who was standing by the pit.

"The door will be opening…very soon, Dragonrider," said Chul as he watched Diamond pacing. "They were in position to open it, when I came in here. The only thing that they're waiting for now, is some of the Supreme Tribunal members want to be here to witness his *coming out*."

Kovarin nodded. "Are there many dragons out there...to welcome him to the world?"

"Supreme Commander Dozzbin, would not allow anything smaller than a forty-five to be here...at this time. He figures that any of Diamond's first challenges, should be from the largest dragons. He's hoping that Diamond will be totally humiliated."

Kovarin let out an evil chuckle. "I can hardly wait."

He was still wearing the uniform that had been made for him. A uniform showing the rank of Wing Commander. The Tailors had not been informed of what the new rank was going to be, so this uniform was good for now. The Supreme Tribunal would make the ruling of the new rank, once they got the certified paperwork from the Ringmasters and the Master Flying Trainer. There was going to be more than one demotion.

Kovarin nudged Chul. "You said that only the biggest are here? Whose is the smallest?"

"Uh...that would be...Battle Division Sub Commander Tollor, with his blue-gray dragon, Slam."

"Hold on...there are eight dragons that are size forty-five...you say that all eight are here?"

"Yes, along with all of the Battle Division Commanders."

Again Kovarin let out a chuckle. "The top fourteen dragons are here. My, my, my, what a welcome to the outside world...

for my Diamond. Thunder, Glutton, Bloodletter, Monster, Eating Machine, Purge, Protector, Fang, Scrambler, Endeavor, Treat Grabber…who else?"

"Sky Dancer, Castle and Slam," said Chul as he continued keeping a close watch on Diamond.

There was a sudden scraping noise on the door side of the chamber. Diamond heard it, looked toward the noise, raised his head and had his neck flares spread out in their full glory. He was on the opposite side of the chamber. He turned and made a direct line to where the scraping noise was taking place. He stepped right through the sand pit on his way. Kovarin remembered how, as a new hatchling, he had barely been able to look over the edging bricks that surrounded the pit. Now, the step up and down was virtually unnoticeable as he headed for the origin of that scraping noise. He left huge claw prints in the wet sand.

"Here Dragonrider," said Chul as he handed some cotton to Kovarin. "Put this in your ears."

"What's that for?"

"You'll find out…very shortly. Just stick some in each ear…if you plan on being able to hear anything…tomorrow."

He remembered that challenge that had taken place when they had moved Diamond. The two dragons had bellowed at each other and that noise had been quite loud. They had been on top of the cliff…Diamond was going to be right here…beside Kovarin. He stuffed the cotton in his ears.

Kovarin could not hear the scraping very well anymore,

because of the cotton, however, he could see the giant door moving up...slowly. Diamond had his head down near the ground, attempting to look through the ever widening slit at the bottom of the door. He could see dirt flying up as Diamond was doing some sharp exhaling near the opening.

Kovarin leaned towards Chul and shouted. "What's he smelling?"

Chul laughed. "Fresh air, for one thing."

Kovarin had not thought of that before, however, it did make sense. Diamond had been closed in, all that there had been of his short life. Now, for the first time, that he was aware of, he would be going out into the world and would never have to worry about stuffy air again.

The gap between the floor and the door kept getting wider. Diamond was looking both ways and digging his claws deeper into the dirt in anticipation. His attention went off to the left, seeing as how that was the only movement that he could currently observe. Twelve men were straining as they turned the large wheel that opened the great stone door.

"Get hold of a ring," said Chul. "Take control of him and lead him out."

Kovarin did not question the order. He went over took hold of one of the rings and started scratching Diamond's head. The big dragon did not respond in the normal manner to getting the head rub. He seemed too excited at what was happening to the wall of his, soon to be, ex-home.

The door continued up. They could now see some other people milling about on the other side of the canyon. All eyes were on the door as it rose.

The long black pennant that was outside the door was hanging somewhat limp. There was very little wind currently in this part of the canyon.

They could see the upper torsos of the men who were turning the wheel. Their arms were bare and covered with sweat as they continued the arduous task. Now they could see the shoulders. Now they could see their heads. Their faces were dripping with sweat as well.

Kovarin checked his position and decided to lead Diamond to the closest point near the center of the door. Diamond had his wings stretched out and Kovarin figured that it would be a more impressive site if he could exit the chamber with both wings fully deployed. Diamond did not seem to like the move, however, with the tug that he was getting on the jaw ring, he gave in and moved.

The door was finally open wide enough for Kovarin to start leading Diamond out. Kovarin had to duck a little to come out. Diamond was mainly length and width so he had no trouble walking through the low threshold.

As Diamond was led out, a man called to the twelve on the wheel: "He's out now…you can stop."

All twelve men stopped pushing on the wheel and looked at Diamond as they panted and wiped the sweat away. They each got a good look at Diamond and now were gawking in awe at the spectacle.

Kovarin brought Diamond out further on the floor of the canyon. He was completely out and his wings were fluttering a little as he tried to look around…in spite of the pain in his jaw.

"Now, Dragonrider," said Chul. "Let him go and let him have his wings…and get out of the way."

Kovarin let loose of the ring and beat a quick retreat, with Chul, away from Diamond.

Diamond stood there for several moments taking in the landscape. He looked high and low, left and right. He was seeing things that he had never seen before…including other male dragons. He raised his head and his wings started flapping even harder when he saw the other males, up on the edges of the cliffs above, sunning themselves. His wing buffets were sending clouds of dirt everywhere.

Instinct took over. His neck flares were spread out, displaying their full glory. His neck went straight, his chest expanded and he bellowed a challenge to all of the males on the cliff above. Kovarin was standing a good distance from him to observe what was going to happen. When Diamond roared, Kovarin felt the ground beneath his feet vibrate. Most of the males above showed their flares, however, they did not roar back at him…yet. He pushed his wings for all they were worth and he was airborne. As he rose up off of the floor of the canyon, his bellowing seemed to get even louder…and the dust cloud was nearly blinding. A few of the males looked in his direction and let out a growl or two. Until it was clear to them, which one was the exact one being challenged, they seemed somewhat lackadaisical about the whole thing. He flew up and hovered for a moment as he looked over the candidates for his challenge. He chose. He got a little closer to the dragon that was on the highest perch and let out another deafening cry of challenging.

Thunder appeared to be insulted. He raised his head and looked at the upstart that was challenging him. His neck flares blossomed and he bellowed back at Diamond, accepting the challenge. He spread his wings and was ready to go airborne to meet this young unknown in combat. He was coming out with no fear at all because he had never been defeated. That was why he was on the highest perch above the canyon.

Before Thunder could really get flying, though, Diamond attacked. He flew directly at Thunder and, using his body, slammed the big brown back onto the perch.

When Diamond hit Thunder, he disappeared from view to the people down in the canyon. There were people up on the top of the cliffs who had come to see the spectacle and they got to see a full view of the fight.

Thunder landed hard back on the perch and was thrashing around trying to regain his feet (and senses). Diamond had struck and was coming around for another attack. Thunder again attempted to take off and this time was broadsided by Diamond and knocked completely off of the perch and down into the canyon. He flapped his wings furiously as he fell. He was able to regain some control before hitting the ground. He was ready to bellow back at Diamond again, however, he never got the chance. Diamond came down from above and behind and put all of his weight into a full bludgeoning body blow on top of Thunder. This time Thunder could not stop from hitting the canyon floor.

The people who were watching from the bottom of the canyon were scattering as the big brown lived up to his name and came down with a thundering crash.

Kovarin looked at Chul. "How many bones do you think are broken?"

"None," said Chul with a shrug.

"What!? How!?"

Chul threw his hands out. "No one knows why…but… no matter how hard they hit each other and no matter how hard they hit the ground…or tumble…they never end up with a broken bone."

Kovarin looked at the floundering brown. "But…how?"

"No one knows. If you can figure it out, you're a much more intelligent man than anyone else who has ever asked that question."

Kovarin backed away from the new cloud of dust that had been stirred up when Thunder hit the ground. He looked up at Diamond who was hovering while looking down on his fallen opponent. Kovarin looked at the other people on the canyon floor. Most of them were at the ready - they were prepared to jump and run in any direction to get away from falling…or thrashing dragons.

The growling and thrashing noises coming from the cloud of dust subsided. Soon all that could be heard was heavy panting.

The people in the canyon started assuming a more relaxed stance. Kovarin decided that these were the experienced ones and their example was a good one to follow. They all looked to the cloud of dust, waiting for it to settle and see what was going on with the loser of the battle…other than panting.

Diamond slowly descended to the perch that had been occupied by Thunder. He came down on all fours and once again, with his flares out full, issued another deafening challenge to all of the males in the area. None of them answered. They had just seen Diamond demolish the dragon that had defeated all of them. That former king was now laying defeated in a cloud of dust. Diamond was the new king - and none of the other males were ready to question that fact. Only one challenge and Diamond had the undisputed victory.

Kovarin was looking up at Diamond, giggling with delight. One challenge was all it took and Diamond had established himself completely. He could hardly wait until Dozzbin was given *all* of the news regarding the *one and only* black dragon.

Chul tapped Kovarin on the shoulder. "There…" he pointed up to the top of the central portion of the cliff. "Vollost is taking Diamond's certifications to the five Tribunal members who are up there."

"Only five of the fifteen showed up? That almost seems insulting," said Kovarin.

Chul looked at Kovarin in shock. "What!? Usually it's only one member of the Tribunal who shows up…and that's not the Supreme Tribunal member. Tremyath himself is up there…of course, he's the only member of the Tribunal who's a Dragonman."

"Why isn't Shondark or Challoo taking the paperwork to

them?"

Chul laughed. "They wanted to see the fight. They wanted to see how soon Diamond would challenge Thunder. They sure didn't have to wait very long, did they?"

"Okay, so where are they?"

"Shondark is…somewhere over on the other side of the dust cloud." Chul looked around for a moment. "There's Felshon." He pointed off to the left. "He's over there stuffing his fat face." He looked around some more. "There's Tulluck…he did go up to the top." He was pointing to a spot just to the left of the five Tribunal members. "I'd recognize that tall, skinny wisp of a man anywhere." He looked around some more. "I have no idea at all where Challoo is…right now."

They watched as Vollost passed behind an enraged Dozzbin as he approached the Tribunals. He walked up to the first one and bowed. He said something and handed the paperwork to the man. The Tribunal member took the paperwork and started perusing it nonchalantly. He started to hand the paperwork to the next Tribunal member. His head suddenly jerked back to the paperwork and he held it close to his face as he looked at something…in particular. He lowered the papers. He looked at Dozzbin. He looked back at the papers. He looked at the other Tribunal members. He looked at the papers. He looked back at Dozzbin and put his right hand over his mouth and leaned over as if he were trying to cover a good hearty laugh. He handed the papers to another Tribunal member, who looked at the first man as if he had lost his mind. He held his arms out in a questioning manner. The first Tribunal pointed to a spot on the paper. The second looked at it closely. He then held the papers out at full arms-length as he looked over at Dozzbin and he lost control.

The antics of the first two Tribunals had Tremyath's attention. He looked over at them and gave some kind of admonishment that Kovarin could not hear from his position. The two laughing Tribunals gave the paperwork to Tremyath. He and the other two attending Tribunals looked at the paperwork together.

The man to Tremyath's left did not try to hide anything. He turned away from Tremyath leaned over and let out a good hard laugh that echoed down through the canyon, as he held his sides.

Tremyath was shaking his head and looking confused. The other Tribunal to his right pointed at a spot on the paper. Tremyath's jaw went slack. He looked over at Dozzbin. He handed the paperwork to the Tribunal to his right. He checked himself and straightened out his ceremonial robes. He ran his hands through his hair. He held out his hand for the papers. He got them back and headed for Dozzbin, with a grin on his face that even Kovarin could see from the bottom of the canyon.

Tremyath stopped just to the left of Dozzbin. He said something. Dozzbin's shoulders sagged and he looked away from Tremyath. The Tribunal got directly in front of Dozzbin and held up the papers. Dozzbin put his fists on his hips and leaned his head down looking with a little disdain at the smaller man. Tremyath pointed to a spot on the papers as he held them up in front of Dozzbin's face. Dozzbin looked with some disinterest at first. Then his entire body jerked. His arms dropped to his side as his shoulders and jaw dropped. He looked over at Diamond in shock. Kovarin could see the whites of Dozzbin's eyes.

Dozzbin held his clenched fists up high and let out a scream that made almost all of the male dragons in the area react, including Diamond, by blossoming their neck flares. Most of them were looking in Dozzbin's direction trying to figure out who the challenger was. When they saw no dragon in that area, they all settled back down to sunning themselves.

Chul had his arms crossed across his chest as he was observing the show up on the cliff. "It turned out to be a very nice day for a *coming out*, wouldn't you say?"

"Oh, yes," said Kovarin with equal sarcasm. "It's such a nice day. It's so nice that Dozzbin isn't overreacting to the fact that he now has the *second* largest dragon."

"Yes," said Chul with a giggle. "His puny little size fifty-one, brown, Thunder, is now second to the magnificent size *fifty-five*, black, Diamond."

They continued watching as Tremyath and the other Tribunals walked over to Tulluck for confirmation. Tulluck simply nodded to all of their questions as he stood there calmly with his hands clasped behind his back.

"When do you think they'll have the change-of-command ceremony?"

"As soon as possible," said Kovarin with a smug, evil grin.

14

Kovarin was once again being checked over by the Tailor. This time, however, he was also being measured carefully by the Master Armorer as well. Before, his rank had not been fully established. Now, they had to make the breastplates that would fit and show the proper status of the new Supreme Commander of the War Forces of High Country. It was a slow boring process.

It was satisfying though, because Dozzbin now had to be fitted for a lesser rank. As soon as Dozzbin decided which Division he wanted to be the Commander of, that would cause an upheaval among the six Battle Division Commanders. Since Division 3 Commander, Ayponch had the smallest of the Division Commander dragons, he would then be kicked downstairs to Sub Commander. He would decide which one he wanted and that would knock Sub Commander Zadusk down to Group Commander. He would decide which one he wanted and that would leave Group Commander Aj with the decision of which Wing he wanted to Command…and so on.

It all seemed so confusing. It was the rules. It was the rules that High Country had adopted long ago when they started the program to use the dragons as a very effective national defense strategy.

He looked around the luxurious quarters that he now occupied. He was told that he had a choice of five different ones that he could choose from, including the one that was currently occupied by Dozzbin. He decided that he did not want the one Dozzbin had because he could not stand the idea of living in a place where Dozzbin had left his…essence.

There was a knock on the door. He had no idea who would be visiting at this time, however, it would help kill the boredom. "Enter!"

Battle Group Commander Aj walked in still wearing the full uniform of his soon-to-be ex-rank. He walked up to Kovarin and saluted.

Kovarin was not sure what to call him, so he went generic. "What can I do for you, Commander?"

"Before the official ceremony…I wish to put in an application, Supreme Commander."

Kovarin was confused. "Application…for…what?"

"It is traditional for the Supreme Commander to have an Aide. With Dozzbin, his Aide was Wing Commander Kevrong. Now, Kevrong's brown dragon Master Gamer, is only a size twenty-nine. When Dozzbin gave him the task of Aide and gave him the rank of a Wing Commander…it made quite a few waves. A twenty-nine doesn't even rate a Unit Commander and Dozzbin gave him Wing Commander status. If I am your Aide…you don't have to make any waves…letting me keep my current rank… because my blue-gray Dastardly…is large enough…for that rank, Supreme Commander."

Kovarin smiled. "Is there any other reason that you want to become my Aide?"

Aj chuckled. "If…there is a sudden influx of, oh say five or more size forty-ones…that would leave all five of the forties… being demoted to Wing Commander. If I am your Aide…I could still keep the rank, Supreme Commander. It would not really be that much of an insult to anybody…I hope."

Kovarin stood there laughing. "You say that Kevrong was his Aide. Would you believe that I owe one to Kevrong?" He saw the confused look on the face of Aj. "Someday, I may have to tell you what happened."

Aj smiled. "Yes, Supreme Commander, some day. For now, what are my chances of becoming your Aide?"

"Very good, since you have such a good attitude and from what I hear have done a rather good job as a Battle Group Commander. You've shown that you know the rules and are not questioning them. You accept what is and are not arguing over what you cannot change. I understand not wanting to lose what you already have and I will give strong consideration towards your request. Would there be much of a change…to your wardrobe?"

"The insignia would change. Right now I am affiliated with a specific Group. Once I become your Aide, that designation would no longer apply and the numbers on my uniform would be changed to a small silver sunburst…to indicate the Supreme Commander's Aide. Kevrong is the one who would be…losing the most prestige."

Kovarin contemplated for a moment. "Not really

Kevrong's fault, is it? He just has the wrong friend. Too bad. Oh well, that's part of life."

Aj nodded.

"Do you think that there will be others…trying for… Aide?"

"I…really don't know. Dozzbin has had some…influence. He's never hidden his…repulsion for you. I just don't understand why…he hates you so much."

Kovarin sighed. "Several years ago, we made a wager. It involved some of those sporting events…that you participate in, in school. The two of us were entered in five different events… against each other. The wager was that either he or I would come out on top…in the majority of those same events."

Aj shook his head. "Wasn't it normal to compete in seven events?"

"Yes, but remember, there are a total of twelve to choose from. Of the seven that I chose, only five of those were the same as Dozzbin's choices. Each of us had two that didn't match."

"Sorry, I didn't think of that."

Kovarin gave an understanding smile. "Yes, well, anyway, after four of those events, we were tied - 2 to 2. The fifth event was the one where you carry that great big stone ball and run with it. Dozzbin had a bit of a lead on me and…just might have won it. Then he tripped and fell flat on his face. Now, of course, he has to pick the stone up again, and get back into the rhythm of running…with that stone. By the time he'd picked it up and got moving again, I had already passed him…and was too close to the finish line for him to catch up. I won. I won the wager: 3-2. He tried to say that someone had tripped him. The judges of the race wouldn't listen, because there was no one close enough to have touched him at all. He refused to pay off on the wager, because he said that someone…who I'll never know…got out there and tripped him up. I called him out on that and he lost a lot of his egotistical prestige as a result. He's hated me ever since."

Aj was staring at Kovarin slack-jawed. "All of this… animosity, over a school…sporting event?"

Kovarin shrugged.

Aj shook his head. He sniffed, cleared his throat and came back to the original subject. "So, what do you think is the possibility of my becoming your Aide?"

Kovarin chuckled. "Very good! You have an excellent attitude and you're the first to apply. So far, so good."

Aj smiled. "Thank you, Supreme Commander. Is there anything that you require…now?"

"Is there any way that you can speed up this boring process of getting fitted by the Tailor and the Armorer?"

Aj laughed for a few moments. "Unfortunately, no. They do want to get it done correctly…especially for someone of your exalted rank. Any mistake would be a permanent blemish on their reputations."

Kovarin sighed and shrugged. "Then…I guess that there's nothing I need…at this time. I'll let you know, if I think of anything, later."

Aj gave a polite bow and departed.

The Tailor and Armorer were doing…something with their tools and the clothing. They were not paying much attention to Kovarin at this time. He used this time to go back and look at the new (temporary) list of the status of the breeders. Diamond the size fifty-five, black was now listed first. Thunder and Dozzbin were second. Since Dozzbin had not made up his mind which Division he wanted, the six Division Commanders were still in place. As soon as Dozzbin got over his emotional tirade and made a decision, they would be able to make a good list…until another size forty or higher broke into the ranks.

A knock on the door.

Kovarin stretched from the boredom. "Enter!"

The door came open. Onjono and Teeha entered.

Kovarin threw his arms out smiling. "Aunt Teeha, Uncle Onjono, so good of you to come. Is there any news of Erashan and his Candidacy?"

Teeha came up and hugged Kovarin. "It's good to see you too." She leaned her head back. "Erashan won't graduate for another two days at least. He's still doing quite well, though."

"Good, I wish him success. Uncle, how are you doing?"

Onjono smiled and shook hands. "I'm here on a different matter."

Kovarin raised his eyebrows. "Oh, what's that?"

Onjono cleared his throat. "There is the matter of the prissy lit…uh…the young ladies. They're all harassing me…wanting to know anything."

Kovarin sighed. He was trying to think of something clever or evasive to say. Then he got a somewhat evil idea. "Tell them…all that I have decided…that I want ten children. I'm trying to decide which one of them…I should *allow* to have all ten of my children. That's what I'm considering at this time."

Onjono looked off to the side, failing miserably, in trying to not laugh.

Teeha was disgusted. "We can't tell them that! How can you expect a girl to accept…the thought of bearing ten children… before she's married?"

Now both Onjono and Kovarin were enjoying a good laugh.

Kovarin turned to her and through his chuckling, he told her: "If a woman can read off a list of demands, as to what she wants in a marriage, why can't I?"

"Because…it's just not…done that way," sputtered Teeha.

"Why?"

"Bu…because it isn't"

"Why?"

"She has to have more say than you…in bearing children."

"Why?"

She looked at Onjono exasperated. "You explain it to him!"

Onjono had a tear running down his cheek from laughing. "How? I don't understand what you're explanation is."

She turned away and let out a grunt of frustration. "Men! You just don't understand!"

"Because you women never explain...anything," said Kovarin through his chuckling.

Onjono sat down on a fat sofa laughing helplessly.

Teeha was even more disgusted over the fact that she noticed the Tailor and the Armorer were both getting a good laugh as well. She let out another disgusted grunt and left the apartment in a huff.

After most of the laughing had subsided, Kovarin sat down next to Onjono. "Uncle, are you going to suffer...a little at home...for this?"

"Oh, absolutely! She'll forgive me...sooner or later... probably later than sooner...but it's worth it...for the laugh I got out of it."

Kovarin got serious. "Would you like...something a little more honest to tell those...its?"

"Something honest would be better...not much, but it would be better - in the long run."

"Tell them that I will *not* be dictated to, as far as how many children or how many times I am allowed to have relations with the woman that is to be my life companion…my wife. If they're ready to get their heads out of the clouds, stop dictating terms and listen…I'll have another discussion with them. Until then… whichever one you're talking to…the answer is a very loud, no."

"They won't like that."

"I didn't like what they said to me…and how they said it. If you're talking romance…you don't do it in a business manner. You do it with a softer and more civil tongue."

The two men sat there staring at each other, contemplating the discussion that had just taken place. Their cogitations were interrupted by another knock on the door.

Kovarin grunted in despair. "Enter!"

Aj came walking in. "The Flag Makers are here to get your approval, Supreme Commander."

"My…approval of what?"

"Your banner, Supreme Commander."

Kovarin looked at Onjono in a questioning manner. "My… banner?"

"Oh, yes," said Onjono. "You have to have a banner… to show at all of the functions that you attend…and at your headquarters."

"Oh! All right, bring it in…let's take a look at it."

Aj turned and signaled someone who was standing outside the front door. A very small, frail looking, gray-haired man, with a big smile on his face came walking in. Behind him came two younger men who held the flag up in front of Kovarin for him to see. All four edges of the flag had the stripes of the High Country flag on them - one gray stripe, one blue-gray stripe and one brown stripe. Most of the rest of the flag was black. In the center of the elongated piece of cloth, was Kovarin's family *crest*, very meticulously embroidered in silver and black. It appeared to be a perfect circle with all of the symbols and pictograms in their proper place.

Kovarin stared at it for several moments. "Very… accurately…and very tastefully done. Your work is…remarkable."

The old man cackled with glee. "Thank you, Supreme Commander. We always aim to please. If you like, I can have several more of these made up…in a jiffy…as many as you please."

"I…don't know how many I'll need…yet."

"At least four," said Onjono.

"Oh?"

"Yes, one for your home, one for your headquarters office and two that you travel with. A second one is always handy, on an inspection trip…in case one gets damaged."

"Okay," said Kovarin with a smile. "Sounds good. Four it is…for the moment."

The old man waved at his two apprentices. "This one will be set up for your Change of Command ceremony. We'll start work on the others immediately."

Kovarin gave him a warm smile. "Outstanding."

With that, the Flag Makers and Onjono departed.

Aj stood at the door. "It there anything else that you need, this evening, Supreme Commander?"

Kovarin shook his head. "Nothing I can think of at this time, Commander."

"I'll stop by in the morning, to pick you up for the ceremony."

They gave each other a polite bow and Aj departed.

The Armorer had come back in. "Can we get back to sizing now, Supreme Commander?"

Kovarin sighed. "Yes, I suppose that we must get everything exactly as it should be…for the ceremony. It'd be a shame to have something go wrong…on, what is so far, the most important days of my life."

The next morning, Aj came in while Kovarin was having breakfast. He was ready to escort Kovarin to the ceremony. Kovarin had to wear the Wing Commander's uniform that he had received earlier. He could not wear the Supreme Commander's uniform until Dozzbin had been officially relieved of command.

First, they headed for the cliffs over the hatchling canyon. Kovarin was eager to greet Diamond and make sure that everything was still all right with the big beast. Diamond seemed content to sit in the morning sun (on the highest perch) and sun himself with his wings spread out completely. He did seem glad to see Kovarin (especially after he got a big glob of *treat* smeared on the front of his beak).

Kovarin was informed, at that time, by Shondark that he would soon be riding Diamond in the air. The training would start the next day, because after the banquet, he might be too intoxicated to do any aerial moves, without injuring someone.

Aj was able to check on Dastardly at the same time. The big blue-gray dragon got a smear of *treat* as well.

They went to the banquet hall. Most of the drapes and decorations were brown. This was for the out-going Commander. As soon as the ceremonies were ended, Kovarin could see that they had all kinds of banners and decorations (in black) that would be unfurled for the new Commander.

The dignitaries started filing in. All fifteen of the Supreme Tribunal entered. All fifteen of the Supreme Judges were ushered in. Numerous priests from the different Temples, that were scattered all over High Country, entered. All six of the Battle Division Commanders were present. There were over forty members of the Senate that were in attendance. The three Ringmasters, and Master Flying Trainer, Shondark had their own special places in the hall. Onjono was one of the special guests along with Teeha. Then there were three of the "possible" brides: Vaya, whose relatives were in the Senate, Teevasha whose father owned the winery and the little scamp Jeendala (who Kovarin still believed that she could not possibly be over ten years old). Last but not least, Dozzbin and Kovarin.

A High Priest from the local Temple came out and started the ceremony. The first thing he wanted was the testimonial from the Ringmasters that Diamond was the largest dragon, currently in the land. They had to testify that he was the largest and had been the dominant one in a battle with any and all other male dragons. After receiving satisfaction from the witnesses of the battle for dominance, the priest blessed and anointed Kovarin and had satisfied his part of the ceremony.

The Military went through their ritual of rolling up the outbound Commander's flag and unfurling the inbound Commander's flag. Then came the changing of the uniform. Kovarin received the breastplate and helmet of the Supreme Commander, while Dozzbin was given a breastplate and helmet of a Battle Division Commander. When asked which Division Dozzbin wished to be the Commander of, he stated that he had not made up his mind yet. He was given an ultimatum of five days to give his final decision.

Now the Supreme Tribunal member, Tremyath stepped up along with the Supreme Justice. They administered the "Oath of Office" for Kovarin.

Now, a toast. Everyone (except Dozzbin) took a healthy swig of the wine. Dozzbin just wet his lips.

Now Kovarin was the Supreme Commander and Dozzbin was an unassigned Battle Division Commander.

Now the party!

Kovarin and Dozzbin were seated side-by-side. Neither one of them was too happy with this arrangement.

Dozzbin did not wait, he picked up a large piece of meat

and took a rather large bite.

Kovarin leaned over to Dozzbin: "Just think, if any of the other nine eggs that I had, had hatched…someone else would have gotten that egg that Diamond hatched from."

Dozzbin choked on a hunk of meat he had and spit some of it across the table as he hacked up another piece from his windpipe. He turned and glared at Kovarin, partially in fear, partially in hate. Kovarin simply smiled back.

'Yes, I know what happened, you nefarious dastard,' thought Kovarin. 'I just haven't thought of the best way or the time to expose you.'

After some eating and drinking, Kovarin ended up having to dance with those "Prissy Little Its" from the other banquet.

Vaya looked at him with her nose a little out of joint as they went through the motions. "Ten children? Are you serious? You can't be!"

"Why not?"

"It…it's not practical. I would spend so much time… with child and child bearing and child rearing…I can't imagine spending that much time doing that."

"That's what a mother does….isn't it? She loves and cares for her children. Why should you be any different?"

"But…*ten*?"

"Yes," he said with a big smile. "I think that's a good number. It represents the fact that Diamond was my tenth egg."

Vaya groaned.

Jeendala had to get her dancing time in. She seemed a little awkward and not very proficient at dancing. "I know that you're just joking about ten children…"

"No, I'm not," he said with as much seriousness as he could muster. "I see no reason for there to be only one or two children."

"No," she said. "I know you and I can tell you're joking."

"You don't know me at all then. I don't joke about things like that."

She finished the dance with a rather pained look on her face.

Teevasha did her best to show even more of her substantial cleavage than she had before. "You'd have to use a lot of Daddy's wine to get me drunk enough for five…maybe six children. You couldn't possibly get me to bear ten of them."

He gave her a sinister smile. "I wouldn't worry about whether you were drunk or sober…there would be ten children… no matter what." He made a special effort to stare directly in her eyes and avoid her cleavage after making that remark.

She departed from the dance floor looking just as uncomfortable as the other two girls.

The last dance that Kovarin had was with his Aunt Teeha. That dance was very enjoyable and civil.

After the banquet was over, Aj escorted Kovarin back to

his quarters.

"You didn't get as drunk as I thought you would," said Aj looking a little perplexed.

"I remember that I have an appointment with Shondark… first thing in the morning. I will finally get to fly…on Diamond. You have no idea how much I've been looking forward to that."

"I'm a Dragonrider as well, Supreme Commander." He chuckled. "Yes, I *do* know," he said with a big smile.

Kovarin was told that the next ten days would be very busy. He would spend a lot of time with Shondark and Diamond. His first flight was somewhat nerve wracking. He had to use every part of his memory of what he had been taught in order to keep Diamond flying level and even, or steering him in any direction or changing his altitude.

"Don't yank on the reins, just give him a hint. Say what you want, at first, and see if he responds. If he doesn't then you use the reins and say the order - loud! Don't push him too hard on the first day. He's not used to being airborne for long lengths of time…yet. When you're ready to land, just let the reins go limp. He will head back to his dominant perch position by himself. Make sure that you reward him when he lands…otherwise you may have a difficult time ever getting him up there again."

When Diamond did land, Kovarin noticed that the dragon was panting very heavily. After just a few moments on the ground, his breathing went back to normal, though. Kovarin made mental note to see if this was normal. According to Shondark, it was. They breathe heavily when they are exerting themselves. When they come to rest, they breathe normally.

After landing, he unhooked himself from the saddle, went to Diamond's head and smeared a big glob of *treat* on his big blunt nose. He stood there rubbing Diamond's head as the dragon licked the goo slowly from his beak.

Shondark walked up. "I complement you on your first flight. You paid attention to detail, and I didn't see any head jerking or hear him growl at you."

"Why would he growl at me?"

"He would complain if you jerked on the reins…more from pain than anger."

Diamond started moving his head a little and was pushing Kovarin. "What…what's he doing?"

Shondark snickered. "Hold out your right hand in front of his nose."

"What for?"

"Do it!"

Kovarin scoffed and held his hand up. Diamond started licking his hand. "What…what's this for?"

Again Shondark snickered. "You've got *treat* all over your hand and he can smell it. Let him have it and he'll stop pushing you."

Kovarin looked at Shondark a little surprised. "That

tongue *is* rough. No wonder Namanti was complaining about it.
He was licking more than her hand…a *lot* more."

"Serves her right," said Shondark with a malicious grin on
his face.

"So now what?"

"After he's finished cleaning your hand, we'll let him rest.
We'll try another flight after midday."

They heard a loud bellowing going on to the left of
Diamond's perch. Diamond's flares spread out to their full glory
for a moment. When he saw that it was two other males bellowing
at each other, he let his flares relax and just watched.

Shondark scoffed. "Glutton and Bloodletter - Those two
are always bellyaching at each other."

"Aren't they the two forty-eights?"

"Right. Number three and four…behind Diamond and
Thunder."

"Uh…speaking of which…where is Thunder?"

"Dozzbin is still upset over his loss of rank. He took
Thunder out to fly around the countryside, while he pouts and
decides which Division he wants. He'll probably be back…some
time tomorrow…or the next day."

Diamond had finished cleaning Kovarin's hand. Now he
was lackadaisically licking his chops, looking for the taste of any
more *treat* on his carapace beak.

Shondark stretched. "Let's go get some lunch."

"Good idea."

They went to a small tavern, where the owner fawned all over the new Supreme Commander. He could not do enough for them and was getting a little irritating by the time lunch was over. They both left shaking their heads and chuckling.

Once back at Diamond's roosting spot, they noticed that Glutton and Bloodletter were still snarling at each other. Glutton, however, did always seem to have the dominant position.

As Kovarin got back up on the saddle, Diamond looked back at him and there was a rumbling that came from deep in his chest.

"I felt...a vibration," said Kovarin wide-eyed.

Shondark smiled. "He's just recognizing that it's you."

Kovarin went through the ritual of buckling himself in to the saddle. "Are all of these clasps necessary?"

"Oh, yes," said Shondark with a grin. "This morning, all you did was baby him. You took small turns and mostly level flying. If you ever make a hard sharp turn...you'll see just what all those safety belts are for."

"Should I try a few sharp turns?"

"Do what you think you are ready for. Don't push yourself...or him."

'Sound advice,' thought Kovarin. He took hold of the reins and let them hang loose. "Up!" he shouted.

Diamond responded by spreading his wings and flapping

hard as he got his tonnage off of the ground.

Kovarin gave him the "Up" order several more times. He continued gaining altitude, until he was given the order: "Level". He held his wings out and just soared on the wind. The adrenalin was coursing throughout Kovarin's body and he just let the thrill of the flight take over. He gave an occasional bank to the left or right and felt like he did not want to ever go back down. He knew he would, because Diamond was still not a very experienced flyer.

All of a sudden, Diamond banked hard to his right and was flapping his wings furiously. Kovarin now got a first-hand demonstration as to why the safety harness and all those buckles were necessary. He wasn't sure what to do and remembered that, no matter what, you don't jerk on the reins.

He saw what Diamond was after, however, he couldn't understand why…yet. There was a big brown dragon flying along, with the two big blue-grays, Glutton and Bloodletter flying close behind. The two big males were flaring and snarling at each other as they flew along behind the brown. Diamond ignored the two combatants, as he passed them, and went straight for the brown.

'Oh great,' thought Kovarin. 'A fight for dominance and I'm right in the middle of it…shackled onto this saddle.'

He saw Diamond's front legs spread out wide as the big black came down on top of the brown and his legs were clamped around the other dragon. He had not slammed onto the brown the way he had when he hit Thunder. He just clamped on. Their descent was rather rapid and Diamond would not let go of the other dragon.

Then Kovarin noticed - the brown had no neck flares. The brown was a female. He closed his eyes and pursed his lips. Three dominant, breeding males chasing after a female that was large enough for breeding...here at hatching headquarters. The natural urge had taken over. Kovarin could do nothing but ride it out.

The landing was not as hard as he thought it would be. Diamond still had his legs clamped around the female. As soon as they were on the ground, he started licking her neck. She responded with growls. After a few more growls, licks and a few odd movements Kovarin realized that this was definitely a mating ritual.

After several moments of movement, Diamond flared at Glutton and Bloodletter. They were pacing around angrily growling at Diamond. Diamond lay there panting for a few moments and then started breathing normally. Glutton was a little ways off, in front of Diamond and the brown, complaining over the fact that Diamond had gotten there first. Bloodletter was off to the right voicing his disapproval as well. Kovarin had not noticed the two of them landing. They now just paced around complaining.

The one that was really complaining was the female. Diamond had finished doing his business and was still laying on top of her. She was struggling to get out from under.

Kovarin decided to try and help her. "Up, up, up!"

Diamond responded by loosening his grip on the female and standing. She stopped her growling and pulled herself free. Glutton and Bloodletter started moving closer...until Diamond blossomed his flares and bellowed at them. Bloodletter folded his flares back, turned and went airborne. As he flapped his wings, he stirred up a huge amount of dust. Glutton stopped but did not fold his flares. Diamond bellowed again and started advancing in a menacing manner. Glutton got the message, turned and flew off, still growling. Again there was an enormous cloud of dust raised as he flapped his wings to get airborne.

Diamond looked around for any other opponents. When he saw none, he flopped down on his stomach. The big brown was laying on her stomach as well. She did not seem to be in a hurry to go anywhere now.

Kovarin let out a long sigh of relief…and then got startled.

"A very good afternoon to you, Supreme Commander."

He looked off to his left. A somewhat tall man, dressed in brown, with long brown hair was approaching. The man seemed friendly and was smiling, so Kovarin responded. "Uh…good…afternoon, Sir."

"I see that your dragon is not one to waste time. He got down to business…rather quickly."

"Yes, he did…uh…may I know your name…Sir?"

He came closer with his hand out in friendship. "I am Dragonholder Cwal. That brown female over there is my charge: Attitude…and she now has the honor of being the first female to breed with your famous black."

"Yes, I guess so." He looked around helplessly. "I wonder if he wants to do any more flying today."

Cwal laughed out loud. "I'm afraid not. We're going to

have to walk both of them back to the canyon. Neither one has enough left in them to fly now."

Kovarin sighed and started unbuckling himself from the saddle.

"Here let me give you a hand with that, Supreme Commander," said Cwal.

"Thank you…Dragonholder." He loosened and unbuckled all of the straps and dismounted. "You…called her…Attitude?"

Cwal chuckled. "Yes…from the way she acted when she was a hatchling. She never thought that I fed her fast enough and she always seemed to want more oil on her skin. Now, she doesn't like mating."

Kovarin shrugged. "There are a lot of females like that… not just dragons."

Cwal went over to Attitude. He gave her a few coaxing nudges on the side of her head. "Up…up, up!" She snarled and got to her feet.

Kovarin decided to try the same method. Diamond growled at him. He took out his pouch of *treat* and spread a finger full of it onto Diamond's nose. Diamond got up on slightly wobbly legs. Kovarin smeared some more on the blunt nose and started leading him back to the canyon.

Cwal came up. "I seem to have forgotten my pouch. Could I get some *treat* from you…for a loaner?"

Kovarin held the pouch open while Cwal got some on his hand. He went over to Attitude and smeared it on the left side of her beak. She started licking the stuff off.

Cwal turned back to Kovarin. "It's quite a ways back… might as well get started."

Kovarin smiled back. He let Cwal "semi-lead" the way, because he did not have a clue where he was or how far away the canyon was. He made another one of his mental notes that he was going to have to pay a little more attention to the surrounding area…on each of Diamond's next flights.

They walked for quite a while. Having a quiet conversation was a little difficult seeing as how they had to keep a little distance between them because of the size of their dragons. He learned that Attitude was currently the tenth largest and fourth oldest breeding female of the twenty-two females at present. She did not have any siblings among the other breeders, like Diamond. Her parents were both deceased, so there was very little problem with these two mating. She had come up with many eggs in her sixteen years of breeding, however, never another breeder.

Cwal had also been prepared for a long walk, because he knew that Attitude was close to her time of going into heat. He said he was not quite sure how soon it was going to be so he had kept a canteen with him…just in case. It came in handy.

Off in the distance, Kovarin heard the roaring of two males, challenging each other. He saw a brown and a blue-gray fly up above the rise as they rammed into each other and attempted to out maneuver each other. The blue-gray was knocked sideways and plummeted down. The brown hovered for a few moments bellowing at the fallen rival.

Now Kovarin had a good idea of which way to go and approximately how far. As they finally came up on the canyon, he realized that they were on the south side, where the smaller males had their roosting places. When Diamond saw where he was he snarled. Kovarin let go of his jaw ring and he took off, heading for his roost on the north side. As soon as he got to his perch, he looked around, showed his flares to the other males, roared and then flopped down for a nap.

Cwal let out a heave of relief. "It's been a pleasant, albeit a *long* walk, and I'll see you around. Right now, I have to take her to a hatching cavern…for some rest and…see how many eggs we get."

"I'd like to know…how many myself…if you would be so kind."

"I'll be sure and get a message to you."

They parted. Cwal had to go east to his destination.

Kovarin had to walk all the way around the upper rim of the canyon to get to his apartments. On his way around he saw Shondark over there checking on Diamond. Chul, Vollost and Yoll were working on unsaddling Diamond. 'They probably wanted me in on that task,' thought Kovarin. 'Oh well, can't be helped. They're almost done…and I'm tired.' He continued on. He walked past several of the breeding females that were on the west end of the canyon rim. A few of them sniffed at him. Other than that they seemed disinterested.

He finally made it to Diamond. The big beast was sleeping soundly with his flares and wings held tightly up against his body.

Shondark looked at Kovarin with a bit of a mocking look on his face. "Did you have a nice walk, Supreme Commander?"

"No, Master Trainer," he cleared his dry throat. "It was long...and dry...and Cwal had just so much water. I need something to wet my throat...and then I'm going to bed."

"Yes, I don't doubt that. After Diamond had his little... *rendezvous*...I'm not surprised at yours, and his, exhaustion. Forget about the training session, tomorrow morning. He won't be in any condition to do it then. He's physically drained from the mating and the long walk. Wait until tomorrow after midday for the next flight."

Kovarin sighed. "I'll be more than happy to wait." He took another look at Diamond. "Everything okay here?"

Shondark bowed his head and smiled. "Yes, Supreme Commander, all is well. You may retire to your apartments."

Kovarin gave him a polite bow and stumbled on to home, somewhat relieved that he did not have to get up early.

15

Kovarin walked into his apartment on some very sore feet. He sat down on the nearest chair. He was tired from the walk, however, he was still exhilarated over the ride of his life. Diamond had taken his inaugural flight, outdoors, and Kovarin had been in the saddle steering him with, what seemed, great ease…until an unforeseen incident occurred. If Diamond had not been a breeder, someone might be a little upset. Kovarin wondered if the entire situation had been somehow set up by the Dragonhandler Cwal.

A knock on the door.

"Enter!"

The door was slowly opened and there stood Namanti. "My, you sound so different…after just a little while as a bigwig. Has anything else changed?"

He sat there and chuckled. "Yes, something else did change: I was able to fly on Diamond and he was able to breed. This all happened in the first day…since…Commander and flyer."

She walked in slowly looking wide-eyed around at his new, big apartment. "He…got to breed?"

"I took him out for a flight and before I realized what was

going on, a female, in heat, was in the area and he chased her down. He beat two other males to the female and in a few days, I'll find out how many eggs are here from his first mating."

"Nice place you got for yourself."

"It *is* nice…and mine…until a fifty-six comes along."

"If a fifty-six *ever* comes along." She got an evil grin on her face. "Speaking of Ex-Commanders, what did you say to the Tribunal and the High Command about Dozzbin?"

He closed his eyes and grunted as if he had been hit. "I… haven't…uh…said anything…yet."

Her jaw dropped. "WHAT?" She threw her arms out. "How long are you gonna…let him get away with it?"

"I…just haven't…figured out the best way…to do it." He cleared his throat nervously.

Her arms flopped down to her sides. She closed her eyes and shook her head while making a few grunts of disgust. She opened her eyes and huffed at him.

"I don't want him to get away with it…I just…am trying to figure out the best way, and time, to commit to the accusation."

She heaved a deep sigh. "Okay…so…you're going to wait." She smiled and held her arms out. "As long as I'm here, do you mind if I look around?"

He smiled at her. "Why not?"

She looked around and lost her smile. "Uh…where's…the bed…or any of the other…necessary?"

He raised his eyebrows. "In...the bedroom."

She got a huge smile on her face. "You...you've got more than one room...here?"

He placed his fists on his hips and looked abashed. "I *am* the Supreme Commander. I *do* get certain...special accommodations commensurate with the rank."

"How...how many rooms...do you get...have here?"

"This is the main room. There's a bedroom. There's a dressing room. There's a kitchen. There's a...uh...indoor outhouse." He cleared his throat. "There's a dining room. There's an office. There's also a couple of spare bedrooms...just in case I have some...visitor...who is invited to spend the night."

She was looking around in wonder, as if not sure what to do next.

"Go ahead," he said with a big smile.

She ran around the place looking in each room, giggling as she explored. She came back and walked up to him with a sexy swagger. "I see that you have some armor...and suits...in *your* bedroom. I don't see any women's clothing...and your *crest* is still hanging on the wall...haven't you chosen a wife yet?"

His shoulders sagged. "No."

"So no one should mind if I visit you...occasionally."

He smiled back. "No one at all who could complain."

He still woke up early the next morning. He started thinking about some of the training that was originally scheduled for today, however, might be changed drastically because of what happened yesterday. He stretched and yawned with a loud moan. Then he remembered that Namanti had asked to stay in one of the guest rooms for the night. There were a few people who had been looking for her because they wanted to drop some of their responsibilities on her. If they could not find her, they would have to get off their duffs and do the jobs themselves…as they were supposed to do originally.

He threw his robe on, went to the guest room and knocked lightly on the door. There was no response. He slowly opened the door. He looked at Namanti lying on the furs. She was on her back with her right arm up over her head and the left down by her side. Her big red mane of hair was covering a large portion of her face. She was still wearing that colorful blue, green and orange dress. He crept in quietly, reached down and lightly brushed the hair off of her face. She did not stir. He stared at her face for several moments.

He stretched again and worked some of the kinks out. He went around to the other side and stared at her face again. Bodily needs took over his contemplations and he headed for his indoor-outhouse. He relieved himself in the "hole". With that crisis taken care of he went back to the bedroom. He made his decision. He went to the wall and stared at his *crest* for several moments. He sighed and took it down from the hook on the wall, where it had been waiting…for a decision. He went back to her. He reached down and lightly picked up Namanti's head. He slipped the golden chain around her neck, carefully let her head back down and straightened the big medallion on her chest. He leaned down and kissed her on her forehead. He stood there staring at her with a smile on his face. He sighed. "The moment of truth," he whispered softly. He lightly took hold of her lower jaw and shook her a little.

It took several shakes before she finally started to wake up. She opened her eyes and sniffed. She saw him and smiled. She stretched, yawned and made one of those grunting noises that usually comes with just waking up.

After she closed her mouth and smiled at him again, he kissed her. She returned the kiss. After he leaned back he smiled at her. "Look down, my precious one."

She looked confused for a moment, raised her eyebrows and looked down at her body…and finally noticed his *crest* on her chest. She gasped in horror and tried to grab for it and take it off. He immediately hugged her so that she could not remove it.

She was almost panic stricken. "I don't know…how it got there! I didn't do it! I didn't touch it! Oh, by all that's holy, I didn't touch it! I wouldn't…!"

He fell on the furs with her. Holding her body and arms trapped against him with his left arm, he placed his right hand tightly over her mouth. "I know you didn't…I did it."

The look in her eyes changed from panic and terror to panic and confusion.

"I put it there…on purpose."

The look in her eyes was still confusion. Then she started

looking a little desperate and her body started jerking. He realized that he was covering her nose as well. He pulled his hand away from her face as she noisily sucked in a full large lung full or air.

She panted several times and gave him a very angry and confused look. "You...you put it there?"

"On purpose," he said as tenderly as he could.

"Are you...CRAZY?" No more confusion on her face, just anger.

"What...do you...mean?"

"What did you want? Did you just wanna see what it looked like, hanging down there on someone...just to see it being worn?"

"No...I...!"

She started wriggling, trying to get out of his grasp. "Let me up, I don't like these kind of jokes!" She seemed to be getting even angrier.

He put both arms around her, squeezed a little tighter and moved his right leg so that he was on top of and pinning her down. "I put it there on purpose, because I want it there and I want it to stay there," he said adamantly.

Her face showed desperation again. Her eyes and mouth were wide open. She spoke in a croaking manner. "Get off! You're crushing me!"

He huffed and quickly rolled so that she was on top, however, he did not let go of his bear-hug on her. "Sorry about that," he said quickly as he grimaced. "But I want you to be the one…who wears my *crest*…for the rest of *our* lives."

She leaned her head back. She still had a look of anger and confusion in her eyes. She panted several times before she shook her head. "You're crazy. No one wants to marry me!" Her voice trailed off and she laid her head on his chest and cleared her throat nervously. "I'm just a nothing…who takes care of…whatever someone else doesn't want to do," she said quietly.

"I do," he said flatly. "I want you and I can't think of anyone else that I could possibly want…sharing my life."

She lifted her head back up. "No one will accept me."

"They'll have to. You will be the wife…of the Supreme Commander of the War Forces."

She flopped her head back down. "Big deal! They still won't like it. They'll talk about me…and you behind our backs. Both of us will be a prime subject for all kinds of jokes."

"I'm not letting go of you, until you agree to keep my *crest*."

She lifted her head back up. "Well, then…we're gonna be here for a long, long, *long,* time, mister. …and I've gotta use your special indoor-outhouse…or at least your chamber pot. Now, are you gonna let me go and…let me take this thing off?"

He sighed. "Look…my Uncle Onjono gave me some advice about whom I choose to marry. You're the only one who fits the list."

She gave him a disgusted look. "He told you to marry a

nothing?" She clenched her eyes and lips. "A low life nothing?" She looked off to the side. "You don't marry someone like me unless…you're nothing as well. You're not nothing, you're the top man in the Dragon Forces."

"He told me three things…"

"Yeah…what are the other two?"

He grunted in disgust. "Stop talking and listen! He told me that I should look to someone that I like and would want to care for…for the rest of my life."

Her expression went from a disgusted stare to surprised joy. "You would…want to…take care of…me…forever?"

"You fit that bill a whole lot better than any of those 'Its' that I came across at that banquet."

She giggled. "Go on."

"Second, he said that I should find someone who has helped me."

"WHAT? I give you an occasional piece of paper or… some supplies. That's what I'm paid to do! What's so great about that?"

"That's not what I'm talking about."

"Well, then…what?"

He closed his eyes and growled. "Do you remember the temperature rods? If you hadn't brought me those good ones… Diamond would've been cooked as well. When you gave me those rods, you saved Diamond's life…and mine."

She lay there looking thoughtful for a few moments. "I… guess…I did…do something…really worthwhile…for you."

"Yes."

She pursed her lips. "So…what's the other thing?"

"That one is very important…to a Dragonman! He told me to find someone that Diamond approves of."

She clenched her eyes in total disgust. "You mean…I gotta let that big beast…keep on licking me…for the rest of my life?"

"It…might come to that."

She sighed and laid her head back down on him. She spoke softly: "You…really want to…take care…of *me*…for the rest of my life?"

"Yes," he said tenderly.

She raised her head back up and showed him her clenched teeth. "Then let go of me! I gotta use the chamber pot! If this is gonna be my permanent bed as well, I'd rather pee in the pot than on the furs!"

He laughed helplessly as he finally released his grip. She crawled off of him, off of the bed, found the chamber pot, squatted on it and sighed with relief as she emptied her bladder. She looked at him and sighed again. "You need this thing?"

"I already took care of it. I went to the *other* room."

She snickered. She put her arms on the edge of the bed and rested her chin on her arms. "You're still crazy…and other folks are still gonna…talk behind our backs."

He rolled over on his stomach and turned to where their faces were very close. "They'll think differently of you...when we lower the axe on Dozzbin."

"You think maybe...they will?"

He smiled. "I'm sure."

"You're sure...you want me to keep the *crest*. You're sure that you want me...to be your wife."

He put his hand behind the back of her head, pulled her close and gave her a long loving kiss. He pressed his forehead against hers. "I'm *very* sure."

She put her hands on the sides of his face. She sighed. "Dear Husband, what's for breakfast?"

He chuckled. He cleared his throat. "There's some fruit preserves in the larder. That's the best I can do...for right now."

She smiled, got up and headed for the kitchen.

He got up, and did a little scratching. He headed for the kitchen.

She had gone through the kitchen and was searching the larder for what she wanted.

He saw the confusion on her face. "Any problem?"

She scratched her head. "Where's...the fruit?"

"It's in those dark jars...on the shelves...to your left."

She checked the jars and started reading the labels. She picked the one that looked the best to her. She turned to him.

"Which one did you want?"

"We'll share one," he said.

She opened her mouth to say something.

"There's far too much, in any one of those jars, for one person."

She looked at the big jar, shrugged and headed out of the larder. "Got some bowls?"

He chuckled. "In that big closet over there."

She looked where he was pointing. She walked over opened the door and gasped in surprise. "Plates, cups, mugs, bowls and…everything you need."

They had each had three mouthfuls of the fruit when she started looking closely at the *crest*. She lowered her head and looked at him out from under her eyebrows, trying to look coy and innocent. She spoke in a tiny voice. "Do you mind…if I take it off for a few moments…to get a better look at it? I promise that I'll put it right back on." She smiled.

"Go ahead, my Love."

She got another spoonful of fruit, shoved it in her mouth and took the *crest* off while she was chewing. She ran her fingers over the different words and emblems on the front side. She swallowed and turned it over. She read what was on the back and got a concerned look on her face. "The back here…uh…it has the names of your parents…and grand…parents."

"Yes."

"Uh…so…if there's…any sons…of ours…their *crests*… should have the same…information on them…Right?"

"Of course."

She looked a little scared. "I…don't know…if you want the name of my…father…on this thing."

"What…do you mean?"

She sighed and put the gold chain around her neck again. "I'm the daughter of a…criminal. Do you really want that on…a crest that any son of ours will have?"

Kovarin shook his head. "Uh…you say that you're…the offspring of a criminal. Who is he?"

She sighed. "My mother…told me what happened. He…and my mother were starving. They couldn't find any job anywhere. He tried to be a Dragonman Candidate but…failed miserably. The two of them tried…jobs just about…anywhere. Nothing worked. Then he…tried to rob someone and…killed the man." She sighed. "They hung him." She looked off to the side. "Five months later…I was born. When I turned seven years old… Momma told me what happened."

"How was she able to…support you…and her?"

She cleared her throat. "She was able to…use her widow status and…get a job in the main offices of the Dragon Force. I kinda grew up…under her desk. Do you still want me?"

"I'm the Supreme Commander. I've made my decision. I want you."

"Did your mother…teach you…how to do the job?"

"Yeah."

"Where is she now?"

"You remember that flood…two years ago? My mother… disappeared…during that flood. I didn't have anyone or anything. I had to survive…so…I took up where she left off."

He sat back in his chair.

She walked up to him and straddled his left leg. "I didn't have anybody to take care of me. I did the only thing…I knew how to do. I didn't have any place to go." She took his face in her hands and looked at him fearfully. "Are you…changing your mind?"

He threw his arms around her and hugged her close. "NO! I said that I wanted to take care of you…love you…keep you safe. I mean it…even more…now, than I did a few minutes ago."

"So…we're still…husband…and…" She got a big grin again. "…wife?"

He stared into those big blue eyes. "Absolutely," he said quietly and emphatically. He had wanted to take care of her anyway. He had wanted to keep her permanently and love her. Now, since he knew her history, he was appalled at the idea of sending her back to those hallways to work herself to death, ever again.

She returned the hug. She hugged him as hard as she could. They sat there in the embrace for quite a while. He heard her sniffling a little. He pulled back and looked into her puffy eyes.

"You've…You're crying?"

"This is happiness. I hated…having to put up with…all those things that…some of them wanted me to do." She sniffed hard. "Now, I don't have to do them…anymore." She kissed and hugged him close again.

There was a knock on the door. She looked at him in panic. She got up and ran to the bedroom.

He waited until he did not hear her running anymore. He headed for the main entrance. "Enter!"

The door opened and Aj walked in. "Good morning, Supreme Commander. I hope you had a good night's rest."

Kovarin looked thoughtful for a moment. "It *was* a good night."

Aj looked a little confused at the enigmatic statement. Then he saw Namanti coming out of the bedroom. He smiled. He started to say something and suddenly noticed that Namanti was wearing Kovarin's *crest*. His expression turned to shock and he looked back at Kovarin confused. "Is she…uh…wearing… your…"

"Yes, she is, Commander. I put it on her. I plan for it to stay there."

Namanti walked up to Kovarin and put her arm around his waist. He responded by putting his arm around her shoulder.

She smiled at Aj. "Aren't you going to congratulate us,

Commander?"

"I…uh…yes…certainly…uh…congratulations to you… both of you on this wonderful occasion." He swallowed hard and looked even more confused. "Supreme Commander, does anyone else…know about this?"

Both Kovarin and Namanti smiled.

"Not yet, Commander," said Namanti with a mischievous grin.

Aj chuckled nervously. He cleared his throat several times before he could talk again. "It looks as if your uncle, Commander Onjono, has won the pool."

Kovarin raised his eyebrows. "Pool? What pool?"

Aj cleared his throat. "It seems…that there was a pool… going around. We were taking…bets on…who you'd…give your *crest* to. I bet on…Teevasha. Your uncle…bet that you would marry someone…other than *any* of those ten girls that you…met at the banquet." He cleared his throat again and gave them a weak smile.

Kovarin smirked. "My uncle had some inside information. He also gave me some very good advice. As a result of his advice… none of those girls could meet the standards of the one I chose." He looked down at Namanti and smiled.

"Yes…Supreme Commander. Is…there anything that I can…do for you…at this time?"

"Yes, you can arrange for the Sanctification and Confirmation Ceremony of our marriage union at the temple."

Aj smiled. "I can do that. Oh, I also was asked to inform you…that Dozzbin has not made up his mind…which command he wants…yet."

Kovarin smiled. "In a little while…I don't think that's going to be a problem."

Namanti giggled.

Aj stood there even more confused. "Not…a…problem?"

"No, Commander," said Kovarin with an evil grin. "For now, remember…the temple?"

Aj smiled. "Yes…the temple…right away, Supreme Commander." He saluted, spun on his heel and departed.

After the door was closed, Namanti looked up at Kovarin. "When are you gonna expose that…criminal?"

He spoke hesitatingly: "I'm trying to think of the best way…the best time…and to whom." He looked worried. 'And how to get more evidence,' he thought.

She grunted in disgust. "I hope you don't wait too long."

16

Namanti got herself as presentable as possible. It was a little difficult seeing as how she had some very bad taste in clothing, either in color or design. He called on one of the tailors to, quickly, get something for her that was more appropriate for a wedding. Since it was going to take several turns to notify all those who wished to attend the sanctification and confirmation ceremony, the dress was ready before all of the plans were finalized.

They headed to the Temple for the administration of the marriage ritual.

It was late afternoon and again the training session with Diamond had to be postponed. Kovarin had been worried about any feeding, however, Shondark assured him that since Diamond was finished growing, he would only eat once every three or four days…whenever *he* felt hungry.

Of the ten "Prissy Little Its" only four attended: Vaya, Natiski, Imathaka and Teevasha. Three were there because of the status of their fathers - Senators, Tribunal members and Judges. The fourth was there because her father was catering all of the alcoholic beverages that were being served at the function. The girls were not pleased. Kovarin did not care.

There was a lot of gossiping going on in regards to who Namanti was. It was buzzing all over the sanctuary that she was definitely one of the low paid workers from the hatching halls.

Namanti looked up at Kovarin. She whispered to him. "What are you going to tell those prospective girls that you turned down?"

He looked at her. "I'll tell them that I took a step *up* in the world," he said with a malicious grin.

"What about their demands? What are you going to say as to how I wasn't so...picky?"

"I'll tell them that you don't mind having ten...or more children...if it comes to that. I'll also tell them that you will do things that they wouldn't dream of."

"Like what?"

He thought of the most perverted thing he could. He leaned down, got close to her ear and whispered very softly.

After he finished she looked up wide-eyed in shock and glared at him. "*That* will *never* happen...and don't you *dare* tell any of them that I'd ever consent to *that*...in any way, shape or form...or at any time!"

"I'll tell them that, only as a last resort...if they don't shut up."

She jabbed him in the ribs with her elbow and grimaced in pain. He was wearing the breastplate of his dress uniform, so the only thing that she accomplished was to nearly fracture her elbow. He chuckled while she rubbed her sore elbow and gave him a dirty look with her mouth clenched tight.

The dignitaries were all in place. Kovarin and Namanti walked up the steps and were standing in front of the huge alter. The Priests came out and started the ceremony. Three of the Priests looked at Namanti with complete confusion in their eyes. Two others would not even look at her. The High Priest, either did not know or care, about her status. He conducted the ritual with all of the consecrated respect it deserved.

Kovarin held Namanti in his arms and kissed her. He let her lean back and looked deep into her eyes. It was over. They were officially married. He sighed. The two of them turned away from the altar and he led her down the steps to the main sanctuary.

As he passed by them, Vaya, Natiski Imathaka and Teevasha all had their noses out of joint over not being chosen. By now they knew, from all of the murmuring and whispers going through the sanctuary that they had lost out to a low level office worker. How revolting! How impudent! How embarrassing! HOW?

According to the tradition, as soon as they got to the center of the sanctuary, Kovarin would go to one side and Namanti was to go to the other side. The guests would file by the newlyweds and give them the congratulations (and possibly a few gifts or tidbits of advice).

Kovarin smiled, shook hands (or returned a salute) and greeted each one who passed by. The first one was Battle Division 6 Commander, Brashtok. Why not - he was the Dragonman for Glutton...the third largest dragon currently in existence.

The other Battle Division Commanders each came by, in

order of the size of their specific dragon. After the salute, the handshake and the congratulations, from the last of the Battle Division Commanders, he now had to shake hands with other dignitaries that he was completely ignorant of their status or office. He tried to be polite as possible. Members of the Supreme Tribunal, the Senate and the High Court filed by. Kovarin felt that he was going to need to know a lot of these people, since he was now one of the elite upper-crust as well.

Shondark was one of the people who came by. "Congratulations, Supreme Commander. I won't judge why you picked her…but Diamond approves…of her…so I can't and won't argue with that. I'm also here to let you know that Yoll is out there keeping an eye on Diamond."

"Why…Yoll?"

"Because, of the four of us Trainers, Yoll and myself are the ones with female dragons. If we were to take Chul or Vollost's male dragons up there to Diamond's perch…the results could be disastrous…for their dragons. My dragon, Gray Bonnet, is afraid of Diamond, while Yoll's Flapper has a rather good rapport with Diamond. So…as inexperienced as Diamond is, we still need to watch him closely…for another ten days at least and Yoll and Flapper will cause the least amount of problems."

"You do a fantastic job, Master Trainer. You live up to your title admirably."

"You are most kind, Supreme Commander." He bowed his head and walked away for the next guest to talk to Kovarin.

Natiski came up to him to congratulate him (and, in a huff,

find out why she had not been chosen). "Why did you choose… that…person?"

Kovarin thought about the perverse thing that he had told Namanti. No, it was better to be nice. "She, like me, is in favor of ten…or more children."

Natiski gave him a look of distaste at the thought. She tried to smile as she walked away, with shock and disgust on her face, she silently voiced the word: "Ten?"

The reactions of Vaya, Imathaka and Teevasha were very similar.

A woman came up to congratulate him. Like many of the people here, he had no idea who she was…until she introduced herself. She was wearing a *crest* that looked somewhat familiar. She had long brown hair that was braided and hung down below her waist. She had on a brown outfit with a pin indicating that she was married to a Dragonman.

"Good afternoon to you, Supreme Commander," she said with a big smile. "I'm here to wish you all the best…in your marriage. I wish I could wish you the same in your rank, but my husband is very upset over it."

"Your…husband?"

"Yes, Dozzbin."

Kovarin was taken a little by surprise. "You're…the… wife of Dozzbin?"

"And mother of his two sons. I'm the Lady Chesesa."

"Oh." Kovarin was feeling a little uneasy. "Whe… where…is he right…now?"

She shook her head with a smile. "Oh, he's in the back of the room, somewhere, sulking. He wanted to be the Supreme Commander for the rest of his life. I told him that this could happen…without notice. He's just…having a problem accepting it."

"Yes, it's part of the life of a Dragonman. We know it from the beginning of training."

After shaking several hundred hands and being congratulated until he was tired of hearing the word, the entire room had paraded past him. Namanti had not had as many go past her, however, she was not too upset over that fact when she saw Kovarin rubbing his sore hands.

"So, husband…when are you gonna tell them?"

"Tell who, what?"

"About Dozzbin…and the cooked eggs?"

"I'm trying to figure out the right way and time and the right people to…"

She growled in disgust, turned around and hollered: "Everyone, I need your attention!"

Before Kovarin could do anything she walked away from him and made sure that she was clearly heard throughout the large room: "Ex-Supreme Commander Dozzbin is a traitor! He's responsible for cooking or destroying dragon eggs…and he's done it at least nine times!"

Kovarin looked up and stared off into space. "Or... someone could just open up their big mouth and blurt it out for everyone to hear," he said flatly. He sighed and looked around the room at gaping mouths and equally wide eyes.

The only one who did not have a gaping mouth and wide eyes was Dozzbin himself. He advanced slowly towards Namanti with his fists clenched tight by his sides. "I knew it," he said menacingly. "I knew that if I gave you enough time and space... you would eventually let your rise to power go to your head...and now...you've done it. Trouble is you don't have the courage to do it yourself. You have to have your tramp of a wife come up with some scurrilous rumors...that I know you cannot substantiate."

Kovarin started advancing towards Dozzbin, trying to look just as, if not more, menacing. "I accuse Dozzbin of being a dragon killer - nine times over. I call as a witness for the charges, Senior Tribune Tremyath. I call as a witness for the charges, Senior Administrator Vock. I call as a witness for the charges, Dragonman Kevrong. I call as a witness for the charges, my wife, the Lady Namanti. I may call other witnesses as well, as soon as I determine if others have been as wrongly treated as I was. I demand that from this day until the trial, that all of Dozzbin's movements be chaperoned, in order to make sure that he has no opportunity to destroy any evidence without being seen doing it."

Dozzbin gave an evil chuckle. "Bring on the chaperones. Bring on the charges. Bring on the witnesses. Bring on the trial. I have nothing to fear. I have nothing to hide. You can't prove anything. After this scam of yours is totally exposed, I will have you stripped of your rank *and* I will have you stripped of your dragon. I will have that beast reassigned and you will be banished from my sight and any true Dragonman, FOREVER!"

Kovarin chuckled back. "The only reason that you will never see me again…forever, is because you will be punished according to the law of the land. My only regret is that you can only be executed once…if that is the final verdict…which I am sure it will be."

One of the members of the High Court came up between the two men. "I am Arthrin, the Senior Justice of the High Court. It is witnessed by all in here that charges have been spoken… witnesses claimed…and trial accepted.   Since Commander Dozzbin has agreed to chaperones, in front of witnesses, we shall assign them. The chaperones will be chosen from the Division Sub Commanders. Are the Division Commanders here?"

A chorus of "ayes" were heard as the six Division Commanders came forward.

Arthrin looked at the men. "You will each choose one of your Sub Commanders to act as chaperones. Division 1 Commander, name yourself and name who your two Sub Commanders are."

One of the men, dressed in brown, stepped forward. "I am Battle Division 1 Commander, Heth. My two Sub Commanders are Commander Hobaro and Commander Frand."

Arthrin looked him up and down. "Which shall be a chaperone?"

"I choose Commander Hobaro."

"Is he the junior one?"

"No, Justice Arthrin. I choose Hobaro because Frand rides Sky Chaser. That dragon is a sibling of Diamond. I do not want to leave any appearance of favoritism...either way."

Arthrin's eyebrows went up. "Commander Hobaro is the better choice then. He will make himself available for the task."

"I am here, Justice Arthrin, and I make myself available," said Hobaro as he came forward.

Arthrin turned back to the Division Commanders. "Division 2 Commander, who are you and who are your Sub Commanders?"

A man dressed in blue-gray came forward. "I am Battle Division 2 Commander, Nossiturm. My Sub Commanders are Commander Rantad and Commander Rempen."

"Whom do you choose, Commander?"

"I'll let them choose between them, High Justice. I trust their judgment."

Another man came forward dressed in gray. "I am Sub Commander Rantad - rider of the gray dragon, Fang. I will accept the task."

The ritual continued on. From Division 3, the chaperone was Chocha. This was a man who had once been the Supreme Commander himself...thirty years ago. From Division 4, the choice was Zadusk. From Division 5, the choice was Jeshko. From Division 6, the choice was Ondegador. With the six chaperones assigned, it was up to them who would take which shift.

Arthrin looked around the room looking as if he wished the

accusation had never been uttered. "We will start the proceedings in ten days' time. All persons named as chaperones and witnesses will make themselves available at that time."

Dozzbin glared at the judge. "Why not tomorrow? Let's get this nonsense over with."

"Fine with me," said Kovarin. 'What am I saying,' he thought? 'I don't have a clue, or evidence, other than the temperature rods.'

Arthrin looked back and forth at the two antagonists. "It is not done that way. I said: Ten days from now, in the great Justice Hall...and I *meant* it!"

Kovarin did everything he could to look even more menacing to Dozzbin. "Ten days!"

Dozzbin scoffed and walked away. The six chaperones followed quickly. All six went with him at this time because none of them had decided what the shifts were going to be, yet.

Tremyath stormed up to Kovarin. "Are you...insane? You called me as a witness against Dozzbin? I...don't know..."

"You know more than you think you do, Tribunal," interjected Kovarin loudly! "You have seen something and you, at this time, don't realize the significance of it."

Arthrin came up and placed his hands on the shoulders of Kovarin and Tremyath. "I advise you two to *not* be discussing the case at this time. It could appear that you are conspiring."

Kovarin gave Arthrin an angry glare. "Anyone in this room can hear us. They can hear what we say. If someone wants to question it, they may. What have I said that would make Senior Tribune Tremyath perjure himself? I have told him that he does know something, he just doesn't realize the full significance of it. He will once he is under oath and hears the questions put to him."

"I await those questions…with great curiosity," said Tremyath with a concerned and confused frown.

Vock had walked up, somewhat unnoticed. "As do I!"

Kovarin smiled. "You both know certain things. Neither one of you has the full story. That's why you're so confused. Once the trial starts and you hear all of the information, it'll all be *very* clear to you…" He looked directly into the eyes of Arthrin. "…*all* of you."

Arthrin sighed. "You are coming close to conspiracy."

Kovarin grunted in anger. "Why? Have I given anyone any instructions to fabricate? Have I tried to steal away with anyone in private? I can see at least three members of the High Court standing here listening. It'd be impossible to hide something from all of them."

Arthrin sighed. "Granted, Supreme Commander."

Kovarin smiled and clasped his hands behind his back. "May I do a minor fact finding questioning at this time, good Judge…for the purpose of gathering evidence?"

Arthrin studied Kovarin's face for a few moments. "Yes, Supreme Commander, as long as I am here and am able to ascertain that you are not doing anything…illegal or inappropriate."

"Excellent!" Kovarin turned to Vock. "Senior

Administrator Vock, prior to Dozzbin becoming the Supreme Commander, when was the last time that a Candidate failed on all ten eggs?"

Vock was a little surprised by the question. "I…I…would have to check…all of the archives…in order to answer…"

He was interrupted. "That would have been twenty-one years ago," said a man wearing a Sub Commander uniform.

Arthrin looked at this new comer. "And you are…?"

"I am Battle Division 4 Sub Commander, Eevek. Twenty-two years ago, my brown - Scrambler, defeated Chocha's gray - Endeavor. They're both size forty-five dragons, but my Scrambler proved to be the dominant dragon. Less than a year after I took the Supreme Command position, I had the unfortunate occurrence of seeing the first Candidate, in fifty-six years, fail on his tenth attempt."

Kovarin leaned a little closer to Eevek. "How long were you the Supreme Commander?"

"I only held that position for three years. Before I could really get comfortable with it, Commander Invelton came along with his big gray - Eating Machine. I've watched the comings and goings of the Hatchery. There were no more failures…until Dozzbin became Supreme Commander. Since the beginning of his tenure…three Candidates failed. You were nearly the fourth."

Kovarin grunted. "One failure…over seventy years ago. One failure twenty-one years ago. With Dozzbin in the office… three *have* failed and there was nearly a fourth…in such a short time." He leaned close to Vock. "Senior Administrator, I would like you to see if you can find those three Grounders. Bring them in. I'd like to talk to them. If Dozzbin did to them, what he tried to do to me, there may be a lot more than…the destruction of nine eggs that I'm leveling against him."

Arthrin cleared his throat. "That sounds as if you're searching for something to throw at Dozzbin."

Kovarin moved up so that he was directly face to face with Arthrin. "If Dozzbin tried it with me…there's a chance he's done it before. If what they say is relevant and exposes more evidence against that traitor…"

Arthrin interjected. "*Alleged* traitor!"

Kovarin smiled and cleared his throat. "If what they say is relevant and exposes more evidence against that…*alleged* traitor…it shows even more of how evil the man is. If what they say is irrelevant…" He shrugged. "…they go their way and that's the last we worry about them. They will not be brought into the courtroom."

Arthrin stood there contemplating. He turned to Vock. "Senior Administrator, can you find these men?"

Vock smiled. "I shall make every effort to do so, Judge."

Arthrin turned back to Kovarin. "How long will the questioning be…on these men…*if* they are found, to determine whether or not they are witnesses for the prosecution?"

Kovarin gave him a smug grin. "It should not take much time to determine that."

Arthrin looked as if he had just had his face slapped. He closed his eyes and shook his head. He looked at Kovarin bewildered.

Kovarin smiled again. "Such is the evidence and such is the case."

Arthrin looked off to the side and clicked his tongue. He turned back to Vock. *"Please* find these men!"

The next day, Aj woke Kovarin to get him out training with Shondark. Kovarin was going to be with Shondark, doing some training with Diamond (and Namanti).

The morning was uneventful. This time there were no females (in heat) that left the area in, what many called, their "egg run".

Kovarin took Diamond on a somewhat long flight, to and from the area.   While Kovarin was flying, Shondark was giving Namanti instructions on how to fly the dragon.

Namanti looked at Shondark, with her nose out of joint. "Why do I have to learn this stuff? I'm not gonna be flying in battle!"

Shondark lightly put his hands on Namanti's shoulders. "If anything - tragic - happens to Kovarin…you'll be the one… who will then be taking charge of Diamond. You won't fly in battle, or patrol, that is a certainty. Diamond however, will still be a breeder. You will be a Dragonhandler and keep him in line. He likes you…he approves of you…and other than Kovarin, no one else would be able to control him…without several months of intensive training."

She stood there with her eyes wide in shock. "Uh…let's hope that I…don't have to take over."

Shondark smiled. "Amen! Hope for the best…prepare for the worst."

Three days later, the first of the three Candidate failures was found. He was brought to the capital and to Kovarin. He was a bit upset over being dragged in from his home, however, when the Supreme Commander of the War Forces gives an order…no one dare question it. If necessary, Kovarin could have sent an entire unit to drag the man in. After a five minute conversation with Kovarin, the Grounder - Chedobo, was more than willing to give evidence against Dozzbin. It carried with it the strong possibility of starting over as a Candidate, with a clean slate - no egg failures.

Two days after that the second man was found. Emkorm was just as agreeable as the first man.

The third man was found on the ninth day. Tahbahk was just as angry about being yanked into Dragon City, against his will. Again after just a five minute session, his attitude changed completely and he was more than ready to testify against Dozzbin.

The table was set. The trial was tomorrow. Tremyath, Vock and Kevrong were still in a complete befuddlement over why they were being called as witnesses for the prosecution.

Tremyath could not understand why he was called as a witness for the prosecution. What could he possibly know that could help? Granted, he had absolutely no love for that manipulative scoundrel Dozzbin, he still could not grasp what he could possibly know that would help this situation in any way at all. He shuffled through the papers, the numerous edicts signed by Dozzbin, some of which were turned down and some of which were reluctantly allowed to pass. Was there something in these papers that led to a crime committed by Dozzbin?

Vock thought that as soon as he had found the three "Grounders" that it was over for him. When he found out that he was still on the prosecution list, he gave up trying to speculate why and decided to wait until the questions were asked and the axe would fall where it would. He just hoped that it did not fall on his own neck. Bring on the trial and see where he was involved. He hoped that it did not include anything…that would bring him down.

Kevrong was totally baffled. He had, so far, been loyal to Dozzbin. He had done everything, no matter how insulting or trivial that Dozzbin had asked. Now, Dozzbin was giving him a rather maligned silent treatment. It had to be some manipulation by Kovarin to turn him against Dozzbin…did it not? He had seen Dozzbin do some twists, manipulations and other such things. Some people might see them as criminal…until you look at things in long term situations. All these things were designed for improvements in the military. Was that not the ultimate goal of the Supreme Commander? He would have to wait until he heard the questions before he could find out anything.

Kovarin desperately wanted to have Vock and Tremyath look over the bad scroll. He still kept it safe. According to the law, he could not let either man see it yet. That might be considered a compromise of a witness. He still had the two bad temperature rods. He still had the good scroll, accidentally dumped on him by Kevrong along with the three good temperature rods given by Namanti. The only person that he could talk to, among those named as witnesses for the prosecution was Namanti. They could not stop him from talking to his wife. Kevrong was just a pawn and did not need any great questioning - just: What happened to his instructional scroll?

17

The day arrived. Kovarin and Namanti got into their coach and made their way to the Great Hall of Justice. When they arrived, Kovarin sat in the coach surveying the area. He was able to spot all six of the Battle Division Commanders. There were at least four of the Sub Commanders - these four were not among the chaperones chosen to watch over Dozzbin. Other than Tremyath, there were ten other members of the Supreme Tribunal who were attending. He saw numerous men wearing the scarlet vest of the Senate members - he stopped counting them when he got to 25. There were 275 members of the Senate and for there to be more than 5 Senators here meant that this was getting a lot of attention.

He noticed also, that there were several other dignitaries here as well. Governors of Provinces and Mayors of Towns and villages, all proudly displaying the giant heavy medallions that clearly showed their office.

The last three men that Kovarin noticed were the three Grounders: Chedobo, Emkorm and Tahbahk. They came up to the coach, all three grinning with delight. All three wearing a large black sash to honor the color of the Supreme Commanders dragon. All three, absolutely elated over the fact that if Dozzbin was convicted, they would be able to start their Candidacy all over again…with no blemishes, of failed hatchings, against them.

Battle Group Commander Aj came up to the coach and pushed his way past the three Grounders. He still could not understand why these three pieces of riff-raff had been brought in. They were an insult to the entire Dragonman community. They were failures. They were nothing. He treated them with complete contempt. He held out his hand to assist Kovarin and Namanti out of the coach. "Supreme Commander, I welcome you to the Great Hall." He leaned a little closer to Kovarin and spoke in softer voice. "I sincerely hope that you are ready to bounce Dozzbin from wall to wall. If he wins, there will be a lot of regret…among many."

Kovarin stepped down out of the coach with a smile. He whispered back to Aj. "Get ready for a *big* storm. Dozzbin thinks that he can get past anybody. I've uncovered some things, in the past few days, that I didn't even know about. It helps immensely in thrashing and trashing that traitor."

"I can hardly wait, Supreme Commander." He turned and held out his hand for Namanti and smiled. "Milady, good morning to you."

She smiled back as she stepped out of the coach. "Good morning to you, Commander." She was tired and it showed. Over the last few days, because of the fact that she might end up with Diamond, if anything tragic happened to Kovarin, Shondark had been running her ragged, teaching her how to handle Diamond. The only thing that had not happened so far, was her being able to take Diamond up for a flight by herself. She was very grateful for the existence of the *treat*. She was able to keep that huge tongue at arms-length, and lick only her hand, instead of giving her a complete bath.

Another coach came up. It was full. Dozzbin and his wife Chesesa were in it. There was also a woman who was holding a baby. Three of the chaperones were in the coach as well: Ondegador, Zadusk and Jeshko.

Kovarin noticed that they were all wearing their dress uniforms. Dozzbin was wearing his brown uniform while all three of the Sub Commanders were wearing bluish-gray. Kovarin thought of it as a humorous coincidence that all three of these chaperones had the same color dragon.

Ondegador got out first. He held out a hand for Dozzbin and then Chesesa. She kissed the baby and then a small boy that was in the coach as well. Kovarin was aware of the fact that Dozzbin had two sons. He had never seen either child until now. Zadusk and Jeshko got out on their own.

Dozzbin glared at Kovarin with nothing but pure hate in his eyes. "Hey you, Grounder…yes I'm talking to you Kovarin! Get used to that title! When I fully expose this scam of yours, I'll strip you of that dragon, that you don't deserve, and claim him for myself. Then you and your whore can go wallow in the trash with the rest of those Grounders, which is exactly where you belong. I'm going to rename that black dragon and make sure that you never know what its new, *real* name is. You hear me… Grounder?"

Kovarin looked at him with equal hate. "All I hear is the ravings of a traitor! Once the evidence and testimony is exposed, losing your dragon and your title will be the least of your problems. Do you hear *me*, TRAITOR!?"

Kovarin headed up the steps to the Great Hall of Justice entryway. His group followed him. Before following, the three Grounders all gave Dozzbin a vulgar gesture, grinned and then followed.

Dozzbin looked at Ondegedor. "Remember who those three Grounders are. When this is over, I'll have the skin whipped off of their backs for daring to show their faces in Dragon City."

Ondegador sighed and headed up the stairs.

After they got to the top, Namanti had to lean against one of the great columns to catch her breath. "Why…are there…so many…steps?"

Aj smiled at her. "There is supposed to be some symbolism to the number of steps and a story that goes with each one. In order to become a High Justice in this court, you have to climb the steps, one at a time, recite the symbol and take an oath to the law and the symbol."

She pulled a handkerchief out of a sleeve and wiped the sweat off of her forehead. "I'd never make it." She took Kovarin's arm and headed inside.

They passed through a long hall that was lined with statues.

Namanti looked at some of the statues a little perplexed. "Who are those guys?"

Kovarin smiled. "Those are the Supreme Justices from the past. There's an inscription under each statue giving name, a little history, when they were a Justice and some of them have an additional inscription if they were a Dragonman."

"Looks like they've got plenty of room for more statues," she smirked. "What happens when they run out of room?"

"They'll find something," said Kovarin with a chuckle. "Consider how much room there is...they won't run out of space for a long time."

"Were many of them Dragonriders?"

"I doubt it. Both jobs - Dragonrider and Judge - can keep you very busy."

They got to the end of the long hall of honor. Aj motioned for them to go into a specific courtroom. Kovarin walked in and was a little surprised at the size of the room as well as the Judges bench.

"Commander Aj, isn't this the gallery for the Supreme Justices?"

"Yes, Supreme Commander, it's a big case," said Aj with a smile.

An elderly man wearing a long gray robe approached them. "I am Court Officer Frosht. Who are you and what is your purpose on this day?"

Aj stepped up. "This is the Supreme Commander of the War Forces for High Country, Kovarin and his wife, the Lady Namanti. They are here to state accusations of treason against the former Supreme Commander, Dozzbin."

He stepped sideways to his right and pointed at a large marble table down front. "The accusers are to go to that specific place in order to make their accusations in front of this court, Supreme Commander."

Dozzbin came in. He was instructed to go to the defense table on the left. He glared at Kovarin as he headed for his assigned spot. He looked around at the entire room and then plopped himself down on the marble bench behind the table and crossed his arms. He did not move until the High Justices came in. His wife Chesesa sat on a bench behind him.

Kovarin and Namanti sat down on their marble bench.

Kovarin groaned. "Uh! I guess they don't want us to stay here very long. This bench is…soooo uncomfortable."

"It's cold too," said Namanti.

Aj looked back into the gallery. "It appears, Supreme Commander, that all of your witnesses have arrived."

Kovarin smiled. He turned to take look for himself. Tremyath and Vock were sitting several rows back. Kevrong was sitting near Dozzbin. The three Grounders - Chedobo, Emkorm and Tahbahk were sitting directly behind Kovarin. He smiled and nodded to each of them. They returned the smile and nod. He turned back towards the bench and sighed. "Now, we wait for the leisure of the High Justices." He frowned. "Commander Aj, how many of the fifteen Judges are hearing this case?"

Aj chuckled. "All of them, Supreme Commander."

He looked up at Aj in shock. "What?"

"Yes, Supreme Commander, it's a big case," said Aj with a smile.

Three rather elderly looking men went to a desk, directly in front of the center of the Judges bench. They set up several scrolls, quills and ink bottles, before sitting down.

A rather large man came from behind a curtain that was behind the Judges bench. He was carrying a very large gavel.

"That thing looks more like a maul than a gavel," whispered Kovarin.

The man with the gavel slammed it down on the Judge's desk. The sound echoed and hurt the ears a little. All talking abruptly ceased. "All who are in the Great Hall, will stand for the High Justices."

The Judges started filing in all wearing their white robes and a medallion from their Province. They all entered from the same place the man with the gavel had come from. As each one entered, he went either to the left or right of the central high seat. They came in randomly and stood at their specific seat.

Namanti tapped her finger against Kovarin's hand and whispered to him. "Why are there fifteen of them?"

"One for each Province," whispered Kovarin.

The last one to come in was Arthrin, the Senior Justice. He looked both ways down the bench to make sure that all were in attendance. He cleared his throat. "The Highest Court for the great nation of High Country is now in session." He gestured to the man with the gavel.

Again the gavel was brought down with an ear hurting echo on the bench. The gavel man took one step forward. "Be seated!"

Namanti looked up at Kovarin. "If he keeps hittin' that desk with that big hammer, he's gonna bust it."

Kovarin glared down at Namanti. "Shut up!" he whispered through his teeth.

She looked as if her feelings were a little hurt as she looked back at him with her lips clenched.

Arthrin picked up a smaller gavel and twirled it in his fingers. "What case do we have before us today?"

The Court Officer Frosht came forward between the two marble desks, to a marble podium that was centered between them. He had a large staff in his hands, which he banged against the floor fifteen times. He then gave a long-winded oration of the charges that were being leveled against Dozzbin and by whom. Down in front, the three scribes were scribbling away as fast as they could with their fancy plumed quills.

After Frosht finished, Arthrin, staring at nothing in particular, said: "Is the Party for the Accusation, present?"

Kovarin stood up. Before he could say anything, Frosht started speaking. "This is the Supreme Commander of the War Forces for High Country. He is the one who makes the accusation."

Arthrin looked down at Kovarin. "Supreme Commander, are you ready to proceed at this time?"

Kovarin cleared his throat. "I am ready, High Justice."

Arthrin again stared off into space. "Is the accused here?"

Dozzbin stood up and gave a dull look at Frosht.

Frosht did not waste any time answering. "This is Battle Division Commander, Dozzbin. He is the accused."

Arthrin looked down at Dozzbin. "Division Commander, are you ready to proceed at this time?"

"I was ready ten days ago, when that mendacious fool…"

Arthrin slammed his gavel down. "Commander that is a yes/no question! Are you ready to proceed at this time?"

Dozzbin clenched his fists and teeth. "I…am…ready!" He glared at Arthrin as he sat down.

Again Arthrin surveyed the people in front of him. "I see no legal representation…for either of you…don't you want any?"

"None needed, High Justice," said Kovarin.

"I need no help in my defense against these lies, High Justice," said Dozzbin mockingly.

Arthrin looked at both with his eyebrows raised. He shrugged. "So be it! Bring in the Inquisitor!"

A door opened off to Kovarin's right. A short, very fat man waddled in carrying one of those smelly little truth boxes. He had virtually no hair on his head at all and what looked like a permanent grin on his chubby face. The box was already giving off the foul smelling blue smoke. It trailed behind him and rose to the ceiling as he came along. He grunted as he took the three steps up to the podium and placed it on the center of the podium. "All is ready, Milord High Justice," he said breathlessly.

"Thank you, Inquisitor."

The fat man nodded. He again grunted as he took each step down. There was a small bench in front of the podium where he sat down.

Arthrin banged his gavel. "The Accuser will approach the..." He turned back to the man with the giant gavel. "What is that foul smelling thing called again?"

The Gavelman leaned down close to Arthrin, trying somewhat unsuccessfully to not laugh. "Just call it a truth box, Milord."

Arthrin grunted. "The Accuser will approach the...truth box."

Kovarin stood up and walked up to the podium. As soon as he got to the steps, he understood why Arthrin had called it "foul smelling". The stench was incredible. He walked up the three steps and was having a hard time breathing. His eyes stung and he turned his face away from the box.

"You must face the box," said Arthrin.

Kovarin swallowed hard. He took in a deep breath, held it and turned his face back to the box, while squinting his eyes.

"State your name and title," said Arthrin.

"Supreme Commander of the War Forces for High Country, Kovarin. I am the rider of the black dragon, Diamond."

"Now, state a fabrication," said Arthrin.

Kovarin was shocked. "Milord?"

Arthrin leaned forward. "Give us a big fat whopper of a lie…NOW!"

Kovarin shrugged. "I…am…not now, nor have I ever been a citizen of High Country." He was even more shocked as he watched the blue smoke momentarily turn green and then a bright yellow.

"Now state a truth," said Arthrin.

He stared through the tears in his eyes at the smoke. "I… uh…I am a Dragonrider…I ride the largest dragon in existence, Diamond, the black dragon." Again, the smoke momentarily turned green and then back to the original blue. Kovarin shrugged and cleared his burning throat.

"Thank you, Supreme Commander," said Arthrin. "You may return to your seat."

He stumbled a little going down the three steps. He walked back to his seat trying to clear his eyes. As he sat down, a youth came up to the desk and placed a small bowl of water and a kerchief in front of Kovarin.

"You may clean your nose and eyes, Supreme Commander," said the youth.

Kovarin picked up the kerchief and blew his nose. He then dipped his fingers in the bowl of water and used the water to clean out his eyes. It took a few tries, however he was finally able to stop the burning and see clearly again.

Arthrin looked at Dozzbin. "The defendant will approach

the…truth box."

Dozzbin stood up and walked to the podium. Before going up the steps he took in a deep breath and then climbed the stairs.

"State your name and title," said Arthrin.

"I am an unassigned Battle Division Commander, Dozzbin."

"Now, state a fabrication," said Arthrin.

Dozzbin looked at Kovarin and smirked. He turned back to face the smoke. "I have nothing but respect for the pretender, Kovarin." The smoke wasted no time turning yellow. Dozzbin again looked at Kovarin with a smug smirk.

"Now state a truth," said Arthrin.

"I am the rider of the great brown dragon, Thunder." The smoke went back to blue.

"Thank you, Battle Division Commander," said Arthrin. "You may return to your seat."

Dozzbin returned to his seat where another youth gave him a bowl and a kerchief. He cleared his nose and eyes the same way that Kovarin had done.

Arthrin banged his gavel. "The Accuser will call his first witness!"

Kovarin stood up. "I call as witness, my wife, the Lady Namanti."

Frosht slammed his staff against the floor. "The Lady

Namanti will approach the podium!"

She looked up at Kovarin with fear in her eyes. "I don't wanna go sniff that stinky thing...right now."

"You're going to have to do it sooner or later. You might as well get it out of the way now."

She looked at the blue smoke and let out a tiny little, desperate squeak. She sighed and headed for the podium. At the base of the three steps she sighed again and stepped up. As soon as she got to the top she turned her head to the side and nearly gagged as she stuck out her tongue and closed her eyes in disgust.

"State your name and title," said Arthrin.

She coughed twice. "I...am...Lady Namanti...newlywed wife...of the Supreme Commander...Kovarin." She turned her head away from the smoke and took in a deep breath and held it with her eyes and mouth clenched tight.

"Supreme Commander, Kovarin, you may proceed," said Arthrin.

Kovarin stood up. "Thank you, My Lord, High Justice." He turned to Namanti. "On the day before I received the egg, from which Diamond hatched...what did you do?"

She turned to face Kovarin.

She was immediately admonished by Frosht. "You must face the smoke, Milady!"

She grunted in disgust and turned to the smoke. "I...went to your room. I decided to see...if you needed anything...before you got your dragon egg." She pulled back and coughed. She took in another deep breath and faced the smoke. "I noticed that it was extremely hot in your chambers. You…told me that it was in preparation for the egg. I've been in some of those chambers… before and…it was never that hot in any of them…before." She pulled back to get another breath of air. There were tears pouring down her cheeks. "We went to the sand pit and looked at the temperature rod. According to it, the temperature was 44 or 45 Abfar…I don't remember which. That's within the range required, but I knew that it was actually a lot hotter." She leaned back again.

"So what did you do?"

The look in her eyes was full of fear. She grimaced, took another breath and faced the smoke. "I left your chambers and went back to mine." Another breath. "I found some temperature rods…that I had gotten…from some of the other…Dragonmen."

"Why did you have those temperature rods in your possession?"

She looked at him with her mouth hanging open. She hung her head. She took another deep breath. "There were times that… some of the Candidates did not pay me…for…certain services or favors that I did for them. I kept *something*…of theirs…as collateral, until they…were ready to pay me." She turned away panting, with her eyes shut.

"So there were three who had not paid you."

"Yes," she said meekly.

"What did you do with those temperature rods?"

"I gave them to you…to compare against the one you had."

"Do you have anything else to add to your testimony, at this time?"

She took in another deep breath. "When I later went back to your chambers…it was a lot cooler. And you got an egg that hatched."

"Thank you. My Lord, High Justice, I have no more questions for this witness."

Arthrin looked at Dozzbin. "Defendant, do you have any questions for this witness?"

Dozzbin scoffed and crossed his arms. He did not bother standing up. "She's a low-life tramp and a confessed thief. It appears that she is also a very well-practiced liar. I hear testimony, but I see no evidence. She's figured out a way to defeat the truth box. Her presence here is an insult to every decent person in attendance. I do not wish to hear any more of her filthy lies."

Arthrin looked a little disgusted. "Lady Namanti, you may step down."

Kovarin looked at Aj and gave a jerk of his head. Aj read it and headed over to Namanti to help her back to her seat.

"Supreme Commander, your next witness," said Arthrin.

"I call Dragonman, Kevrong to the stand."

Frosht slammed his staff against the floor. "The Dragonman Kevrong, will approach the podium!"

Kevrong headed for the podium. He looked at Dozzbin

and shrugged. He took a deep breath before walking up the three steps. He involuntarily let out a grunt of disgust when he got to the smoke.

"State your name and title," said Arthrin.

"Wing Commander, Kevrong. Aide to Commander Dozzbin and rider of the brown dragon, Master Gamer."

Kovarin gave Dozzbin a sly little side glance before he started the questioning. Dozzbin was still sitting there with his arms defiantly crossed. The expression on his face did have a little concern on it. "Commander Kevrong, when your dragon had finally matured, what did you do with your instructional scroll?"

Kevrong grimaced and grunted. He looked up and through clenched teeth he said: "I lost it."

"How did you lose it?"

He hung his head. "I…accidentally threw it away?"

"HOW!?"

Kevrong growled again. "I…thought that…I threw it in your meat chute. I…didn't need it any more. I had forgotten that I had to sign the thing out and was supposed to return it to the Administrators."

"So you were mocking me, by giving me *your* instructional scroll?" Again he stole a furtive glance at Dozzbin. The man's eyes opened up in shock for a moment and then closed again and his shoulders sagged a little.

"Yes, Supreme Commander, I thought I gave it to you,

but…you couldn't find it…in your meat chute."

Kovarin chuckled. "You mocked me, by throwing the scroll into my meat chute - I mocked you by telling you that it hadn't been there." He reached down and pulled it out of a pouch on his side. "Here it is, Wing Commander…the scroll that was lost."

Dozzbin's arms dropped down to his side and his chin hit his chest.

Kevrong looked at Kovarin with hatred and anger on his face. "That's…the…that's my instructional scroll? You said…"

"You were mocking me. I mocked you back," Kovarin shot at him angrily!

"I had to pay for that thing! Do you know how expensive they are?"

"No, but I imagine that you do."

"I want that back…I want my money back!"

"You'll get it back and you will get your money back… later! At this time, it is evidence!"

Arthrin banged his gavel. "Gentlemen, please! We do not need some ridiculous argument as part of the testimony. Supreme Commander, if you are trying to make a point, please make it… otherwise, move on."

"Of course, High Justice," said Kovarin. "Now, Commander Kevrong, I am going to hand you this scroll. Remember, that at this time, it is evidence. You will get it back, later, for proper compensation."

The youth that had brought the finger bowls grabbed at the scroll case. "Uh...Supreme Commander...you're supposed to stay at your station. I...am supposed to move the evidence...from place to place."

Kovarin felt slighted for a moment. He shrugged and handed the scroll case to the boy. "Then give it to him."

The boy quickly took it and almost ran to the podium. He handed it up to Kevrong.

Kovarin was noticing that Dozzbin was not looking as smug as before. "I would like you to pull the scroll out and see if you can recognize it as the one that was in your possession."

Kevrong gave Kovarin a disgusted look. He then looked at the scroll case. "The symbol of the Hatchery is on the cap." He pulled the cap off and pulled the scroll out. "Yes, it is the instructional scroll that was in my possession, when I had the successful hatching of Master Gamer."

"How can you be so certain?"

Kevrong sighed. He pointed to a spot on the scroll. "When I first got this scroll, I made a mark...on the back...at the beginning. I marked it as the scroll that...I had...when I got my charge, Master Gamer."

Kovarin smiled. "We are finished with that scroll...for the moment."

Arthrin interrupted. "You say that this scroll is evidence?"

Kovarin responded. "Yes, High Justice."

"Then, for the moment, it will be placed on the evidence table as Accusation exhibit number 1."

"As you wish, High Justice."

After Kevrong put the scroll back in its case, the youth took the scroll to a table where the scribes each took a quick look at it and continued writing.

"Commander Kevrong, I have another scroll for you to look at."

"Huh...what for?"

"I'm asking the questions, Commander."

"As you wish, Supreme Commander."

Kovarin handed the scroll case to the youth. He ran it to Kevrong.

"Now, Commander Kevrong, what is this scroll?"

Kevrong looked the outer case over. "This case...has the symbol of the Hatchery on it...as well."

"How about the scroll, itself?"

Kevrong pulled the cap off and pulled the scroll out. He unrolled it a little and looked aghast. He unrolled a little more, then some more. "This is a...a mess! This childish scribble...looks like Dozzbin's writi..." He now had a totally shocked look on his face. He looked over at Dozzbin who was slouched over with his arms hanging limp between his legs. "Uh...it...uh, closely resembles…" The smoke turned yellow. Kevrong noticed it and grimaced. "It most definitely…looks…exactly…like Commander Dozzbin's writing." The smoke turned blue.

Kovarin continued: "If you will notice, Commander Kevrong, there is a small piece of paper that has been introduced into the scroll itself."

Kevrong looked at the side of the scroll. "Yes, Supreme Commander."

"Please unroll the scroll to that section."

Kevrong cleared his throat and took another glance at Dozzbin. He started unrolling the scroll while rolling up the upper portion as he went. When he got to where the paper had been inserted, he looked confused for a moment. "The…uh…foreign paper has nothing on it."

"The foreign paper is nothing more than a marker," said Kovarin flatly. "What I want you to do is start reading that portion of the scroll - out loud - in regards to bathing the hatchling."

Kevrong looked back at the scroll. "Bathing…bathing… bath…oh here it is. 'At the earliest possible moment, after hatching and the first feeding, the hatchling should be given a long bath in a strong alkaline solu…' WHAT?" He looked at Kovarin in horror. "You don't get alkaline anywhere *near* a fresh hatchling. That stuff would burn the skin *right off* of a fresh one."

"So, Commander Kevrong, from what you know of caring for a hatchling, this would be a very bad set of instructions to follow…is that what you're saying?"

"That example *alone* makes it a bad set of instructions."

"What would you say if I told you that that is one of many bad instructions in that scroll?"

"If someone were to go by this set of instructions…I doubt that their hatchling would survive…to coming out."

"Thank you, Commander Kevrong." Kovarin turned to Arthrin. "That is all of the questions I have, at this time, for this witness. I might call upon him, at a later time for more… expertise."

Arthrin looked at Dozzbin. "Defendant, do you have any questions for this witness?"

Dozzbin looked up. He had a bit of a scowl on his face. "I didn't realize just how far that…Kovarin's conspiracy went against me. He used my own Aide against me. I don't ever want to lay eyes on that spy again."

Arthrin shook his head. "Commander Kevrong, you may step down."

Kevrong turned and went slowly down the three steps. He looked back and forth from Kovarin to Dozzbin. He walked back to the gallery looking very concerned.

Kovarin looked up at the Judges. "At this time, High Justice, I would like this other scroll to be labeled as Accusation evidence number 2."

"So be it. Supreme Commander, your next witness," said Arthrin.

"I call Senior Tribunal, Tremyath to the stand."

Frosht slammed his staff against the floor. "The Senior Tribun...WHAT?" He looked up at Arthrin astonished.

Arthrin was looking equally astonished. "Supreme Commander...are you aware of the fact that a member of the Supreme Tribunal cannot be called to testify?"

"They cannot be *forced* to testify, is my understanding of the law, My Lord, High Justice," said Kovarin with a little bit of a smile. "I think that possibly because of the testimony, so far, that Senior Tribune, Tremyath may *want* to voice his testimony...in this case."

"Very well...we shall see what his goodwill is...in this case." Arthrin signaled to Frosht.

Frosht swallowed hard. He slammed his staff against the floor. "The Senior Tribune, Tremyath, will approach the podium!"

Tremyath was already on his way, with an Aide following him. He walked up, next to the podium. "My Lord, High Justice. Yes, I realize that I cannot be..." He looked at Kovarin. "... *forced* to testify." He looked back at Arthrin. "It seems that in this case...my curiosity is piqued. I was told, earlier, that I had certain information, in regards to this case. I was just not aware of the significance of...what I know. On one hand, there is a charge of treason - on the other hand a charge of conspiracy. If I can give testimony that exposes the guilty party...and I do *not* testify... someone might say that I am a part of the evil. In good conscience, High Justice, I must testify."

"Very good, Senior Tribune." Arthrin cleared his throat. "Please assume the position at the podium, then. State your name and title," said Arthrin.

"Senior Tribune of the Supreme Tribunal, Tremyath.

The Aide helped Tremyath climb the three stairs. Tremyath coughed several times as he was affected by the smoke.

Kovarin felt a little smug. He did his best not to show it. "I thank you for your cooperation in this case, Senior Tribune."

Tremyath gave a polite nod to Kovarin.

"Senior Tribune, the day that you were there to perform the ceremonial distribution of the eggs, when it came to the egg that I received - the egg that Diamond hatched from - did anything occur…that seemed odd to you?"

Tremyath now was looking at no one. He had his eyes shut, because of the smoke and there were tearstains going down both cheeks. He answered the questions keeping his eyes shut. "Yes, Supreme Commander, there was an oddity. When I asked you if you were ready, you informed me that your temperature rod had been broken. Upon hearing that your rod was broken, it was Commander Dozzbin - not an Administrator - who gave you a new temperature rod. He produced the thing so fast…there was no time to call an Administrator…to do the replacement."

"Has this ever happened before?"

"What part?"

"Has Dozzbin ever handed out…supplies…that would normally be given out by the Administrators?"

"Uh…yes…as I recall, it has happened…several times that I can remember."

"Do you remember the names of these Candidates?"

Tremyath shook his head and gave a helpless smile. "I… am very bad with names. I might remember the face…I couldn't possibly remember the names."

Kovarin looked up at Arthrin. "High Justice, I ask at this time, that Senior Tribune, Tremyath, be allowed to clear his eyes… for a possible identification."

Arthrin pointed to one of the youths that was running evidence and other errands. The boy reached down and grabbed a bowl and kerchief and headed to the podium. The Aide took hold of one of Tremyath's hands. The youth reached the podium, dipped the kerchief in the water and handed it to the Aide. The Aide transferred it to Tremyath's hand who took it and wiped his eyes. He nearly stepped back off of the top step. The Aide caught him and steadied him. Tremyath looked back at why he had been grabbed.

"Oh, my!" He nodded at his Aide. He handed the kerchief back to the youth. "Thank you, my boy."

The youth took the kerchief and stepped back two paces.

Tremyath looked at Kovarin through bloodshot eyes. "Why are my eyes being cleared…before my testimony is over?"

"I would like you to look around the gallery, Senior Tribune. See if there is anyone you recognize…in regards to the odd occurrence that I went through, at the Hatchery."

Tremyath's jaw dropped. "It…it's a huge gallery." He held his arms out taking in the entire gallery. He had a sound of desperation in his voice. "How could I possibly find one face in all of…?" His expression changed to shock. "Oh my! There is one!"

Kovarin was feeling more confident. "Where?"

"He…he's almost directly behind you, Supreme Commander." Tremyath pointed.

"To whom are you pointing at, Senior Tribune?"

"That…rather disheveled man…behind you…with the very dirty brown vest."

Arthrin interjected. "Who is this man?"

Kovarin looked behind him as the man indicated stood up. He turned back to Arthrin. "This man is identified as Grounder, Tahbahk."

Arthrin looked stunned. "A…Grounder? You brought a… Grounder, here…in this court…for what purpose?"

Kovarin leaned forward with his fists on the marble table. "I commanded him to be here, High Justice. I commanded him to be here to give critical testimony against the accused."

Arthrin looked at some of the other Justices who were equally insulted. "It had *better* be critical. If it is not…you will be held in contempt, for bringing a…*Grounder* in front of our presence."

Kovarin stood back up and clasped his hands behind his

back. "I assure you that it is critical. May we continue?"

Arthrin sat back in his chair. "Yes," he said, still with a look of disgust. "By all means, continue…with haste…so we can get…*that*…out of here."

Tahbahk gave Arthrin an evil glare and sat back down.

Kovarin looked back at Tremyath, feeling very good about himself. "Senior Tribune…are you sure that there is absolutely no one else, in this room that you recognize…in regards to the oddity?"

Tremyath shook his head. "I am quite certain…I do not recognize anyone…else."

"Are you still certain, that it did happen to at least one more person - other than myself?"

"Yes, Supreme Commander, I am very certain."

Kovarin looked up at Arthrin smiling. "I am finished with this witness, My Lord, High Justice."

Arthrin looked at Dozzbin. "Defendant, do you have any questions for this witness?"

Dozzbin looked up. He looked whipped. "The conspiracy against me has even gone into the Tribunal itself. That old fool actually believes the lies that he has just insulted this court with. I am facing a trial against sorcery. I don't care to hear any more lies from this…*person!*" He hung his head back down.

Arthrin looked at Tremyath. "Senior Tribune, Tremyath, you may step down."

Tremyath bowed his head to Arthrin. "I thank you, High Justice." He turned and took his Aide's hand as he went down the three steps. At the bottom, he immediately beckoned the youth with the water bowl. He cleared his eyes and nose before leaving the podium area.

"Supreme Commander, your next witness," said Arthrin.

"I call Senior Hatchery Administrator, Vock to the stand."

Frosht slammed his staff against the floor. "The Senior Hatchery Administrator, Vock, will approach the podium!"

Vock came to the podium with a large satchel slung over his shoulder. He gave Kovarin a sideways glance and patted the satchel several times. He walked up the steps and started coughing as he smelled the smoke.

"State your name and title," said Arthrin.

"Senior Hatchery Administrator, Vock."

Kovarin was feeling rather good about the way things were going. He was hoping that Dozzbin did not have any form of a backup plan that would be sprung back. "Administrator Vock, have you looked for the evidence that I requested?"

Vock got a pained look on his face and grunted. "Yes, Supreme Commander, I did…and I am terribly embarrassed."

"I will prove to you, during the course of this trial, that the embarrassment is not yours. Now, you told me, at the time you gave me Diamond's birth certificate, that you could not find… certain paperwork on me."

"Yes, Supreme Commander…it is just…not anywhere in my offices."

"Has this happened with any other Candidates?"

Vock let out a long sigh. "Yes…it did."

"How many?"

"It happened to three other Candidates."

"Name them, please."

"Chedobo, Emkorm and Tahbahk."

"What was the final outcome…for these three Candidates?"

"All three became Grounders."

Arthrin (and at least three other Justices) gave off an audible, pained grunt.

"Did any of these three men requisition any supplies?"

"Only the time candles for the turning of eggs and the coal blocks for keeping the sand pit warm."

"No other supplies…at all?"

"In thirty total eggs…not one live hatching…they didn't need anything to care for…a *live* hatchling."

"If one or more of them, were to have broken a temperature rod, would the replacement be annotated…somewhere in your paperwork?"

"Oh, absolutely. We *must* keep track of them…the ones that we use in the Hatchery are terribly expensive."

"What about the instructional scrolls?"

"In…uh…regards to what?"

"What would happen if a Candidate…somehow damaged… or *lost* a scroll - is that expensive as well?"

"Yes, the scrolls are expensive as well. We go through great pains to make sure that they are written, only by the finest, artists. All writing is to be very legible and all illustrations are to be exact."

Kovarin looked up at Arthrin. "High Justice, may we allow Administrator Vock to look over exhibit 1?"

Arthrin nodded. "Granted."

One of the youths took the scroll and ran it over to Vock. Vock accepted it with a nod and a smile. He looked at Kovarin. "What am I looking for?"

"Is this an appropriate instructional scroll, for a Candidate?"

"Oh." Vock opened the scroll case and took it out. He laid it in front of him and unrolled a good portion of it. He rolled it back up and placed it back in the case. "It appears to be one of our good instructional scrolls. It would take at least a day to go over it thoroughly, in order to make sure that it *is* a valid one."

"Thank you, Administrator, you may put it back."

Vock handed the case to the youth who ran it back to the evidence table.

Kovarin looked up at Arthrin. "High Justice, may we allow Administrator Vock to look over exhibit 2?"

Arthrin nodded. "Granted."

The youth grabbed the other case and ran it over to Vock.

Vock took it out and started looking it over. After just a few moments, he let out a disgusted grunt. "This…this is an atrocity. This barely legible scrawl…it looks like Dozzbin's writing. I'd recognize that mess anywhere. I have four grandchildren who are all under the age of six and yet they have better penmanship than this."

"Why are you so sure that it is Dozzbin's writing?"

Vock looked over at Dozzbin and scowled. "I have seen dozens of *edicts* that have been written by that man. He has done everything he can to undermine my authority by taking away my responsibilities and giving them to himself."

"Did you…immediately obey…all of these edicts?"

"No, we challenged every single one of them…to the Tribunal."

"Did the Tribunal force you to enact all of them?"

"No, thank the Great Maker, there were very few that we were forced to obey. The rest, thank the Great Maker, were thrown in the trash."

Kovarin felt the thrill of exhilaration. He had heard, by rumor, that every edict, from Dozzbin, had been enacted - no matter what. Now he found out that it just was not true. He momentarily lost track of his thoughts. Kovarin tried to think of what he wanted next. He had a plan of attack, however, this wonderful news was just too good to not wallow in, for a glorious moment, or two.

Arthrin brought Kovarin back to reality. "Supreme Commander, do you have any more questions for this witness?"

"Uh…yes, High Justice…I do…have some more…inquiries." He collected himself and turned to Vock. "Administrator, look at me."

Vock turned away from the smoke looking confused. "Yes, Supreme Commander."

"Watch what I do."

Vock nodded.

Kovarin reached into his belt and pulled out two temperature rods. "From where did I pull these out?"

Vock shook his head baffled by the display and the question. "From inside…your belt!"

Kovarin held the two rods up high. "High Justice, at this time, I would like for Senior Administrator, Vock to examine these temperature rods."

Arthrin nodded and made a motion to the youth. The youth ran to Kovarin, took the rods and then ran to Vock, who took them still looking confused.

Kovarin continued. "What are those items, Administrator?"

Vock looked at them quickly. "They're temperature rods that are used to make sure the Hatchery sand pits are kept at proper temperatures."

Kovarin raised his eyebrows. "Are they?"

Vock let out a grunt of exasperation. "What else would they be?"

"What is the current reading on these two rods?"

Vock rolled his eyes and then took a close look at one of the rods. His face changed from annoyance to surprise. "Uh… this one…is showing a reading…that's IMPOSSIBLE!"

"What is impossible?"

Vock stuttered for a few moments. "You…you had…they were inside your belt! They should…the reading should be… somewhere around normal body temperature."

Kovarin put his fists on the table. "What is the *reading*?!"

Vock scoffed. "The reading on this…thing…shows minus 10 degrees Abfar."

"What is the reading on the other one?"

Vock rolled his eyes. He took a look at the one in his other hand and his jaw dropped. He looked back at Kovarin totally stunned.

"What is the *reading*?!"

"Uh…this one…is also…showing…minus 10 degrees… Abfar."

"So, what, in your expert opinion, is wrong?"

"These rods are faulty…they…" He took a very close look at one and then the other. "Uh…very strange…"

"What is strange?"

"The…the…uh…liquid level…inside the rod…looks where it should be…for normal body temperature…but the numbers…are in the wrong place!"

"What would happen if…oh say someone…who is not really familiar with those rods, were to use them…in a hatching sand pit?"

"With this…these?" Vock shook his head. "They'd probably get the sand pit…way too hot…and…" He looked at Kovarin with total horror in his eyes. "…cook…the egg."

Everyone in the room was silent. Kovarin let the silence go on for several moments. He again stood up straight and clasped his hands behind his back. He then smiled. "Who would be the party responsible for the death of the egg?"

Vock looked angry. "Who ever made these…fraudulent and unholy contraptions," he said through his teeth.

"Those are the temperature rods that were given to me… by Commander Dozzbin. The edicts that were allowed to be enacted by the Tribunal…violating your authority…did it include the distribution of the instructional scrolls and temperature rods?"

Vock was almost shaking with anger. "No! The main thing that Dozzbin took from me was the random distribution of the eggs."

"Please give those…faulty rods to the boy." He waited until the youth had the rods. "High Justice, at this time I enter those two…faulty rods as evidence."

The youth headed for the evidence table with the rods.

Arthrin looked down at the scribes. "These rods are now marked as accusation exhibits three and four."

Kovarin looked at the youth. "I have three more items for Administrator Vock to look at."

The boy ran back to Kovarin. He received three more temperature rods that were pulled from under Kovarin's belt. He quickly ran them over to Vock.

Kovarin let Vock look at them closely for a moment. "What do you have in your hands now, Administrator?"

Vock did not look up from the rods. "I now have three… *accurate* temperature rods. I saw you pull these from under your belt…and all three are showing normal body temperature."

"Those rods are the ones that were given to me, by the Lady Namanti, just before I received the egg from which Diamond hatched. When I received those…that was the first time that I had seen an accurate temperature rod."

Kovarin stole another side glance at Dozzbin. He was a little surprised at what he saw. Dozzbin was sitting there with his head on the marble table. Chocha and Ondegador were standing behind Dozzbin. The two Sub Commanders were standing there, holding a position that would normally be for a guard watching over a prisoner. They had a dagger in their right hand, with the right arm across the chest…and watching the prisoner…very closely. Chocha and Ondegador were convinced. Dozzbin had done something *very* illegal. As he was looking, Sub Commanders Rantad and Zadusk joined as guards with daggers ready. The four men formed a semi-circle behind Dozzbin.

Kovarin looked back at Vock. "Do those appear to be accurate rods?"

Vock looked at the scene at the defense table with total hate in his eyes. "Yes, Supreme Commander…they are good ones."

"Thank you, Administrator." He turned to Arthrin. "I ask that these three temperature rods be entered as evidence, and I am finished with this witness, for the moment."

The youth took the three rods and ran them to the evidence table.

Arthrin looked at Dozzbin. "Defendant, do you have any questions for this witness?"

Dozzbin did not look up from the table. He simply waved his hand at Vock as if shooing him away.

Arthrin cleared his throat. "Senior Administrator Vock, you may step down."

Vock stepped down and gratefully accepted a bowl of water and kerchief.

"Supreme Commander, your next witness," said Arthrin quietly.

"I call…Grounder, Chedobo to the stand."

Frosht slammed his staff against the floor. "The Grounder Chedobo, will approach the podium!"

Chedobo got up and walked to the podium. There was a lot of murmuring going on in the gallery. Why would the Supreme Commander talk to, let alone allow, a Grounder into the capitol city…let alone the court? He climbed the three steps and glared at the Judges on the bench.

"State your name and title," said Arthrin.

"Grounder Chedobo."

Again there was considerable murmuring.

Arthrin slammed his gavel down. "SILENCE!" He glared at Kovarin. "There had better be a *very* good reason for this."

"All will be cleared up, My Lord, High Justice."

Arthrin leaned back in his chair again. "Continue."

Kovarin looked back at Chedobo. "Were you a Candidate in the Hatchery, some three years ago?"

"I was," said Chedobo flatly.

"When you officially became a Candidate, did you receive an instructional scroll from one of the Hatchery Administrators?"

"I did not."

"Did you receive a temperature rod from one of the Administrators?"

"I did not."

"Who gave you an instructional scroll?"

"Dozzbin."

"Who gave you a temperature rod?"

"Dozzbin."

"After losing all ten eggs, who collected the instructional scroll and the temperature rod?"

"Dozzbin."

"At any time, during the ten attempts, did you accidentally break a temperature rod?"

"Yes - twice."

"Who gave you a replacement rod?"

"Dozzbin."

"Both times?"

"Yes."

"When you were preparing the sand pit, on each occasion, did it seem rather hot in the egg chamber?"

"It was *very* hot, in both the egg chamber and in the bed chamber."

"What temperature, according to the temperature rod you were given, was the normal temperature, in the sand pit?"

"According to the temperature rod, it was usually between 43 and 45 Abfar."

"And…you lost ten eggs."

"Not one hatched."

"Yesterday, you were taken into the Hatchery again. When you were escorted into one of the hatching chambers, was there an egg in the sand pit, at that time?"

"There was."

"Did it seem as hot, in the egg chamber, as when you were there?"

"Not even close. This time the temperature was very tolerable. The times when I had an egg to care for, I was sweating the entire time."

"Were you allowed to check the temperature rod?"

"Yes."

"What was the reading?"

"44."

"Have you ever had an argument or contest, of any type, with Commander Dozzbin, any time in the past?"

"Yes. In school, I was always getting better results than Dozzbin. There were times that some others showed better than me, but, Dozzbin never did. I always got better scores than him."

"Why did you wait until after Dozzbin was the Supreme Commander, to apply to be a Dragonman?"

"I wasn't sure that I could make it. After I found out that Dozzbin had made it, I was sure that I could make it with my eyes closed. So I applied and made it."

Kovarin looked up at Arthrin. "At this time, I would like this witness to closely see exhibits 1 and 2."

Arthrin grunted and signaled the youth to comply. The boy grabbed both scroll tubes and went to Chedobo and handed them to him. Chedobo took the tubes. He opened the one marked "2". "This looks like the scroll that I was given. It's hard to read because whoever wrote it has some very sloppy writing."

Kovarin smiled. "Please look at the other one."

Chedobo opened it and immediately started handling it with, what appeared to be, reverence, at first. "This…this is… beautiful. I can read this. I don't have to sit there and study any one word…to try and figure out what it is. I love this one."

"Please give them back to the boy."

Chedobo seemed reluctant to stop fondling the good one. He shook his head rolled it back and placed it, carefully, in the tube. The bad scroll was dumped in the tube.

Kovarin looked up at Arthrin. "At this time, I would like this witness to closely see exhibits 3 and 5."

Arthrin nodded consent. The boy grabbed the two rods in question. He ran them to Chedobo. He surrendered the bad one first.

Chedobo looked at it carefully - and scoffed. "This one…" He held it up high. "…it looks like the thing that I was given… each time by Dozzbin. It doesn't look like it's been used, it looks as if it were misused." He was handed the other one and he studied it. "This one, I have never seen the likes of. The numbers are easy to read, the lines are straight. I wish I had had one like this second one."

"So, Commander Dozzbin never gave you a good looking one."

"What he gave me was always something that looked as if it had been used to hammer nails into planks."

"Please give them back to the boy."

The youth took the rods and ran them back to the evidence table.

Kovarin looked up at Arthrin. "I have no more questions for this witness at this time."

Arthrin looked at Dozzbin. "Defendant, do you have any questions for this witness?"

Dozzbin looked up and scoffed. "A whore, sorcery induced liars and now a mongrel. I have no reason to speak to that thing."

Arthrin looked a little nauseous. "Grounder, you may step down."

"Supreme Commander, your next witness," said Arthrin.

"I call Grounder Emkorm to the stand."

Frosht slammed his staff against the floor. "The Grounder Emkorm, will approach the podium!"

Emkorm stood up and swaggered his way to the podium. He was a very large man with huge bulging muscles.

"State your name and title," said Arthrin with disgust in his voice.

"Grounder Emkorm."

Kovarin cleared his throat. "Were you a Candidate in the Hatchery, some two years ago?"

"Yes."

"When you officially became a Candidate, did you receive an instructional scroll from one of the Hatchery Administrators?"

"No."

"Did you receive a temperature rod from one of the Administrators?"

"No."

"Who gave you an instructional scroll?"

He looked at Dozzbin. He sneered. "Dozzbin!" He spat the name out as if it were a curse word.

"Who gave you a temperature rod?"

Again he spat: "Dozzbin!"

"After losing all ten eggs, who collected the instructional scroll and the temperature rod?"

"The same Dozzbin," said Emkorm with unhidden disrespect.

"At any time, during the ten attempts, did you accidentally break a temperature rod?"

"Yes - three times."

"Who gave you a replacement rod?"

"Dozzbin."

"All three times?"

"No one else but him."

"When you were preparing the sand pit, on each occasion, did it seem rather hot in the egg chamber?"

"I've never been that hot, before or since. It was incredibly hot."

"What temperature, according to the temperature rod you were given, was the normal temperature in the sand pit?"

"I did everything I could to keep it at 44 Abfar…according to the rod that I had at the time."

"And you lost ten eggs."

"Every one."

"Yesterday, you were taken into the Hatchery again. When you were escorted into one of the hatching chambers, was there an egg in the sand pit, at that time?"

"Yes, beautiful thing."

"Did it seem as hot, in the egg chamber, as when you were there?"

"I didn't sweat at all. It was nothing like when I was there."

"Were you allowed to check the temperature rod?"

"Yes."

"What was the reading?"

"44."

"Have you ever had an argument or contest, of any type,

with Commander Dozzbin, any time in the past?"

Emkorm chuckled. "All the time, in school. He was always trying to show how tough he was. He never beat me. I bested him in fisticuffs and wrestling. I played with him like a toy. There were at least three times, after I finished whipping him that he left the arena, crying."

"Why did you wait until after Dozzbin was the Supreme Commander, to apply to be a Dragonman?"

"My father died. I had to help my mother and sisters, until they could handle things on their own."

Kovarin looked up at Arthrin. "At this time, I would like this witness to closely see exhibits 1 and 2."

Arthrin nodded. The boy grabbed both scroll tubes and ran them back to Emkorm. Emkorm was given the bad one first. He opened it. "This looks…like…" He started unrolling the scroll. He unrolled it quite a ways, while rolling up the first part. He got to a certain point. "It is! This is the scroll that I was given. I remember it because, one night I was studying it while sipping some wine. The wine went down the wrong tube and I coughed some of it up…onto this scroll. Here's the wine stain right here."

Kovarin smiled. "Please look at the other one."

Emkorm opened it and stood there staring for a moment in shock. "What…what's this? I've never seen the likes. This one…it can be read…without guessing what is written there. This is what should be given to the Candidates, not that other…useless piece of experimental trash."

"Please give them back to the boy."

He put them back in their cases and gave them to the boy.

Kovarin looked up at Arthrin. "At this time, I would like this witness to closely see exhibits 3 and 5."

Arthrin again nodded consent. The boy grabbed the two rods and ran them to Emkorm. As before, he gave the witness the bad one first.

Emkorm handled it very casually. "It looks as if the person who made that bad scroll, also made this...thing." I remember it well. Each time I got a new rod...it looked as if it were in worse condition than the one I'd just broken."

He was handed the good one.

"Now, this is more like it. Using this one would...wait a minute...the numbers are in different places. I'd like to see these things...used side-by-side. The outcome might be very interesting."

"So, Commander Dozzbin never gave you a good looking one."

"What he gave me looked in horrible condition....always."

"Please give them back to the boy."

The youth took the rods and ran them back to the evidence table.

Kovarin looked up at Arthrin. "I have no more questions for this witness at this time."

Arthrin looked at Dozzbin. "Defendant, do you have any questions for this witness?"

Dozzbin shook his head. "Questions? For another mongrel? That thing insults our integrity, get it out of here."

Arthrin sighed. "Grounder Emkorm, you may step down."

"Supreme Commander, your next witness," said Arthrin.

"I call Grounder Tahbahk to the stand."

Frosht grunted in disgust. He then slammed his staff against the floor. "The Grounder Tahbahk, will approach the podium!"

Tahbahk walked up to the podium. He gave an evil glare to Dozzbin as he passed by.

"State your name and title," said Arthrin.

"Grounder Tahbahk."

Kovarin smiled thinking about what was happening. He had not asked the other two Grounders why there was an argument between them and Dozzbin when he first met them. The results of the question had been very satisfying. "Were you a Candidate in the Hatchery, last year?"

"I was."

"When you officially became a Candidate, did you receive an instructional scroll from one of the Hatchery Administrators?"

"Not at all."

"Did you receive a temperature rod from one of the

Administrators?"

"Not at all."

"Who gave you an instructional scroll?"

He looked at Dozzbin and growled the name out. "Dozzbin!"

"Who gave you a temperature rod?"

Again the growl. "Dozzbin."

"After losing all ten eggs, who collected the instructional scroll and the temperature rod?"

"The same Dozzbin."

"At any time, during the ten attempts, did you accidentally break a temperature rod?"

"Yes - six times."

Kovarin was a little rattled at this answer. That meant that Dozzbin had been able to replace eleven rods...at that time. "Uh...each time...who gave you a replacement rod?"

"The same Dozzbin."

"Every time?"

"Yes."

"When you were preparing the sand pit, on each occasion, did it seem rather hot in the egg chamber?"

"Miserable! Absolutely horrible. I've never seen the like, before or since."

"What temperature, according to the temperature rod you were given, was the normal temperature, in the sand pit?"

"I tried to keep it at 44 Abfar at all times."

"And you lost ten eggs."

He hung his head. "Yes."

"Yesterday, you were taken into the Hatchery again. When you were escorted into one of the hatching chambers, was there an egg in the sand pit, at that time?"

"Yes."

"Did it seem as hot, in the egg chamber, as when *you* were there?"

"I liked that temperature. It was very nice. It was *nothing* like when I was in there."

"Were you allowed to check the temperature rod?"

"Yes."

"What was the reading?"

"44."

"Have you ever had an argument or contest, of any type, with Commander Dozzbin, any time in the past?"

"Yes, in the past and in the present: My wife. When we were growing up, Dozzbin was constantly chasing my love, Feenala. She couldn't stand him…she still can't. Neither could I…or can I. She took my *crest* at an early age, in order to try to get him to stay away. He didn't then, he still doesn't now. He has continually tried to go after her to take my *crest* off, even after the confirmation ceremony. A few years ago, I tried to discourage him, by telling him that there was that other woman…I believe her name was…Chesesa. She was chasing after him and throwing herself at him all the time. He told me that he wanted Feenala and he would marry the hag, Chesesa, only as an *absolute* last choice."

Chesesa had been looking away from all of the other witnesses. She could not have turned her head to look at Tahbahk faster if she had been slapped. A myriad of emotions crossed her face as she was contemplating what she had just heard. She looked closely at the smoke to see if there was any indication of a color change - none. She finally slouched down and buried her face in her hands.

"Why did you wait until after Dozzbin was the Supreme Commander, to apply to be a Dragonman?"

"I had to find a safe place to hide Feenala. I knew that that monster would probably try to go after her again. Once I was sure that she was safe I applied. After…" He sighed. "…I lost the tenth egg…I left the capital. I ended up in the same place as all the other…Grounders. Even today, though, Dozzbin has been there chasing after my Feenala. She has told him over and over that she would rather be married to a Grounder than him, for any reason."

Now Chesesa was hatefully glaring a hole through the back of Dozzbin's head. He was sitting there, somewhat slouched over, with his eyes and teeth clenched tight.

Kovarin looked up at Arthrin. "At this time, I would like this witness to closely see exhibits 1 and 2."

Another grunt of consent. The boy again shuttled the two scroll tubes to the witness. Again, he was given the bad one first. Tahbahk grunted. "Same piece of illegible trash I had before."

Kovarin smiled. "Please look at the other one."

Tahbahk opened it. He, like the other two men, was startled by what he saw. "Why wasn't I given something like this? I can read this one. It's very clear...and there are...illustrations."

"Please give them back to the boy."

Tahbahk placed them back in their tube. He handed them back to the runner.

Kovarin looked up at Arthrin. "At this time, I would like this witness to closely see exhibits 3 and 5."

The boy was off and running with them before he got consent from Arthrin. Again, he handed the bad one to Tahbahk, first.

Tahbahk looked at it disgusted. "This looks like one of those, handed to me by Dozzbin. It's scratched up, it is missing lines...it needs badly to be retired." He was handed the other one and he looked at it very closely. "This one is beautiful. This is what should be issued to a Candidate."

"So, Commander Dozzbin never gave you a good looking one."

"No, what he gave me was trash."

"Please give them back to the boy."

The youth took the rods and ran them back to the evidence

table.

Kovarin looked up at Arthrin. "I have no more questions for this witness at this time."

Arthrin looked at Dozzbin. "Defendant, do you have any questions for this witness?"

Dozzbin growled. "A third mongrel. When is this idiotic parade of fools going to end? Get that *thing* out of my sight!"

Arthrin sighed. "Grounder Tahbahk, you may step down."

Tahbahk left the podium. He gave Dozzbin a vulgar gesture as he went back to his seat.

"Supreme Commander, your next witness," said Arthrin.

Kovarin put his arms out with a smile. "Me!"

Frosht stood there a little confused. He did not move, other than his head as he followed Kovarin slowly walking to the podium. All fifteen Justices leaned forward a little, most of them with their mouths hanging open. It seemed that their interest in this testimony was very high.

Kovarin walked up to where the smoke was. He cleared his throat. He blinked his eyes a few times because they were burning.

"State your name and title," said Arthrin.

"Supreme Commander of the War Forces of High Country, Kovarin."

"Proceed, Supreme Commander."

"When I finally passed all the tests for Candidacy, I went to the Hatchery. When I arrived there, I was met by Commander Dozzbin. At that time, *he* issued me an instructional scroll - the one that is currently marked as exhibit 2. He...very loudly *commanded* me to take care of it. He also handed me a temperature rod - the one that is currently marked as exhibit 3. He again, very loudly, *commanded* me to take care of the rod as well. An Administrator, I can't remember his name, assigned me one of the chambers for hatching an egg. At no time did any Administrator bring me anything, initially.

Through nine unsuccessful attempts at hatching an egg, I sweated in those same two rooms. Then...while preparing for the tenth egg, I had the encounter with the Lady Namanti. She was the one who informed me that it was just *too* blamed hot in there. She left the chambers and came back shortly with the three temperature rods, that are marked as exhibits 5, 6 and 7. When I compared the three new rods with the one that I had been using... all the times before, I noticed that the differences were striking. I now realized that the sand pit *was* too hot. I immediately remedied that situation, by getting rid of excess coals and pouring in some cool water.

Another thing that happened was that the Dragonman Kevrong, decided to be facetious. He had forgotten that the instructional scroll was an accountable item, and, to mock me, he threw his scroll down my meat chute and informed me of it in a very derogatory manner. I was a little upset at the time. I pulled the scroll - which is currently marked as exhibit 1 - out of my meat chute and tossed it across the room. Later on, when Kevrong came back, I, in a vengeful manner told him that I knew nothing of that scroll. He left, rather irritated.

On a whim, I opened up the scroll to see what his looked like. I was astonished…and sickened by what I saw. The scroll that I had been using was messy, childish scribbling. The scroll that Kevrong had vindictively thrown at me…a thing of beauty, a work of art…a totally different set of instructions than what I had been following through nine unsuccessful attempted hatchings. I now had a good set of instructions to follow…and I did…to the letter. With a good set of instructions and a good temperature rod, I had a successful hatching on the first attempt: The great black dragon - Diamond.

I need to digress. When the ceremony of presenting the egg to the Candidate took place, I informed the Senior Tribunal, Tremyath, that I had just broken my temperature rod. I now know that the procedure would have been for one of the Administrators to assign a new one. This did not happen. Dozzbin immediately produced another temperature rod from his person and gave it to me. A breach of protocol. I noticed, at the time, that Tribunal Tremyath was surprised by the act as well, but since he didn't say anything about it I let it go…at that time.

I checked this…" He cleared his throat again. "…*new*… temperature rod with the other four that I had in my possession at that time. This *new* rod, was exactly the same as the one that Dozzbin had originally issued to me. This rod is currently on the table as exhibit 4."

He let the information sink in for a few moments. "Several years ago, I myself, had an argument with Commander Dozzbin… while in school. There was a seven challenge tournament. As you know, each of the contestants chooses seven, of twelve, challenges to participate in. Dozzbin and I had five of those challenges in common. He initiated a wager between us, saying that he was the better competitor. I took his wager. Of the first four contests, he took two and I took two. It came down to the 'stone walk'. Once around the track, carrying that heavy round stone. He was ahead of me…at first. He faltered and dropped the stone. As you know, in the rules, you have to pick the stone up, at the exact same place you dropped it. He had to roll the stone, back to the 'dent in the ground' and pick it up there. While he was trying to get the stone back and pick it up, I passed him, and I finished ahead of him. He complained that someone had tripped him and that the wager was forfeit. The referees all stated that no one had touched him, he faltered on his own. I accused him of a reneging and that I *had* won the wager. He, to this day, has refused to pay off."

Kovarin was very pleased with himself. The entire time he had been talking, he had kept his eyes open to watch the smoke. Even though it was just a blur, through his tears, he was able to see the color and it had never changed from the bright blue that indicated "truth".

"All these years, and Dozzbin has carried a monumental grudge against…myself, Chedobo, Emkorm and Tahbahk. Because of this infantile attitude, he has treasonously destroyed 39 eggs, just to keep the four of us from becoming Dragonmen. Because of childish vindictiveness, he has betrayed me…three others…and his country.

I was…initially going to wait, to execute my accusation. I wanted a little more time to gather more evidence and possibly witnesses to bring forward today…my wife, the Lady Namanti… was impatient. That is why we are here…now."

Kovarin stood there, looking down the row of the faces of the Justices. "With that, My Lord, Justices…the Accuser… retires."

After a rather long silence, Arthrin looked at Dozzbin. "Defendant, do you have any questions for this witness?"

Dozzbin stood up. "Why? To hear more lies? To irritate this room with more twists and manipulations of the truth? I don't want to hear another word from that reprehensible scam artist. I can't even stand to look at…*it*!" He sat down.

Arthrin frowned at Dozzbin. "Supreme Commander Kovarin, you may step down." He took a deep breath. "Defendant, you may now present your case."

Dozzbin chuckled and shook his head. He stood up and crossed his arms. He drew in and let out a deep breath. "My case…my case is that…there is no case against me." He scoffed. "That…that 'pretender', that…scam artist has collected, as so-called witnesses, a mendacious, thieving whore…a Tribunal member, who has obviously been put under the spell of a sorcerer…a senile old fool, who makes feeble attempts at being an Administrator…but should have retired…years ago. Himself and his own lies…" He shook his head and scoffed again. "And to top it all off, he brings in three Grounders. Three failures who come up with some insignificant thing from the past and blow it completely out of proportion. That scroll up there…the bad one - I could just as easily prove that he wrote it. The temperature rods…yes, I gave him two rods. The whore says she gave him three. Which two did I give him? Which three did she give him? I put it to you that I gave him two good ones and she is the one who aided in the conspiracy against me, with him, to embarrass me and invent these scurrilous accusations, by creating those bad ones…herself. Circumstantial evidence, coincidences, rumor, fabricated evidence, Grounders who want to blame someone else for their failures…lies, twists, spins and manipulations!" He put his fists on his hips. "There is not one single piece of evidence that can factually be put against me…not one." He growled as he shook his head. "I could waste more of the court's time by fighting each one of these charges, but, I am weary of listening to the manipulations. My total defense is…that there is not one single piece of substantiated evidence against me. No one can put any of this…fabricated junk in my hands or prove that I ever handled it." He sat down.

Kovarin stood up. "Commander Dozzbin, will you stand at the podium and make these comments? We want to see if they are true or not."

Dozzbin chuckled. "I don't have to do anything that you tell me to do. You are the one who has fabricated this entire scheme. You are the one who is going to have to answer for how you did it and why. You have proven *nothing* against me. I'll do as I please."

All that Kovarin could think of was: 'Oops!' The case could fall apart on those facts. The fact that only Kovarin saw *which* rod was handed to him by Dozzbin. All Tremyath could prove, is that Dozzbin handed a temperature rod to Kovarin. Vindictive acts of the past that might have been forgotten...by Dozzbin, while being remembered by the other side of the argument.

Arthrin contemplated for a few moments. "What the defendant says is true. The evidence, while compelling, is still... very circumstantial. There must be something, stronger, that can be attributed to him and him alone...otherwise...your case is based...mostly on speculation. You have not supplied anything that is his alone."

Chesesa stood up. "Maybe I can supply you with what you need to...hang this...thing!" She started heading for the podium while glaring at Dozzbin contemptuously.

Dozzbin grabbed Chesesa's arm and held her back. "High Justice, you can't allow a woman to testify against her husband!"

Arthrin scowled at Dozzbin. "You cannot *force* a woman to testify. If she comes forward of her own free will, neither you nor I, can stop her."

"I will *not* let her," shouted Dozzbin.

At that moment, the Sub Commanders who had been the chaperones came up. Ondegador slammed the hilt of his knife onto Dozzbin's wrist. Chocha and Zadusk both held the blades of their knives up to Dozzbin's throat.

Chocha looked at Dozzbin in the most sinister way he could. "She wants to testify...you cannot and will not stop her," he growled through his teeth.

Jeshko grabbed Dozzbin's arm. He placed his knife on top of Dozzbin's wrist. "Let her go, or she'll go up to the podium, with your dismembered hand, hanging on her sleeve."

Hobaro placed his knife next to Jeshko's, on Dozzbin's wrist.

Dozzbin looked at Chesesa fearfully. "Don't do this," he whispered angrily.

Chesesa looked at Hobaro. "Cut his hand off, he won't need it after he's been condemned."

Hobaro looked more than ready to start carving. Dozzbin pulled his hand back while still looking at Chesesa with some desperate pleading in his eyes.

She stormed up to the podium. She made the mistake of waiting to inhale when she got to the smoke. She gagged and coughed for a few moments while she cleared her lungs.

Before Chesesa could speak, Arthrin interrupted: "Lady Chesesa, I must have it on the official record - do you voluntarily waive spousal privilege for this testimony?"

She stood there with her fists at her side. "I waive it voluntarily and willingly! I also petition the court, at this time, to allow me to take this wretched *crest* off and throw it into the sewer."

Arthrin gave a pained look. "That petition will have to wait. We will hear your testimony…at this time…in regards to this case."

Dozzbin screamed at her. "Don't do this!"

Hobaro and Zadusk forced Dozzbin back to his seat. As

soon as he was seated, Chocha put a knife to his throat. Jeshko grabbed his hair so that he could not get away from the knife.

Chocha got in real close and whispered. "The Justices may not be convinced...but we *are*. Keep very still...or I will have an accident...with your throat."

Once Chesesa saw that Dozzbin was corralled, she turned back to face the bench. "All the time that we've been married, he keeps on talking about this...Feenala. He told me that she was dead. He told me that she had been killed in some...catastrophe... years ago. When we're under the furs, he calls *me* Feenala. Now, I find out that she's alive and he's still chasing after her...even though she prefers being married to a Grounder, rather than consorting with him. That makes me wonder what other tall tales he's telling." She gave him another evil glare. "He has this secret office at home. When he goes in there, we are not allowed in, not I or my sons are allowed to go in there...for any reason. We're not even allowed to knock on the door. When he comes out, his fingers are stained with either ink or paint. I've seen him carrying scrolls in there. I've seen him carrying several boxes in there, large and small.

The entire time, since the accusation, where he has been under close scrutiny from the chaperones...he has gone nowhere near that secret room. I understand that the chaperones would have had to go with him. He is hiding something in there and he won't even let the chaperones know about the room, let alone allow *them* in."

Dozzbin screamed at her. "What I do in there, deals with military issues! It is none of your concern!"

She turned and screamed back at him. "No, it doesn't. When you fill out all of your ridiculous edicts, you do it at that desk that's next to the bed. Your fingers are covered in ink after you do your writing there. You're writing *something* in that secret room and it has nothing to do with your silly edicts." She turned back to the bench. "Each time he writes an edict, he has to go through several different drafts He has never been satisfied with the first one. He always wants to make them sound…as if the world will end if they aren't enacted immediately. He's doing some kind of other writing in that secret room. It might explain that…phony instruction scroll.

As to the temperature rods, I've seen them up close. The writing on them was done in a white paint. Sometimes when he comes out of that secret room, he has white paint on his fingers and a little spattered on his face."

Arthrin looked around the room in contemplation. "Lady Chesesa, are you finished?"

"Yes, High Justice."

He looked both ways down the bench at the Associate Justices. He stood up. "We will retire to the back room for a few moments. We will bring a decision out shortly."

Frosht slammed his staff against the floor. "All in attendance will stand!"

As the Justices filed out through the central door, Aj walked up to Kovarin.

Aj chuckled…then whispered: "They'll be back when?

Have you ever heard of any judge making a quick decision?"

Kovarin sighed. "We don't have much of a choice."

After all fifteen had exited behind the curtains, people immediately began talking. It started out as a minor rumble and then built up to a bit of a din.

Chesesa turned around and sat down on the top step of the podium. She received a bowl of water and a kerchief right there, which she gratefully used. After clearing her eyes, she sat there glaring at Dozzbin, with hurt and hate in her eyes. While sitting there, she ended up having to move out of the way of the very fat Inquisitor. He had chosen this time to check his little truth box. He again grunted as he went up each step. He looked the box over, opened a small latch near the bottom and put some kind of rock in the bottom of the box. He smiled, turned and grunted his way down the steps again.

Dozzbin glared back at Chesesa...at first. He then appeared as if he were trying to think his way out of this mess. He looked at the Sub Commanders that surrounded him. They all stood ready with a dagger held high - ready to strike, if necessary.

Before any of the people in the gallery could really get comfortable with just sitting and waiting and speculating...until who knows what, the man with the large gavel slammed it down on the Judge's desk. Most talking abruptly ceased. "All who are in the Great Hall, will stand for the High Justices."

All talking ceased and everyone stood up. The fifteen Justices slowly filed in and went to their seats.

Arthrin, again, was the last to come in. He looked around at the large gallery, picked up his gavel and sat down. "Be seated." He sat there for a few moments letting everyone stew and fret. "While the charges against Commander Dozzbin have not thoroughly been proven...there is *great* suspicion. There is, at this time, no witness that he is the author of the false instructional scroll. There is witness that says it *appears* to be his handwriting. This means that it bears further investigation. There *is* witness, that he has broken protocol, in the Hatchery on several occasions. While in and of itself, this is not a crime, it still proves suspicious activity. The Lady Chesesa has given us more things to contemplate." He twirled his gavel in his hand. "While we cannot convict on what we have heard, we can still order further investigation. The two scrolls that have been entered into evidence, will be compared. Find out if there are discrepancies and if there are - how bad are they? This...secret room...while any person in this country can have a private place for themselves...if there is any...criminal activity or intent going on, it must be investigated. Commander Dozzbin has claimed that it is for military duties and secrets. I can understand the need for the military to keep certain secrets from the populace. That is *very* necessary. The Lady Chesesa, however, has introduced us to a bit of a conundrum. If he is writing his edicts, right next to her, what *is* going on in this secret room? The question that arises here: Who will investigate this private room? Since it is the Supreme Commander who brings the charges against Commander Dozzbin, it cannot be the Supreme Commander who investigates the room. There is a need for at least one of the other Battle Division Commanders to aid in this investigation, along with a trained investigator from the Constabulary.

In three days from now, we will reconvene this trial. During those three days, the Administrators from the Hatchery will compare the scrolls.

If there are any Battle Division Commanders here, will you please identify yourselves and come forward."

Two men stood up and came down from the gallery.

The first one to arrive near the podium introduced himself. "I am Battle Division 1 Commander, Heth. I am the rider of the great brown dragon, Monster. I will aid in the investigation."

The second one arrived, stood on the other side of the podium and introduced himself. "I am Battle Division 3 Commander, Ayponch. I am the rider of the great gray dragon, Protector. I will aid in this investigation."

Arthrin nodded to both men. "During the investigation of the…room in question, Commander Dozzbin will not be allowed to go near it and possibly compromise any evidence. The chaperones who are currently watching him will continue with these duties for the next three days." He looked around. "Are there any questions?"

Chocha turned away from Dozzbin. "I have a question, My Lord, High Justice."

"Yes, who are you and what is it?"

"I am Battle Division 3 Sub Commander, Chocha. I am the rider of the great gray dragon, Endeavor. My question is: Do we keep him away, *only* from this secret room, or do we keep him away from anything else?"

Arthrin cleared his throat. "Since it is the wife of Commander Dozzbin, who has brought this…*situation* to light, I feel that it is best that he be kept from the Lady Chesesa as well. It is suggested that he be kept away from his home, altogether. He will be temporarily lodged elsewhere, for the duration of these three days. Are there any other questions?"

There was nothing but a few coughs heard in the gallery.

Arthrin heaved a sigh. "Then we are adjourned, for the three day duration of the investigation. May the Great Maker watch over our activities and may justice prevail." He banged his gavel on the desk. He stood up.

Frosht slammed his staff against the floor. "All in attendance will stand!"

The Justices all filed out silently. After they had all gone behind the curtain, Frosht again slammed his staff against the floor. "Depart in peace, all of you! Let justice prevail in all of our lives!" He headed for the same area where the Judges had gone.

Mass noise arose as almost everyone seemed to start talking at the same time.

Chesesa glared at Dozzbin as she walked by him. After she had passed by, she did not look back.

Kovarin leaned down to Namanti. "Now you see why I wanted to wait. We didn't have enough of the information to slam him down in one shot. Maybe next time, you'll be more patient."

Namanti just gave Kovarin a sour and hurt look.

The six chaperones all stood there giving Dozzbin the evil

eye. They escorted him to a temporary facility that would keep him, far away, from Chesesa, the secret room and Kovarin.

18

During the three day investigation, Kovarin was scrutinized as well, by the Constables, in order to make sure that he was *not* fabricating any new evidence. He used that time to get in more flight training with Diamond. One thing that he found out about a fully mature dragon was that the eating habits changed radically. When he was flying Diamond, if the dragon started doing his "hunger cry", you start looking for one of the pastures where they have a lot of ovine or bovine running around. You tell the dragon to eat and do not try to steer him at all. Once Diamond had decided on which of the livestock to use for his next meal, Kovarin found out what those claws were for. Diamond swooped down from above onto a steer. He dug his front claws deep into the neck of the *very* surprised steer, while using his rear claws to dig in deep and pick the steer up. By the time Diamond had found a place to dig in and eat, the steer had either bled to death or died of shock from the pain or trauma. Another thing that was different was that Diamond was now able to digest bone as well. He did not care what he bit into or off of the steer. He was able to swallow everything. Kovarin now knew that the control he had over Diamond, included the fact that no matter how hungry he was, the big dragon would not eat until given permission, by his handler.

Another thing that happened during those three days was that Namanti got to take her first solo ride on Diamond. The purpose of this was to get both Namanti used to Diamond and vice versa. When she came back, she was in a state of euphoria. Kovarin knew what she had gone through, because of that first ride he had taken, so long ago, with Onjono, and then his first solo ride on Diamond.

Namanti was so excited that she could not finish a sentence. "I took him…he…*whoosh*…and the…and then I…he…we went *wheee*…and then he…I went up…he was…and *whoom* we…" She used her arms to show, in wild, animated, exaggerated movements the different twists and maneuvers and turns that they had gone through as she tried to orate. Namanti was learning just what it was like to be a handler…if the worst should happen to Kovarin.

After hearing all of her gibberish, partial sentences and wild ravings, he, with a flat monotone and a blank stare said: "So, did you enjoy yourself?"

She was momentarily stunned. Her shoulders sagged and her jaw dropped. She then realized that he was joking and screamed at him. She threw her arms around his neck. "Oh, thank you for picking me. I'll wear your *crest* forever. If you want ten children, you got em'. Thank you, thank you, thank you, I love you." She planted several kisses all over his face.

He chuckled. "Thank you, and I love you too."

She giggled and started caressing his neck. "Do you want to start on the first of our children…now?"

He smiled.

The fateful day arrived to reconvene the trial.

When they arrived, they were met by Aj on the way in. "Supreme Commander, I was asked to convey a message to you… by a Dragonhandler, named…Cwal?" He shrugged. "Anyway, he told me to tell you that four eggs, all size eight, have been distributed to the Candidates. Does that mean…anything?"

Kovarin smiled with pride. "Diamond's first breeding! Four eggs! You said that all of them were size eight? Wonderful!"

They went inside. Frosht and all those other people went through the same pomp and circumstance and rituals of the court, before anything could get done.

Kovarin and Namanti took their seats as the Accusers. The three Grounders were back, sitting directly behind Kovarin.

Dozzbin was there looking a little haggard. The six chaperones were there, looking no less ominous than before, with daggers at the ready.

Chesesa took a seat - behind Kovarin.

After everybody was where they were supposed to be, Arthrin heaved a sigh and then looked to the Accuser's desk. "Supreme Commander, are you prepared to continue?"

Kovarin was a little surprised at the question. He stood up. "High Justice, I assumed that you were the one who would preside…at this time. I mean…it was at your command…the further investigations were ordered. I was commanded to stay out of it…in order to avoid any compromise."

Arthrin looked a little surprised and disgusted. "I told you to stay out of the investigation itself. I did not tell you to be totally ignorant of what was going on."

"Well, High Justice, I'm afraid…that's what happened." Kovarin shrugged helplessly.

Arthrin groaned in pain. "All right." He shook his head. "Inquisitor, there has been a charge that that truth box had somehow been tampered with, magically. Is there any truth to this?"

The little fat man stood up. "Oh, no, Milord High Justice. There are several indicators, if that sort of thing happens. None of those indicators were present."

"So when it was blue, that was the truth and when it was yellow that was mendacity?"

"Absolutely, High Justice."

"Thank you. Now! Whom is, or are, the person or persons, who took on the task of investigating this faulty scroll?"

Five men stood up.

Arthrin looked them over. "One at a time, state your name and title, for the record, please."

"Vock, Senior Administrator for the Hatchery"

"Acong, Secondary Administrator for the Hatchery."

"Nathak, Secondary Administrator for the Hatchery."

"Bruthik, Secondary Administrator for the Hatchery."

"Paligon, Constable Detective. Primary expert in

investigating forged writings."

Arthrin nodded. "We will go with the ranking man from the Hatchery first."

Frosht slammed his staff against the floor. "Senior Administrator Vock, will approach the podium."

Vock headed for the podium. As he passed by Frosht he gave the man a dirty look. "Do you always have to be so loud?"

Frosht ignored the comment.

Vock got to the top step and coughed a few times from the smoke.

Arthrin leaned forward. "Administrator Vock, have you… finished scrutinizing the entire scroll?"

"No, High Justice, we stopped at a certain point…it was useless to continue."

Atrhrin looked appalled. "I told you to go over the entire thing, why did you stop?"

"It was pointless, High Justice. At the beginning, we found three glaring discrepancies. Any one of the three, by itself, could have prevented the hatching of the egg. All three combined…it would take a miracle for the egg to hatch. The hatching is virtually impossible as a result. We continued on. When the hatchling first comes out of the shell, we found four more discrepancies. Two of these discrepancies would interfere or totally destroy the bond that is supposed to be there in order to control the dragon. The other two would injure…possibly fatally, the hatchling. If the hatchling survived those atrocities, there are more down the path…that are equally as diabolical…if the hatchling survives this long. It would be sickly, it would be in constant pain, and it would be, at best, lethargic. At a certain point, the Ringmaster would go in to take care of his responsibilities. One of those responsibilities is to make sure that the young dragon is in good health. Once he saw the condition of the dragon, he would report it and an investigation would begin. We would go over the scroll with the Candidate to find out what went wrong. Once the Candidate showed us that horrible document, we would have discovered the conspiracy, right then and there. If the egg never hatches…no investigation is warranted and you end up with a ten time failure. We found a total of 135 atrocious discrepancies before we finally said: Enough! No dragon could suffer that much…and live."

Arthrin sat there thinking.

One of the other Judges spoke up: "If, as you say, the egg should never hatch, why do you think a conspirator would even bother with the rest of the scroll?"

"My Lord, Justice, when the Candidates are in training, they are told that they will be receiving *one* scroll that has *all* the instructions. If they were to receive a scroll that stopped at a certain point, before the *coming out*, even the dumbest Candidate should realize that there is something dreadfully wrong with the scroll that they have in hand. They are told to read the entire scroll. That way, when the dragon gets to a certain point, they are not totally ignorant of what can or does happen."

Another Judge spoke up: "So, at the beginning, hatching is thwarted, and even if, by some unforeseen accident, the egg hatches, each following instruction is designed to bring about the death…or ill health of the youngling. Is that what you're saying?"

"Absolutely, My Lord."

Arthrin looked both ways down the bench. "Anybody else?"

Nothing.

Arthrin turned to Kovarin. "Supreme Commander, do you have any questions for this witness?"

"No, My Lord Justice, I believe that he has satisfied my curiosity completely."

Arthrin looked at Dozzbin. "Defendant, do you have any questions for this witness?"

Dozzbin did not move…anything.

Arthrin shrugged. "Thank you, Senior Administrator, you may step down."

Vock smiled, nodded, turned away from the smoke and staggered down the steps to a welcome bowl of water and a kerchief.

Arthrin looked at the others who had worked with Vock. "Are there any more comments or any additions to the testimony from any of you?"

The three Administrators shook their heads.

Paligon stood up. "Yes, Milord High Justice, I have something to add."

"What was your name again, Sir?"

"Constable Detective Paligon, Milord."

Frosht slammed his staff against the floor. "Constable Detective Paligon, will approach the podium."

Paligon flinched when the staff hit the floor. "All right, all right, you don't have to get cranky about it." He headed for the podium, trying to clear his left ear with his pinky finger. He climbed the three steps to the smoke. Apparently he was used to testifying and the smoke did not seem to bother him…much.

"State your name and title again, for the record," said Arthrin.

"Constable Detective, Paligon."

"And, good Constable, what have you to add?"

"I have examined many passages throughout the faulty scroll in question. I have also examined many of the edicts that we know *were* written by Commander Dozzbin. In my expert opinion, this faulty scroll *was* written by Commander Dozzbin, from beginning to end."

One of the other Judges spoke up: "How can you be so sure? If a forger wanted to make it look as if Commander Dozzbin had done it, how can you be so sure that someone else did not, in fact, write this scroll?"

"Even the best forger, in doing something that long, has a tendency to get bored or tired of copying someone else's style. They would tend to drift or get lazy and go back to their own normal style of writing. I find no drifting or any other form of inconsistency. This faulty scroll *is* consistent and had just one author - Commander Dozzbin."

Arthrin again looked both ways down the bench. He turned to Kovarin. "Supreme Commander, any questions?"

"None, My Lord, High Justice. I am quite satisfied."

Arthrin looked at Dozzbin. "Defendant, do you have any questions for this witness?"

Dozzbin still sat there motionless.

Arthrin cleared his throat. "Constable, you may step down," he said quietly. He again looked at the other three who had investigated the scroll. "Is there anything else that any of you three may want to add?"

All three shook their heads.

"All right," said Arthrin. He took a deep breath and let it out slowly. "So, on to that secret room thing. Are those two Commanders in court today?"

Heth and Ayponch both stood up and moved towards the podium. A third man was headed for the podium as well. He was in the uniform of the Constabulary. The three men stood next to the podium looking up at the bench.

Arthrin sniffed. "Which one of you is the ranking Dragonman?"

"I, Battle Division 1 Commander, Heth, rider of the great brown dragon, Monster."

Frosht slammed his staff against the floor. "Division Commander Heth, to the podium."

Ayponch looked back at Frosht. "We're right here, there's no need to shout."

Frosht glanced at Ayponch. "Protocol, Milord."

Ayponch grunted and rolled his eyes as he turned back to the bench.

"I would tell you to state your name and title…but you already have," said Arthrin. "So, what do you have to say about this…secret room? Is it military secrets that we may not know about, or is it something else?"

Heth coughed a few times as he got near the smoke. "It is something that is much more…sinister, High Justice. We found four scrolls in the room. Two are fabricated instructional scrolls that have been written by the hand of Commander Dozzbin. One is an unfinished fabrication and the other is not yet started. There are also twelve temperature rods in the room as well. Nine have been tampered with, one is in the process of being changed…two are still good."

Arthrin shook his head. "Are there any other objects in the room, Commander?"

Heth cleared his throat and coughed. "High Justice, There are several dozen worn out quills along with several empty ink bottles. There is a supply of new quills and eight unopened ink bottles. There is also a knife that shows signs of being used to scratch the good numbers off of the temperature rods. There are at least a dozen paint brushes that are small enough to paint new numbers on the rods, along with a large bucket of paint that is consistent with the colors of the lines on the temperature rods. All of the information I have just given you, is in this affidavit..." He pulled a small scroll tube out of his belt. "...signed by myself and Battle Division 3 Commander, Ayponch."

One of the other Judges spoke up: "Just how detrimental are these...so called *bad* temperature rods?"

"We did an experiment, Milord, Justice. We took all of the finished *bad* rods and went to an empty hatching room in the Hatchery. We got all of the necessary coals and other equipment for heating the sand pit. We obtained twenty eggs from different fowls in a barnyard. Once we had the pit up to 43 Abfar...according to the *bad* rods, we placed the fowl eggs into the pit. Using a time-glass, we took one egg out at each turning of the glass. We cracked the egg open and talked to a kitchen maid and asked her how well cooked the egg was. By the time we got to the sixth turn of the glass...all of the eggs were fully cooked." He closed his eyes and turned his head to the side. He cleared his throat again and looked back to the bench. "If a dragon egg, especially a small one was put in that same sand pit...by the time the 32 days was up...it would be thoroughly cooked. The smaller the egg, the faster...or greater certainty...of it being...totally cooked."

Arthrin leaned forward. "Commander, is that information in the affidavit, as well?"

"Yes, High Justice...it most assuredly is."

The room was very silent.

Arthrin again looked both ways down the bench. He turned to Kovarin. "Supreme Commander, any questions, from you for this witness?"

"None, My Lord, High Justice."

Arthrin looked at Dozzbin. "Defendant, do you have any questions for this witness?"

Dozzbin still sat there motionless.

Arthrin hung his head. "Commander, you may step down."

Heth stepped down looking for the merciful bowl of water and kerchief.

Arthrin turned to Ayponch. "Commander, do you have anything to add...to what your colleague has said?"

"No, Milord, High Justice - as he said, it's all in the affidavit and signed by both of us."

Arthrin nodded. "And...who...is this third man?"

The Constable took one step forward. "Constable Detective Zlah, Milord."

"Constable, do you have anything to add?"

"Oh, absolutely, High Justice!"

Ayponch covered his ears and grimaced as Frosht slammed his staff against the floor. "The Constable Detective, Zlah to the podium."

Zlah climbed the three steps.

"Again, I would tell you to state your name and title...but you already have," said Arthrin. "So, what is this extra testimony?"

"High Justice, I am a colleague of Constable Detective

Paligon. While Paligon was examining the scroll that has been placed in evidence, I was examining the two scrolls found in the secret room. I compared the writing, in these scrolls, to some of the edicts, written by Commander Dozzbin. The writing is totally consistent with the aforementioned Commander. Upon reading many of the passages in the two finished scrolls, I was assured, by the two Commanders who were with me, that no dragon could have survived the ordeal of being taken care of…by those atrocious instructions."

Arthrin looked both ways down the bench. He turned to Kovarin. "Supreme Commander, any questions from you for this witness?"

"None, My Lord, High Justice."

Arthrin looked at Dozzbin. "Defendant, do you have any questions for this witness?"

Dozzbin sat there motionless.

Arthrin shook his head. "Constable, you may step down." He put his elbows on the desk and covered his face with his hands, for a few moments. He sighed. "Is there…any further… testimony…from either side?"

Kovarin stood up. "None, My Lord, High Justice."

Dozzbin did not move.

Arthrin looked at the other Judges. "We will retire to the deliberation room. I don't think that the decision will take a very long time. Until we come back…the defendant will be kept under close guard." He banged his gavel on the desk and stood up.

Frosht slammed his staff against the floor. "All in attendance will stand!"

The Justices all filed out silently. After they had all gone behind the curtain, Frosht again slammed his staff against the floor. "Lord High Justice, Arthrin has requested that you all stay in place, until they come back to the bench. If they cannot make their decision today, I will let you know." He headed for the same area where the Judges had gone.

Heth and Ayponch joined the six, with daggers ready, who had been assigned as chaperones, in guarding Dozzbin.

Kovarin looked back at the three Grounders. Chedobo was staring back to a certain place in the gallery. He did not move the entire time they were waiting. Emkorm simply sat there slouching, looking as if *he* were the one who had been put on trial. Tahbahk was sitting there with his eyes closed, silently mouthing some kind of prayer.

Namanti glared up at Kovarin. "You made me confess...to taking those rods...illegally! What are they gonna do to me? Did you think of that before you asked me those questions?"

"Yes, I did. I'm not worried. What you ended up doing... *ended* up being something for the greater good. If they want to bring any punishment against you...I'll fight it hard...in your favor, my Darling."

She grunted, crossed her arms and just sat there brooding.

He put his arms around her and held her tight, trying to reassure her...and himself.

The man with the giant gavel slammed it down on the Judge's desk.

Namanti let out a yelp of surprise when the hammer sound echoed through the entire great hall. She had fallen asleep while waiting for...

"All who are in the Great Hall, will stand for the High Justices."

Kovarin helped Namanti get up.

The Judges started filing in. Once again, Arthrin was the last to enter. He gave both Kovarin and Dozzbin a rather stern look. "We are back in session. You may be seated." He banged his gavel. "Are there any more comments before we render the decision?"

"I have one, High Justice," said Dozzbin.

Arthrin almost looked indignant. "What is it?"

"I'd like to know what punishment that the whore Namanti is going to get for stealing and tampering with those temperature rods?"

Now Arthrin really *did* look indignant. Several of the other Judges scoffed. A few of them shook their heads. One sat there trying to hide the fact that he was laughing.

Namanti squeezed Kovarin's hand to the point where he almost winced in pain.

Arthrin cleared his throat. "It is the decision...*unanimous* decision of this court…that the actions of *Lady* Namanti are being viewed as divine intervention in an atrocious situation."

Namanti let go of Kovarin's hand and let out a long sigh of relief.

Dozzbin growled. "High Justice, that woman stole rods from Dragonman Candidates! She deserves some kind of punishment for this repeated crime!"

Arthrin had a look on his face as if he had just tasted something very bitter. He sniffed loudly and then cleared his throat. "Supreme Commander Kovarin!"

Kovarin stood up. "Yes, My Lord, High Justice."

"When you get home tonight…turn your wife over your knee and spank her. Three swats for each transgression. That is the ruling of this court."

"I assure you that it will be done, High Justice." He sat down and looked down at Namanti, trying desperately not to laugh. "You heard him," he whispered.

Namanti gave Kovarin a dirty look, slouched down and crossed her arms.

Dozzbin growled again. He started to say something else.

Arthrin banged his gavel. "The accused will sit down and SHADDUP! We will hear no more comments from you!" He looked around the gallery. He took a deep breath and let it out slowly. "From all the testimony and evidence that we have, it appears that the total charges against the defendant are: Four counts of fabricating an instructional scroll that would virtually guarantee the death of a dragon. Twenty or more counts of fabricating a temperature rod that would virtually guarantee the death of an unborn dragon. Thirty-nine charges of willingly and maliciously causing the death of an unborn dragon. For the moment we will look past the false scrolls and tampered rods." He shook his head and pursed his lips. "Never, in the history of High Country, has there ever been a criminal who...so totally insulted the entire realm, so badly. For the thirty-nine counts of purposeful and malicious destruction of a dragon egg, we the members of the High Court, by unanimous decision, do find the accused guilty of all charges. We sentence the accused to the mandatory death penalty. The only disgrace here, being that we can only execute this traitor once. As to the fabrications and forgeries...any sentence would be trivial and a waste of time talking about it, compared to what was done to the eggs. So, we shall not bother wasting our breath. Since this man has been found guilty of killing unborn dragons, we find him guilty of treason as well...thirty-nine times. From this day forth, his name will not be spoken and if it is, it will be a synonym for traitor. In consideration of what our verdict is, we must look to the Lady Chesesa. She has petitioned this court, to allow her to lawfully remove the *crest* of the traitor. This court unanimously supports that petition. The Lady Chesesa is allowed to remove and destroy the aforementioned *crest* at her whim. It is also the ruling, in conjunction with the verdict against the accused, that the Lady Chesesa now has full charge and care of the great brown dragon, Thunder. The Lady Chesesa may also refuse to put the name of the father on the *crest* of any male child that was sired by the traitor. It has come to our attention that the traitor was quite adept at issuing all forms of edicts. From this day forth, *all* edicts, authored and enacted by the traitor are now officially null and void." Arthrin took several breaths and collected his thoughts. "Because of the actions of the traitor, it seems that the person, known as Grounder Chedobo, was completely cheated…when it came to being given a fair chance of hatching a dragon. The traitor made any successful hatching, completely impossible. We turn the decision over to the Supreme Commander of the War Forces of High Country, as to the whether or not, this Grounder Chedobo, should be given another chance as a Dragonman Candidate. Supreme Commander, do you allow it?"

Kovarin stood up. "I don't allow it, I *command* it, High Justice."

Chedobo fell to his knees and buried his face in his hands. The way his body was jerking, it was hard to tell whether he was laughing or crying…or both. A short gray-haired woman ran up to Chedobo sobbing and threw her arms around him and rested her head on top of his. The two of them were there for some time, crying in the arms of each other.

"Because of the actions of the traitor, it seems that the person, known as Grounder Emkorm, was completely cheated… when it came to being given a fair chance of hatching a dragon. The traitor made any successful hatching, completely impossible. We turn the decision over to the Supreme Commander of the War Forces of High Country, as to the whether or not, this Grounder Emkorm, should be given another chance as a Dragonman Candidate. Supreme Commander, do you allow it?"

Kovarin smiled. "I don't allow it, I *command* it, High Justice."

Emkorm stood up and threw his arms up in triumph, with a huge smile on his face. A large man and a woman came down from another place in the gallery and the three of them had a very tearful group hug.

Arthrin continued: "Because of the actions of the traitor, it seems that the person, known as Grounder Tahbahk, was completely cheated…when it came to being given a fair chance of hatching a dragon. The traitor made any successful hatching, completely impossible. We turn the decision over to the Supreme Commander of the War Forces of High Country, as to the whether or not, this Grounder Tahbahk, should be given another chance as a Dragonman Candidate. Supreme Commander, do you allow it?"

"I don't allow it, I *command* it, High Justice."

Tahbahk and Aj both shouted a cry of joy and the two men hugged each other.

Arthrin sighed. "Normally, I do not allow that kind of… carrying on, in my courtroom. Considering the circumstances, though, I will not hold anything against them." Another long sigh. "Since the condemned is of the military and the crime is a military one, I will now turn the condemned over to the Supreme Commander, for the purpose of carrying out the sentence. The only suggestion that I will make to the Supreme Commander, at this time, is that the military uniform be stripped off of the condemned. Said traitor is an insult to said uniform."

Kovarin turned to the chaperones and nodded. They did not hesitate to start pulling parts of the uniform off of Dozzbin. They also did not try to be polite about it.

There were four members of the Constabulary who came up to the prisoner and supplied the chaperone Commanders with some shackles to hold the prisoner.

Once Dozzbin was on the floor, totally restrained, Arthrin stood up. "This case is over. Let justice prevail at all times." He banged his gavel and the Judges all started filing out.

Dozzbin looked up and tried to say something to Kovarin. Before he could utter one sound, Rantad punched him in the side of the head and Zadusk savagely kicked him in the ribs.

Ondegador yanked Dozzbin's head back, by his hair. "No one is interested in anything that a convicted and condemned traitor has to say, so keep your putrid hole shut!"

"Get that *thing* out of here," said Kovarin flatly.

Dozzbin was dragged out by some of the Sub Commanders with the help of a few Constables.

Kovarin turned to Aj. "Is this man…an acquaintance…of yours?"

"My cousin," said Aj as he wiped away some tears. He looked at Tahbahk. "My cousin, *Candidate* Tahbahk!" he stated proudly!

Tahbahk was standing there with his arms around a rather small woman who had a huge smile on her face and tearstains running down both cheeks. "Supreme Commander," said Tahbahk joyfully, "let me introduce my wife, Feenala."

The little brown haired woman turned her head to look at Kovarin. She let go of Tahbahk and threw her arms around

Kovarin. "Oh thank you, Commander, thank you. We can come back to civilized society again, without having to worry about that…monster…or what people are saying about us."

Kovarin gave her a few pats on the back. "You're quite welcome, dear Lady.

Feenala held on to Kovarin for several moments sobbing before she let go and went back to her husband.

Kovarin moved to the next man. "Candidate Emkorm, how are you doing now?"

Emkorm started laughing. "I haven't felt this good…in quite some time, Supreme Commander. Thank you, for…doing this. Thank you for exposing that…*thing*. Thank you for the reinstatement."

Kovarin looked at the two people hugging him. "Do you know these people, Candidate Emkorm?"

Another round of laughing. "Yes, Supreme Commander, let me introduce you to my Uncle Hochkon and my mother, Zindeema."

It was now Zindeema who threw her arms around Kovarin and started sobbing as she got a few words of gratitude out in between all of the crying.

Kovarin patted her on the back as well as he nodded to and shook hands with the Uncle.

After Zindeema finally let go of him, he went to Chedobo. "Candidate Chedobo…uh…please stand."

The little gray-haired woman was kissing him on the top of his head and caressing his back as she repeated, several times, "my baby,' back."

Chedobo tried to stand up, however he could not break the hold his mother had on him. He finally put an arm around her waist and stood up. "Uh…Supreme Commander…this is my mother…Ansheea. She and I would just love to thank you for what you did."

Kovarin smiled. "It wasn't all me, Candidate. I had help from you, the two other victims of Doz…uh, the traitor, as well as some much needed assistance from the Hatchery Administrators."

"Nevertheless, it was you who exposed and prosecuted that…*wretched* thing. Again, thank you, Supreme Commander."

Kovarin gave him a polite nod and stepped back. "CANDIDATES, your attention!"

The three men stopped what they were doing and snapped to attention.

"You three gentlemen will make yourselves available to the Hatchery Administrators, at the earliest possible time…or when it is most convenient to you, for uh…refresher information, in the task of hatching and caring for a dragon. Any questions?"

The three men saluted.

"May you and your dragon fly high and long," said Emkorm.

The other two echoed the sentiment.

Kovarin returned the salute. "May your hatching be a success."

Kovarin and Namanti arrived back at their home.

He walked in and flopped himself down on a chair with a loud exhalation. "What a day!"

She chuckled. "What a day, indeed! I'm going to go take a bath."

"Before you go, my Love, will you help me unlatch this breastplate?"

She giggled. "Where's Commander Aj?"

"By now, he and his Candidate cousin are probably half way to getting *roaring* drunk."

She snickered some more as she unlatched the plate. He took it off and laid it on the table.

"I need to clean this thing…now."

She looked at it with horror. "What *is* all of…*that*?"

He huffed. "Snot, spit, sweat and tears - any other questions?"

She turned away and pointed as she left. "A bath!"

He shook his head as he got some clean rags and started wiping the "liquids" off of the breastplate. It took longer than he thought it would.

Namanti came out with a towel wrapped around her body. She had another on she was using to dry her hair. "Haven't you finished with that thing yet?"

"There were several, grateful women, who…used it as a crying hanky. I couldn't really…push them away."

She snickered. "What did you think of that ridiculous thing that the Judge said?"

"What? Ridiculous…? What thing?"

She bent over to wrap the towel around her head. "He told you to spank me." She scoffed. "What utter…"

She was cut off as he grabbed an arm and threw her over his lap, on her stomach. He put his left arm across her back to keep her from escaping and gave her bottom, nine *hard* smacks…as had been ordered by the High Justice. She screamed or squawked with each lick. He then let her go.

She stood there facing him. Her face was red with anger. Her breath was going in and out very rapidly as she angrily glared at him, while rubbing her buttocks. "You didn't have to hit that hard, didja?"

He put his arms out and shrugged. "The High Justice ordered it. What was I supposed to do?"

"You didn't have to enjoy it," she spat. She turned and stormed off to the bedroom and slammed the door.

He sat there contemplating. He sniffed and cleared his throat. "I wonder if she'll ever forgive me." He heard a few more grunts and squawks of exasperation come from behind the bedroom door. Something hit the bedroom door. He shrugged and sighed. "No, not tonight…at least."

He decided that now would be a good time to go check on Diamond. He threw a cape around his shoulders and left the house. He made the climb up to the high roosting place that Diamond had won from Thunder. Diamond was laying there letting out a few snorts. As Kovarin approached, Diamond lifted his head up and growled.

"Easy, big fella," said Kovarin calmly.

Upon recognizing the voice, Diamond laid his head back down on the ground.

Kovarin went up to him and smeared a little *treat* on Diamond's snout. The big dragon calmly started licking his snout. Kovarin started scratching the top of Diamond's head. Diamond started rumbling again, however this time it was a contented growl.

"I think I'm safer sleeping with you tonight, my friend," said Kovarin while he was chuckling. "You don't know of the trial…or any of that, do you?" He turned, sat down next to Diamond's neck and made himself comfortable.

19

Nine days after the trial was over, Kovarin woke up from a sound sleep.

Namanti was standing over him. "Someone's knocking on the door…Supreme Commander."

Kovarin growled a little as he got up from under the warm furs. He put a robe on and headed for the door. He scratched himself in random places and yawned. He got to the door and opened it.

Aj was standing there looking a little concerned. He was holding a large satchel that he put down as he saluted Kovarin. "Supreme Commander, there's a problem…at the execution site, in regards to Do…uh the traitor."

"What, he refuses to die?"

"I don't know, Supreme Commander, I just know that they need your presence there…immediately."

"Okay, Commander," he yawned. "Where is it?"

"The execution site is on the western coastline, just south of Dragonfort Sunset."

Kovarin groaned. "Why there?"

"It's in the edict, Supreme Commander."

Kovarin shook his head in disbelief. "It's in the edict...
and there's no other...place...that it can be carried out?"

"No other place...according to the edict."

Kovarin growled. "Come on in. Let me...wake up." He
stretched and tried to shake the sleep out of his head. He closed
the door behind Aj after the man walked in. "Have a seat...
somewhere, while I get ready for the day." He followed Aj into
the living room. "Just...flop...anywhere. It's gonna take me a
few minutes to get ready."

Aj sat down.

Kovarin went back to the bedroom. "Commander Aj is
waiting out there...to give me some more information."

Namanti looked at him through still sleepy eyes.
"Information...about what?"

He sighed. He sat down on the bed. "It seems that
they're...having some kind of problem. For some reason, there's
a problem with the execution of...the traitor. They feel that I am
the only one who can solve this...*problem*."

She stopped cleaning and threw the rag in the water in the
tub. "I'm going with you."

He looked at her through bleary eyes. "Why?"

She walked over to him, placed her hands on her hips,
leaned down and got her face right into his. "It's because of *his*

bellyaching, *I* got *spanked*. I wanna be there…to watch him suffer and die!"

He stared back at her for several moments. He shrugged. "Okay."

She stood back straight. "Thank you," she said flatly. She turned and was headed for the kitchen.

"Stop!"

She turned around confused. "What?"

He scoffed. "Commander Aj…is *still* out there…put a robe on…NOW!"

She let out a little squawk of frustration. She went to the wardrobe, pulled out a robe and put it on. She held her arms out. "Is this good enough?"

He gave her a bit of an insincere smile. "Yes, my love."

She stuck her tongue out and left the bedroom.

Kovarin put some pants and boots on. He donned his shirt and headed out of the bedroom before he buttoned it up. He walked into the dining room and witnessed a little of Namanti's "lack" of finesse.

She was holding a pitcher in one hand and a glass in the other. She was holding the glass up to Aj. She snarled at him through clenched teeth. "I've already poured it! So whether you want it or not - *drink it*!"

Aj gave Kovarin a bit of a helpless sideways glance. He took the glass from Namanti. "Thank you, Milady." He took a quick sip from it.

Kovarin walked up and put his arm around her shoulder. He smiled at Aj and led Namanti back into the kitchen. "You *must* learn a few more things about being gracious, as a host... especially since you're the wife of the Supreme Commander."

She snarled back. "Okay, what do you want for breakfast?"

"Just some eggs will do, my love." He kissed her on her forehead.

She smiled back.

He pulled some plates and flatware out and took them to the dining room table. "Commander Aj, please come in here."

Aj walked in with the glass still in hand. "Yes, Supreme Commander."

"You say that they gave no clue as to what the problem was?"

"None!"

"Okay, so how long does it take to get there?"

"If you go by coach, it will take six or seven days... depending on weather and which bridge over the Divider Gorge is still in good enough shape to cross. If we try going north of the gorge, by coach, it would take an extra five days."

"Are there problems with the bridges?"

"Yes, it's difficult to maintain them. Apparently after each rainfall, there is some erosion...on one side or the other. This tends to make a need for a new expansion on the existing bridge. If they don't get to it in time then…there could be a collapse…and they have to start over again…with a new bridge."

Kovarin closed his eyes and growled. "Six or seven days."

"Of course…it would take only two to three days…by dragon."

Kovarin looked at the grinning Aj. "Right! With the dragons, we don't need to worry about that gorge."

Aj bowed his head a little, with a smile, in approval of the statement.

"I'm not sure…how to get there. I've seen it on a map, but I've never been there…personally."

"We'll have a guide to get us there."

"Namanti wants to go as well."

"Why?"

"Doz…uh…the traitor made several nasty comments about her. I think that she thinks that she'll enjoy watching him be executed."

"He made a lot of nasty comments about a lot of people. There's a *huge* congregation of people who want to watch him *get it*."

"Do you think that Diamond can carry both of us…all the way to Sunset?"

Aj smiled. "I've taken my wife, on a few long excursions,

with Dastardly. You need to stop more often and get him fed. After we get there, he'll be more tired…than what you're used to seeing."

"Is that because he's still kind of young and inexperienced?"

"No, Dastardly *is* experienced and I still see him get exhausted after a long flight…especially since we have to expedite our move to the fort."

Namanti walked in with a skillet full of scrambled eggs. She served up the eggs for Kovarin and herself. She looked at Aj, trying to be cordial. "Did you want any…breakfast, Commander?"

Aj smiled at her. "No, thank you, Milady. I've already had my breakfast. You enjoy yours."

She smiled back. She picked up the pitcher and poured a glass of fruit juice for Kovarin and herself.

Kovarin took a mouthful of eggs. He chewed for a moment and then swallowed. "What did you say? We have to expedite… why?"

Aj cleared his throat. "It seems that one of the females is about ready to go into heat. If Diamond is still here, when she flies…he is most likely to chase, and as strong a flier as he has shown himself to be, he would probably catch her, mate with her…and not be able to depart…for a day or two."

Kovarin looked at Namanti. "Hurry up and eat, so we can pack some clothing, and get out of here."

She looked up with a big grin. "How much can I pack?"

"Not very much," said Aj. "We still don't know Diamond's full capabilities on weight and distance. True, he's the biggest thing that has ever come along…but…there are still some unknown's."

Namanti wolfed down her eggs, quickly drank her juice and headed for the bedroom.

"I don't think that she's very excited about this trip, Commander," said Kovarin sarcastically.

Aj chuckled. "I have something for you, Supreme Commander."

Kovarin looked at Aj suspiciously. "Okay, what, Commander?"

"I left it in the living room, I'll go get it. You finish your eggs."

Kovarin shrugged. He packed some more eggs in his mouth and chewed. He was finishing the last of the juice when Aj walked back in with that satchel he had brought with him. Kovarin stretched, yawned and belched. "What is it?"

Aj pulled two smaller black satchels out of the big one. "These are for packing your clothing that you're taking with you, on this excursion."

Kovarin was a little shocked. "They…they're not very big."

"Again, Supreme Commander, we don't know what Diamond's full capabilities are…yet."

Kovarin sighed. "I better get that thing in the bedroom.

No telling how much Namanti is already planning on taking."

"Yes, Supreme Commander. I'll leave you to that task. Right now, I'll go and make sure that Diamond is saddled and that there are at least two of those small kegs of *treat*. We don't know how much you're going to have to bribe him with the *treat*."

"Yeah, you coward. You're leaving me with the dirty job of limiting Namanti on how much she can take."

Aj chuckled all the way out the door.

Kovarin walked into the bedroom. Namanti had several drawers opened as well as the wardrobe. There was a rather large amount of clothing spread out on the bed.

He chuckled and held up the two satchels. "My love. Here are the bags that we will pack our clothing in. If it doesn't fit in one of these bags…it doesn't go."

She held up a fancy evening gown. "But…I…what about…"

"WE'RE NOT GOING TO A FORMAL BANQUET! We are not going to any kind of gala shindig! We are going to an execution! We have to get there, using Diamond. We can't pack a lot of weight on him, yet, until we know just what he can carry and how far."

She hugged the dress to her body and had a pouting look on her face. "I can't take…any nice clothes?"

He walked over to her to hand her one of the satchels. "We're going to be gone for several days. Pack only what you *absolutely* need. Remember, it's not a party - it's an execution.

She dropped the dress on the bed and took the satchel. She shoved her hand inside it to see just how big it was. She looked up at him with a pleading in her eyes. "This isn't a…bag for a long trip…it's a…I don't know what it is."

"It's all you're going to get for this trip. May I suggest a few changes of underwear and a nightshirt?"

Her arms dropped to her sides. She looked rather concerned. "But…I don't…have any…currently clean…night… shirt."

He went to one of his drawers and pulled one out. He held it up to show it to her. "This is my nightshirt. You can use it. If it'll fit me, I am positive that it'll fit you."

She stared at it. She had her nose out of joint. "This and some underwear…and that's all."

He smiled and tossed it to her. She looked at it distastefully. She started stuffing it into the valise. She then went to try and put some underwear in the valise as well.

She grumbled at him. "What're we gonna do for, changes of clothing…or lodgings?"

"When we get there, we'll be right next to Dragonfort Sunset. I'm sure that they'll have some kind of lodgings for the Supreme Commander."

She crammed as much as she could into the small bag. Every few moments she looked up at him and snarled.

He looked at her with a big smile. "Now, get dressed… and don't try to get away with wearing two or three pairs of pants or shirts."

Her shoulders sagged and she huffed.

They got dressed and headed for Diamond's roosting spot. When they got there, Shondark and Aj were finishing up the cinching of the saddle straps.

"All in place and ready to go," said Shondark. "Two small kegs of *treat* and some vouchers that you can give to…whoever ends up losing some livestock for feeding Diamond, plus some money for you to purchase any food you need."

"We do need to get moving," said Aj. "As soon as possible."

As Namanti was lashing her valise in place she scoffed at Aj. "What's the hurry? We're not going to get there today. Why the rush to leave so quickly?"

"There's a female that is just about to go into heat. If Diamond - or Dastardly - are here, they may try to compete in chasing her." He pointed off to his left. "Over there you see the brown dragon Scrambler and the gray dragon Sky Chaser…they're the two who have been chosen to compete for this breeding. We have to get out of here, before she flies or Diamond and Dastardly *will* compete."

Namanti pointed at two others. "I see a blue-gray and a smaller brown…who are *they*?"

Aj smiled. "The blue-gray, is my Dastardly. That smaller brown belongs to a Unit Commander named Discoro, who knows the most direct route to the fort as well as all of the best places for us or the dragons to get something to eat on the way. He is our guide."

Namanti chuckled. "Always best to plan ahead, isn't it." She went to look down into the canyon. She forgot that she was close to Diamond's head. He turned his head and gave her a big lick. She let out a cry of disgust. "Ooooh...there's that... TONGUE!" She quickly headed away from his head, to the saddle, still giving off a few grunts and squawks of disgust.

Shondark handed Kovarin a small horn. "If Diamond starts getting tired, or gives off his hungry cry, just give a toot on this horn, to Discoro or myself and give them the necessary signal for what is needed."

Kovarin chuckled. "The last time I saw one of these little things, was in Candidate school. They made us play with them for a couple of days. They never did tell us what they're supposed to be used for." He stuffed it into his belt. He helped Namanti get up on Diamond and buckle her in. He then climbed aboard and buckled in as well.

Aj started running to his dragon. He had to pass by Scrambler and Sky Chaser to get to Dastardly. Both dragons watched him and blossomed their neck flares at him. There was no growling, so it was just a warning. They still watched him cautiously as he passed by. As he approached Dastardly, he gave a shout. A man, who had been resting, hidden from view by his dragon, stood up. As soon as he saw Aj, he mounted his dragon and started attaching all of the buckles. Aj mounted Dastardly and started buckling himself in. When Aj was finished he looked at Discoro. Discoro pointed straight up. Aj looked to Kovarin and pointed up. Kovarin gave the command to Diamond to fly.

All three dragons unfurled their wings and started flapping, stirring up a lot of dust as they took off. Once they were up above all of the dust, Kovarin looked to see where Aj and Discoro were. They were both giving a signal by pointing their arm, to take a heading, going west southwest. Kovarin steered Diamond and the three were soon flying in formation, with Kovarin in the middle, Aj to the right and Discoro to the left.

The difficulty for Kovarin was that Diamond refused to follow another dragon. He had to be in the lead. The other two men were fully aware of the dominance factor between the male dragons, so they had no choice but to tolerate it. They would simply give a toot on their little horn, if Diamond was straying from the course. Once Kovarin looked back, they would get him back on the proper heading by pointing. They were keeping the morning sun just over the back of the left shoulder.

Namanti kept up an almost incessant giggling as they were flying along.

Kovarin huffed. "What's the matter with you, what's so funny?"

"I love being up here, "she said in an excited manner. "It's so…I don't know, it's…wonderful." She continued giggling.

"It's wonderful…in spite of his tongue," chuckled Kovarin.

"Oh, shut up!" She smacked him on the back of his right shoulder.

Kovarin smiled. He understood the feeling. There were

not that many people who could experience this incredible feeling of riding one of the big battle dragons. As she had said: It is wonderful.

Kovarin looked to each side to watch as Diamond flapped his wings. Sometimes he would do hard flaps to gain altitude (when ordered), other times it was an easy flap or two, other times his wings were held out stiff, just to glide.

The wind in his face and the scenery that sped by below him added to the euphoria of being one of the Dragonriders. He hoped that he would never lose the thrill of being up in the air on Diamond's back.

They were airborne for over a full turn before Discoro tooted his horn and gave the signal to land.

Kovarin was concerned at first as to why they were landing so soon. He decided to wait for any fretting about why they were landing until he found out why. He brought Diamond down for a smooth easy landing. As soon as they were down, he could feel Diamond panting heavily. The heavy breathing only lasted for a few moments and then the breathing was back to normal.

Kovarin looked back at Discoro. "Commander, why are we landing?"

Discoro was unbuckling himself from his saddle. "It's a routine rest, Supreme Commander. We have to rest them from flying, whether they need it or not. This way they stay fresh and don't get too tired. We'll walk them for a while."

Namanti started unbuckling herself.

"Milady, you don't have to get down…unless you want to," said Discoro.

Kovarin finished unbuckling himself and got down. "You can stay on the saddle if you like, my love. When we walk them, we're up front leading them. If you're up there, you're within range of his tongue."

She looked at him with shock on her face. She quickly re-buckled the ones she had undone, wrinkled her nose at Kovarin and folded her arms across her chest.

"It's best to give them a little *treat* right now. Let them know that they did a good job…especially since they were flying that long," said Discoro. "Supreme Commander, has your Diamond ever flown that long…at one time that is?"

"Not that I recall," said Kovarin as he smeared some *treat* on Diamond's snout. "If we reward them, each time we land, we may run out of *treat* very quickly."

"Not to worry, Supreme Commander. There's plenty more at Dragonfort Crossroads. That one is located at approximately at the half-way point to Dragonfort Sunset."

They started walking towards their destination, leading the three big reptiles.

Kovarin looked over to Aj. "Commander Aj, there were only two other male dragons back at the Hatchery. Where are the rest of the breeders?"

"Most of them are at the execution site."

"Most of them?"

"Yes, Supreme Commander. It has something to do with a lottery, in regards to who participates in the execution."

'I need to read this edict,' thought Kovarin. "When you say *most of them*, approximately how many do you think that is?"

"Oh, probably between twenty and twenty-five."

Kovarin growled. "Twenty to twenty-five! Battle Division Commanders, Battle Division Sub Commanders and Battle Group Commanders...and none of them can make a decision without me! I can hardly wait to see what this problem is."

"Yes, Supreme Commander," said Aj chuckling.

After walking for nearly one half turn, Discoro called to them. "It's time to mount up again."

Kovarin walked back to the saddle and found Namanti nodding off. He chuckled as he quietly climbed up and buckled in. He looked back to his left and Discoro gave the signal to fly. Kovarin gave the command and Diamond obeyed with a leap and strong flaps of his wings. Namanti yelped in surprise and wrapped her arms around Kovarin's midsection.

"You did that on purpose," she scolded.

He just laughed as he started enjoying the scenery while mentally mapping the route to Dragonfort Crossroads.

There were three more rest walks for the dragons before they stopped for lunch. Discoro directed them to a large paddock. They saw numerous bovine running in the paddock...away from the dragons. They landed in the paddock and rode the dragons as they directed them to a large building in the middle of the paddock.

A door opened and a large heavy set man with brown hair that was showing streaks of gray came out to greet them. The man stopped and waited for them. He stood there with his fists on his hips and a big smile on his face. "By the Great Maker! That dragon *is* black. I never thought I'd see the likes." He dropped his arms to his side and came out to get a closer look at Diamond. He just stood there grinning and shaking his head. He turned back to the building. "Mother! Come look at it! It *is* as black as they said it *is*."

An old woman, half stooped over, came out. She hobbled along with her cane and walked up to Diamond, showing a toothless grin. "I seen some dark grays before," she cackled. "But this…well I never!" She came a little closer. Diamond looked her up and down and then gave her a big long lick that nearly knocked her over. The old woman cackled with glee as her son caught her and kept her from hitting the ground. "He likes me too!"

The next thing that Kovarin knew, there was an entire family coming out of the big building. The caretaker, named Arkeron, lived in this big building with his mother, his wife, two sons, a daughter, their spouses and five grandchildren. All of which had to come out and gawk at Diamond.

None of them seemed afraid of coming close to the big dragon, because one of the sons was a Dragonman himself. He had a little male, size ten, brown named Frisky. The little dragon came out of a hiding place under the porch, under the front door. He blossomed his flares and growled at Diamond, and everyone covered their ears. Diamond blossomed and bellowed back. Frisky ran back under the porch and no one saw him again for the rest of the day (or at least no one in Kovarin's group).

Kovarin found out that this place was a good stop over that was a half-way point between the capitol city and at least five Dragonforts. You stop here, have lunch, rest your dragon, feed the dragon something (whether he needs it or not, to keep him from grumbling from starvation later), and then you are on your way.

The people who took care of the rest station were able to make a little money on the side, selling the meat (that the dragons or the guests did not eat), as well as selling the hides of the different livestock that was slaughtered for the guests.

When they departed the feed station, they headed a little more westerly than before. These stations were all over High Country, just for the purpose of taking care of the needs of the dragons during their patrols and movements around the country.

Finally seeing some of the ways that the entire economy of the nation revolved around the dragons, first hand, Kovarin was wondering just where the Grounders were sent. They were to be kept as far away from any dragons as was possible. With all of the Dragonforts and these comfort stations, littering the countryside… where did they go?

They used most of the afternoon to fly, rest, fly, rest, in the regular intervals, to get to Crossroads. They arrived and found that there were currently three other members of the military in at this station. The three that were there consisted of two size twenty-six and one size twenty-eight. Some people were worried, at first, wondering if there were going to be any challenges between the dragons that had not met each other before. Diamond was able to make just about any of the other dragons slink away with a single deafening bellow. Diamond was, again, the center of attention because of being the one unique black dragon (and of course because of his size).

The fort was a rather large stone enclosure that had a few buildings inside the walls and a few large dirt mounds (so that the dominant male could take the high position and glare down at the weaker opponents). Diamond, of course, planted himself on the highest mound and after getting fed an entire ovine, he promptly went to sleep.

Kovarin and Namanti were given the best suite (of course), for the night.

Namanti walked in, flopped down on a chair, with the valise in her lap. She looked down at it a little disgusted. "Well, love, how long do you think it's going to take to unpack this thing…for our one night stay?"

Kovarin just chuckled. "Remember, this is *not* a pleasure trip. This is entirely business. If it were some pleasure trip, we would have made some additional plans for luggage."

Namanti sneered. She got up and started exploring the suite. "Hey, this place has a balcony and there's some kind of ropes that go across the thing."

"Since we don't have any change of clothing, we hang our garments on those lines for the night to air them out. That way, we don't smell too bad, when we get to our destination."

She went to the fireplace and added a few logs to build up

a little more flame.

He was a little confused. "Are you cold?"

"No, I just want a good sized fire, so I can heat up some water for a bath."

'Good idea,' he thought.

She went to the tub, stopped it and started pumping water into the tub. After she got it half full, she used a bucket to take some of the water to a large cauldron that hung near the fireplace. While that water was heating up, she stripped her riding outfit off. She then transferred the warmed water to the tub, making it tolerable as not too hot or cold. She gave him a smug look. "If you want a warm bath, you're going to have to heat your own water." She climbed in for a nice bath.

He snickered as he picked up her clothing, took it out to the balcony and hung all of it up for airing. He stripped his shirt off and hung it up as well. He went back in to hear her moaning a little.

"What's wrong?"

She huffed. "When you take those turns of walking while resting Diamond from flying, I'm going to walk as well, tomorrow."

"Any particular reason?"

She sneered at him. "I sat all morning, in that saddle. I sat at lunch time. I sat in the saddle all afternoon. My 'sit down' is 'sat out'."

That night, after both were bathed, she got her first experience at wearing one of his nightshirts to bed. She did not like it. It was difficult to walk in it, because it was way too long, it bunched up while she was in bed and the sleeves were too long as well. He reminded her that it was one of his nightshirts and that as soon as they got back to the capitol, she would be able to get some that would be a better fit for her.

The next day was more of the same of the fly, walk, fly, walk, fly, walk, lunch. During this one, Namanti did walk. At first she tried to keep from being licked by putting some *treat* on her hand and let him lick it off. When he did finish cleaning her hand, she ended up getting her posterior licked and realized that that particular method was not going to slow Diamond down. He still liked her and was going to show affection his way. Fly, walk, fly, walk, fly, walk - final destination.

When they arrived at the final destination, just south of Dragonfort Sunset, they had to land the dragons early because of a very strong wind that gave the dragons no end of difficulty in trying to fly against it. Walking was the only option. They were all a little upset over having to walk the last portion. Discoro had told them, several times, about the view of the ocean. He had suggested that they fly over the water and come in for a landing over the cliffs that were in this area. The wind made that little side trip impossible.

As soon as Kovarin, and entourage arrived, his banner was raised on the highest flagpole and there was a general salute for the Supreme Commander, by all in attendance.

Kovarin was a little disgusted when he saw just how many

Dragonriders *were* in attendance. Aj had estimated that there were between twenty and twenty-five. No, it appeared that there were at least fifty dragons wandering around, flaring at each other, while all of their riders were wandering around, drinking or drunk.

There was a somewhat ornate pavilion in the middle of all of the reptiles, however it was just too windy to have a meeting of any type there. One of the Wing Commanders that was there met Kovarin and led his group to a small building. He slammed his fist against the door several times, waited for a few moments and then opened the door. All of the people who were inside this one room building, were holding papers down on tables as Kovarin was ushered inside. When the door was closed, they all relaxed from holding papers and saluted.

"All right," said Kovarin in a patronizing manner. "Why is it with all of these Division Commanders, Sub Commanders, Group Commanders, Wing and Unit, no one can make a decision without me?"

Battle Division 1 Commander Heth was the first to speak up. "Because the decisions that have to be made, cannot be made...by anyone below *your* rank, Supreme Commander."

Kovarin was taken a little aback. He looked around the room at all of the faces, who seemed to confirm what Heth had just said. "Well...it seems that I need...an explanation. Possibly a long one. Should I make myself comfortable?" He decided that he had better hear the entire story before making any...incorrect decisions.

"I suggest you do, Supreme Commander," said Heth. "We

have some wine, if you wish to imbibe at this time."

"No, I want to stay sober during this explanation."

There was a loud pounding on the door. Everyone in the room that was standing near a table immediately pounced on any loose papers that were on the tables and held them down. Whoever was knocking finally opened the door and entered. Kovarin saw all of the papers flapping under the hands that held them and fully understood (what seemed strange) about knocking and giving everyone a chance to keep the papers from being blown around.

The man who entered was Battle Division 5 Commander Invelton, the man who rode Diamond's father, Eating Machine. He exchanged salutes and pleasantries with Kovarin and it was he who was to do the explaining.

"Our main problem," started Invelton, "is that *one* ruling from the Supreme Justices. They said that any edict that had been initiated by…that traitor…were now officially null and void. We didn't know, until we got here and were well on our way to beginning…when the Chief Executioner informed us that it was the traitor who came up with this form of execution. Since you are now the Supreme Commander, it falls in your office, as to how we go about this. Do we go back to the old method of, either the gallows or the block, or are you going to sign on to *this* new form of execution?"

Kovarin sat there digesting the information for several moments. "So, this form of…execution has…never been done before. The traitor dreamed it up and…now we're sitting here…" He looked around at all of the faces that were waiting for an answer. "Before I make any final decision, I think I would like to read this...invention from a traitor."

"It could take a little while to read it, Supreme Commander," said Invelton. "Perhaps I could give you the short form?"

Kovarin sighed. He again thought for a few moments. "Okay, Commander, give me the short form."

"Yes, Supreme Commander. The basic premise behind it is that if a man has been found guilty of maliciously and willingly killing dragons...the dragons should participate in his execution."

Kovarin raised his eyebrows. "How?"

"The condemned is tied up and then put on a tether. The Dragonriders, who have won a slot in the lottery, take turns, dragging the condemned through the ocean water, near the beach."

"So, he gets wet - what's that supposed to do?"

"The edict gives a very specific location as to where your start and stop is...on the dragging. When the wind dies down a little, we'll go to the edge of the cliff and you'll be able to see it very clearly."

"Why are we waiting for the wind to die down?"

Invelton let out an ominous growl. "I have no intention, whatsoever, of going anywhere near the edge of the cliff, in wind this strong. You could be blown over the side...so easily."

Kovarin looked down and cleared his throat. "Okay, I'll take your word on that. I've never been here before...how long does this wind usually last?"

"We have these windstorms…from time to time. There's no way of telling how long it'll last. It could be a few turns…or several days."

"So, why can't the dragging be done, in spite of the wind?"

"Again the edict is specific. According to what is written, the dragons are to be flying from south to north. If you look outside, you can see all of the banners, standing straight out and pointing due south. If a dragon were to attempt to fly against that wind…all they'd do is back up."

"Does it give any allowances to make a few simple changes…due to weather or…any unforeseen situation?"

"I'm afraid not, Supreme Commander."

Kovarin grunted in frustration. "Since we can't do a flaming thing, right now, I'm going to read this wretched thing and see if I approve or if we're going to go back to the *old* methods."

"As you wish, Supreme Commander," said Invelton as he handed a scroll case to Kovarin. "It's all in there."

Kovarin smiled. "Thank you, Commander." He took the case and slid it down under his belt. "I'll see you after I read this thing."

Invelton stood up. "Gentlemen, someone is about to open the door."

Once again, all the men near tables pounced on the papers. They all watched Kovarin as he went to the door. He opened it and nearly got the edge of the door slammed in his face. He took control of it, went through the doorway and fought the thing closed.

He had to fight his way against the wind as he headed for the spot that Diamond was sitting. Diamond was easy to spot, being the only black dragon.

He noticed that all of the dragons were crouching as low as they could get to the ground. They all had their legs splayed out as much as possible and their claws were dug deep into the soil. Their wings and flares were all being held very tightly against their bodies.

He finally got to Diamond. He saw that Namanti was sitting beside Diamond, using the big dragon to shield her from that powerful gale force wind. She had braided her hair into one long pigtail and was holding on tight to the tail to keep it from whipping back in her face.

She looked up at him squinting. "So...what's the plan?"

He patted the place on his belt where the scroll was. "I'm going to read this thing and see if I approve. If I do, we'll carry out the execution - if or when this infernal wind dies down. I may have to make a few changes of my own...depending on what I read."

She scoffed. "You're gonna try to read a scroll...in this wind?"

"No, I'm going to the fort. I'm going to get in a room, without wind and read it there."

"What about Diamond? Where's he gonna go?"

"Don't worry about the dragons," said Discoro. "My

Dustmaker has been through at least a dozen of these horrendous winds. If we were talking about a dragon that was a size twelve or less...those little ones would have a problem. The big ones will survive it. They just won't get very much sleep and when the wind dies down, they'll be very hungry."

Kovarin looked around. "So, we are able to just...leave him...here?"

Discoro smiled. "They've all dug their claws in...deep. They're not going anywhere...none of them."

Kovarin grunted. "I hate to just...abandon him."

"Give him a big smear of *treat*. He'll be okay."

Kovarin went to the saddle and pulled one of the kegs of *treat* off. He broke the keg open and got a huge hand full. He walked up to Diamond's head and spread it wide and thick. Diamond wasted no time in getting his big tongue right in the middle of the smear and lapping it off of his snout.

Kovarin and Namanti grabbed their little valises and joined all of the other Dragonriders in fighting their way through the wind to the fort. They were all nearly exhausted when they finally got within the walls of the fort and were partially shielded from most of the wind. Once they got into a room, the only reminder of that powerful wind was the noise. They were able to settle down, do some cleaning, eating, drinking and resting.

20

Kovarin spent most of the rest of the evening looking over the edict. Seeing as how he had spent so much time deciphering Dozzbin's haphazard scrawl, by way of the bad instructional scroll, he was able to read the edict rather easily. He was a little bit disgusted with the fact that Dozzbin would use four paragraphs to say something that could be stated completely in one sentence. Dozzbin liked to show how smart he was by using a lot of big words that most people had not heard of...or used...or wanted to use.

He read until his eyes burned. He gave up thinking about it after a while and joined Namanti under the furs. She had already been asleep for some time when he went to bed. He put his nightshirt on and crawled under the furs with her. She did not stir.

He was rather rudely awakened by Namanti as she was pushing hard, against him with both hands.

"Go answer the door," she croaked at him.

He sat up. There was a light knocking on the front door to the suite that was somewhat persistent. He got up and looked back at her. She was mostly uncovered, so he re-blanketed her with two large furs. He stretched and yawned as he went out of the bedroom, through the sitting room, to the door.

He opened the door. Two men stood there with (almost) silly looking smiles on their faces. One was shorter than Kovarin. The long stringy hair on his head was totally gray. He was rather skinny and his blue-gray uniform hung rather loosely on his body. The other man was eye-to-eye with Kovarin. This one had white hair (what little there was of it) and was dressed in a gray uniform. He was a little overweight, however not enough to be called obese.

A very small blue-gray dragon jumped off of the smaller man to Kovarin and clung to the nightshirt. The little dragon started climbing up the fabric.

The little man reached out and got hold of the tiny dragon and tried to pull it away without tearing the nightshirt. The dragon was adamant in trying to hold on. "Naughty, naughty, you nosey little thing. You can get acquainted later. I'm awfully sorry about that, Supreme Commander. She's just…very curious."

Kovarin did everything he could to help pry her tiny little claws out of his nightshirt, without hurting the little beast. She let out a bit of the scared yeep as she was finally pulled away from him.

Once the little man had full control of the feisty little beast, he smiled again. "Supreme Commander, I am Tambont and…this little pest is Nosey, my charge."

"Nosey? I think she earned her name." Kovarin looked at the little squawker and backed away a little.

The other man spoke up. "Supreme Commander, my name

is Whiym and this little girl on my leg is my charge, Cuddles."

Kovarin looked down and saw a little gray dragon with the forelegs wrapped tightly around the right leg of Whiym. He snickered a little thinking about when Diamond had been terrorized and was wrapped around a leg.

He composed himself. "May I help you...gentlemen?"

"We're here to assist you, Supreme Commander," said Whiym. "If you wish to rewrite that style of execution edict and put your name to it, we are the local scribes who can assist. If you're going to abolish it completely, we'll assist in getting the word out in that case as well."

Tambont looked at him with eyebrows raised high. "Have...you made up...your mind yet...as to which of those choices you plan to make?"

Kovarin looked thoughtful for a moment. "I...have decided to...try this one. It was the traitor who came up with it. It is...somewhat ironic that he's the first one who is...tested...using his method. I have a few problems with...some of the wording... some of the rules. I think that it needs to be rewritten."

Both of the scribes smiled.

Tambont spoke up. "All of the necessary blank documentation, quills and ink are in a desk, right here in your suite, Supreme Commander. If you allow us to come in and set up, you may dictate your ideas...if you want to leave it as is, or change it...according to your pleasure."

Kovarin yawned. "Go ahead and set up...while I get...

more appropriately dressed."

"As you wish, Supreme Commander," said Whiym with a smile.

Kovarin went back to the bedroom. Namanti was still asleep. He reached down, picked her up and then dropped her on the furs. She was awakened and was looking around, while flailing her arms a little.

"Oh, you're awake," he said merrily.

She looked up at him through glassy eyes trying to figure out what had happened. "I…guess…I am," she mumbled.

"I have two scribes in the sitting room. See if you can scare up some breakfast for us, while I'm talking to them."

She looked around, trying to get completely awake. She moaned as she stretched. She got up off the furs, looking for the chamber pot.

"Remember, my love, we have guests. Make sure that you're properly dressed before you leave the bedroom."

"Yeah, yeah," she waved her hand at him.

He went to the balcony to retrieve his 'aired out' uniform. He noticed that the wind had died down completely. He also saw that Diamond was perched on a part of the west wall of the fort. Diamond was currently biting chunks off of a steer that he had "obtained". There were several people, in front and behind Diamond, on the wide wall, gawking at him as he sat there eating.

He got dressed and headed back to the scribes. They

were sitting on one side of the desk, scrolls out, quills ready and ink bottles open. Nosey was running around on top of the desk, investigating everything up there. The other little dragon, Cuddles, had her back feet on the floor, her front legs wrapped around Whiym's leg and her head in his lap. Kovarin sat down, opposite them at the desk.

Nosey now had to investigate the newcomer. She started running over to him. Her run was cut short when Tambont grabbed hold of her and pulled her back. He smiled and shook his head. He attempted to put Nosey in his lap, however the little beast was back on the desktop within a few seconds. He kept a hand on top of her, trying to keep her in one place. She let out a few of those "panic" yeeps in protest.

"First, the title," said Whiym. "Is there any problem with that?"

"No," said Kovarin. "The title is adequate. We don't need something that sounds congenial, beneficial or altruistic for an order of execution."

Tambont attempted to write the title down. Nosey was out from under his hand and following each movement of the quill with her nose. "Oh dear, this is not going to work. We need to have her distracted...somehow." He looked at Kovarin with a helpless pleading in his eyes. "Could you...do something to distract her?"

Kovarin was trying to keep from laughing out loud at the antics of the tiny dragon. He coughed a couple of times to cover up any laughter. "Uh...like what?"

"Well, since we have to use both of our hands to do the scroll, if you could get some *treat* on your fingers that would keep her away from the scroll." He produced a thick pouch of *treat* from his belt. "If you would be so kind?"

Kovarin took the pouch, still trying to stifle his laughing. He wondered what kind of an unholy terror Diamond would be if he were this nosey and hyperactive. He shoved two fingers deep into the pouch and then put the sticky fingers in front of Nosey. She followed as he pulled his hand back and set it down on the edge of the desk. Nosey started licking the *treat* off of his fingers. Her tongue was darting in and out so quickly, it was hard to see. He mainly felt the little rasping tongue as she cleaned the goo off of his hand. She put her claws up on his hand. She did not dig in, it was more to steady herself than latch on.

Tambont looked up from his writings. "Is there any problem...or changes in the first paragraph?"

"No," said Kovarin. He tried to concentrate on what he wanted, however he was getting a little distracted himself, because of the way Nosey was cleaning his hand off. "I quite agree with the idea that if someone willingly and maliciously kills one or more dragons, the dragons should take part in the execution."

Tambont started writing. Whiym scrutinized as the writing continued.

Meanwhile, Nosey had cleaned all of the *treat* off of Kovarin's hand. She was looking around at other parts of his hand, sniffing for more of the stuff. She finally gave up looking and turned her attention back to the document and the movement of the quill.

Tambont grunted. "Supreme Commander, if you would be so kind as to distract her again."

Kovarin got more goo on his hand, got her attention and led her away from the document.

While Tambont was writing, Whiym smiled at Kovarin. "As to the next part: The lottery of ten, chosen to carry out the execution…"

"Ten is not enough," said Kovarin emphatically. "If it takes longer than we think, the dragons could get tired. Make it twenty and have five more standing off to the side…in case one of the twenty does get overworked from the ordeal."

Both scribes nodded their heads and wrote in the changes.

Whiym raised his eyebrows questioningly. "The… physician's check?"

"I like that the way it is," said Kovarin flatly. "The physician checks the condemned after every ten drags. This way, no one knows exactly who was responsible for the final, *fatal* drag."

Again, while Tambont was writing Whiym went on to the next paragraph. "Are there any problems with the path that the dragon must follow?"

"Yes, there's a huge one," said Kovarin as he watched Nosey in her greedy little endeavor. "That wind could cause all kinds of things to go wrong. Put a…something in there that states that we can change the direction…depending on wind direction…

and speed."

Both scribes nodded again.

Nosey was slowing down. She seemed a little unsteady. Kovarin remembered the story of the dragon Glutton, getting into a storeroom and devouring over a dozen kegs of *treat*. Glutton was a size forty-eight - Nosey was a size two. Nosey could drown in one keg. He realized that they were trying to get her too drunk to bother them. She shifted her stance a little to get at a different patch of the stuff on his fingers. She was definitely slowing down. She was slowing, however she was determined to get all of it... before possibly passing out.

Kovarin now noticed that Cuddles had raised her head and was doing her own scrutiny of what was going on with Nosey. "Excuse me, Scribe Whiym...does she get any?"

Whiym looked down and snickered. He got a bit on his finger and smeared it on Cuddles' snout. She lowered her head back to his lap as she slowly licked the stuff off.

After finishing what he was writing, Tambont looked up. "Is there anything else that you want to change?"

Kovarin frowned. "Before I do, I'd like to know some more about the location...between the two...spires?"

The two scribes looked at each other confused. Tambont spoke up. "Didn't you get a look at it...yesterday...when you arrived?"

"No, no one wanted to go anywhere near the edge of the cliff in that powerful wind."

"Oh, yes," said Whiym. "That wind was…unusually strong yesterday."

Tambont sat there nodding in agreement. "That was not normal at all."

Whiym continued. "We've had some strong winds in the past…but absolutely nothing…compared to yesterday. That was…very unusual."

Tambont again nodded. "I don't ever remember a wind like that."

There was a knock on the door. All three men looked up. Namanti went to answer the door. Kovarin was mildly surprised at first. He had not heard or seen her enter the room. She had been quietly sitting off to the side listening. She opened the door and her gaze went almost directly up. She backed up gawking with a look of fear and surprise on her face.

They all heard a deep bass voice: "May one enter?"

Kovarin was not sure how to take Namanti's reaction to this stranger. He shrugged. "Yes, you may." Now he gawked a little.

The tallest man that Kovarin had ever seen ducked his head as he came through the doorway. He had short scraggly, dark brown hair on top of his head and his beard was identical. He had muscles on top of muscles. He was wearing a dark brown leather sleeveless shirt. His pants were of the same material. His skin looked as if he spent most of his time out in the sun. His dark eyes looked tired and apprehensive. "I'm sorry to disturb you at this time, Supreme Commander…but there are some people who are getting a little impatient."

Kovarin stood up, trying to *not* appear frightened or awed. 'If I wanted to get some information,' he thought, 'this is the man I would send to get it.' "And you are…?"

The giant closed his eyes and grunted. "My apologies, Supreme Commander." He bowed his head slightly, "I am Quong, the Chief Executioner."

Namanti backed up out of the room.

"What is it that people are…getting impatient about?"

"They wish to know, if you are going to use this form of execution or are you going to use something else?"

"We…I am going with this form…of execution, with a few modifications."

The big man nodded. "If I have your word, that you are going to use this form of execution, is there anything that I can start on now, such as the lottery of ten, to speed up the process… once you have ratified it with your signature?"

Kovarin smiled. "Yes, my good man, as a matter of fact you can! I've changed the lottery to twenty…with five alternates standing by, in case one of the twenty gets…tired. You may rest assured that I will ratify it and you may start the lottery choosing… right now."

Quong raised his eyebrows and looked up. "Twenty…plus five." He nodded. "I will." He looked at Kovarin and smiled. "Again, Supreme Commander, I apologize for interrupting, and I will leave you to finish your work."

Kovarin gave him a polite bow.

The big man again ducked through the doorway as he departed.

After Quong was gone, Kovarin sat back down and shook his head. "Wow! I've never seen anyone...quite so..."

"Yes, Supreme Commander, he is...*quite*," said Tambont sarcastically. "May we continue?"

Kovarin looked confused. "Continue? Uh...where were we?"

Tambont leaned forward a little. "The spires!"

"Oh...yes...what about them?"

Tambont smiled. "When you go out there and look over the cliffs, the two rock spires, in question, are very noticeable. Even during a high tide and heavy surf conditions, those two can always be seen. The time that it would take for a dragon to fly between the spires...oh...forty to fifty-five beats...depending on a head wind or tail wind...or no wind."

"Okay," said Kovarin, "but what's so special about the area between them?"

"Rocks!" Tambont looked thoughtful for a moment. "When there's a high tide, the rocks are completely submerged. When there's a low tide, you can see all kinds of jagged rocks... between the two spires. There don't seem to be any rocks... outside of the spires...or none that would make any difference."

Kovarin closed his eyes in contemplation. "So, the condemned is being dragged behind…on a tether…over jagged rocks…again and again…until declared dead by a physician."

Both scribes nodded.

"I want one more thing in there."

Tambont picked up the quill. "Yes?"

"Make an annotation…that certain minor things can be changed…if the situation warrants it…be it a tired dragon, a sudden weather condition or if…some unforeseen circumstance comes along."

At that moment, Nosey's body convulsed. There was a loud bodily noise that came out of the little dragon. Kovarin was not sure which orifice the noise came out of and was not really sure that he wanted to know.

Tambont chuckled a little as he made the final addendum. Then the signature block.

Kovarin signed it, rolled it up and put it into a scroll case. "So, you have to make a few more copies of this and then we proceed."

"Oh, no," said Tambont. "While we were working, we made two copies. The second one is ready for your signature. We can give that one to the Chief Executioner and then proceed."

Kovarin signed the second copy. "Let's get this…morbid thing underway.

The two scribes nodded as they cleaned up. Tambont

picked up the drunken (and passed out) Nosey and cradled her in one arm as he left. Whiym walked around with the clingy little Cuddles still holding on to his right leg and walking behind him.

Namanti watched them leave. "I wonder if that guy sleeps with that charge of his…wrapped around his leg."

"I don't…really want to know," he said shaking his head. "I'm just glad that Diamond is not…anything like…either one of those…little ones. I'd be terrified to go to sleep. He could crush you if he rolled over. You'd have no privacy…in an outhouse, in a bathtub…anywhere."

"So," she looked up at him. "When is this…*not a party* supposed to get going?"

"Probably tomorrow…depending on the weather."

21

Kovarin and Namanti went out the next day to the location of the execution. They saw several dragons taking off and departing the area entirely.

"I thought that this was supposed to be a big show," said Namanti. "How come they're leaving? Don't they want to at least watch?"

"The ones that are leaving are probably the ones who did not get a slot in the lottery. They have duties to perform and since they're no longer needed here...off they go to take care of their business."

Discoro walked up to Kovarin and saluted. "Supreme Commander, I have a list of those who are going to participate in the dragging." He held out a piece of paper for Kovarin.

After looking it over a little, he frowned. "I only see one person here, below the rank of Battle Group Commander. Was there some sort of fix going on?"

"Oh, no Supreme Commander. There weren't that many Wing Commanders or Flight Commanders that entered their name in the lottery. Most of them were a little squeamish about having to carry the weight of two men by a dragon that was smaller than a size forty. That Executioner, Quong, he stated that he didn't want any dragon smaller than a thirty-five on the list at all."

Kovarin looked at Discoro. "You're dragon is what... size...?"

"Thirty-three, Supreme Commander."

Kovarin grunted. "Never in the running."

"Yes, Supreme Commander."

Namanti smacked Kovarin on his back. "Why didn't you enter in the lottery?"

"I just enacted this...*mode*. It just didn't seem right...for me to participate...as a dragger. I need to observe...to see if there are any changes that need to be made. After this is over, I may abolish it altogether. Who knows?"

Namanti grunted in disgust. She then looked around. "Where's Commander Aj?"

"He's one of the alternates. He's probably setting off to the side, waiting to see what happens."

Namanti wrinkled her nose. "While you're doing whatever preliminaries are necessary, I'm going to check on Diamond."

Kovarin stopped and watched her heading for the wall where Diamond was perched. Rarely did she ever volunteer to watch over or take care of him. He had a suspicion that she was up to something.

It was a bit of a walk to the spot where the dragons were gathered. Kovarin was finally able to walk along the cliff top and look down to where the two primary spires were located. It was quite a site. It would have been quite a distance between the two spires if you were walking. A dragon could fly that distance in very little time. He observed that there was a rather heavy surf pounding at the cliff face. He could not tell whether the tide was coming in or going out.

As he got closer to where all of the Dragonriders were waiting, it was very easy to spot the Chief Executioner. The man towered above everybody…and just about everything else in the area. He headed for the group that was crowded around Quong.

Someone called the group to attention. Most of them turned and saluted Kovarin. The only ones who did not were Quong and a man dressed in the blue, green and white of a physician. Kovarin returned the salute and kept on his direct path to Quong.

Kovarin looked around at the faces as he walked up to Quong. "Chief Executioner, is everything ready for this… spectacle?"

Quong bowed his head slightly. "Yes, Supreme Commander. We have the Physician Palhagath ready to do his duty. All of the participants know their number and are ready."

Kovarin and the Physician Palhagath exchanged polite head nods.

"Physician, are you fully aware of what is expected of you?"

Palhagath raised his eyebrows and stood in thought for a moment. "I am…unfortunately *well* aware of what is going on. I don't like it…however, I do realize what has happened and…yes I'm aware." He looked away rather disgusted.

Kovarin nodded. "Where's the traitor?"

Quong pointed to a spot that Kovarin had not looked at before. He saw Dozzbin on his knees, between two men who looked as if they were almost as tall as Quong. Dozzbin's legs and arms were tied tightly. There was a tether rope attached to a harness that was around his chest.

Kovarin shook his head. "He looks as if he is going to accept it in silence. I've never known that man to not want to get the last word in."

"He can't," chuckled Quong. "He was giving us a lot of guff, and I figured that no one was interested in anything that a traitor had to say, so about five days ago, his tongue was cut out."

Kovarin looked up and frowned. He then shrugged. "I guess…he won't be needing that…any more…not at all."

Quong shook his head. "No, he won't."

Kovarin took in a deep breath and sighed. "Let's get on with this unhappy situation."

Quong raised his right arm up high and signaled his two aides. They started dragging Dozzbin to the starting point. Quong then pulled out a piece of paper. "Number one on the list, Battle Division 1 Commander Heth, with your dragon - Monster…to the starting point."

All of the men started heading to their dragons. The dragons were all lined up and had tethers tied between their jaw rings and some rather large poles. They were in a situation where they could not flare at each other without causing themselves considerable pain, so no one was worried about any challenges.

Aj walked up to Kovarin. "I wonder if I'll be needed, Supreme Commander."

"Who knows? We've no idea how long the traitor will last, but I don't want to see anything go wrong because of a tired dragon."

"I was told, by some of the folk who live around here that the tide should start going out..." He looked up toward the sun. "...very soon. The water will be deep, but the waves should slacken a little during the drags." He got a serious look on his face. "Are you hoping that it will be...fast?"

"I don't know what to hope for. The traitor...brought this on himself. I don't really like executions...but...the law is the law."

Aj grunted an approval.

Heth had reached Monster. He un-tethered the big beast and mounted the saddle. He started steering Monster toward the spot where Dozzbin was waiting. As he passed by Kovarin, he saluted.

After returning the salute, Kovarin looked back at the other dragons and saw that they were all being moved up on the poles. He leaned over toward Aj. "The next one in line...who is that?"

"That's Battle Group Commander Hassurm."

Kovarin grunted. "Let's go to the edge of the cliff...and

watch. I don't know if I want to watch…very much of it…but I feel it…my responsibility to do just that."

Kovarin, Aj and Discoro made the walk to the edge of the cliff. They got there just as Monster was taking off to do the drag. The big brown dragon flew directly up while Heth was looking back at Dozzbin. As soon as Dozzbin was lifted off of the ground, Monster was steered out over the cliff. Heth took him on a wide turn and brought him down to where Dozzbin hit the water, almost next to the spire. Heth kept Monster on a level flight, while Dozzbin was being buffeted around, on and between the curling waves.

Kovarin slowly counted to 45 before Monster was steered up, to keep from hitting the spire himself. Dozzbin nearly came in contact with the spire.

Quong called out: "Number two on the list, Battle Group Commander Hassurm, with your dragon - Grinder…to the starting point." Heth took Monster back around and flew him back to the starting point. The entire time that Dozzbin was on the return trip, he was spinning on the end of the tether.

Aj grunted. "If he's not dead, he'll be dizzier than ever before."

Kovarin cleared his throat. "Does anyone know who number three is?"

Aj checked a piece of paper he had with him. "That would be Battle Division Sub Commander Ikong."

Monster landed just as Hassurm got there with Grinder.

The two brown dragons flared at each other and each got a bit of a painful yank on their jaw rings. They both folded their neck flares back. Quong's aides removed the tether from Monster's saddle and quickly moved it to Grinder's saddle. Before Monster was led away from the starting point, Grinder started flapping his wings and leapt up into the air.

Quong called out: "Number three on the list, Battle Division Sub Commander Ikong, with your dragon - Chubby...to the starting point."

Grinder had a near flawless flight, just like Monster. When he was flying back to the starting point, Kovarin could hear Dozzbin hacking and coughing as he spun on the tether.

Quong called out: "Number four on the list, Battle Group Commander Emkash, with your dragon - Charge...to the starting point."

Chubby performed his flight. Kovarin was wondering if this might take longer than anticipated. So far, all he could see was that the condemned was getting wet. He wondered just how long it would take for the final...death flight to occur. He shook his head. 'This is only the third flight,' he thought. 'Wait and see what happens. Don't get negative thoughts in your head...yet.'

Quong called out: "Number five on the list, Battle Division 3 Commander Ayponch, with your dragon - Protector...to the starting point."

Quong called out: "Number six on the list, Battle Division Sub Commander Rempen, with your dragon - Sky Dancer...to the starting point."

Quong called out: "Number seven on the list, Battle Group Commander Yolonj, with your dragon - Singe...to the starting point."

Quong called out: "Number eight on the list, Battle Group Commander Onjono, with your dragon - Bird Eater...to the starting point."

Quong called out: "Number nine on the list, Battle Division Sub Commander Eevek, with your dragon - Scrambler... to the starting point."

Quong called out: "Number ten on the list, Battle Group Commander Monkusk, with your dragon - Robust...to the starting point."

Quong called out: "Number eleven on the list, Battle Group Commander Naytor, with your dragon - Eager...to the starting point."

Before the tether was moved from Robust to Eager, Palhagath went to check on Dozzbin. Just before he reached the condemned man, Dozzbin moved his legs and coughed. Palhagath turned to Naytor and gave him the signal to continue.

Quong called out: "Number twelve on the list, Battle Group Commander Nezzur, with your dragon - Protester...to the starting point."

Quong called out: "Number thirteen on the list, Battle Division Sub Commander Hobaro, with your dragon - Castle...to the starting point."

Quong called out: "Number fourteen on the list, Battle

Group Commander Udosk, with your dragon - Air Walker…to the starting point."

Quong called out: "Number fifteen on the list, Battle Division 2 Commander Nossiturm, with your dragon - Purge…to the starting point."

While Kovarin was watching Air Walker do his drag run, Aj started tapping him on the arm. Kovarin looked at Aj, a little irritated, wondering what could be so important. Aj was looking up into the sky with a look of alarm on his face. Kovarin looked where Aj was staring.

Kovarin now was a little shocked. "Oh…my! Is that…the Lady Chesesa, riding Thunder…heading our way?"

Aj cleared his throat. "Yes…Supreme Commander. That is most definitely the Lady Chesesa…and Thunder."

Kovarin turned to watch as Air Walker made the final turn to land.

Quong called out: "Number sixteen on the list, Battle Division Sub Commander Ondegador, with your dragon - Treat Grabber…to the starting point."

Chesesa landed Thunder on the field between the line of dragons and the starting point. She dismounted and walked towards Kovarin leading Thunder. She smeared a little *treat* on his snout as she walked along. She reached Kovarin and just stood there watching the exhibition going on in front of her. The only sound was that of Thunder licking his snout.

Quong called out: "Number seventeen on the list, Battle

Group Commander Azzitok, with your dragon - Crunch…to the starting point."

Quong called out: "Number eighteen on the list, Battle Division 5 Commander Invelton, with your dragon - Eating Machine…to the starting point."

Chesesa sniffed. "We're only up to number eighteen?"

"Yes, Milady," said Kovarin. "Eating Machine, as the eighteenth one in line, gets the next drag."

She pursed her lips. "How…often…does the Physician check…to see if that…*thing* is still alive?"

"Every ten drags," said Kovarin flatly.

Chesesa grunted and led Thunder away.

Aj stammered a little. "Wha…what do you…think…she's going to do?"

"I'm not even going to hazard a guess as to what she's doing or planning on doing," said Kovarin without looking back.

Aj sniffed and grunted in agreement.

Quong called out: "Number twenty on the list, Battle Group Commander Chachur, with your dragon - Rampage…to the starting point."

Quong called out: "Number one on the list, Battle Division 1 Commander Heth, with your dragon - Monster…to the starting point."

As soon as Rampage landed, Palhagath went to check on

Dozzbin. He saw the man's chest heaving and heard him coughing. Palhagath hung his head, turned and gave the signal to continue. Dozzbin was tethered to Monster for the second time and off he went.

Quong came up to Kovarin. "Uh…Supreme Commander… we have a bit of a problem."

Kovarin looked at Quong. The big man was pointing at the ready line. Kovarin looked where he was pointing. Chesesa had broken in line, in front of Battle Group Commander Hassurm. She stared at Kovarin defiantly. Kovarin grunted and started walking to where she stood.

Quong sounded worried. "What do I do, Supreme Commander?"

"Call the next *valid* dragger to the line."

Quong called out: "Number two on the list, Battle Group Commander Hassurm, with your dragon - Grinder…to the starting point."

Hassurm got a bit of a worried look on his face and looked at Kovarin with his mouth wide open.

Kovarin looked at Hassurm angrily. "Move it!"

Hassurm immediately started Grinder heading for the starting point.

Kovarin stopped about five paces from Chesesa. The two of them stared at each other for several moments, neither one moving a muscle.

"This…is unprecedented," said Quong. "You…are going to have to make a decision…Supreme Commander."

Kovarin took in a deep breath. "Lady Chesesa…" he said quietly. "With your dragon, Thunder…to the starting point. You will drag…after Hassurm."

She gave him a cordial nod of the head and started walking, leading Thunder behind her.

Quong let out a bit of a frustrated grunt. "Supreme Commander…this is…totally…without precedent. What is on your mind?"

The next man in line, Ikong, chuckled. "Oh, come on, my good man. Haven't you ever taken a chance on something?" He walked up to Quong. "Here, my tall friend, have a drink." He held up a flask to Quong.

Quong looked back and forth between Kovarin and Ikong several times. He finally shrugged and took the flask. He took a long draw from the flask, swallowed…and started hacking uncontrollably. He collapsed to his knees with loud coughs and labored breathing. He held the flask up to give it back to Ikong, with his other hand on his chest as he continued coughing.

The next man down the line, Emkash, stood there chuckling. "Don't tell me! You brought some of that rancid 'rodent snot' that you get from that Grogmaster in Joktel."

Ikong looked at Emkash indignantly. "Rodent snot? You call this….rodent snot?" He took a sip and looked back at Emkash again. "Rodent snot! I don't think that I've ever heard of anyone talk about this stuff…with such high regards." He took another sip. "Yes, it is the stuff I get from that Grogmaster…so what?" He took another sip, put the stopper back in, belched and placed it in a pouch on his side.

Quong looked up at Ikong and signaled him to get to the starting point. He was still gasping for any air that he could inhale.

Kovarin looked at Emkash. "Rodent snot?"

Emkash snickered. "Have you smelled it?"

Kovarin looked disgusted. "I don't think I want to." He turned to head back to the cliff.

Chesesa on Thunder was just taking off. As she made the big turn to get to the starting point, she threw something shiny off into the water.

Aj saw it and gaped for a moment. "What was that?"

"That was the *crest* of a traitor," said Kovarin.

"Ah! Of course."

It took a while before Quong could find his voice again. He stood back there just using hand signals for the next few members of the drag team. When he finally was able to talk again, he headed for the cliff to observe the draggings.

Kovarin looked at Quong. "So, you're finally able to talk again?"

"Yes, Supreme Commander. Remind me, please, to never touch…that horrid concoction again."

"I don't think that you'll really need a reminder. What you just went through…should be enough."

Quong grunted. "You're right." He checked his sheet. He called out: "Number seven on the list, Battle Group Commander Yolonj, with your dragon - Singe…to the starting point."

After drag number thirty, the Physician did a very short check and gave the signal to continue. He walked away with his head hung low.

They continued down the line. Thirty-one, thirty-two, thirty-three, thirty-four, thirty-five. Each one of the Dragonriders taking their second turn. Chesesa had upset the count…slightly. She got back in line with the others to take another run herself.

Run number forty. Palhagath checked Dozzbin. His breathing was now getting very ragged and labored, however he was definitely still alive. The Physician gave the signal to continue. He did not hide the disgust on his face or the contempt when he glared at Kovarin. He simply walked back to the pavilion and sat there waiting for the end of run number fifty.

Forty-one, forty-two, forty-three…

Quong walked up to Kovarin. "I know that you allowed the Lady Chesesa to participate…I was wondering about any continuance in the changes…?"

"I authorize it," said Kovarin through his teeth. "Let it continue."

Quong shrugged. "Very well, Supreme Commander." He turned back to the line. He called out: "The Lady Namanti, with the dragon - Diamond…to the starting point."

Now Kovarin did look back shocked. Namanti was leading Diamond to the starting point (getting her posterior licked several times). She ignored the licks and kept on going to get ready. He saw that Chesesa was the next one on the line after Namanti. He shrugged and sighed and turned his attention back to the cliff.

Aj turned to Kovarin looking a little worried. "How much longer…do you think that this will go on?"

"I don't know," said Kovarin in a disgusted manner. He turned to Aj. "Commander…go get your dragon ready. Tell the other alternates to do the same. We're in the third round and that traitor is still alive. This may take a *lot* longer than anticipated."

Aj saluted and headed off to the pavilion at a dead run.

Run number forty-four ended. Namanti was saddled, buckled and ready.

Quong called out: "The Lady Chesesa with your dragon - Thunder…to the starting point."

After run number fifty. Palhagath made the walk back to inspect the condemned. This time he had to get closer to check. He knelt down and touched Dozzbin's throat. He stood up with his shoulders sagging. He was looking up, shaking his head. He turned back to the pavilion and gave the signal to continue.

Kovarin sighed. "Chief Executioner!"

"Yes, Supreme Commander."

"Once the primaries have finished their third round…if

they finish the third round…call the alternates to the line."

"Yes, Supreme Commander." Quong called out: "Number nine on the list, Battle Division Sub Commander Eevek, with your dragon - Scrambler…to the starting point."

Run number fifty-two, fifty-three, fifty-four, fifty-five…

Quong called out: "The Lady Namanti with your dragon - Diamond…to the starting point."

This time, Kovarin did not look back. He just accepted it as Namanti lined up for run number fifty-six.

Fifty-seven, fifty-eight, fifty-nine…sixty. This time the Physician had to do an even closer examination. He stood up, headed back to the pavilion and gave the signal to continue.

Battle Group Commander Azzitok took his third run with Crunch.

Kovarin was fighting back his revulsion. "Chief Executioner, How many…of the primary…dragons are left…to do their third run?"

"Three, Supreme Commander."

"Are the alternates ready?"

"Yes, Supreme Commander. They have made their own line…and are standing ready."

"Thank you."

As Chachur, riding Rampage, took off for their third run, the sixty-fourth overall, Quong looked at the bottom of the list for the alternates. Quong called out: "Alternate number one on the list, Battle Group Commander Hajahoy, with your dragon - Standard…to the starting point."

Hajahoy took run number sixty-five. Chocha on Endeavor took number sixty-six. Aj on Dastardly took number sixty-seven.

As Dastardly landed, Discoro leaned close to Kovarin. "Supreme Commander," he whispered. "I don't think it's going to be much longer. I can see the traitor's entrails dragging behind him."

Kovarin had to fight to keep from throwing up.

Klabool, the only Wing Commander to get a slot in the lottery took number sixty-eight on his dragon - Chomp. Minjell on Respect took run number sixty-nine. Chesesa took run number seventy.

Hajahoy was at the starting point, ready to take his second run. Palhagath did a long examination of Dozzbin. He stood up and waved Hajahoy away. He gave Kovarin and Quong the signal that it was over. The traitor was dead.

Kovarin and Quong took a slow walk to the body. From the cliff top, it had appeared that Dozzbin was only bouncing off of water. When they saw the body closer, they realized that he had hit the rocks…several times. Both legs were broken, the left arm was broken, a portion of the left side of his head was caved-in. The right eye was staring up at the sky…lifeless.

Quong cleared his throat. "Supreme Commander…what do we do with…the corpse?"

Kovarin was fighting off a wave of nausea. "In this area…
aren't there…uh…several different kinds of…wild animals…
birds and bugs that eat…carrion?"

"There are," said Quong quietly.

Kovarin let out a deep breath, still trying to keep from
regurgitating.   "Why…should we cheat…those creatures…of
their…nutrition?"

"No reason not to."

"Good. Leave this…mess…here. From what I hear, the
prevailing winds will keep the smell away from the fort. If the
wind changes…and they start smelling it…we can always send a
detail out here to shove this mess over the cliff."

"As you wish, Supreme Commander."

They all walked back to the fort in silence. Diamond flew
back to the highest perch possible (for holding a dragon of his
size) on the wide west wall of the fort. The other dragons all
settled down for the rest of the day and the night. Each dragon got
a large snoot full of *treat*.

When Kovarin got back to the fort, he called for the
scribes. He ordered them to get a statement from every individual
who was involved in the execution, Dragonriders, Executioners,
the Physician, as well as Chesesa and Namanti. He wanted to
find out what each one of them thought of the proceeding…before
deciding as to whether or not it should be a permanent fixture in
the laws of High Country. He sat alone in the suite, lost in his own
thoughts about what had taken place. He sat there with a blank

piece of paper in front of him and a quill in his hand.

The Physician was the only one to barge in and interrupt his thoughts, in regards to what his impression was. He came through the door without knocking. He seemed to be in a bit of a rage.

"Supreme Commander! Do you really want to know what I think? I'll give it to you, without any written word!"

Kovarin slammed his fists down on the table as he stood up. "I don't want to hear it!" The look on his face made Palhagath take a few steps back. "I said that I want it written down. Everyone's impression of what happened out there today. I want it written down so that everyone knows, first hand, from the people who were involved. The dragon is a major part of our society. This man maliciously *killed* thirty-nine eggs, before they had a chance to hatch. How many of them would have been breeders? How many of them might have been bigger than Diamond? We'll never know! He hurt our national defense network. He was a traitor. I know that you didn't like it. NEITHER DID I! Sometimes, things that we don't like...are painfully necessary. Your observation, the observations of the Dragonriders, the Executioners...and myself...will become a part of our historical archives. Now, go... if you can't write it down, dictate it to the scribes."

Palhagath frowned. He turned, hung his head and silently walked away.

Kovarin sat back down and started writing.

Namanti came in and started writing as well.

Kovarin looked up. "My Love, why…did you take part… in the execution? What did Doz…the traitor do…that made you want to be a part of this…spectacle?"

She looked up with anger in her eyes. "I got spanked! I got spanked because of what he said. I don't like being spanked. I can't…do anything nasty to you…so…I did it to him. Any more questions?"

He shook his head and sighed. They both went back to writing.

It was three days before he received all of the statements from all of the persons involved in the execution. Over and over he saw words like: Disgusting, sickening, nauseating, repugnant, offensive, despicable, objectionable, odious, reprehensible, and atrocious. He also saw words like: Necessary, important, substantiated, vital and fundamental. They did not like it, however, they did see that it was necessary to keep order and make all attempts to stop anything like that from ever happening again.

Many of them had been very interested or even thrilled to participate in the execution of a traitor. According to what was written, any thrill or strong desire was almost gone by the end of the first round of dragging. It became something grotesque by the end of the second round.

From what he read, the only ones who really wanted to continue…were the women. He understood why Chesesa was so angry…but Namanti…why was she being so vindictive…over a spanking? Hopefully she will grow out of it.

He wrote an edict, that all of the statements were to be entered into the historical library in the capital city.

After finishing his edict (which he hoped no one would object to), he stretched and headed for the bed in his suite at Dragonfort Sunset. He was a little surprised to see Namanti… wearing a nightshirt…that fit.

"Where did you get that nightshirt, my Love?"

"They have a local seamstress here. I got tired of trying to get around in that cumbersome bag of yours - it's just too big."

"Now that the execution is over and all of the paperwork is in, we can go back to trying to some kind of normal existence."

She walked up to him slowly and put her arms around his waist. He put his arms around her and held her close in the embrace.

She sighed, looked up and rested her chin against his chest. "I've talked to the local midwives. We don't have to try making a baby any more. We've achieved the first part of the goal." She gave him a big grin.

His heart started pounding for joy. He felt a little like crying from hearing the thrilling information. He kissed her forehead and rubbed his hands up and down her back.

She started giggling. "I don't want to sleep standing up… can we go to bed now?"

He started chuckling as he still held her in the embrace and walked her backwards to the bed.

Epilogue

Diamond won every challenge from any other dragon. One: Because he was very aggressive in battle - Two: There never was another dragon larger than he…NEVER! He was the largest to have ever existed and the one and only true *black* dragon. The normal life span for the dragons of High Country was forty-eight to fifty-three years. There were a few that lived to their seventies… Diamond lived to be ninety-one. He was able to fly and breed all the way up to the day of his death. A life size statue of Diamond was carved and placed on the cliff overlooking the Hatchery…any dragon that tried to use the statue as a high perch, got instantly admonished.

Kovarin, because Diamond being the only size fifty-five dragon (that ever existed), was never ousted from the rank of Supreme Commander. He rode Diamond and held his rank for fifty-nine years, until his death at age eighty-five.

Namanti was the Dragonhandler for Diamond for another six years after the death of Kovarin until she passed away. After Namanti joined her husband in death, one of the daughters of Kovarin and Namanti became Diamond's new handler for the last twenty-six years of Diamond's life.

During their long marriage, Namanti gave birth to twelve children (seven boys and five girls). After the birth of the third child, most of the "Prissy Little Its" stopped complaining about not being chosen as the wife of Kovarin. When it was known that Namanti was pregnant for the seventh time, all of the "Its" stopped their belly-aching completely. After the birth of the twelfth child, Namanti actively started chewing *chatl root*. This was some kind of herb that prostitutes chewed to keep from getting pregnant.

All seven of the sons of Kovarin became Dragonmen. Four of the daughters married Dragonmen. The fifth daughter never married, because she was the final handler for Diamond and once you have flown biggest and the best, nothing else is worthwhile.

Because of the ruling by the Supreme Court, where all of the traitor's edicts were nullified, the Hatchery Administrators, once again, had full control of the Dragon Hatchery. The specific sand pit that Diamond had hatched in was made into a shrine.

Grounder Chedobo, now Candidate Chedobo had a live hatching on his first try. It was a size forty-two, brown male that he named: Restitution.

Grounder Emkorm, now Candidate Emkorm had to wait until his second egg for a live hatching. He got a size forty-four gray female that he named Miracle.

Unfortunately, Candidate Tahbahk had to wait until his fifth egg, before he came up with a live one. A size thirty-nine brown male named Pride.

The statements from the execution of the traitor became mandatory reading in the Candidate school. The atrocious form of execution for the crime of destroying dragon eggs is still on the books and has never had to be used again.

Chesesa never remarried. Both of her sons grew up to be Dragonmen. They never questioned why their *crests* were incomplete.

Many of the women who worked in the Hatchery became wives of Dragonmen. It became extremely difficult for any of the "Prissy Little Its" to outdo the secretarial staff in obtaining the *crest* of a Dragonman.

Because of their *big bluff* of the capabilities of the dragons, High Country was never invaded. No despot, dictator or conqueror was crazy enough to try to take on a force of flying dragons...who flew around the top of all of those huge cliffs surrounding High Country.